Baja Air & Sea

A Novel

by RICK ZAZUETA

Published by Revom Press
Copyright 2020 by Rick Zazueta
First Edition

Revom Press
P O Box 430381
San Diego, California, 92143

Cover Design by Itamar Lilienthal, Casa Tamarindo
Edited by Kelly Davis
Author Photo by Alan Cisneros

Baja Air & Sea is a work of fiction. Any references to historical events, real people or real places are used fictionally. Other names, characters, places, and events are products of the author's imagination, and any resemblance to actual events or places or persons, living or dead, is entirely coincidental.

Copyright Registration Number TXu 2-111-459

ISBN: 978-1-7349076-0-5 (Ingram Spark paperback)
ISBN: 978-1-7349076-1-2 (KDP paperback)
ISBN: 978-1-7349076-2-9 (eBook)

For media or booking inquiries, please contact:
STRATEGIES Public Relations
jkuritz@strategiespr.com

First printed in the United State of America.

For my mother who rode horses, flew airplanes,
and dared to walk on water.

– RZL

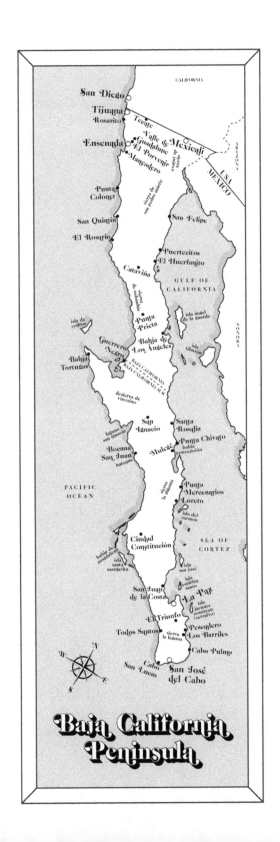

Baja California Peninsula

List of Chapters

PART II - The Business

PART III - Tandem

PART IV - Payoff

PART V - Underworld

"The wealth of the wicked is reserved for the righteous."
                                        Proverbs 13:22

PART I

The Cecilia

CHAPTER 1

La Capitana

THE SUN HAD JUST RISEN as Julian Mayorca gazed upon the Sea of Cortez from *La Capitana*'s skybridge. His bloodshot eyes, three-day beard, and uncombed hair matched his raspy voice as he hummed loose verses of Cromwell's pirate song. With certain nostalgia, the forty-two-year-old took a deep breath and scratched his chest through the worn out v-neck he was wearing. Looking down, he noticed Denise, a cute brunette wearing impeccable yachting attire, climbing up the ladder. She was holding a satellite phone in her left hand.

"Is it him?" Mayorca's voice cracked.

Denise nodded and handed the phone over.

"Julian, my hands are tied. Sons of bitches don't want to budge; the vote's tied at six to six. I just found out *I'm* the swing vote," said the voice on the other end, Admiral Gomez, head of the Mexican Navy in Baja California.

"Who's against me?" asked Julian.

"Cabo and Ensenada," said the Admiral.

"*Pinchi* Valdez... *pinchi* Samper."

"I told you, you should've cut them some slack on their fishing licensing deal. You were too harsh."

"Well, *padrino,* at least I can count on you. Or do I need to ask which way *your* vote is going to swing?"

Admiral Gomez took a moment. "It's not that easy. Obviously, they know you are my godson, but they're holding me over a barrel."

"What?"

"It's not them. I have no problem voting in your favor. I don't care what Valdez and Samper have to say. But I'm being pressured from within the Mexican Navy, and it's coming down from the top. They want me to vote against you."

"What? Why?"

"I don't know. I get the feeling somebody big is betting against us."

"Well, let's show them how strong our bond is. Let's show them we're together. Keep supporting me Admiral. Vote in my favor. Let's finish what we started."

Admiral Gomez took a second. "This is the thing—they have some intel that can benefit my chances of becoming Secretary of the Navy if my party wins the next election."

"Wow. So that's what it comes down to, huh?"

"No, it doesn't. But, Julian, you've been president of the Baja Port Captains Association five years already. Nobody has ever achieved that!"

"Nobody has ever achieved what I've achieved; not just in five years, but ever! Look how much it's changed? You remember how the association was before I got in? It didn't even have a real budget. I made it what it is today," said Julian, with a taste of anger in his mouth. "I've cleaned up more coasts, patrolled more harbors, and continue to log more sea hours than all those other tar-heads combined."

"Listen, here's what I can do," said Admiral Gomez. "This just got to my desk this morning. I'm about to embark on an expedition. I'll be off the grid for some time. Legally, I have up to thirty days to respond. Let's stall them and see how the cards play out upon my return. In the meantime, you talk to Valdez and Samper."

"Yeah, I'll talk to them alright. And *padrino*?"

"Yes?"

"Thank you for the call," Julian said as he watched the horizon change with the sunrise.

After the phone call, Julian took a quick shower. He looked at himself in the mirror, shaved his beard, and put in eye drops. He combed his hair, sprayed a little cologne on his neck, and walked out of the head. Clothes were laid out for him on the master stateroom bed. He put on a clean v-neck undershirt, blue shorts, and khaki top-siders. He strapped on his watch and placed a yellow waterproof envelope in his back pocket. He then put on his sailing shirt, which read: *Julian Mayorca, Port Captain.*

La Capitana was the name of the La Paz Port Captain's ship. It was a beautiful seventy-footer, running on two twin diesel engines, and sporting a refinished deck. With three staterooms, an ample galley, and a salon that had been redesigned as a sea office, she was more than seaworthy. The exterior of the yacht was bone color, and she sailed under Mexican and South Baja flags. Julian's claim to *La Capitana* began when he was just coming into his own as Port Captain of La Paz, ten years earlier. With the help of Admiral Gomez, he'd spearheaded negotiations with various government agencies to release to his office the beautiful yacht that had been confiscated from Goar Salazar, a tax-evading millionaire. For Captain Mayorca, it wasn't only about the job; it was about the sea life that came with it. He didn't just understand the sea, he breathed it. He himself was made of ocean; 185 pounds of seaworthiness. As captain, his soul and heart were part of his ship.

At 0815 that morning, the yacht was anchored at Balandra Bay. Julian was finishing breakfast on deck with his first mate, Denise, and Ernie Jordan, the deckhand. Even though Denise and Ernie were married, they never acted like it, and certainly never talked about it with their captain. They were a no-nonsense crew, hardworking and honest.

Ernie had made his way to Baja as a teenager, under strange circumstances. When Julian first met Ernie, he was homeless, hiring himself out as a dockhand. Julian gave him a job, a boat to live in, a craft to learn, and a career. Ernie was truly grateful. Julian, being a man of integrity, had never brought up Ernie's questionable past, and Ernie was loyal to his captain for having done so much for him. He respected Julian, and Julian trusted his deckhand.

Denise was brought to Baja at age eleven. Her mother, Camille Johnson, a Realtor and a Cabo legend, known for her parties and romantic affairs, thought it was a good idea to put some space between her and Denise's father. Denise was Canadian by birth, Mexican by heart, and Baja Californian by fate. As a teen, she took refuge in two things: the Baja Christian Church, and sailing. She became an exceptional sailor, and even had a documentary film made about her travels from Baja California to Patagonia, and back through the Panama Canal, at age eighteen. True adventurers and seafarers, Denise and Ernie lived a romance that was pure, tender, and very private. Julian respected them both and, as they'd met while working for him, they had a special bond with their captain.

"Ten boats are coming into port today sir; five that we've cleared, three that we've identified, and two that we haven't," Denise said.

"Any supermodels coming in?" Julian asked.

"No, sir, I don't believe you'll be so lucky today."

"Well that's too bad."

Ernie pulled up anchor.

"Why don't you take us over to Valderrama. Let's see if you can handle her," Julian said.

"Aye, aye, Skip," answered Denise.

Julian enjoyed the breeze on the helm. He needed the sea air to clear his mind.

The tide's changing; the wind, choppy...

"It's a day to ride her a little steep," he told Denise as the weather turned slightly overcast.

The conversation with Admiral Gomez that morning made Julian think of the job he loved. The position required captains to patrol the twelve different ports, marinas, and the coasts of the Baja California peninsula; a stretch of land west of mainland Mexico and south of California.

Baja is divided into North and South. Since the two states were always fighting for money, they agreed to form a coalition—the Baja California Port Captains Association. Through the years, the association misplaced funds and was involved in scandal after scandal. After it had lost all prestige, no politician wanted to authorize a decent budget. That's about when Julian Mayorca had just managed to get *La Capitana* released to his office.

The amount of political engineering that took place during that operation impressed the right people. So Admiral Gomez convinced Julian to run for president of the Port Captains Association. Julian won a tight race and took the association's helm with a strong stance. He worked hard for five years, putting resources to work efficiently and growing the association's budget year by year. He was days away from getting $50 million USD approved by the Mexican senate for the following year.

And now that I'm finally working with a decent budget, of course they want to come in and take it from me, he thought.

He turned on the radio, hoping to distract himself from maritime politics.

"Samuel Bracho, renowned boss and gruesome criminal, has escaped from Almoloya prison in central Mexico," said the newscaster. "Originally convicted for a series of twelve murders, terrorism, and arson charges related to the burning of the Gazeta newspaper building in the city of Tijuana five years ago, Bracho was serving a 120-year sentence."

"Aghh! Criminals!"

He changed the radio to a classical music station.

Julian remembered the day he saw the headlines about Samuel Bracho's capture. He was grateful that Baja was separated from central Mexico by an inland sea, a paradise that he sailed daily.

Julian smiled and glanced at Denise, who held the helm. She let Julian know about the commercial fishing vessel, *Azul,* coming in through Bay of the Dead.

He looked at his watch. "Give her thirty knots."

Denise answered with a smile.

Thirty knots can seem fast on the right yacht, and *La Capitana* was running smoothly. As they approached Bay of the Dead, they spotted *Azul*, a beat-up fishing boat.

"Funny name for a pinto," said Denise

Julian chuckled.

The crew consisted of humble fishermen who helped Julian and Ernie tie the tender to their stern. The ship's captain introduced himself as Cano, and Julian asked him if they had any weapons.

"Only our spearguns," said Cano as he took Julian and Ernie down to see the yellowtail tuna they had caught. Julian loved the sight of all the tuna and asked him where they caught it.

"About seven clicks off Cerralvo Island." Cano gave Julian a big tuna as a gift.

"I'm only taking this if you promise that if you see anybody fishing with nets, you call me. These are line-only waters! You understand?"

"Yes, sir."

Julian, acting as Port Captain, waived the standard $15 per fish license fee, only asking them where they were headed, to which they replied, "San Felipe."

Julian wished them luck and warned them about the San Fernando flats—underwater sand dunes that had caused many ships to capsize.

Julian entered *La Capitana*'s galley, holding the tuna as blood dripped through his hands onto the floor. Jose Rubio, the cook with an eyepatch over his left socket, took the tuna from Julian's hands and began cutting it up.

"I'll make sashimi, some *ceviche* with the mango I've got left over, and my signature poké," said the cook.

Julian grabbed two bottles of Pilsner from the fridge and handed one to Rubio.

"Ah, that hits the spot," he exhaled in satisfaction. "How about you? Are you hung over?"

"Me? I was born hung over. It's my natural state," Julian replied. They both laughed as they drank their beers.

"Cheers," Rubio said. "Always a pleasure to have a beer with you, Skip."

"Yeah, well, you're the only one. I've got a Christian first maiden and her dry husband for a deckhand," said Julian.

"Well, I've got a couple of drunks you can hire, but they won't be all business."

Julian laughed. "True. We'll gladly drink their portion."

Bottles clinked and the friends finished their beers.

Julian walked onto the deck with a smile on his face; he could always count on Rubio and a beer to do that.

Denise was on helm going about twelve knots per hour and finishing up a conversation over the CB. She took off her binoculars and handed them to Julian, who spotted two luxury yachts approaching.

"One is an eighty-foot, *Azimut Carat,* and the other is a sixty-two-foot, *Sunseeker Manhattan,*" said Denise.

Julian kept looking through the binoculars.

"I talked to the captain. He wouldn't reveal the shipmaster's identity, but he assured me they're wealthy businessmen on leisure. The captain said he knew you. His name is Axel Cuevas."

"My cousin?" A smile.

The two yachts were coming in fast. Julian hit the siren and Ernie lowered the tender. Julian jumped on and asked Ernie to untie him.

"Want me to come with?" asked Ernie.

The two yachts were slowing to a halt and Julian spotted what very well could have been a couple of supermodels tanning on the bow of the *Sunseeker.*

"I can handle it. Stay here with your wife." Both men looked up to the bridge and saw Denise overlooking.

As Julian was leaving *La Capitana,* he grabbed the tender's CB and radioed Ernie. "Have all the rods, reels, and bait ready, because when I get back, we're going fishing for dorado."

"10-4."

Julian pulled up to the *Sunseeker's* stern and peeped overboard. "Ahoy!"

A perfect ten of a woman—a dark-skinned, long-legged beauty

—looked up and removed her sunglasses. Simultaneously, a topless brunette turned around to hide her breasts, embarrassed, as if topless tanning on a yacht was taboo.

A red-bearded man came down from the bridge.

"Don't be frightening my girls." He turned to Julian. "I know you're ugly, but shit, I didn't think you would scare the talent!" he said.

"I'll be damned. When I heard 'Axel Cuevas,' I knew there couldn't be two of you," Julian said as he threw the rope over. Axel helped him aboard.

They hugged each other hard.

"It's been too long," said Axel.

"Incredible. How the heck are you, cuz?" said Julian.

Axel looked at the supermodels. "Can't complain."

"You know, these are two of my favorite yachts?" said Julian.

"You've got good taste. You've always had good taste."

"So what are you doing? Why didn't you tell me you were coming?"

Axel chuckled. "Do you really have to ask so many questions being port captain?"

Julian relaxed. "It comes with the job, Axel."

"Well, come in for a beer and we'll chat," Axel said as he opened the door to the salon.

"It's a gorgeous boat," said Julian as he stepped into the yacht.

Axel closed the door behind them.

A man holding a shotgun hit Julian on the back of the head.

Down on his knees, through the pain and blurred vision, Julian noticed Axel pretending not to know what was going on. Such a bad actor.

Julian tried to get to his feet, but another man slapped him in the face. Julian had never seen him before. He didn't remember seeing a picture of him, but in that particular moment, when he looked up and saw that fat face wearing those ridiculous photochromic lenses that change colors with the sunlight, everything clicked. He sensed it, felt it, like a revelation. He knew that man was Samuel Bracho, the crime lord who had escaped from prison.

"Well, if it isn't Julian Mayorca, port captain of La Paz, president of the Port Captains Association of Baja California," said Bracho. "Highest authority on the Sea of Cortez, is it?"

Julian stared with disgust.

"Aren't you going to ask any questions? Who we are? What we want? What your cousin is doing here?"

Julian looked at Axel with all of his rage.

"If looks could kill, huh?" There was a long pause. "I'll tell you what, since I can see that you are a man who knows when to keep silent, and I know you are a man of great leadership and character—I mean, you are the only port captain we haven't been able to buy off in this part of the world. What's the matter? Don't you like money?"

Julian stared at Bracho with utter disgust.

"Well, today you are going to make a choice. Either you die, right here, right now, and we kill all of your crew; or you sign this letter that says you resign as port captain, and you, and your crew, everybody lives."

Julian couldn't believe this was happening. He thought of the association's election. He couldn't give his enemies the privilege of quitting.

Hold your tongue, Julian, hold your tongue, he thought to himself in anger.

"You think it would be hard? Sinking your boat? Disappearing your crew into the blue?"

A laugh from Bracho's goons.

"You see, the new port captain," everyone looked at Axel Cuevas, "knows you very well. He told us that you would die before signing, but not if we torture your crew in front of you. Are you gonna let me do that? Or are you going to sign?"

A sigh from one of his goons.

"And please don't insult me. I'm not a very patient man. I am doing all this out of courtesy for your cousin, who begged me not to kill you."

Julian looked at Axel with disbelief.

"If you were anybody else, you wouldn't have the luxury of choice."

Julian remained silent, looking down at the carpet.

Bracho got angry. "Cock that gun," he told the gunman.

Cold twin barrels grazed the hairs on Julian's head.

"You have five seconds to decide. What's it going to be?" asked Bracho.

"One."

Julian looked up.

"Two."

He got to his feet.

"Three."

He yanked the letter from Bracho's hand.

"Four."

He thought about ripping it up. *Maybe death is only a door, but what about Rubio, Denise, and Ernie?*

"Five."

Julian pulled out his pen. His hand did not shake when he signed.

CHAPTER 2

Seattle

THAT EVENING, JULIAN HAD A meeting with his crew. He thanked them for their years of loyalty and service, forewarning them of many changes to come. He handed out letters of recommendation and encouraged them to look for employment opportunities outside of the Port Captainship.

When the crew wanted to know the truth, Julian told them he was able to negotiate severance pay for all of them, even if they chose to stay. He cut them all checks out of the Port Captainship account. The last check he signed as Port Captain was his own severance pay for eleven years of work. Later, Ernie and Denise, in a private conversation, commented on Julian's genius in steering the conversation toward severance when they pushed for facts.

Julian resigned and lost faith in a system that he had upheld his whole life. He was so furious, he vomited in the alley behind the harbor office as he walked out for the last time. He didn't know what to do, so he went looking for Jose Rubio, his only friend. Julian told Rubio the truth about his cousin's betrayal. This led to a drinking binge that peaked with them making plans to sink *La Capitana*.

"I put that boat together. It kills me that they can just take it from me," Julian told Rubio

Rubio suggested they think things through before being so radical. He took Julian back to his place where he cooked and cared for him. The next day, Julian hugged Rubio and thanked him for being his loyal friend. Rubio was glad Julian hadn't insisted on sinking *La Capitana*, because he knew that if Julian had asked him to do it, they would've sank that ship together.

Three days later, Julian hitched a ride on a commercial vessel to Seattle with the sole intention of disappearing from Baja for a while. He chose Seattle because it had the word *sea* in it; he figured it was a good place to lie low. He didn't know for how long—at least until the news of his resignation and all the accusations journalists were making blew over. Julian knew he couldn't stay in Baja because the media kept wanting interviews, accusing him of corruption and nepotism due to his family ties with the new port captain, Axel Cuevas. At first, it infuriated Julian that he was being looked at as the bad guy; he also couldn't believe how many of his friends in power turned their backs on him. But soon enough, his anger turned into profound sadness.

Seattle was cold and wet. Julian got a small place downtown. He would walk around in the rain and drink coffee during the day. At night, he would go out for dinner and drink wine. He met a lady named Michelena, and made love to her one night at her place by the lake.

Michelena fell in love with Julian, but he walked out on her. Summer came and Julian began to frequent the marinas in Seattle; in particular, he liked Shilshole Bay. Sometimes he would drink Pinot Noir at the marina bar and smoke cigars on the terrace before catching a cab back to his place. He rarely talked to anyone. He would sit in silence and gaze upon the cold Pacific Northwest.

It was as if Julian was in mourning, because a part of him had died. It wasn't just losing the job, the yacht, and its perks. It was Axel's betrayal that had damaged him. Axel and Julian had grown up together; Julian's parents had died while scuba diving off the cave of Asunción when he was nine years old. Luisa, Julian's maternal aunt, and her husband, Gene, had embraced Julian as their own son. Axel, only two years younger, practically became Julian's little brother. At the time, Julian didn't know how to mourn the death of his parents, so he developed a strong and silent character. This gave him the ability to focus and excel in a lot of areas, particularly in sports, and later in sailing.

Julian became an exceptional seaman before the age of thirteen. He enrolled in the Mexican Naval Academy in Veracruz when he was sixteen and ranked top of his class. Gene and Luisa were proud of Julian and loved him greatly. Axel always tried to follow Julian's footsteps but never came close. With all the history they shared, Julian could not bear telling his aunt and uncle about Axel's betrayal. Even though they never talked about it, Gene and Luisa knew Axel had double-crossed Julian. It was a very sad situation for all of them, and Julian felt incredibly alone.

During the middle of summer, Shilshole Bay was full of boaters and yachties. Julian became a regular at the marina bar, and the staff was intrigued by the dark-skinned man who drank upscale wines and stared at the sea. One Tuesday evening, Julian was sitting on the terrace, glancing at the sunset, when a pit bull came up, demanding to be petted. The lovely creature, in all of her innocence, wagged her tail, encouraging love.

"Reyna, get down!" a man said from afar.

"Reyna, what a beautiful name you have," said Julian, as he pet the dog.

"Sorry. She can be a hassle," said the dog's owner, a sixty-something man with a ponytail.

"No big deal," said Julian as he continued showing affection toward the dog.

The man, who introduced himself as Boyd, ordered a beer and talked to Julian about Seattle in the summer. Before long, Julian and Boyd were talking about Baja and the Sea of Cortez. It turned out Boyd had been to Baja on his yacht plenty of times and loved it there. Julian insisted on picking up the tab, and Boyd invited Julian for another drink aboard his yacht, the *Almost Heaven*.

CHAPTER 3

"Pirate Blood"

THE *ALMOST HEAVEN* WAS A fine yacht, an off-white ninety-foot masterpiece that radiated life. Julian was mesmerized by the attention to detail that had been poured into every inch of the ship. Its logo, imprinted on the metal bars and wood trim on deck, looked like a wave wrapping around the sun. The salon was a masterpiece of comfort and style, putting Julian in a delightful mood.

Even though it was luxurious, the yacht had a down-to-earth realness. With a flat-screen TV connected to a hard drive with thousands of movies and albums ready to play on demand, a black couch that sat sixteen and turned into a bed for four, the yacht was built for entertainment. Boyd played Steely Dan's *Countdown to Ecstasy* out of speakers designed by an ex-NASA engineer. The track sounded like God's calling as Boyd sang along and poured drinks. He handed Julian a vodka cranberry, and Julian felt like himself for the first time since he had left *La Capitana*.

"*Oh no, Guadalajara won't do*" sang Boyd as Julian watched with a big grin on his face.

"You know why Guadalajara won't do, right, Boyd?"

Boyd kept jamming out to Steely Dan.

"Because it has no ocean!"

"You're right, you're right. You're goddamn right!" said Boyd, still humming to the music with closed eyes.

That night, Boyd called over some girls he had met at a party weeks before. Julian kissed a girl named Amber on the bow of the yacht. Amber wrote her number down on the whiteboard by the fridge, and Julian slept by himself in the stateroom that had the bed with the amber-colored sheets.

The next morning, Julian awoke aboard the *Almost Heaven* as it started to move. A smile grew on his face as he realized they were taking her out to sea. He rinsed his face with cold water and made his way up to the bridge, barefoot. Boyd was on helm, chewing a cigar. A bald white guy, who introduced himself as Timbo, assisted him.

"Good morning, sailor," said Boyd as he pushed her to about nine knots.

"Good morning, Captain," said Julian as he sat down.

Timbo poured coffee; Julian drank it while enjoying the cool breeze and warm sun. At noon, they had lunch while cruising at sea. Boyd cooked and Julian assisted him while Timbo was on helm going five knots. Boyd grilled steaks and vegetables astern, while Julian mixed greens with potato salad in the galley. They had lunch outside and Boyd opened a bottle of Cuban rum. They had some on the rocks.

"Yeah, I sold my real estate business, traded it for the yachting life ten years ago. Now, I mostly do yacht charters," said Boyd, with a hint of pride.

"It's a lovely yacht. It reminds me of one that I used to skipper," said Julian with a faraway look.

"Yeah, what was she called?"

"*La Capitana.*"

That afternoon, when they arrived at the marina, Julian jumped to the dock and tied up the *Almost Heaven* with one hand. Boyd saw his knots, and realized Julian was no ordinary seaman.

Boyd and Julian kept this up for many days—going out during the morning, having lunch at sea, and returning dockside in the afternoon to hang out with girls. Julian liked Sundays because Amber would come aboard the yacht with them. Amber and Julian began to date. She even introduced him to her son, Michael William Michaels, a very nice, nine-year-old boy who went out with them on the yacht once.

Boyd loved having Julian aboard his yacht. He would tell everyone that he had "the best first mate from Baja."

Julian noticed that Boyd began drinking hard liquor at lunch each day and wouldn't stop until he passed out, usually by 10:30 p.m. He would also repeat what he said over and over and this began to drive Julian mad.

Julian talked to Boyd about sobering up, and Boyd spent three days in Julian's apartment, getting off the liquor. When he came out, Boyd was motivated and began changing his diet and exercising. This helped Julian stop drinking as well, and they both experienced a period of healthy, clean living. Boyd wanted to focus his efforts on his business, and began going to benefit galas in Seattle and Vancouver to promote himself and his yacht. Sometimes Boyd would ask Julian to accompany him, but Julian wouldn't, since he was spending more and more time with Amber.

At the end of the summer, Julian was at peace with his life. He was healthy and had made a family for himself with Amber and her "little frog," as Julian called Michael William Michaels. He had a great friend in Boyd, whom he yachted with at least three times a week. He didn't have a job, but he didn't really need one. One morning, when they were out at sea, Boyd asked Julian to accompany him to Vancouver to the Ladies of British Columbia Annual Gala. He told Julian that the summer was coming to an end and he needed to get one big client to move south, to warmer weather, with his yacht.

"Just come work for me, bro."

Boyd had been joking for weeks about Julian being his first mate, but nothing serious had ever been established between them.

"What do you need me to do?"

"I need a first mate. A real one. Somebody who knows this ship and knows the ocean."

"I'll have to think about it."

"Think about what? You ain't doing shit."

"Yes I am. I'm detoxing," said Julian.

"*Detoxing*? Ha! Plus, you know this ship told me, she asked me to hire you."

"You're crazy."

"Bro, ships speak, you believe that?"

"I'm not superstitious," said Julian

"You don't know nothing. You should be grateful there's someone looking out for you."

Julian took that comment to heart. "So what do you need me to do?"

"I'll give you a small salary to work around the boat, you know, keep her clean, greased, and waxed," a chuckle.

"How small of a salary?"

"A hundred bucks a week." He took a sip of his coffee.

"Fahh… man…"

"What? I'll pay for your room and board, all the meals, all the costs. I'm basically paying you to hang out with me and to do what we already do."

Julian liked the idea of living back on the water.

"I'll give you 6 percent of any charter that comes in."

A smile from Julian. "Make it 10 percent and you've got yourself a deal."

He stretched out his hand. Boyd shook it, then hugged him.

A couple of days later, Julian moved out of his apartment and into the cabin aboard the *Almost Heaven*. The day they left for Vancouver, Amber and Michael William Michaels ate lunch aboard the yacht with Boyd and Julian, while Timbo served them. Amber and Julian kissed dockside as Boyd and Timbo whistled and teased. Julian smiled, got aboard, and waved goodbye to Amber and her son.

The ride north to Vancouver was a little choppy. They didn't see much of Vancouver since they arrived the same day as the gala. Julian hadn't been to a gala since he was Port Captain, but he knew the routine—look good, smile, make acquaintances, and talk about whatever good cause they were supposed to be endorsing. Julian was certain they could get a client that evening.

When Julian came out of the cabin wearing his impeccable Mexican Naval Academy whites, Boyd was already waiting for him in the salon, wearing a tux and chewing on a cigar. Julian radiated confidence with his medals and shiny shoes. Boyd complimented his look.

The Ladies of British Columbia Annual Gala was a nice event. Julian and Boyd shook hands and exchanged a brief word with the Honorable Ann Lambert, premier of British Columbia. Boyd disappeared for a moment as Julian met with the Mexican Ambassador to Canada, a very nice man by the name of Gilberto Alarcón. It turned out, they had a mutual friend out of Ensenada, the nautical attorney Alberto Fontana. Gilberto Alarcón and Julian talked politics, and Julian was taken aback by how well-versed Gilberto was in Baja California matters.

Boyd had a drink in his hand when he introduced Wendy Samson to Julian.

There goes sobriety!

Gilberto excused himself as Wendy spoke to Julian.

"So I hear you're from Baja." said Wendy as Boyd disappeared again.

"Yeah, from La Paz, originally."

Wendy grabbed a glass of red wine from the server's tray and convinced Julian to do the same. Julian treated the wine rather well; smelling it, sipping it, smelling it, and tasting it. The distinct dark plum and spice tones reminded him of his childhood when he would run around the great Baja outdoors. He took a prolonged sip.

"It's fantastic," he said.

"I am glad you like it, because it's from Baja."

Julian smiled and repeated treating the wine; smelling it, sipping it, smelling it, and tasting it.

"It's from my ranch in Valle de Guadalupe, in Baja wine country, east of Ensenada," Wendy said.

Julian reached over and touched her forearm, looked into her sixty-year-old gray eyes, and said, "A woman that makes wine this good must have a lot of heart."

Wendy Samson, the recent widow of Ryan May Samson, founder of Samson Athletics, told Julian that she was going to be in Baja at the end of the month to host her annual *vendimia* wine party. After a long talk, Julian suggested that she arrive in style, and offered her the option of chartering the *Almost Heaven* to Ensenada. Wendy was intrigued; she agreed to consider the charter, granted they moved the yacht from the Burrard Marina to the Heather Marina in downtown Vancouver the following day so she could inspect it at 15:00. Boyd was very excited about this potential charter and wanted to make sure the yacht was spotless.

The following day, when Wendy arrived fashionably late at 5:00, she fell in love with the *Almost Heaven* and made arrangements with Boyd to get picked up four days later at the Genoa Bay Marina on Vancouver Island. Boyd agreed and asked for a 50 percent advance. Wendy wrote a check for $110,000. That night, Julian, Timbo, and Boyd got incredibly drunk.

Boyd told Julian that bringing him along had proven what he always knew—that they were both one in the same, "pirates, with pirate blood."

"But how did you manage to charge her over $200,000 for a three-day charter?" Julian asked.

"Three day charter? What are you talking about? I'm gonna take at least a week getting down there. What? Do you think we'll be going twenty knots? No, we'll be going ten, and we're anchoring at night."

"You old seawolf," said Julian with a laugh.

"You should see how much they charge for charters in the Mediterranean. A yacht like mine is worth at least as much as the ones over there," said Boyd as he took a swig of rum. "If not double."

"I don't know about that."

"Always double it!"

They both laughed.

Over the next couple of days, Boyd, Julian, and Timbo cleaned the yacht, fueled her up, and went through the meticulous list of provisions and safety measures required for a thousand nautical mile journey.

"Always overstock, that's why you overcharge," Boyd would say as he focused on every detail.

CHAPTER 4

Baja Bound

JULIAN THOUGHT VANCOUVER ISLAND WAS a wonderful place; he loved the way the King Beaver Seaplanes landed on the water. The morning they arrived at the Genoa Bay Marina, Julian and Boyd walked Reyna around town and had quiche-salad sandwiches for lunch at a French place. Julian called Amber, who was concerned because she hadn't heard from him since Shilshole Bay.

"Yeah, we picked up a charter to Ensenada. Don't know when we'll be back," he said.

Amber silently wept goodbye, knowing she would never see Julian again.

Wendy arrived at the Genoa Bay Marina, a little bit after 1:00 p.m., with her personal assistant—a cute girl named Monique.

Boyd told Wendy they had prepared for only one passenger, but Wendy insisted on bringing Monique along. Boyd almost lost his temper, saying they had made arrangements for one passenger to be treated to the highest standard in comfort, luxury, and safety. But now, with two people, his crew of three was "totally outnumbered."

"You need to learn some basic math. In what world does two outnumber three?" Wendy asked.

"In the nautical world. Do you understand the scope of our journey? I'm trying to give you an experience unlike any other!"

"You're getting too bossy. I don't like men when they get too bossy. You can ask my late husband."

"Well, all I know is that a sixteen-day yacht charter down the Pacific coast is no small endeavor."

Julian chuckled when he heard sixteen days. The old hustler was at it, stretching out truths, just so he could make more dollars.

"Okay, what do you suggest we do?" Julian stepped in.

"Well, I can stop in Oregon to pick up a deckhand and cook," said Boyd.

"Sounds good to me."

"It's gonna be an extra fifteen-K," Boyd said.

Wendy took a beat. "Just put it on my tab." She walked into the salon.

By 2:30, they were in open waters.

Wendy was drinking white wine. The sea had begun to cast its spell. The tension from an hour earlier dissolved. Julian was on helm when he realized how great of a yacht the *Almost Heaven* was because he felt a swift glide even when coming up against a wake. He attributed this particular feature to the wide beam of the yacht.

They anchored at 6:40 p.m., and Boyd cooked a delicious dinner of mussels *au* white wine, crab bisque, and filet mignon. Wendy and Monique watched black and white films and fell asleep in the salon before they went to their respective staterooms. Julian slept in the cabin, while Timbo slept on a sleeping bag on the bridge, and Boyd and Reyna slept in the Captain's Quarters.

When they got to the Warrenton Marina in Oregon, there were two new crew members Timbo had recruited; Elsa, a thirty-five-year-old Chilean woman, and Matt, a twenty-seven-year-old deckhand from Maine. Boyd made sure Wendy paid him the remaining amount. Wendy had an associate of hers deliver a briefcase that she gave to Boyd. He put the cash in the safe behind the closet door in the Captain's Quarters. Boyd and Julian studied the weather and mapped their journey south. They made calculations and were looking forward to coasting down to Ensenada without a rush.

Even though Julian had been on plenty of vessels and had worked with a lot of fine yachtsmen and captains, he began to admire Boyd.

Not his seaman skills, as Julian realized that he came up short on these, but the passion, craft, and touch that he put into his yacht. Boyd ran a smooth operation and was also an incredible cook; his crew responded to him immediately and he began to trust Julian at the helm.

Wendy Samson was a great guest. She would mostly sit around, look at magazines, and read books. She drank white wine on most nights, but sometimes she would drink red. Monique was a different story. She drank vodka on the side and took pills.

"It's for seasickness," she would say whenever somebody saw her grabbing an orange bottle out of her purse.

At around 11:00 p.m., she would start to get sloppy. Wendy would go to her stateroom around that time and Monique would look for attention. She began flirting with Matt, but quickly learned that Matt was gay. She kept him as a friend and began confiding in him certain things about Wendy and her eccentricities. One day, Julian was on helm and Boyd was next to him making smalltalk when Monique came up, drinking a beer. She had another closed can in her left hand.

"One of you boys better drink this beer with me. I'm getting bored," she said.

Julian looked ahead, letting the open ocean do the talking for him.

"I'll never turn down a drink from a lady," said Boyd, who smiled and took the beer from her. He opened it, took a swig, and exhaled in satisfaction.

Boyd told Julian to move over and asked Monique to hold the helm. He rubbed up against Monique's behind as they held the helm together. Before long, Boyd and Monique were in his quarters. Julian was happy the two were getting laid, and Wendy didn't seem to notice anything. The next morning, Wendy listened to an audiobook on her silver headphones while Monique gave her a pedicure. Boyd didn't come out of his quarters until noon, and he already had a beer in his hand. Boyd's drinking over the next couple of days began to get out of hand. He would slur his words, stumble, and, worst of all, his cooking waned. Julian began to feel embarrassed toward Wendy and went out of his way so that she wouldn't notice Boyd's alcoholism.

Wendy and Julian spent a lot of time together talking about topics of mutual interest— preserving the environment, sustainable development, and international politics. They also talked a lot about the future of Baja California, which gave Julian very mixed feelings. He loved his homeland and cared about its development, but he definitely didn't want to be back there. Everything he and Wendy talked about reminded him of Axel Cuevas and Samuel Bracho. The closer they got to Baja, the more hate Julian harbored in his heart toward his cousin. Sometimes, when Julian was alone at night, he would pick imaginary fights with Axel. Julian usually caught himself going into these bizarre, vengeful fantasies. In order to get away from those thoughts, he would put on some music, talk to the crew, or whisper prayers on deck.

It was a beautiful Southern California morning when Julian spotted the U.S. Coast Guard coming at them from afar. He asked Timbo to hold the helm as he ran downstairs and knocked on Boyd's quarters. Boyd could barely get himself to open the door. Reyna was in there with him and the room smelled like dog, alcohol, and sweat. Julian told Boyd the U.S. Coast Guard was approaching, but Boyd went back to sleep, hugging Reyna.

"Look, they're gonna wanna know who the captain is, and they are going to want to see boat papers," said Julian.

"Tell them it's my boat," slurred Boyd as the yacht began to slow down significantly.

Julian slapped Boyd's leg and yelled at him, "Boyd! Papers!"

Boyd reacted a little bit and answered, "What, bro! They're in the safe."

Julian opened the blinds to let some light in, and Boyd complained as he swerved in bed.

"Just open the safe, bro," said Boyd.

"You open it. It's your safe," said Julian.

"Eleven, twenty-four, eighty-nine," murmured Boyd.

Julian went over to the large safe in the closet and typed in the numbers. The safe opened after a long beep. A tacky gold Rolex and a stash of cash were the first things he noticed. Behind the bills was an unmarked VHS tape that intrigued Julian. Next to the tape, he spotted a Smith & Wesson .45 caliber pistol and some ammo. Julian chuckled at the sight of the pistol. He pulled out a yellow, waterproof folder and assured himself the boat's papers were in there. He locked the door on his way out of the Captain's Quarters.

Julian was waiting on the stern when three U.S. Coast Guard officers came aboard. The three of them had guns on their belts and only one of them spoke. Julian was very respectful to the lawmen. He handed the ranking officer his U.S. passport and Baja yacht captain's license.

"Mayorca," said the ranking officer, "it says here you were born in Baja. How did you become a U.S. citizen?"

"My mother was from Santa Fe. Well, born in Albuquerque, but from Santa Fe, sir."

"Let me see your boat papers," said the ranking officer.

The other men roamed around the boat. Julian handed the officer the boat papers and he radioed in all of Julian's information. "What flag is that you are sailing under?"

"It's a Cayman Islands flag," said Julian.

The other two officers had all of the crewmen lined up and checked their passports.

"This ship does not have a departure permit. We are going to have to pull you into port," said the officer.

Julian shrugged as he heard Wendy's sharp voice, "What's going on here?"

"Ma'am, please identify yourself," responded the officer.

"I'm sorry officer. My name is Wendy Samson, and I am this ship's commander." Wendy handed the officer her Canadian passport. "I have chartered this vessel to Ensenada. As a matter of fact, I notified Admiral Jerry P. Bamp III, commandant of the U.S. Coast Guard, of my journey. You see, Admiral Bamp is a personal friend of mine. He and his wife Maggie spent Easter at my place on Vancouver Island this year."

The officer looked at Wendy briefly and returned her passport. He made another radio call and, soon enough, called off his men.

Julian was surprised Wendy's influence worked. He had never seen U.S. officials give into the kind of power-play he was used to seeing in Baja.

But then, *It's the same, the world over*, he thought.

This brief encounter with the Coast Guard reminded him of his days as port captain; this made him nostalgic and mad at the same time.

After the incident, Julian was fed up with Boyd's antics. He'd begun harassing and irritating the crew members. The next morning, Timbo, Matt, and Elsa held a meeting with Julian while Wendy and Monique tanned on the bow.

"We just don't think he's behaving in a professional manner," said Elsa. "He told me he wanted me to come to bed with him. He's lucky if I don't press charges against him for sexual harassment."

"Elsa, that is horrible. I promise you that it will never happen again. And if it does, I'll throw him into the ocean myself," said Julian.

"It's not that, it's that he has been drinking for days. He has forgotten his duties and has compromised this whole journey."

"I was about to kick his ass yesterday," said Timbo. "He kept repeating himself over and over about the U.S. Coast Guard coming aboard his yacht."

Julian's calm demeanor assured them he would keep Boyd in check. "There's only a couple of days left in the charter. Let's give it all we've got. Wendy's a great guest. She deserves our best. Even if Boyd is not up to standard, *we* have to be," he said.

The night they crossed into Mexican waters was a particularly starry night. Julian was very anxious about being back in Baja. He was talking to Wendy on the stern when he heard Frank Sinatra's *Watertown* begin playing loudly.

Boyd behaved a little better and he sang the words to the songs "What a Funny Girl" and "What's Now is Now."

That night, the whole crew and their guests came together for a family-style dinner. Most of them drank to excess, and Wendy was happy everybody was enjoying themselves.

"It's incredible how everything seems less tense already," Wendy was heard saying. "I can feel we're already in Baja."

Julian smiled and nodded, but deep down inside, he knew he was going to leave Baja as soon as he could. He thought about spending some time in South America after this journey came to an end; Chile and Argentina, in particular, were places Julian wanted to visit. The next morning, they arrived at the Marina Coral in Ensenada.

Even though Ensenada is on the Pacific side, and technically belongs to North Baja, Julian still felt too close to home. He didn't want to call the attention of the Ensenada port captain, Hector Valdez, a man he had battled fiercely against at the Port Captains Association. He made every effort to remain as invisible as possible, since he was certain he could run into a lot of people that he knew in this town. Although Boyd had reached an alcoholic plateau and was respectful with the Ensenada Port Captainship, Julian handled the registration upon arrival at the marina.

Boyd asked him to use his name.

"Why do *I* have to register *your* boat?" asked Julian

"Honestly, I slept with the dude's wife," said Boyd, dead serious.

"What?"

"I slept with the wife of the dude that owns this marina."

Julian laughed and shook his head. "Well, you're one in a million."

"Billion," said Boyd. "So be careful."

"Why's that?"

"Because there are six more like me out there in the world."

They both laughed.

Boyd looked at his watch-less wrist. "Oops, the seventh one is being born right now."

They erupted in laughter.

An hour later, the friendly dock master asked Julian for his identification. He showed him his Mexican passport.

Julian could almost tell that the dock master had identified him as the once-powerful port captain, but nothing was mentioned.

Boyd was very charming when the guests departed. He hugged Monique and kissed her on the cheek while Wendy invited Julian to her *vendimia* party at the Acorazado Vineyard later that week.

"What's a *vendimia*?" asked Boyd.

"It's a wine-harvest party that celebrates the end of summer," said Wendy.

Her same associate who dropped off the cash in Oregon came up to the yacht for her bags and loaded them into a black SUV.

The guests had finally left. The crew was happy about getting off the vessel, and Julian made sure to pay them out of the cash Boyd had in the safe. Boyd, at first, didn't want to pay them until they cleaned the yacht, but Julian assured him he would do the cleaning.

"The crew has done enough, Boyd. They want to leave," said Julian.

"Shit, I've done enough!" answered Boyd.

"I'll never work with Boyd again," said Timbo on his way out.

"Yeah, screw him. Drunk bastard!" said Elsa.

Julian had considered leaving that same night for a hotel, but he felt sad for Boyd and didn't want to leave him alone in his drunken state.

Over the next couple of days, while they were docked at the Marina Coral in Ensenada, Julian cleaned the yacht, waxed her, ran maintenance, and left her spotless. In the afternoons, he would walk Reyna, then drink a little bit with Boyd, who kept asking about Monique every five minutes. He also had the word *vendimia* stuck in his head and kept asking when the *vendimia* party was going to be. Julian was very patient with Boyd and made sure he ate at least twice a day.

The night before the *vendimia*, Boyd opened up to Julian about his alcoholism. He told him he had been drinking for over thirty years, since his daughter Josephine had committed suicide and his wife had left him.

"You know why this yacht's called the *Almost Heaven*?" asked Boyd.

"Because it's so comfortable?" answered Julian.

"No," said Boyd. "Because that was life when my daughter was still alive. That was my life with Josephine and Ciara, her mother."

He told Julian how his daughter's suicide had led to a downward spiral in his life, and since then, little by little, he had lost everyone.

"If it wasn't for my yacht and the sea, I would've died a long time ago," Boyd said.

Julian just listened to Boyd as he painfully admitted that he had no one left in the world except Julian and Reyna. Even though he felt a lot of compassion and empathy for Boyd, Julian was very aware of an alcoholic's manipulation skills and didn't want to be pulled deeper into Boyd's problems. He knew he couldn't stay in this environment much longer. Julian made up his mind to leave Boyd and Baja right after the *vendimia* party.

CHAPTER 5

Cecilia

Julian dressed casually for the *vendimia*: khaki slacks, a white and red buttoned-up shirt, blue Top Siders, and a light blue blazer. Boyd, however, dressed like a frustrated cowboy. He wore tight jeans, stingray boots, and a Stetson hat. Julian laughed a little when he saw Boyd's outfit.

"What, bro? Don't I look good?" Boyd asked.

"You look great!" answered Julian.

They hired a black car service to take them to the *vendimia* and back. Manuel, the driver, was very kind and played the Gypsy Kings on low volume as they drove through the mountains into Valle de Guadalupe.

They arrived at the vineyard at 1:20 p.m. There were already close to fifty people there. Wendy greeted them with a delicious Viognier. Julian thought the wine was fabulous, and Boyd must've had about seven glasses. Boyd asked around for Monique, but Wendy said she had to go back to Vancouver last minute to attend to some business on her behalf. Julian chatted with a couple of members of the Samson family. He was impressed with their simplicity, given how wealthy they were.

Wendy gave a speech, expressing her happiness and gratitude to the attendees. She also publicly thanked Boyd and Julian for the "fantastic charter" that had brought her down from Vancouver. As dusk closed in on the pristine property, the vineyards gave off an enchanting aroma and the red wines began flowing. First, they served a Tempranillo-Grenache blend, then a small batch Cariñana that surprised everyone for the better. To finish off, they poured a ruby-red Malbec.

Uh tannins.

The Malbec was very aggressive and put Julian in a strange mood.

The wine-induced euphoria saturated him with emotion. He tried talking to a gorgeous brunette with long shiny hair by the name of Genevieve, but she didn't give him a shot. The live band was playing a phenomenal fusion of Norte beats with jazz trumpets and Veracruz strings. Julian was very happy roaming around the party. He ran into Benito Pesquera, an old friend of his from the Mexican Naval Academy, who introduced Julian to his wife Marie, an English woman with a broken leg.

"Pardon me for not getting up," she said.

"My wife got her heel stuck in a rug at the supermarket," said Benito.

"Yes, and in Mexico there are no civil damages. I can't sue them for millions," Marie said.

"Well, we could go break the supermarket's windows if you'd like," said Julian.

"Is that how you handle things around here?" asked the Englishwoman.

"It's one way," said Julian with a big grin.

They all laughed.

He talked to Benito for a good amount of time. They mostly reminisced about their adventures at the Academy.

"How's your *primo*, Axel Cuevas?" asked Benito.

Julian felt a rush of anger at the very mention of his name. "Well, last time I saw him, he was taking my job as port captain of La Paz."

"Well at least it stayed in the family," said Benito, as he tried to downplay what obviously sounded like a major betrayal.

Julian and Benito drank more Malbec together and Julian went off looking for Boyd.

Boyd was talking to a group of five people quite loudly. He was telling the story of how he and Julian had met, adding in details that Julian didn't remember. He was saying things like "yeah, I took him in," and other strange comments like, "I saw potential in him."

It wasn't easy for Julian to ignore Boyd's stupid remarks, but Julian came to his senses and remained quiet. He chalked up Boyd's comments to his drunken stupor, and reminded himself that by this time tomorrow, he was going to leave behind Boyd and all of his bullshit.

Julian drank more wine while standing at the server's bar. He stained his blue blazer and khakis with some Malbec and tried cleaning it with white wine only to make a bigger mess. Just after 11:00 p.m., when the live music stopped, Julian asked for a beer because his mouth was purple and saturated with tannins. As he drank the cold craft amber ale, the Simon & Garfunkel song "Cecilia" came on the speakers.

Julian was overcome with emotion and his eyes watered as he listened to the song. Cecilia was his mother's name, and coincidentally, this was her favorite song. She used to listen to it all the time. Julian had memories of his mother getting ready at her dresser, playing this song as she multitasked and took time to talk to Julian about different things. She was a very intelligent woman who encouraged Julian to think things through in a rational manner, but she was also very spiritual and always taught him that when faith and reason clashed, faith was the better alternative. Julian noticed that one of the waiters was staring at him. Julian, who at this point, was shedding one long tear out of his right eye, got embarrassed, wiped his tear, and went off to find Boyd again.

Boyd was talking to a different group of guys. They were all very drunk and loud. Julian didn't like their appearance and tried to convince Boyd to head back to the yacht.

"Everybody's leaving, Boyd. The party's over!" said Julian as Boyd drank a sparkling rosé out of the bottle.

"Nah, nah, these guys are gonna go to the—what's it called, bro?" asked Boyd.

"Paris de Noche," said a fat German-American who introduced himself as Pete.

"They're telling me it's the best strip club in Baja." said Boyd.

"Well, I don't want to go. I'm drunk and tired," said Julian.

"What? We're all drunk. We're always drunk."

Boyd tried to persuade him to head to the club with them, but Julian insisted that he wanted to head back to the yacht. Boyd gave Julian the keys and told him to leave the door open so he could get in later.

"You know I love you," said Boyd with a drunken glaze. He walked away, looked back, smiled at Julian, and left with the guys.

As Julian said goodbye to Wendy, she put her right hand on his crotch and insisted that he stay the night.

"Oh my, you've got a nasty stain. I've got a really good cleaner here," she said, holding her hand on his bulge.

"Probably gonna toss these out anyway," said Julian.

"Toss them out with me," she said

This strategy wasn't working. "Yeah, but I've got a big wine stain all over myself."

She smiled and sipped her wine, her hand still caressing Julian's genitals.

He played dumb to Wendy's advances and left the party by himself. On his way out, Julian saw a case of Viognier that was left out on one of the reception tables. Without a second thought, he picked it up and stole it.

"She assaulted me, it was the least I could do," he drunkenly mumbled to himself as he laughed and put the case in the trunk.

Julian rode in the back seat of the black car and listened to Haydn's *Sonata in B Minor* that was playing on the Baja classical musical station, XLNC1.

CHAPTER 6

The Joker

J̲ULIAN WOKE UP THE NEXT morning with a horrible hangover. He was shaking with cold sweats and barely made it to the head where he vomited a purple and brown stew. He felt a little better, brushed his teeth, and drank two full glasses of water, only to puke again. The second time he made it outside and blew chunks overboard. The people on the yacht docked next to the *Almost Heaven* saw Julian vomit and shook their heads in disapproval. A flock of seven seagulls rushed to the vomit and began picking it out of the water.

"You see, it's bird feed," said Julian.

He walked himself back to the salon, but couldn't find a comfortable position to sit since his head was pounding. He looked over to the bar and saw the case of Viognier he had stolen from Wendy's party the night before. He felt an awful bitter taste rise from within.

Julian fell asleep in the salon for a couple of hours as the after effects of Baja wines wore off. He woke up again at 11:17 and drank more water. He was extremely hungry and felt like making some eggs, but the fridge and pantry were empty. He knocked on the Captain's Quarters and heard Reyna scratching at the door. He knocked again as he called Boyd, only to hear more scratching from Reyna. He opened the door and Reyna ran out of the room, wagging her tail. Julian entered the room and realized Boyd wasn't there. He looked for Boyd in the other staterooms and up on the bridge, but didn't find him.

He probably partied well into the night with Pete and the group of guys he was with.

Julian walked into town with Reyna and had birria tacos from a street vendor. The tacos were so delicious that Julian had six of them. He realized how much he had missed Baja cuisine. Julian bought a small bag of dog food for Reyna and fed her when they got back to the yacht. Boyd wasn't back yet, so Julian showered and packed his bags. At 1600, he was ready to leave.

He felt like renting a car and driving to Tijuana to spend a couple of days there before crossing stateside to San Diego, where he was going to look at his options for South American flights. At 1800, Julian was very irritated that Boyd hadn't arrived. He set the keys on the bar and began writing a goodbye note. When he finished, he tore it apart.

Boyd deserves better than being abandoned via note, he thought, and decided to wait to tell him goodbye in person.

Julian put on an old movie about a father and daughter who conned people into buying Bibles, and slept well into the evening. By 8:00 p.m., he was hungry again, so he got the clerk at the marina office to order a mushroom and olive pizza pie for him. He politely asked the clerk if anyone had seen or heard from Boyd. The clerk didn't even know who Boyd was. That night, Julian slept in the salon to make sure he heard when Boyd came in.

The next morning, Julian felt great. He hadn't realized how bad he'd felt the previous night until he felt himself at his optimum that morning. He hadn't heard Boyd come in all night, but he checked his quarters anyway. Boyd wasn't there. The yacht felt empty and Reyna was transmitting sadness.

Julian began to get angry at Boyd over his irresponsibility. He also wondered if this was Boyd playing an alcoholic's game for attention. As his anger waned, Julian began to feel concerned and decided to go out and look for him. He phoned the Acorazado Vineyard, where he was able to talk to Wendy. Julian told Wendy that he hadn't seen Boyd since the party, and although it was probably nothing to worry about, he had left with an overweight gentleman by the name of Pete.

"Pete's a good friend," said Wendy. "But I'll give you his number so you can talk to him personally." She read the ten-digit telephone number that began with an 858 U.S. area code.

When Julian called, Pete was already back in Carlsbad, California. He seemed surprised to hear from Julian and assured him that they had all left the strip club together. After that, Pete told him that he didn't remember much.

Julian took a cab to the Paris de Noche, but the doors were closed. A sign on the door read, *Open Daily from 7 to 7*. Julian walked around the bars near the club and asked the people who worked there if they had seen a sixty-year-old gringo with a ponytail a couple of nights earlier. One waiter remembered seeing a man who matched Boyd's description, and told Julian to check Caguas, a hole-in-the-wall bar that never closed. Caguas was a real shit hole. The smell of stale smoke and dried alcohol mixed with oversaturated toilets hit Julian in the face as he tried talking to the bartender, who remembered Boyd well.

"A crazy ponytailed gringo that kept talking about his yacht?" said the aging bartender. "The sun was about to come up yesterday when he left with Saulo, one of the locals."

Julian offered another waiter $20 to take him to Saulo. They caught up with him curbside two blocks down. Saulo was a scrawny looking boy. He was no older than twenty-two and looked filthy.

"Yeah, I remember Boyd. Him and I are cool," said Saulo as he struggled to stay awake.

"Do you know where he went after the two of you hung out?" asked Julian.

"He told me he was waiting for Santa to get off work, and that the two of them were gonna go have sex on his yacht."

"Who's Santa?" said Julian.

"A girl from Paris," said Saulo as he giggled.

As Julian observed Saulo closely, he noticed a little bit of white residue on his face. "Did you give him any drugs?"

"What?"

"Drugs! Did you give him any?"

"Uhmm, Boyd bought some drugs; he gave me some coke and weed and left with Santa."

"You saw him leave with Santa?" asked Julian.

"No, he told me," answered Saulo as he sat on the sidewalk and fell asleep with his head against a wall.

Julian wanted to find this Santa girl who worked at the Paris de Noche, but it was barely 1:00 p.m. and the club didn't open until 7. He decided to go to the police station, just to check if Boyd had gotten himself in trouble because of the drugs he had bought. The station in downtown Ensenada was a small building with three police officers, and none of them knew anything about Boyd, nor had they heard about anybody matching Boyd's description being picked up recently. They did advise Julian to go to the police headquarters uptown, where they would have more information.

The police headquarters in Ensenada was a very modern building. There were around fifty cops there and the place was buzzing with activity. Julian asked the officer at the reception desk about Boyd and the officer told him they had picked up an old gringo sleeping on the sidewalk who matched Boyd's description. Julian went back to the cells and spotted a ponytailed man from behind. When he called him, he realized it wasn't Boyd; it was an old U.S. veteran who looked homeless and didn't want to talk about anything. The police advised Julian to go look for Boyd at the major hospitals in town, telling him that if Boyd was still missing after forty-eight hours, Julian should return to file a missing-persons report.

Julian went to three hospitals that afternoon, each more gruesome than the last. He saw a girl come into one of the ERs with a sawed off leg, and a man who had bitten off his tongue due to a seizure, bleeding all over the floor. Julian walked all of the beds in the emergency rooms, but found no trace of Boyd. He asked as many nurses as he could about Boyd, but none knew anything about "an old gringo with a ponytail."

Disappointed, he walked on the boardwalk and had a tuna sandwich for supper at a food truck nearby. He felt like having a drink or two, but concluded that now was not a good time to drink. He stopped at the Little Havana Cigar Shop and bought a case of Cubans. He told the shopkeeper about his missing friend, but the shopkeeper only expressed empathy and offered nothing regarding Boyd's whereabouts.

Julian went back to the yacht to make sure Boyd hadn't returned. The yacht was quiet and Reyna was sleeping on Boyd's bed. Julian showered, because he still felt the hospital on his clothes. Later he put the case of stolen Viognier in the fridge and smoked a cigar on the bow as he waited for the clock to hit 7:00. While smoking his habano, Julian contemplated Boyd's situation and came to the conclusion that if he didn't find him tonight, he was going to have to call in favors from some of the high-ranking government officials he still had connections with.

Julian walked into the Paris de Noche at 7:40. The place was disgustingly tacky, with purple velvet walls and a ceramic Eiffel Tower sculpture-fountain near the entrance. Past the black curtains, blue and red neon lights illuminated a big stage with three poles. A bodacious babe with a redhead weave was swinging on one of the poles, and there were about ten men scattered around the spacious floor of the club. Julian sat down in a casual spot near the stage.

A friendly waiter asked him what he wanted to drink.

Julian handed the waiter a $100 bill. "I only came here for Santa."

He got escorted to a private booth upstairs by one of the bussers, and waited for about ten minutes. The red lights were beginning to hurt his eyes as "Love Song" by The Cure came on the speakers, and a beautiful green-eyed brunette wearing designer lingerie entered.

For a brief moment, Julian forgot what he was doing in the club and allowed Santa to sit on his lap.

As soon as he remembered about Boyd, he smiled and thought to himself, *I can't blame the bastard for wanting this beauty.*

Julian grabbed Santa and sat her next to him. She smiled and removed her bra, putting her breasts to his face.

Julian laughed a little. "I think you are very beautiful, but I only came here to talk."

"Ohh, so you are one of those," said Santa. "I get one every night. Never this early, though." She checked her small wristwatch.

"No, I came here to talk to you about a client you had the other night. An old gringo with a ponytail," said Julian.

"Who, Boyd?" said Santa with a tone of familiarity that was music to Julian's ears.

"Yeah, Boyd! I haven't seen him since the night he was with you, and I'm beginning to worry. Nobody seems to know where he is."

"Well, don't look at me," said Santa, looking at her nails.

"So what happened that night?" asked Julian.

Santa looked from side to side. "You know what, honey, I can't tell you anything else. I respect my client's right to privacy."

Julian took out another $100 bill and held it between his index and middle finger. Santa blushed, grabbed it, and put it in her little, plastic, see-through purse.

"I left him satisfied, and with a smile on his face," she said.

"Where exactly did you leave him?" asked Julian.

"At the hotel," answered Santa.

"What hotel? Why didn't you two go back to Boyd's yacht?" asked Julian.

"Oh, that was true?" said Santa with a laugh. "I thought he was lying. You see, in my line of work, I can't take chances. You know how many guys come in here bragging about their yachts and mansions? Plus, my boss doesn't allow me to make house calls anymore. I've had too many bad experiences." She took a napkin from her purse and cleaned a crumb of mascara from falling into her eye.

"Look, the whole night Boyd was after me. I danced a couple of songs for him, and he became obsessed, bragging about his yacht and telling me he wanted to take me to Barra Navidad with him. Of course I didn't believe him, but he insisted that I party with him on his yacht when I got off work. I told him I would charge him $300 if he met me outside the club at 7 a.m.," said Santa. "He wanted me to get in the cab with him, but I convinced him to come with me to the hotel, where I would be more comfortable. There, we partied pretty hard."

Santa smiled and scratched her nose. "We finished two bags of coke and fooled around a lot, but when we wanted to have sex, Boyd couldn't get it up. So I went down to the pharmacy and got him some Viagra. We had great sex after that, honey," said Santa as she ran her hand through the inside of Julian's leg.

Her touch made Julian aware of the difficulty of remaining focused. "Then what happened?" he asked.

"We smoked a blunt, and I left him while he was still puffing on it. In bed with a big smile on his face."

"What's the name of the hotel?"

"The Joker."

Julian rushed to The Joker Hotel, which was toward the marina on the main road. Out of all of the places in Ensenada, Julian would've never imagined to look for Boyd there. The Joker was a nightmare of a place with light-purple and pastel-green coloring. Outside, it had an enormous clay clown with a big rubber finger pointing to the hotel entrance. The lobby was a cold and spacious cement-color hall with cheap paint chipping off the wall. A middle-aged man wearing round glasses was sitting behind reception watching a small screen. Julian was irritated by the fake laughs coming from the TV as he approached the desk.

"Good evening," said the man as he stood up. "Welcome to The Joker." The man stuck out his hand and said, "I am Publio, the manager here. How can I assist you?"

Julian was disgusted by Publio, but he shook his hand. "I am looking for a guy named Boyd. An old gringo with a ponytail. Is he staying here?"

"That depends on who's asking," Publio answered like a quick-witted little weasel.

"Look, Publio, Boyd's my cousin, and I haven't seen or heard from him for the past couple of days. I am worried and I just want to make sure that he's all right."

"Well, worry no longer mister… Boyd is sleeping soundly in room 214. The maid went in there and tried to clean an hour ago, but I told her not to bother him while he slept."

"Thank you," said Julian as he ran up the stairs.

Julian knocked on door 214 and heard no answer. He knocked harder and still no answer. He saw a housekeeper walk by and asked her if there was anybody in that room.

"Yes, he's sleeping," said the robust aging woman.

Julian persuaded her to open the door with a variation of the same spiel he had given Publio below. When the door opened, Julian was relieved to see Boyd's silhouette. He flipped the light switch and saw Boyd's bare left foot sticking out of the bottom of the sheets. He recognized the cowboy boots and pants that were spread out on the floor. As Julian approached the bed, he saw the leftovers from the partying he had done with Santa: condoms, crumbled bags, empty bottles, and an ashtray with a blunt roach.

"Boyd."

No answer.

"Boyd!"

Still no answer. He touched his leg. It seemed stiff. Julian shrieked when he saw Boyd's face.

He ran downstairs to the lobby and shouted at Publio, "Boyd's not sleeping. He's dead, you idiot!"

CHAPTER 7

The Tape

THE POLICE ASKED JULIAN ABOUT his relationship with Boyd. Julian stuck to his story, calling Boyd his cousin. Julian knew the Mexican judicial system well and little white lies like this came out almost automatically.

"We came down from Seattle for a *vendimia*. I lost track of him after the party and hadn't seen him since," said Julian. "I looked for him everywhere, and finally found him here."

"Did you file a missing-person's report?" asked Officer Benson.

"I actually went to the station and the officer there told me to wait forty-eight hours before filing one," said Julian.

Benson asked him to sign a statement, and to write down a local address. Julian wrote the address of the Acorazado Vineyard and signed the statement.

"Well, you can come by the police headquarters tomorrow after ten. We'll have more information for you then," said Benson as he extended his hand.

Julian shook it.

"Sorry for your loss." The officer cleared the room.

Julian was exhausted when he got to the yacht, which was odd because he couldn't sleep. He opened a bottle of Viognier and drank a glass. He pet Reyna out on the stern and poured the rest of the bottle overboard.

"We'll always miss you, Boyd," he whimpered.

Reyna moaned, and Julian got choked up. At this point, Julian didn't even want to think about all the formalities and paperwork he still had to do for Boyd over the next couple of days. He thought about contacting somebody. But who? Julian fell sound asleep in the salon with Reyna next to him. The next morning he woke up at 10:30 and rushed to police headquarters.

The official ruling on Boyd's cause of death was "drug-induced heart attack." The police did not investigate, nor did they conduct an autopsy; they figured the evidence spoke for itself. Officer Benson was off-duty, so Julian had to talk to Officer Sandra Quintero.

"You can pick up the body tomorrow, once everybody signs off on it. We still need two signatures and we won't get them today," she said. "Since his passport card was in his wallet, we sent a notification to the U.S. consulate in Tijuana about the passing of a U.S. citizen. But because there's no suspected crime or investigation, it's up to the family of the deceased to establish further communication with the consulate if you want to repatriate the body."

Julian left police HQ with a yellow manila folder full of papers and pamphlets. He had breakfast at the Gorilla Cafe, where he ordered eggs benedict and drank orange juice. He went back to the yacht and used the satellite phone to call Shilshole Bay Marina in Seattle. He talked to Burt, one of the managers, and notified him about Boyd's death.

"Do you know if Boyd had any family?"

"No, nothing."

"He had an ex," said Julian.

"Well, he never told *me* anything about her," said Burt. "Let me look up his file."

Julian heard the clacking of the keyboard on the other end.

"He put Timothy Wade as a reference."

"Timbo?" asked Julian.

"I guess," said Burt as he read Timbo's number. Before they hung up, Burt asked, "So what's going to happen to the yacht?"

"I don't know," answered Julian.

He wasn't sure if he wanted to talk to Timbo, but he didn't have anybody else to call. He dialed the number and it was out of service; he dialed a couple more times and got the same result. Julian left the satellite phone on, just in case somebody called. He went into the Captain's Quarters, expecting to find something, anything, that connected Boyd to other people.

He had to have somebody.

He tried opening the safe in the closet, but couldn't remember the combination. Julian looked through Boyd's stuff, but only found old bank statements and random papers of no value to him. Frustrated, he threw himself onto Boyd's bed. He lay there looking at the ceiling for about five minutes, the smell of Boyd all around him.

Give me something. Anything.

As Julian was getting ready to stand up, he noticed a book stuck between the bed and the nightstand. It was tightly wedged in and took some effort to remove. It was an Alcoholics Anonymous textbook. Julian browsed through it and noticed it was heavily highlighted up to the fifth step, which read, "We admitted to God, to ourselves, and to another human being the exact nature of our wrong." Julian kept browsing through the pages and a small photograph with round edges that was being used as a bookmark fell out. Julian picked it up and saw a younger Boyd hugging an overweight teenage girl. Another woman with short hair was smiling next to them. The teenage girl looked a lot like Boyd, but she had the other woman's eyes. Julian figured this was the wife and daughter he had lost. He flipped the picture over and noticed written in cursive, *RIP Josephine Brunswick, you will be forever in our hearts. August 8th 1972 - November 24th 1989.*

Julian lingered in thought about Boyd and his past, and after a brief moment, it finally came to him. He rushed to the safe and typed in the numbers 11-24-89. A long beep. Julian's arm blossomed with goosebumps. The safe opened. Without a thought, Julian began emptying it of its contents. The first thing was the small pile of money — Julian counted $24,320 in cash and put $6,000 of the crispest bills in his pocket.

Dying costs money.

He tried the gold Rolex on his left wrist. It fit perfectly, but flashy gold wasn't Julian's taste. He grabbed the pistol, made sure there wasn't a round in the chamber, and put it back in its holster. He pulled out the boat's papers and went through all of them. He was somewhat relieved to find a phone number for Boyd's insurance company, though he couldn't help but think, *What is Boaters Insurance International going to do?*

He pulled out the final thing in the safe, an unmarked VHS tape.

He went into the salon holding the tape. There was only a DVD player in the entertainment system. He looked through the televisions in all of the staterooms. None had a VHS player. Julian walked Reyna around town and spent three hours trying to find a VHS player. He finally found one in a junk shop and bought it for $20. It was dusk when Julian returned to the yacht.

The image in the video had the date 08/13/1997 at the bottom of the frame in ugly digital orange numbers. There was an empty chair in a small, plain room. The camera shook a little and a younger Boyd, who was recording himself, walked into the frame. Boyd sat down in the chair, took a deep breath, and began:

"My name is John Boyd Brunswick. Everybody knows me as Boyd, and I'm an alcoholic."

Julian listened attentively.

"My alcoholism has destroyed my life, and it has destroyed the lives of everybody that has ever cared for me or loved me. It's been two years, four months, and sixteen days since my last drink. I don't know how it all began, and I don't want to make excuses anymore."

Boyd wept a little.

"I'm part of this program because I genuinely want to get better, and in accordance with the fifth step, there are certain things I must confess." Boyd stared at the floor for a moment.

"My daughter, Josephine, slit her wrists on November 24, 1989. She was seventeen years old." Tears came out of Boyd's eyes. "She had been fighting depression since she was fifteen. I never knew why, until I read her suicide note." Boyd began sobbing.

"She had been raped by a guy that I don't even remember. She described him as a tall man with dark hair and a goatee. She accused me and Ciara, her mother, of hosting parties all the time and not noticing her when she was being molested." Boyd wept.

"Ciara found the body, but I found the note. I didn't show it to anybody. Not to Ciara. Not even to the police, because I didn't want any more exposure."

Julian was heartbroken and a tear ran down his cheek as he continued watching the tape.

"Ciara and I kept drinking well after Josephine's suicide, but things rapidly turned eerie. She began blaming me and my parenting skills every day. Every day! She wouldn't shut up. She drank Bourbon straight and would weep every night. On the anniversary of Josephine's death, Ciara and I went to the graveyard to remember our daughter. That night, we got really drunk at Mel's, and she confessed to me that she wouldn't rest until she found out the reason for her daughter's suicide. I felt awful." Boyd rested his head on his hands.

"A couple of weeks after that, I moved out. I started working at the Keiser Real Estate office and got a small apartment on the eighth floor. I would still see Ciara once or twice a week. This was the first time I tried to get sober. I think I went, like, three months without a beer, but soon enough, I was drinking again.

On Saturday, May 11, 1991, Ciara came to visit me at my place. It was still early, so I wasn't too drunk. She was very sad, but we kept drinking, and eventually, as always, we started talking about Josephine. I remember her saying something, like, 'If I only knew why she killed herself, then I wouldn't be sad all the time.' I don't know why I lost it, but I did. I screamed at her and told her, 'You know why she killed herself? Because she got raped.' I told her I had found a note where she blamed both her and I for our drunkenness, and she completely went crazy on me."

Boyd stood up in almost desperation, but sat back down.

"She started accusing me of abusing my own daughter. I got furious and slapped her in the face. For the first time in my life, I slapped that woman in the face, and I must admit, it felt good." Boyd continued sobbing.

"She got up and told me she was going to the police, that she wasn't going to rest until she saw me pay for her daughter's death. Ciara bolted out the door, and I chased after her. As soon as I caught up, I pushed her."

Boyd wept even louder.

"I pushed her over the ledge. She fell eight stories to her death." Boyd's breathing turned heavy, his tears ripped out of a place deep within.

"My buzz faded away that very second, and I walked into my apartment in shock. I went into the bathroom and took a shower.

"A downstairs neighbor knocked on my door ten minutes later to tell me my wife had fallen. From that moment on, I've been playing the part—the part of the victim that I am tired of playing." Boyd stood up and rubbed his forehead.

"Luckily, for me, my next door neighbors weren't home and the police believed my story—that we had been drinking and having a good time, and that I had jumped in the shower before she left to go change because I was going to pick her up for dinner later. Her funeral was very sad, only her mother with Alzheimer's and I assisted.

I wish this story ended there, but no. I cashed in on her life insurance policy, and sold the dry cleaning stores she had inherited from her father. With that money, I started my real estate business."

Boyd took a moment. The hollow silence set in.

"I am making this video today, because I must confess my wrongs. I know I can't tell anybody. But at least I hope that someday, someone will know the truth. And that this exercise helps relieve some of the guilt that I've been living with all of these years. I am sorry Josephine. I should have been a better father. I am sorry Ciara, you deserved a lot better."

Boyd whimpered and sat in silence. After a moment, he stood up, walked toward the camera, and turned it off.

The television screen went blue.

CHAPTER 8

Atonement

THE BLUE LIGHT GENERATED BY the television created a disturbing environment. Julian turned it off and flipped the lights on. He didn't know how to feel. He went out on the stern and lit a cigar. He must have said the word "fuck" a dozen times that night while he smoked. He asked himself what he should do with the tape, and even though he didn't feel like talking to anyone, he felt incredibly alone. He fell asleep on the bow, gazing at the stars, but woke up in the early morning with mosquito bites all over his legs. He walked over to the salon and slept until eight.

The next morning, he felt anxiety and tension in his stomach. He decided to do something he hadn't done since his second year as port captain. He went on a twenty-minute jog and walked for another thirty. He was in the shower when he told himself he would do the civilized thing and bury his friend before finding out what to do about the tape.

He took a cab to police headquarters. Officer Sandra Quintero released Boyd's body at 1640. Julian contacted a funeral home and they sent a hearse. Julian rode in the front seat as he talked with the undertaker about the various packages available. For a moment, Julian contemplated the cremation package. He thought it would be nice to take Boyd's ashes out to sea and spread them all over the blue. But the thought of the video came to mind and Julian convinced himself that his best option was to handle Boyd's situation as quickly as possible.

At the funeral home, he closed a deal with the manager for their

"Plot Purchasing Package" that included a casket and graveside burial service. Julian picked a nice plot for Boyd, up on a hill, away from the highway with a clean ocean view. The manager lowered the price to $7,800. Julian paid him $5,500 and promised him the rest when he returned the next morning for the service.

"What religion did Boyd identify with?" asked the manager with the calm voice reserved for people in the business of death.

"I don't know," Julian said.

"Let's give him a Christian one. I've known priests that require baptism certificates to do a funeral service."

"Jesus!" said Julian

"Exactly," said the manager with a slight smirk.

That night, Julian had dinner and a beer at Wendlandt. He ran into an old couple from La Paz who were close friends of Gene and Luisa Cuevas. When they asked him what he was doing in Ensenada, he answered, "I'm here for a funeral."

The next morning, Reyna accompanied Julian to the burial service. The pastor's name was Lucas. He was short in stature and spoke with authority. The sermon was filled with beautiful analogies of life, death, and eternity. Julian paid particular attention to the verse, "Let the dead bury the dead." Pastor Lucas explained how this verse meant that the living shouldn't get caught up in death, since death has a logic of its own. The pastor closed with a prayer that Julian repeated. After the burial, Julian hugged Pastor Lucas and invited him for a cup of coffee.

Julian drank an Americano while Pastor Lucas had chamomile tea on the Cafe Tómas terrace by the port.

"Boyd had a deep secret that only I know about. It's a terribly dark secret, and I don't know what to do," said Julian.

"All of the dead have secrets," said Pastor Lucas. "Does this secret pose a threat to you or anybody else?"

"I don't know," answered Julian.

"Do you think that by sharing his secret you could endanger your life, or anybody else's?"

"I don't know if it would endanger me, but Boyd hurt a lot of people, most of whom ended up dead."

"I see." Pastor Lucas took a second. "Did you have anything to do with the people he hurt?"

"No. I only found out afterward, while looking through what he left behind."

"Well, if you remember the verse I shared during the service about the dead burying the dead, God is telling us that when things like this happen, it's important to let go of the dead's burdens. Let me say a prayer for you."

Pastor Lucas put his hand on Julian's shoulder.

"Lord Jesus, I pray that you give Julian strength to endure this loss. I also pray that you give him the wisdom he needs to make the right decisions. Reveal to him your holy plans, and lift this burden that doesn't belong to him."

Pastor Lucas got excited, and was almost shouting. "Lift this burden in the name of Jesus. We lift this burden in the name of Jesus!" He kept repeating it a few times, but then opened his eyes. "Are you a Christian?"

"What?"

"Have you accepted Jesus as your Lord and Savior?"

"Well, my mother made me pray to Jesus when I was a little boy."

Pastor Lucas took a moment. "Repeat after me: Lord Jesus."

"Lord Jesus…"

"I ask forgiveness for my sins…"

"I ask forgiveness for my sins…"

"I accept you as Lord and Savior of my life, and I invite you to come into my heart and rule over me…"

"I accept you as Lord and Savior of my life, and I invite you to come into my heart and rule over me…." Julian had his eyes closed and his head bowed, and although he hadn't prayed like this since his childhood, he felt the burden lift, and he knew exactly what to do.

"You're a Christian now. You're saved. You can never lose that, but you must treasure it, protect it!"

Julian nodded.

"God gave me a word for you, Jeremiah 29:11, 'For I know the plans I have for you, declares the Lord, plans for welfare and not for evil, to give you a future and a hope.' God has big plans for you Julian, do not harden your heart."

He felt a fire spark within. He felt peace and a sense of direction. "Thank you so much."

"My pleasure. God is going to use you, but you have to remain open to Him."

Julian didn't know what to say. He just nodded.

"Promise me you will call if you ever need anything. Here's my card."

"Of course." He put the card in his pocket.

Julian walked around town with Reyna, thinking about everything Pastor Lucas had said. He stopped at a fish market and bought tuna steaks. When he returned to the yacht, he grilled them astern and opened a bottle of Viognier. When he had finished dinner, he lit a cigar and puffed on it. Before putting the fire out, he threw the unmarked VHS tape with Boyd's confession into the burning flames.

"Your secret dies tonight, Boyd. Consider your sins atoned," Julian said as he watched the fire consume his friend's confession.

CHAPTER 9

Agencia Mayorca

REYNA'S SMELL WOKE JULIAN UP. It was something like rancid cheese and perspiration. He took her to the vet and got her a full grooming package, which included an oxygen-induced bath, teeth cleaning, nail trim, and anal gland cleansing. The vet asked him to return before six.

Julian went back to the yacht and showered. He put on khaki slacks, a black t-shirt, and Top-Siders. It was a little breezy but the sun was shining. On his way out of the yacht, Julian threw on Boyd's red Paul & Shark jacket that was hanging by the door.

He walked six blocks, past the small seafood stands and black market, to the municipal dock. When he got there, Julian headed to the upstairs floor and entered a wooden office. There was a sign on the door that read: "Alberto Fontana, Nautical Attorney." The office was filled with old Naval décor. Julian addressed the secretary very properly. He asked if Attorney Fontana was available. The secretary asked his name.

"Captain Julian Mayorca," he answered.

"Oh, so you are the famous Captain Mayorca. I hadn't had the pleasure of meeting you in person; I only talked to you over the phone," said the aging lady. "I am Margot."

"Oh yes, of course," he answered.

"Captain Mayorca!" said Alberto enthusiastically as he opened the door and hugged Julian.

"Alberto Fontana! How the hell are you?" said Julian, with a huge smile on his face.

They entered Alberto's office and Margot brought them coffee. They ate cookies while they caught up.

"I was down in La Paz three weeks ago, and I had a meeting with Axel Cuevas. Man, Julian, I know you two are family, but dealing with that son of a bitch is worse than pulling teeth. He makes everything so complicated. Not only that, he's sticking everybody."

"Hey, don't look at me," said Julian.

"You know how much he wanted to charge me a month for the use of the port for the Topolobampo ferry?" asked Alberto. "Twenty thousand! Twenty fucking thousand Julian! That's five times what you used to charge me. We settled on fifteen, and the motherfucker still tells me that *he's going to keep an eye on me.* I mean, what the fuck is that? *Keep an eye on me.*"

"The Topolobampo ferry? The one that transports scrap metal?" said Julian.

"Yeah, that one. I barely make any money on that operation now. Shit, I'm thinking about closing it altogether."

After both of them had expressed their disdain for Axel, Julian told Alberto that he had met his friend, the Mexican Ambassador to Canada, Gilberto Alarcón.

"Great guy, Gilberto," said Alberto.

"Yeah, I was in the Pacific Northwest after my retirement."

"What were you doing over there?"

"I don't know. Licking my wounds," said Julian.

Alberto laughed. "You know Gilberto is my compadre. I'm godfather to his oldest son. He and I did some business together back in the eighties. We made a shitload of money. We're still good friends and all, but ever since he became a diplomat, I hardly see him."

Julian told him how knowledgeable Gilberto Alarcón seemed about Baja.

"Gilberto is definitely a good guy to know," said Alberto.

"When I was over there, I hopped aboard a yacht charter and helped out as first mate," Julian said.

"You, as first mate?"

Julian smiled. "Times have changed, Alberto."

He took a sip of his coffee while Alberto had a little laugh that was interrupted by a cough.

"We came down from Vancouver Island, and it was a great experience."

He paused for a brief moment, contemplating what to say next. "When we got here to Ensenada, the captain of the yacht, who was also the owner, died."

Alberto became serious and looked at Julian. "He died?"

"Yeah, he was an alcoholic and went on a cocaine and drinking binge that killed him."

"Holy mother. Did he die aboard the yacht?"

"No, he died in a room at the Joker Hotel."

"The Joker Hotel. Huh. He was probably accompanied by someone from the Paris de Noche," said Alberto.

"I'm sure he was," said Julian. "The reason I came to you, other than to catch up, is because Boyd didn't have anyone. I've looked everywhere for a family member, or even a close friend, but nothing."

"Do you have the keys to the yacht?" asked Alberto.

"Yes, I do," Julian said. "Not only that, I've been staying there."

"When did he die?"

"Sunday. I buried him yesterday."

"How long have you been staying on the yacht?" Alberto leaned forward.

"I've lived aboard the yacht for about three months."

Over the next thirty minutes, Alberto questioned Julian on everything about the yacht: size, name, flag, financing, and insurance. Julian answered as best as he could, but there were many things he couldn't answer.

"Why don't we go see it?" Alberto asked.

They drove his blue Land Rover Discovery to the Marina Coral. Alberto was mesmerized by the *Almost Heaven*. He called her a "ladylike no other."

"She rides like a pro, too," said Julian.

"I bet she does with a beam like this," Alberto said as he looked at the polished steel rails that reflected the ocean. "Let me look at the boat papers."

Julian gave them to Alberto.

"Why don't you let me do some research? Let's meet again tomorrow at my office, and I'll have some answers for you."

Julian gave Alberto a cigar on his way out. "Let's go make a copy of the boat papers. I think I should keep the originals," Julian said.

"Relax, Julian. I'm gonna look out for you on this. Do you think I have forgotten all the favors you did for me when you were port captain?"

Julian smiled. "That's why I came to you, because you are a real friend to me, Alberto."

They hugged goodbye, and Julian didn't insist on making a copy of the boat papers. That evening, Julian picked up Reyna from the vet and had fish tacos for dinner. The next day, he arrived at Alberto's office ten minutes after nine. Margot greeted him with the same enthusiasm, and when he entered Alberto's office, the attorney was finishing a call.

"I ran the papers. She is paid for in full, and there are no liens on the boat, 100 percent clean," he said as he hung up the phone. He paused for a moment and looked Julian firmly in the eye. "So, what do you want to do with the boat?"

Julian itched his chest. "Well, if there's nobody claiming it, sell it for some real money."

Alberto smiled and let out a single laugh. "Listen Julian, selling the yacht is simple. All we have to do is come up with some forged documents. That's the easy part. However, we are going to have to cover our asses. If, one day, whoever buys it sells it, they could uncover us, and we could run into all kinds of trouble, and, frankly, I don't think it's worth it."

"What about Tom Loman out of Agencia del Cabo?" Julian asked.

"Loman is a piece of shit; he'll do his own research and find out the truth. Then he'll hold us over a barrel, pay us pennies on the dollar, and he'll chop her up into little pieces. I saw that yacht — she deserves better. Plus, Loman is for yachts that are hot. I checked this one out, she's clean. I mean, you said so yourself, you've been trying to find someone to claim her. But guess what? There's nobody claiming her."

Julian looked distressed, so Alberto stood up, walked around his desk, and sat on the chair next to Julian.

"Listen, you and I are friends. We have known each other for twenty years. I appreciate the fact that you trusted me enough to come to me with this. Let me give you my advice," Alberto said. He waited for Julian to make eye contact. "Keep it. Keep the damn yacht."

The news hit Julian strong. "I would love that, but I can't keep it. The moment someone runs her papers, they're going to see Boyd's name, and they're going to red-flag us."

Alberto shook his head: "Not if the yacht is undersigned to an *agencia*."

Julian smirked and realized what the attorney was saying actually made a lot of sense.

An *agencia naviera* is a Mexican legal instrument that holds power over ships and sea vessels. Like many things in Mexico, the *agencia* has its roots in the Mexican Revolution, and its sole purpose is to underwrite foreign vessels to Mexican citizens, or to a Mexican company while in Mexican waters. Any foreign vessel that holds commercial interests in Mexico must be represented by an *agencia naviera* if they want to conduct business legally in Mexico. Julian knew this, as he had dealt with many *agencias* as port captain, and had even worked for one in his early twenties.

"We'll still need to forge some documents, but that's easy," said Alberto. "Just tell me if this is something you want to do, and if it is, I'll help you."

Julian's mind went all over the place. At first, he was a little frightened over the potential legal problems, but then he thought about the *Almost Heaven* and Boyd's tape came into mind. He realized that if he took Alberto's advice, he was going to be attached to this yacht for the rest of his life.

Julian's heart began to rise and he said, "Let's do it."

"Yes!" Alberto high-fived Julian, who didn't get up from his chair. "Okay, I'll handle all of the paperwork. Just leave me your passport and your captain's license. I need you to do a couple of things. First, we are going to have to change the name of the yacht, just in case somebody recognizes it. Then, I would change a couple of things, primarily the color. I don't know, I'm not some artsy designer, but make it look different."

Julian laughed.

"This is a great opportunity for us. I'm glad you came to me. Better for the yacht to be in our hands than with some insurance company or government."

"So, how much are you going to charge me for all of this?" Julian asked. "I know you aren't going to go through all of this trouble out of the kindness of your heart."

Alberto laughed. "Listen, Julian, if shit ever hits the fan, I am as guilty and as involved as you. However, I am going to make sure that that never happens. Why don't we do this — you pay for the startup costs for *Agencia Mayorca*. The registration, business license, grease a couple of palms to speed up the process, and I'll partner up with you."

Julian leaned back on his chair and said, "*Agencia Mayorca*, huh?"

Alberto laughed a little. "Yeah, I just thought of that right now. You like it?"

Julian smirked. "It's not bad. What split are you suggesting?"

Alberto leaned forward. "First of all, you need somebody that has his naval agent's license." Alberto pointed at himself with his thumb and continued. "Secondly, we are going to have to run some sort of business out of the yacht. And for that, we need a certified Mexican yacht captain." Alberto pointed at Julian. "It makes no sense to have a vessel underwritten to an *agencia* if it's not operating a commercial business. Let's do yacht charters. At first we don't have to do too many, just a couple to keep our books active. Then we can make some cash flow. I won't be able to help you a lot on the operation side, but I'll keep our business address here at the office, along with a phone line—a line that me and my staff will answer, just in case anybody has questions for *Agencia Mayorca*, or any authority wants to double-check our papers. Also, you would have my legal expertise in case anything ever happens down the line."

Julian crossed his legs. "It all sounds great, but you still didn't answer my question."

Alberto laughed. "I don't want much. I just want twenty percent."

Julian looked down and told Alberto: "I appreciate everything you are doing for me. But *I'm* the one that's going to be exposing myself aboard that yacht; I am also going to be the one paying out everything, and all of the expenses and maintenance fees really add up. Or do you intend on giving me some money for the operation costs?"

Alberto shook his head.

"Let's make it ten percent."

Alberto and Julian shook at fifteen percent, and Alberto agreed to send Julian charter referrals.

"I also want two fully catered weeks a year aboard the yacht. You see, I've got this mistress, Tatiana, a real queen," said Alberto.

Julian agreed.

"Oh, one last thing. I know it's obvious, but our *agencia* won't protect us internationally, so that ship can never leave Mexican waters."

"I can live with that. I'll just take her to the Sea of Cortez," said Julian.

"And what about Axel?" Alberto asked.

The loaded question that could sink a ship.

"Well, we can't forget him, but if you and I go into business together, we've got to make a deal. We've got to get Axel back. I'm not talking about a slap on the hand, either. I'm talking about getting him fired and in jail—not just for extorting you and setting me up, but for the good of all of us; he's a huge liability," Julian said.

"That's a deal Mayorca!" said Alberto as he stretched out his hand.

Julian shook it.

"Let's be patient when it comes to Axel. I agree we can't live in fear of him, but we've got to be like tournament poker players and wait. We'll take a shot at him when we get our chance," said Alberto.

CHAPTER 10

Christened

THE NIGHT AFTER JULIAN SHOOK hands with Alberto Fontana, he had a dream in which he walked on the sea, holding his mother's hand. It was very strange, because he had only dreamt about his mother twice before in his life. When he awoke, he was both excited and nervous about the yacht situation. The memory of his dream brought him peace. But as he was sitting astern, he began to question his decision about appropriating the yacht. He began to feel guilty, but he remembered Boyd's tape, and somehow the fact that he knew Boyd's secret gave him enough justification to proceed. He realized that, like Boyd, he, too, was going to have to keep a secret.

Can I trust Alberto to take this secret to the grave? Julian thought as he did a mental inventory.

Julian had never participated in large schemes. He had a spotless record when he held public office; sure, he took and shared favors with friends, but he had always been a hardliner when people tried to bribe him. He remembered the day Axel Cuevas and Samuel Bracho made some goon hold a shotgun to his head. His temper began to rise, and just when the anger had returned, a gentle breeze swept the air. He looked at the ocean and its horizon. He felt embraced by the warm sun, and almost instantly, the weight of anger left him. He stood up with courage and decided to take this golden opportunity and own it.

"Fuck it, this is my yacht," he mumbled as he locked her up and headed into town.

The first thing Julian did was hire Dirk Gonzales and three other dockhands to shave off the name *Almost Heaven* from the back of the yacht. When they had finished, Julian hired Flor, a thirty-two-year-old designer with big curly hair and stunning Mediterranean features who was known around town for her styling.

"I need you to show me various options for style and font for the new yacht name."

"Sure thing. What's the new yacht name going to be?" Flor asked.

Julian stood up and wrote *Cecilia* on her whiteboard.

"My mother's name," his voice cracked slightly.

The designer asked to go aboard the yacht to "soak it in," and Julian hosted her for dinner. Three days later, Flor came up with only one design that had Cecilia written in Zapfino font. Julian loved it, and Flor traced it, painted it black, and gave it a non-glossy finish. The yacht looked gorgeous with *Cecilia* marked on her back.

Over the next two weeks, Julian went through all of Boyd's things. He kept some of his nicer stuff, like his jackets and his gold Rolex, but mostly, he donated everything to charity. He threw out the bedsheets Boyd slept in, and all of his toiletries. He also changed the combination on the digital safe. Julian destroyed the satellite phone and bought a new one that was registered to him. He also changed the GPS, just in case anybody wanted to track the boat.

Julian had a budget done by Flor to change all of the small details that had the yacht's old logo engraved, and to replace them with a letter C. Flor gave Julian what he thought was a very pricey quote, but Julian negotiated her down twelve percent over a bottle of Viognier.

Flor remodeled two of the staterooms—the Captain's Quarters, and the one with the amber sheets. Julian insisted they get new amber-colored sheets, but Flor got light yellow sheets instead. Flor didn't understand why Julian wanted to paint the exterior of the yacht. She thought the off-white was too beautiful to change. She compromised with Julian and painted a sleek black line on the periphery with an even thinner baby-blue line an inch below it. They sat on the dock, looking at the yacht for an hour after all the work was finished. That night, Julian and Flor made love in the stateroom with the light yellow sheets.

Alberto Fontana was pounding on the stern door the next morning. Julian opened it wearing only shorts.

"Good morning, Skip," said Alberto as he entered the salon. He sat down on the couch and rested his briefcase next to him. "I've got the boat papers for you."

Julian made a motion for silence with his finger. Flor walked out of the stateroom, smiled at Alberto, and poured herself a glass of water in the galley. She walked back into the room as Julian remained quiet until he heard the noise of running water.

"Not even a week as a yacht owner and already getting laid," said Alberto as Julian laughed.

"What are you talking about? I've been a yacht owner my whole life," he said.

The attorney handed the Captain boat papers in a folder that had *Cecilia* written on it. Julian signed three copies of *agencia* documents while he joked around with Alberto.

"Now, I have registered with Social Security to give us more legality, but we need to register a full-time employee. I would register you, but it has to be somebody who's not a stockholder. So we need to hire somebody," said Alberto as Flor came out of the stateroom fully dressed and ready to go.

"Flor, this is my partner, Attorney Alberto Fontana," said Julian as Alberto stood up. "Alberto, this is Flor, the beautiful designer who helped us with the remodeling."

"Oh, you did a wonderful job," said Alberto.

They shook hands, and Flor reached down and kissed Julian on the lips. Julian told her that he would call her that night, and she winked at him as she walked out the door.

"Look at you. She's beautiful," said Alberto. "Here, let me sit closer to you. Let's see if some of that will rub off on me."

Alberto moved closer to Julian and began caressing him. Julian laughed and pushed him away.

When Alberto left, Julian picked up his satellite phone and called Jose Rubio in La Paz.

"Hello?" said Rubio with a broken voice.

"I am looking to hire a sailor that can cook, and I'd prefer if he was missing an eye," said Julian.

"Goddammit, Mayorca. I haven't heard from you in over a year."

"No, it hasn't been that long."

Rubio and Julian caught up, and Julian explained that he had finally used his parent's inheritance and bought a yacht.

Rubio was impressed. "Everybody always said that your parents had left you a lot of money in the states, and that your frugalness had always prevented you from actually using it," said Rubio.

Julian laughed. "Well, my frugalness helped me to be patient until I could get a deal that worked for me. And wait till you see this beauty. I named her *Cecilia* after my mother."

Before long, Julian had convinced Rubio to quit his job at Bandidos Fish Tacos and come up to Ensenada for the Christening ceremony later in the week. Julian asked Rubio for a bank account number and promised he would deposit some cash so that Rubio could buy his plane ticket and cab fare to the Marina Coral in Ensenada.

"I am on slip C-13," said Julian.

"I will be there on Friday. It's going to be nice being on the water again," he said before they hung up.

Julian spent the next couple of days acting like a married couple with Flor. For the christening ceremony, they wanted something simple but meaningful, so Julian decided to contact Pastor Lucas.

When Rubio arrived, Julian was making preparations with Flor in the salon. He was so happy to see his old friend that he completely ignored Flor for the rest of the day. She resented this, and left early that evening. Julian didn't care. He wined and dined Rubio at Sano's Steakhouse. They had a marvelous time; the kind of time only best friends can have together, joking around loudly about everything, yet somehow still tender and present.

The next day, they christened *The Cecilia*. Pastor Lucas gave a message about having enough faith to walk on water. Julian vividly remembered his dream about his mother, while Alberto, Margot, Flor, Rubio, and Reyna listened attentively.

After Pastor Lucas prayed for protection and said, "Amen," Julian thanked everyone for helping this dream come true. He asked Rubio to lower the tender, and they went around the bow. To christen the yacht, Julian smashed the last Viognier bottle from the case he had stolen from Wendy's party. Everybody clapped and cheered as *The Cecilia* celebrated her seaworthiness.

CHAPTER 11

Corazón

RUBIO WAS PLEASED TO BE working for Julian again. He went to the local markets and stocked up on everything he could get his hands on: steaks, ribs, shrimp, lobster, marlin, tuna, snapper, and snook. He also got Asian and local spices, chiles, vegetables, noodles, rice, beets, tortillas, beer, wine, liquor, and fruit. Julian had given him orders to manage the galley and cook three healthy meals a day.

On the days following the christening ceremony, Flor kept coming around the yacht. Julian didn't mind this at first, but after some time, he started to get tired of her. She kept pressuring Julian to take her out to sea; Julian had every intention of doing so, but he disliked the way she said things. He felt she had an immense sense of entitlement, and that repelled him. Flor started to complain that they never had any time alone. One day after dinner, she even blamed Rubio for taking Julian away from her. When Flor said this, Julian calmed her down, took her into his quarter's and made love to her.

The next day, Julian made arrangements to take Flor out to a nice dinner at Corazón de Tierra. They dressed their best and got black-car service. The restaurant was glowing in the evening light. Its earthy tones and modern architecture contrasted with the dirt road they had taken to get there. At sunset, the property's vineyards released a magical scent of lavender and roses that fascinated them. The quality of service was impeccable. Julian and Flor got served an impressive twelve-course meal and a smooth Sangiovese-Cabernet blend made by Casa Magoni.

When they had finished dinner, Flor reached out to touch Julian's hand, but he withdrew. Julian took a swig from his glass.

"Listen, Flor, you're really nice and all, but this isn't going to work."

"What do you mean?"

"I don't want you coming around the yacht anymore."

"Is that it? You're through with me? Well, why didn't you just tell me? Why did you take the trouble to bring me all the way out here?"

"Well, I thought about it. I figured we might as well break up in a really nice place. You deserve that. You're a real nice girl. Plus, I've never tried this restaurant before. It's impressive."

"Yeah, you're a real gentleman. Call me if you ever remodel another yacht," she said with disdain as she set her business card on the table.

Flor excused herself, and Julian made arrangements for the black car to take her home. Their last goodbye was Julian waving as the car drove off, dusting the air outside the restaurant. He went back into Corazón de Tierra and got drunk with the chef, who introduced himself as Diego. They drank Robalmas mezcal until four in the morning, and Julian asked Diego to call him a cab.

Rubio was happy that Julian had broken up with Flor.

"I never liked her. She was so controlling," said Rubio.

"Well, we won't have to deal with her anymore."

Julian used this time to familiarize Rubio with the yacht and all of its features. They went through all of the controls, the safety measures, ship procedures, and inspected the engine room. Rubio loved the yacht. However, he was most impressed with the hard drive with all of the albums and movies.

"So, you're telling me I can play any one of these songs on command?" Rubio played "Human Nature" by Michael Jackson.

"Oh god," said Julian.

"That's right," said the cook.

During the next week, cold weather and strong fog began to creep into Ensenada Bay. Julian began to grow tired of the cold and impersonal Pacific. He longed for the Sea of Cortez. He thought about La Paz a lot, mostly about the warm weather, the fishing, and the good people. Sometimes the thought of Axel would enter his mind, but he would tell himself that he wasn't going to be exiled or destroyed by what Axel Cuevas had done to him.

"At the end of the day, I'm pretty much retired. I just want to lay low and be on my yacht," he told Rubio one evening.

"Good for you to enjoy life, Skip. I mean, somebody has to, right?"

On a not-so-foggy day, Julian awoke early and fueled up *The Cecilia*. He stopped by the marina office and paid the dock fee. When he got back to the yacht, he noticed there was almost no wake. He turned on *The Cecilia* and took her out. Rubio met him up on the bridge when Julian was going about nineteen knots in the middle of Ensenada Bay with Todos Santos Island starboard side.

"Where we going, Skip?" asked Rubio.

"Home," said Julian as the wind blew his hair.

CHAPTER 12

Nowhere

THE ENSENADA-CABO SAN LUCAS RUN was a route Julian had skippered before. He was very confident about the journey, even if he only had one other crew member. He made sure to stay coast side, not only because of the view, but because he didn't want to entertain the slightest possibility of straying into international waters. Julian was on helm almost all of the time; he even slept on the bridge. Rubio would bring his food up and keep him company during the day. When they crossed the 28th parallel, the weather embraced them with some warmth. They anchored and rested for a couple of days.

As they continued their journey south, Julian remembered his days in the Mexican Naval Academy. Sleeping very little, boating a lot, grinding out hundreds of hours at sea.

"Only 180 miles to Cabo," he said as they watched the sunset while anchored in Santa Maria Bay.

"You excited?" asked Rubio.

"I'm ready for what's next. Life is about stages, and this one, we're going to enjoy."

"I'll drink to that," said Rubio, as he poured eighteen-year-old Highland Park single malt Scotch whiskey over rocks.

"You know what's better than being port captain?"

"What's that, Skip?"

"Freedom. Axel doesn't have freedom. We do," said Julian.

Rubio nodded.

The next day there was a lot of wake. Julian attributed this to their proximity to Cabo, where two seas meet.

When the winds began blowing strongly, Julian told Rubio, "It's a sign of a good winter."

They abandoned the coast to beat the wake and winds. While on the open sea, everything was smooth. Julian set the GPS coordinates to Cabo Marina and relaxed in the sun. He handed the helm over to Rubio and laid out on the bow. *Everybody Knows This Is Nowhere* by Neil Young with Crazy Horse played over the yacht speakers. As he thought about home, and how cool and breezy it was, Julian sang out loud.

"Everybody seems to wonder what it's like down here... Gotta get away from this day to day running around... Everybody knows this is nowhere...."

As Julian exhaled deeply and stretched his legs, he felt a rumble below. It didn't feel like an engine, so he looked up to the horizon and saw a wall of water coming his way. He jumped to his feet.

"Rogue wave!"

Rubio froze the moment he saw the water wall approaching. Julian climbed through the front and pushed Rubio away from the helm. Out of instinct, Julian steered the ship straight into the wave while lowering her speed. Rubio prayed out loud, holding up his hand like a Mexican Moses wishing for the sea to split. Water splashed aboard. Julian gripped the helm, Rubio hung onto the rail, and the yacht rose over thirty-five feet.

Rubio looked below and whimpered.

The second the yacht plateaued atop the wave, Julian turned it port side and revved both engines. The drop came seconds after that, but Julian managed to get the yacht to slide on the back of the wave. When she hit against its tail, Julian straightened her out and decelerated to a halt. The yacht stabilized, floating aimlessly while Julian and Rubio saw the wave from behind. It was heading nowhere fast.

Rubio was shaking. Julian smiled and hugged his friend.

"Goddammit, Julian. I swear I thought we were done for," said Rubio.

"Well, we would've been if I hadn't jumped on helm," Julian said with a chuckle.

"Screw you, Julian." Tears were running down Rubio's cheeks.

Something below them popped. They headed down to the engine room.

"It's a piston," said Rubio.

"It must've overheated when I forced it," Julian said. "Damn! We're gonna have to kill it and make it down to Cabo on one engine."

They did a complete check of the vessel and realized the electric system was also acting up.

"None of the lights up here work," Rubio said.

Julian got back on helm, committed to not stopping until they reached the Cabo Marina.

CHAPTER 13

Cabo Wabo

THE SUN ESCAPED OVER THE ledge of *The Cecilia* as they pulled into Cabo. The marina was full; boats of all shapes and sizes occupied the slips. Julian pulled up to the main dock, and Rubio tied her down. People walked up and down the pier, almost like it was a public street. Some of them complimented *The Cecilia*. When he got to the marina office, Julian asked for Joan Valencia, the owner of the marina. The manager said she wasn't in.

"I am sorry, sir, but there are no slips available," said the manager.

Julian was frustrated by this, and explained his broken engine situation. The manager showed very little sympathy. Julian made clear to the manager that he was a close friend of Mrs. Valencia, and asked that the manager get his boss on the phone. The manager dialed, but there was no answer. Julian told the manager that he was looking for a lot more than a slip.

"I need a mechanic, an electrician, and a detailed service — maybe even pull her out of the water and check her out. You see, we caught a rogue wave about thirty miles out."

The manager looked out the window at *The Cecilia*. "We don't have a big enough lift for a yacht that size. You need a 100-ton lift. There are only two of those in the whole state. You know who has one? The Circus Marina. Let me call them."

That same night, Julian and Rubio moved the yacht over to the Circus Marina. It was a small and dark marina, dirty because of its industrial nature. They gave him a slip, but couldn't connect him to electricity. Julian arranged to get a mechanic to take a look at the engine the following day.

The entrance into Cabo had been very stressful for Julian and Rubio.

They were sitting on the stern of the yacht in the darkness. "You know what? We almost died out there. Let's go out and have a drink somewhere, maybe even get you laid."

They took half an hour to get ready. Julian wore white and blue striped pants, a white shirt, and docksiders. When he was leaving, he went back into the Captain's Quarters, opened the safe, and put on Boyd's gold Rolex. The Cabo strip was packed with people, Mostly snowbirds from Canada and the midwestern United States accompanied by their twenty-something children. They tried to get a table at The Office, but there was a two-hour wait. Then they tried to grab a cocktail at Mandala, but there was a multitude of people trying to get in.

"Forget this," said Julian.

They settled for street tacos. Julian slipped a $20 to the doorman at Squid Roe and got into the overcrowded club. They each drank a yard of some alcoholic potion known as Green Giant, which finally loosened them up. The music did not agree with Julian's taste. They were playing some sort of rap or trap in an ugly mix of other genres that Julian didn't even know existed. The only song he recognized was a remix of "Sweet Child o' Mine" by Guns & Roses, and even that was a song Julian didn't really like. They left with a mild buzz.

They walked by Sammy Hagar's place, a cantina-lounge by the name of Cabo Wabo. There was a live rock band playing, so Julian thought it would be a good idea to go in for a drink. Cabo Wabo was a fun place where people sang along to The Eagles and other classic rock that Julian found better than the shit they were playing at Squid Roe. Julian and Rubio drank the house tequila and shared jokes with some of the other people there. Two gorgeous ladies, by the names of Jennifer and Amy, walked into the cantina wearing all white. Julian was immediately attracted to them and approached them. The ladies were easy-going, fun, and lively. They called Rubio over, and the four of them seemed to hit it off.

Julian and Rubio were throwing back tequila shots and cocktails as they laughed and flirted with the ladies, who mentioned they were staying at The One & Only Palmilla. Julian went to the restroom, and on his way out, bought some condoms and a cheap cigar from the men's room attendant. When he returned to the table, three guys were talking to Jennifer and Amy. The guys were in their twenties, very well-built and tall. They were all wearing flip-flops and shorts. Julian took his old seat at the table and chewed his cigar.

"Excuse me," said a guy wearing an orange tank top.

"You're excused, young man," answered Julian.

"No, you see, bro, I was going to sit there."

Julian shook his head. "No. You see, you are not my bro." He pointed at Rubio. "He's my bro, so don't insult me. And show some respect for people having a conversation."

The ladies looked and smiled at Julian. The other two guys looked at their "bro," wondering what he was going to do.

"Oh, I'm sorry, I didn't know Captain One-Eye had a retarded brother," said the other bro, as his two friends laughed. Julian realized that this was the main bro.

Julian looked at Rubio and gently bit down on his cigar. He felt a gentle twitch in his left eye.

"You know what, you're right, maybe *I* was the one being rude. Let me buy you a drink. As a matter of fact, let me buy all of you guys a drink."

Julian called the waiter and ordered beers for all of the guys, shots of tequila for him and Rubio, and cosmopolitans for the ladies. When the drinks arrived, Julian paid $100 and told the waiter to keep the change. It was close to a $50 tip.

Everybody had a drink in their hand, and Julian proposed a toast to Cabo. They all said cheers and touched glasses. Julian took his shot quickly and looked at the main bro, still drinking his beer. Julian punched the bottle of beer straight into the bro's cheekbone and continued punching his head and stomach. Rubio threw his shot of tequila into another bro's face, and they all began fighting. Julian didn't move very quickly, but he was landing strong punches. The main bro's face was bleeding. The second bro grabbed the table and hit Julian in the back with it. The ladies' drinks flew into their laps and drenched their white clothes a pinkish red. They ran out screaming. Rubio grabbed a barstool and hit the bro who had hit Julian on the back of the head, knocking him unconscious. With two of the bros on the floor, Rubio and Julian focused on the main bro, who began to apologize.

Julian grabbed the man's face with both hands.

"Listen here, boy," he said. "Never, ever insult a man in the presence of another man who is willing to die for his friend. Are you willing to die for your friends?"

The man nervously shook his head.

"Well, that's the difference between you and us; we are willing to die for each other." Julian turned around swiftly and kicked the man in the stomach. He and Rubio looked at each other and realized the bar had gone silent, and everyone was looking at them. They ran out the door.

The Cabo police were waiting for them. Julian and Rubio tried dodging the officers, but they chased them down. Their hands were zipped-tied, and they were put in the back of a police pickup truck. The truck made a stop en route to the jail, picking up a transvestite named Carmela. She was very funny and asked Julian to forgive her for her appearance.

Julian laughed. "You look fabulous, honey," he said.

When they arrived at the jail, Julian's back began pulsing in pain from being hit with a table.

The officer went inside the small jail and left Rubio, Carmela, and Julian alone in the back of the truck. When he returned, he untied Rubio. As he began untying Julian, he noticed his gold Rolex.

"We are going to have to take this off. We don't want it to go missing while you're in here," he said as he unbuckled the Rolex.

Julian nodded, and when the cop least expected it, he headbutted him with all his might.

"Oh, right on the nose," said Carmela, laughing.

The officer fell down and almost unconsciously reached for his gun. Rubio quickly grabbed the cop's gun out of his belt and helped Julian release himself from the zip-tie. The cop began cursing them out, as two cops came outside to his aide. Rubio pointed the gun at the two cops and they raised their hands. Julian helped Carmela remove her zip-tie. Carmela took the gun from Rubio and pointed it at the cops.

"Run, get outta here," she said.

Julian and Rubio bolted.

"Now, you pigs are going to pay for all of the times you've brought me here for no reason," was the last thing Julian heard Carmela say.

Gunfire rattled the air as the two disappeared into the night.

CHAPTER 14

The One and Only

JULIAN AND RUBIO RAN TO the Circus Marina. When they got there, they tried getting in, but the gate was locked. They yelled out for the gatekeeper, but only Max, the guard dog, came to the door. Julian sensed the police after them, so he advised Rubio to get out of there. They took a dark path through trees and sandbanks. After what felt like an eternity, they found themselves on a remote beach. Julian and Rubio sat speechless in the sand. After a while, they looked at each other under the moonlight and laughed uncontrollably.

By the time they finally got back to the marina, the sun was rising.

The people who worked there made stupid remarks like, "Rough night?" and "I wonder what you guys were up to?"

Julian and Rubio didn't say a word.

When they got into *The Cecilia*, they noticed Reyna had pooped on the salon carpet. Rubio took to cleaning and Julian fell asleep for a few hours. When he woke up, he showered.

"You think we're going to get prosecuted, Skip?" asked Rubio

"Don't think the bastards got any ID. How will they find us?"

Julian dressed incognito as he took Reyna for a walk around town and picked up a local newspaper. The headline read: *Transvestite holds jail hostage for five hours.* The article talked about Carmela, portraying her as brave for standing up to abusive cops that had harassed her for years. There was no mention of accomplices or descriptions of him or Rubio.

He felt bad about how he had gotten himself in such a shit situation, but was proud that he could get away with it.

I can still hold it down.

He had thrown punches and succeeded, that was important for a sailor.

He remembered a song he had heard the night before at Squid Roe. It went, "*Blame it on the ah-ah-ah-ah-ah ah ah- alcohol.*" Julian smirked for a second.

He threw the paper in the trash and walked into Luxury Avenue, a boutique mall with high-end stores. While window shopping, he came across a store named Jacoby & Jewels. There was a gorgeous black-strap, black-face Bell & Ross watch on display. He went in and inquired about the timepiece. When he tried it on, he felt the quality of the automatic movement and the absolute precision it represented; the spotless sapphire crystal, elegant round design, bold forty-two-millimeter black steel case, black dial, and white hands. It had the two chronograph dials off-center, and the date between the four and five o'clock marks. Time on this dial didn't tick, it glided. Just a masterpiece of a thing.

The staff was friendly and even gave Reyna some water out of a red doggie bowl they kept by the register. The sales associate helping Julian was a slim black girl named Colette. She complimented Julian's watch, and said it was much more suitable for a man like him than the shiny gold Rolex he came in with. Julian didn't really like the gold Rolex, either. Somehow, he believed that last piece of Boyd was what had gotten him into trouble the night before. He made a deal with Colette and bought the Bell & Ross watch, with the condition that he would leave the gold Rolex with her on consignment. Colette agreed to notify him when they sold it. Julian gave her his satellite phone number.

When Julian returned to the marina, he was beat-up. His back was aching, and he even felt a fever coming. He asked about the mechanic, and the marina manager told him he had called to say he was booked all day. They were going to have to wait another day for him to take a look at *The Cecilia.*

When Julian entered the yacht, Rubio was asleep and Reyna needed a bath. Julian was not in a good mood, especially since they couldn't turn on any electronics. He woke up Rubio and called a cab. They dropped Reyna off at the Paw Center so she could get her bath, then headed over to the One & Only Palmilla. He got a two-bedroom suite for one night. It was just what they needed, a little bit of beauty and comfort. Rubio slept well into the afternoon, and Julian went to the spa where he had a deep tissue massage followed by a steam bath. Rubio woke Julian for dinner at 8:15 p.m.

The pair dined at the Market Jean-George, and then headed to the bar at Aqua. As soon as they entered the bar, Julian smiled when he realized his plan had worked. Jennifer and Amy, the two ladies at the Cabo Wabo the night before, were sitting at table number three. Julian approached the bar and asked the bartender to send the two ladies a bottle of Champagne. When the bottle arrived at their table and the ladies saw Julian and Rubio, they became ecstatic. They hung out all night, drinking Champagne, red wine, and vodka cranberries. It was a fun night for all of them, two middle-aged couples acting like teenagers in love. Julian took Jennifer to his suite, where he used the condoms he had bought the night before. Amy took Rubio with her.

The next day, Julian woke up and Jennifer was gone. He called the front desk and asked to be connected to Amy's suite. Rubio answered the phone. He told Julian the girls and their luggage were gone. When Julian checked out of the hotel, the receptionist gave him a very large bill that included everything from Jennifer and Amy's room. He tried to argue about the charges, but the receptionist told him Jennifer had said she was his wife. Julian couldn't believe it; he had been scammed by a couple of broads. He refused to pay for everything Jennifer and Amy had spent. The manager arrived and told them that if they had been scammed, the police had to be notified. Julian realized Jennifer and Amy knew they wouldn't press charges against them because of fear of repercussions for the previous night.

"At least we got laid," Julian told Rubio as he signed away thousands of dollars in hotel charges that didn't belong to him.

The pair picked up Reyna from the Paw Center and headed to the Circus Marina. The marina manager informed him that the mechanic had arrived earlier, but since he didn't find anyone aboard the yacht, he'd left. The manager called the mechanic, but he said he was busy until the next day.

"Well, is there any other mechanic that can come and look at the yacht?" Julian asked.

"Unfortunately not. We only work with him since he is the only one that is bonded and insured to work out of here," said the manager.

"You make it sound so professional. But you know what? I figured out why this place is called the Circus Marina. Because it's ridiculous. It's a damn circus, and you're all clowns," Julian said.

He got aboard *The Cecilia* and turned the engine on. Rubio untied the yacht as the marina manager came running up, asking to be paid.

"Pay you for what? You didn't even give me electricity or a decent slip."

"Well, you might be right. How about you fuel up with us, and we call it even?"

Julian agreed, but only fueled it to half. Julian and Rubio left Cabo with the same engine problems they'd arrived with and with a sour taste in their mouths.

"At least I bought a nice watch," said Julian.

"Yeah, what time is it?" Rubio asked.

"11:05."

CHAPTER 15

The Real Baja

THE WARM BREEZE HIT JULIAN's face as they passed Los Barriles, a small town north of Los Cabos. Rubio came up to the bridge with smoked wahoo salad and tostadas. As they ate, they spotted a large group of kite surfers doing tricks off the coast. The Sea of Cortez's power began infiltrating Julian's soul, and a smile crossed his face. North of Los Barriles, the wake and winds simmered down. The sun began to let loose its magical colors on the Sea of Cortez — turquoise and orange tones mixed with baby-blue waters all bathed in a noble yellow that saturated the coast.

"Well, even with a broken engine, you can't beat this," said Julian.

Rubio handed him a Cuban cigar, and Julian just chewed on it. They enjoyed a quiet ride up to La Paz. There was a lingering feeling. It wasn't nostalgia or bittersweetness; it was a kind of introspection that only exists upon these waters. It was all of the memories about the times Julian had been on this sea, memories condensed into one single indescribable feeling.

"Man," said Rubio "these waters have healing powers. I can already feel myself being relieved of all of the tension."

"They sure as hell do," said the captain with a chuckle.

When they passed Espiritu Santo Island, Julian began wondering what La Paz would be like upon his return. He had been gone for less than a year, but it felt like an eternity. He wondered whether the port captain's office still ran the drills that he had commissioned.

"I wouldn't worry too much about the new port captain," said Rubio. "Word on the street is that he isn't doing much except getting rich."

"Well, he's not gonna get rich off of me. I'll shoot him before giving up another inch."

"That's the spirit," said Rubio as they slowed down and entered the Bay of La Paz.

Julian secured a slip at the Marina Palma, a small marina owned by the Aburto family. He knew them well and had maintained a good relationship with them over the years. Felix Aburto received Julian with the utmost attention and guaranteed him all of the marina services he requested. Julian, Rubio, and Reyna stepped onto the streets of La Paz as the sun was setting. "Let's go over to Bandidos and have us some octopus," he said.

Bandidos was the same as he remembered it. The grills were going strong, and people were happy to see both him and Rubio.

Kiko, the owner, came out and greeted them.

"When Rubio told me that he was leaving to go work for you, I couldn't stop him. Even though he's a great cook, I was happy, knowing that you had someone trustworthy with you out at sea."

"Yeah, that makes all the difference," said Julian, putting his hand on Rubio's shoulder. That night they ate like kings. Heavy portions of grilled octopus and lobster, South Baja-style Caesar salad, and tomato gazpacho. The manager offered them some mezcal, but Julian declined.

When they finished dinner, Julian told Rubio, "I'm gonna go back to the boat. Can you take Reyna home with you?"

"Why aren't you going to your place?" asked Rubio.

"Well, I left the keys on the yacht, and I'm pretty sure my house is dirty, and I don't know if my electric bill got paid. Don't want to deal with anything until tomorrow."

"No can do Skip. Either we all stay on the yacht, or we all go back to my place."

Julian thanked Rubio for his solidarity and insisted on some alone time. Rubio understood and left with Reyna as Julian walked back to the yacht.

The next morning, Mauricio, the mechanic, came and looked at *The Cecilia*'s engine. It was burned out and needed a new piston along with an oil change. He suggested a full service on both engines. Julian authorized the work and Mauricio began almost immediately. Julian grabbed the keys to his place and walked home. On his way, he either waved hello or talked to at least a half-dozen people. All were interested in where he'd been. Many were concerned by his political situation, but most were just happy to see him.

Julian felt the warmth of his community and thought to himself, *This is the real Baja, a place where people care for each other and are genuine and nice.*

Julian's place was a condominium-style, two-story house close to the water, part of a residential complex called Baja Terra. There was a new security guard watching over the gate who didn't recognize Julian when he walked up, but Amanda Suarez, his neighbor, drove up in her Mercedes and recognized him. They talked briefly, and her kids ran up and hugged Julian, telling him they had missed him. Julian, who had always been very friendly with Amanda's kids, told them the story about the rogue wave he had encountered off the coast of Cabo. The kids were very entertained, and were glad to hear his tales again.

His house was dusty and there were some clothes on the floor from when he had packed before leaving for Seattle. He opened the windows to let in fresh air, then checked the garage for his car, a green ten-year-old Land Rover Defender. It was still there, so he turned it on. It seemed to run fine. Julian took a shower and changed into a fresh pair of shorts. He tried calling Rubio from his home phone, but it was disconnected. He went next door **to** the Suarez's and used their phone. He asked Rubio to come meet him.

"And bring Reyna," he said.

Julian asked Amanda to recommend a good cleaning lady. She got on the phone at once. Rubio showed up in his beat-up red pickup truck and Amanda's kids ran out to play with Reyna. Julian made arrangements with the cleaning lady. She mopped, swept, and cleaned the house. Amanda's kids begged Julian to let them keep Reyna for a little while, just while he was out running errands.

"Only if your mom agrees," said Julian.

Julian and Rubio ran errands for the rest of the day. They got his home phone reconnected, and also got smartphones for both of them. They stopped at the Banco Santander, and Julian checked his account. It was where he kept all the money he had earned during his adult life, including his port captainship severance. However, that money wasn't the bulk of his wealth. He had US accounts where he kept the money he had inherited from his parents along with the life insurance money that his aunt and uncle had helped him get when his parents passed away.

The Cuevases had been key in getting that money. Julian's parents died scuba diving, which was not protected in their policy. Still, Mr. and Mrs. Cuevas used their connections to make sure scuba diving wasn't mentioned in the official report, which listed the cause of death as *Drowning because of a capsized ship due to bad weather*. This was their effort to help Julian be better off. Julian downloaded an app on his smartphone to check his US accounts, which were healthy as always and growing because he hardly touched the principal. The only purchase he had ever made with it was buying his home, which he had gotten for a great deal directly from the builder.

He got his electricity bill and phone bills automated so they would charge his Banco Santander account directly. He called Alberto Fontana, his attorney and business partner, who was glad to hear that Julian was safe in La Paz. Fontana gave him the bank account number for Agencia Mayorca, and Julian transferred some funds. He also deposited Rubio's paycheck for the past month, and made arrangements for money transfers from his personal account to his business account and direct deposits into Rubio's account on the last day of every month.

Before he went back to the yacht, he stopped at Chaka's mechanic shop and got an oil change for his Defender. Chaka ran a complete engine check and congratulated Julian on keeping such a clean and almost mint-condition engine. They gave him a full car wash and wax. Later, Julian cruised on the La Paz boardwalk with his windows down, while Rubio sat on the passenger side.

"I love this town," said Julian.

"There's no place like it," replied Rubio.

CHAPTER 16

La Paz'd

A MONTH WENT BY, AND *The Cecilia* was still out of the water, held up by metal bars on the marina grounds. After having all of the barnacles removed, Julian had the hull repainted. The La Paz pace of life was settling in. Julian found himself napping in the afternoons and going for evening walks with Reyna. He particularly enjoyed the La Paz *malecón*, the boardwalk where pretty girls rollerblade and old men play chess in cafes. One day he went into the Staz Café and ordered an iced lavender latte. He was untying Reyna from the tree outside the cafe, when he heard someone call his name, It was his aunt, Luisa Cuevas. She was accompanied by her husband, Gene.

"*Tía*, so good to see you." Julian had so much love for his mom's sister, but **a pebble** formed in his thoughts, *her son Axel.*

"I was wondering when we were gonna get around to seeing you," said Gene.

"Well, I was in Seattle. You know, after I left my job."

"And now you're back," Luisa said.

They stood talking underneath the ficus tree for seventeen minutes. Julian told them he had bought a yacht. Luisa was happy to hear that he'd finally done something for himself.

"You have always worked so hard, you deserve that," she said.

Julian gave them both a big hug and left. That whole night he had an uneasy feeling. He felt like a hypocrite; he loved Gene and Luisa Cuevas, but the fact that they were Axel's parents meant they would always side with their son. The next morning he woke up to the high-pitched ring of his home phone. It was Aunt Luisa.

"I was so happy about having ran into you, I could hardly sleep," she said.

"It was so good to see you too, *Tía*."

She invited him over for dinner on Saturday. "I'm cooking your favorite dish, *asado Mazatleco*." She insisted.

Julian accepted the invitation and promised to bring a bottle of wine. As the date neared, he was anxious about going over to his childhood home even though Luisa had told him that Axel was out of town.

Julian arrived at the *Quinta Cuevas* at 7:00 p.m. The decaying white mansion had the aura of a fortune diminished. Once inside, Julian noticed a remodeled living room and kitchen. The Cuevases had finally come back into some money.

Axel being at the helm of the captainship probably made sure of that, Julian thought as he greeted his aunt.

He brought two bottles of Baron Balche's version of the Pomerol blend and decanted them in the kitchen while he talked with his aunt.

"Sometimes, I miss having you around. You were always so helpful around the house."

"But you've always had maids, *Tía*," said Julian as he carried the plates to the kitchen.

"I know. But it's not the same. You know I send them home on the weekends because I've always enjoyed serving personally, especially with the help of my boys."

Julian smiled and gave her a kiss on the forehead.

The *asado Mazatleco* was nothing short of spectacular, and it paired well with the wine. Gene, Luisa, and Julian had some laughs, remembering their life together.

Luisa talked briefly about Cecilia, her sister, and told Julian that she would've been very proud of him.

Gene mentioned Julian's father, Oliver, his compadre. "I hope I have lived up to my duty, because your father," he said. "Oliver was the best friend I ever had, and helping to raise you has been one of the joys of my life."

Julian got teary-eyed. "Thank you guys for having always been there for me."

As Luisa stood up and began taking dishes to the kitchen, the door opened.

"Who's there?" she asked.

Footsteps came toward the dining room, and Axel walked in. He was wearing a gray suit. Julian felt his heart drop. He grabbed his glass of wine and drank the rest of it in one gulp.

"Hey, Axel!" said Gene as he stood up and greeted his son. "Your mother said you were out of town."

"I was. I just got in from a convention in Vallarta," replied Axel as he looked at Julian. "Hey cousin, how the hell are you?" He extended his hand. Julian stood up and shook it.

"Couldn't be better, Axe."

Luisa gave Axel a big kiss on the cheek and asked him to sit down while she served him. As Axel ate, Luisa held his hand and said how happy she was to have her whole family together again. Julian kept pouring wine and drinking.

"Julian bought a yacht," said Luisa. "You know what he named it? *The Cecilia*, after your aunt."

"Oh, that's nice," said Axel as he chewed his steak and potatoes. "What's the LOA?"

"Ninety-two feet," Julian replied.

"I'm glad you finally decided to use some of your money, cousin," he said. "Maybe one day we could all go aboard *The Cecilia* and have a day out. I'll bring some steaks to grill."

"That would be lovely, wouldn't it be, Gene?" said Luisa.

"Yeah, it'll be like when I had my *Hatteras*. Remember how we all used to go out on Sundays?" said Gene.

"I would love that," said Julian.

"Maybe next week can work for you?" said Axel.

"Sure, just call me."

Julian stayed a little longer at his aunt and uncle's. When he excused himself, Axel accompanied him to his car. There was an entourage of people outside waiting for Axel, including a chauffeur and bodyguards. A strange looking one with a strong, almost Middle Eastern accent, came up and asked Axel if he needed anything.

Axel waved off his men. "No hard feelings about what happened between us cuz. It was something that I *had* to do. If you knew the alternative, you would *thank* me."

"I *do* know the alternative. I was given a choice, remember?" Julian said.

"Well, nevertheless, it's all worked out for the best," said Axel.

"Yeah, I bet it has," replied Julian.

"I'll call you next week to go out on your yacht," said Axel.

"Sounds good," said Julian as he shook hands goodbye.

When Julian was driving back to his place, all of the tranquility and joy he had experienced in La Paz over the last month faded. He couldn't believe how cynical Axel had been. He remembered his words, *"If you knew the alternative, you would thank me."* He felt ashamed for having been so passive in front of Axel and wished he would've beat him to death in front of his parents. He didn't know what to do, so he called Rubio and asked him to come over to his house for a drink.

Rubio prepared margaritas and Julian told him about the diner at the Cuevas's.

"I can't live like this, Rubio," said Julian. "I have to get back at this piece of shit, even if it kills me!"

"Then why don't you kill that motherfucker?" said Rubio.

"That would destroy my aunt and uncle, and they don't deserve that," replied Julian.

Rubio sat down next to Julian, lifted his eyepatch, and revealed his empty eye socket. "You know how I got this?"

Julian shook his head. It was a disgusting sight, a shriveled old prune where an eyeball belonged.

"When I was sixteen," Rubio continued, "I left my hometown in Guanajuato in search of a better life. Everybody I knew was going up to the states for work. So I decided to pack my things and try my luck... My sister, who raised me, sold some cattle and gave me $5,000, her life savings at the time. I paid a coyote to take me across the border. We walked for days through the Sierra and desert. One night we couldn't take the cold, so we made a small fire. It was finally warm and we fell asleep. Sometime later, strange noises awoke me. There was a group of about eight people dressed in black. They called themselves the Border Minutemen Vigilantes, and they were holding Pedro, the coyote, with a knife to his throat. I got scared, so I ran. Three of them chased after me. I heard gunshots and hid. But my panting was too strong. The vigilantes discovered me, beat me to a piece of shit, and took my eye out with their knife."

Rubio had a sip of margarita and continued. "Most people assume that it hurt a lot, but to be honest with you, I didn't feel a thing. Maybe it was because so many other parts of my body were in pain, or maybe I just blocked that part of the experience. But you know what *did* hurt? Their laughter. How they laughed at my expense. No humanity. The bastards left me outside of a Border Patrol station. To this day, I have the impression they were in cahoots with the Minutemen, since they laughed at me as well. I was in the hospital for two days, and all I was given was an eyepatch. They deported me to Tijuana, and I decided to make my way down here to South Baja because I couldn't bear the thought of going back to my hometown as a maim and failure. And I have been here ever since."

Julian didn't know how to react to Rubio's story and remained quiet. Rubio took a deep breath and continued.

"For years, I was angry. Angry at the United States for having such evil people. Angry at Mexico for having such a shit system that forces people to migrate. I was even angry at my sister for giving me the $5,000 I used to pay the coyote. But now, over 35 years later, I hold no grudges. You see, I believe that things turn out as they have to. And, in the end, justice will be served. I don't like to call it karma, or God, or—fuck it, I do call it God. The point is, the universe is always looking out for those of us who are outsiders. And you and I, Julian, we're outsiders, outcasts, and we—we'll get our revenge. We just need to learn to be patient."

"I'll drink to that," said Julian.

The pair downed their margaritas, and Rubio stood up to pour some more.

"Plus, if that hadn't happened to me, I wouldn't have met you. I would've never experienced life at sea and the joys of having a brother like you."

Julian thanked Rubio for his advice, and for having opened up to him. He agreed with him and the pair hugged upon Rubio's departure.

That night, when Julian laid down on his bed, right before he fell asleep, he thought to himself, *Rubio's right. I'm going to be patient, but I'm going to destroy Axel when the time is right. I'm going to make sure he is either dead or in jail forever when I am done with him. And when I do it, nobody, especially not my aunt and uncle, will know I was behind it all. And that is a fact. Axel Cuevas has it coming.*

CHAPTER 17

Going Places

HIS ENCOUNTER WITH AXEL HAD given Julian an itch to get out of town fast. Over the next week, he hurried to get his yacht back on the water. The 200-ton lift at the Marina Palma placed *The Cecilia* gently on the sea. Julian ran electrical diagnostics, got both of the engines double-checked by a second mechanic, and steam-cleaned the entire engine room.

He brought in his cleaning lady to mop, sweep, and wash all of the linen aboard. He and Rubio, along with a couple of the dockhands, polished all of the stainless steel, shined the interior leather, and waxed the deck. *The Cecilia* was a $5 million yacht that looked like a $10 million yacht. Yacht owner's pride came over Julian.

"She's a thing of beauty," said Felix Aburto.

The Cecilia was in the best shape of her life, thanks to all of the work, time, and money Julian had put into her. He ordered Rubio to restock the pantry and get ready for a long journey.

"Where we going, Skip?" he asked.

"Places," answered Julian. "We're going places."

Julian forwarded his home phone to his smartphone, and made sure his stateroom was stocked with clean clothes. Rubio did the same, and the pair, along with Reyna, embarked aboard *The Cecilia*. Felix Aburto and the marina staff waved goodbye as they left the dock. Rubio cracked open a bottle of Vena Cava Sauvignon Blanc and poured two glasses. It was a uniquely dry wine, and Julian enjoyed sipping it. *Going Places* by Herb Alpert & The Tijuana Brass began playing over the yacht's speakers as they passed the La Paz boardwalk starboard side.

CHAPTER 18

Wanderlust

SIX DAYS AFTER THEY LEFT La Paz, Julian's phone rang. *The Cecilia* was anchored off the west coast of Isla San José. He didn't answer because it was Aunt Luisa. He figured she was inquiring about his yacht, and Julian didn't feel like talking to anyone, especially if he was going to have to excuse himself. In fact, Julian was prepared to do only one thing: sail the Sea of Cortez.

It began as a strong feeling, a captivating awe that Julian couldn't resist. Wanderlust, the desire to travel deeper into the enchanting sea and its majestic coasts. They would sail days at a time, sometimes weeks, often cruising at speeds no higher than six knots. If they found the right beach to anchor, they would stay as long as they pleased. They were on a meandering journey north. They ate well, drank plenty, swam in the ocean, and smoked cigars. Sometimes they fished in the early morning, and often in the afternoon.

They anchored at Bahia Agua Verde. The emerald waters and the rose-orange sunsets created a pocket of magic that came alive every day. When Christmas came around, they had been anchored there for close to a month. Rubio cooked a wonderful crab bisque and stuffed snook with pasta.

When they finished their dinner, the pair spotted a group of people on the beach. They were bumping good music, had a bonfire going, and were setting off fireworks. Julian and Rubio lowered the tender and brought along leftovers and a couple of bottles of mezcal. The pair arrived like conquistadors on a burning beach. It was a friendly group of college students from Constitucion City.

The guys in the group were stoked that Julian and Rubio had shown up because they were almost out of booze, and the girls were happy to have the extra attention. There was one girl in particular who Julian was attracted to—a brunette named Yolanda. Julian and she flirted the whole night. Rubio was part of the drum circle, and even played a bad ukulele when one of the guys brought it out. Julian and Yolanda cuddled to sleep inside a small REI tent.

The next morning, Julian awoke at sunrise. He rode the tender back to *The Cecilia* and brought provisions to make breakfast and coffee. When he returned, Rubio was already standing on the beach, looking at him.

"I was wondering what you were doing," he said as he helped Julian unload the provisions. "Did you get any last night?"

"A gentleman never tells."

"You are one son of a...."

Rubio made breakfast for ten on the hot coals, and Julian brewed Talega coffee. Little by little, people began waking to the warm smell of coffee. The group was fascinated with the cowboy-style eggs and burritos.

While they feasted, one of the guys said, "Man, you guys sure as hell know how to live."

Before the group left, some of the girls needed to use the restroom, so Julian took a group of three, including Yolanda, aboard *The Cecilia*. None of the girls had ever been aboard a luxury yacht, and their jaws literally dropped. As Julian steered the tender back to the beach, Yolanda held his hand. When they beached, all of the girls got down, except Yolanda, who gave Julian a kiss on the lips.

When the group had all of their stuff packed into the van and pickup truck, Yolanda whispered into Julian's ear.

"Is it okay if I stay with you for a couple of days?"

Julian smiled. "Of course."

He said goodbye to the group and asked Rubio to go into town with them to get provisions.

"But, we've got almost everything we need, Skip."

"Well, you said it. Almost. Get that which we don't have. And don't forget the beer."

Rubio overheard Yolanda tell her friends that she was going to stay. He looked at Julian with a smile and said, "When should I get back?"

"Tomorrow would be fine. Not too early, but not too late, either. You're making us dinner."

Rubio leaned in. "That's cool, But you are going to have to give me all of the details when I come back, especially the dirty ones."

Julian chuckled.

"Hey, amigos, got room for one more?" Rubio asked the guys.

The van and pickup drove off, leaving a trail of copper-colored dust. Julian put his arm around Yolanda, and the two stood watching the cars escape into the warm mirage of desert and sun.

As soon as the quiet sounds of nature took over, Julian slid his hand onto Yolanda's butt through the blue bikini bottom she was wearing. He had wanted to grab it since he first laid eyes on her. It was gorgeous, big, and statuesque. Julian began grabbing and caressing it with both hands. Yolanda enjoyed it, and the two laughed and began kissing intensely. Yolanda stared deeply into Julian's eyes with her mouth slightly open. Her lip would flinch a little as she looked down to his lips, then they would resume kissing and neatly licking each other.

Julian removed her bra and began sucking on her breasts very gently, as if they were soft-shelled milk-chocolate doves. He worked himself into a passionate trance, consumed by the desire of lovemaking. This energy transmitted. He slightly bit the tips of her nipples while fondling them with his tongue.

She pulled away softly and ran to the beach. She threw herself on the sand and held her hair and arms above her head. Julian walked over, laid down beside her, and began kissing her from behind. They rolled, turned and made out like lustful beings enchanted in a heat that rises from the abdomen. Yolanda had her back arched toward Julian, and he reached across and felt her belly button with the tips of his index and middle fingers.

He continued moving his hand down, underneath the lace of her bikini bottom, and when he touched soft hairs, he gently bit her lip. She sighed, and Julian introduced the very tip of his middle finger inside Yolanda. He touched the top of her opening, just gently enough to feel her getting wet. He had his finger on her pulse, on her valve.

He kissed her and she responded with force. He kept rubbing her vulva from the outside of the soft texture of her bikini bottom. This strange game of desire, where he wasn't touching her directly but through a cloth, was even more stimulating for her. He moved the bikini bottom slightly to her side and gently rubbed the outside of her clit with his palm in a circular motion. Then with all the tenderness in the world, and with the tip of his finger, he massaged her small clitoris. She couldn't take it; the ocean was exploding inside her with lascivious waves.

Yolanda reached over and grabbed his hard cock through his shorts. He removed them, and she turned around and began sucking him off. Julian laid back as Yolanda gave him a slobbering blowjob. She was enamored with his penis, fixated by it, all full of saliva and throbbing with pre-cum. She kissed the side of it before continuing her sucking with dedication. Julian was certain that this was the best oral he had ever received. She stood up for a moment, and Julian removed her bikini bottom.

"Let me lick your pussy."

"What? No…"

"Come on. I can't eat it without tasting it."

"You're crazy. I haven't even showered."

"Fine, let me just kiss it."

She bent over slightly and Julian tasted her sacred parts with the tip of his tongue.

She turned around and made him get on the ground. She spread her legs and squatted on his throbbing penis. She sat there, not moving, and giggled. Julian giggled, too, and she leaned down and kissed him. She played and released her muscles for a moment, then that soft and gentle up and down that made time warp into an eternal hole of pleasure disguised as a free exchange of fluids.

Then there was a period of hard, beautiful coitus and vulgar ways in which they positioned their bodies for maximum sexual pleasure. He hit the spot harder, harder, harder, then she paused him and they decomped, Julian still hard as a husk inside her. Yolanda stood up and walked naked on the beach. She had a little bit of sand all over her back; it reflected like gold particles in the hot sun.

Julian stood up and began following her. Watching Yolanda walk naked on that beach as she gave him coquettish glances gave Julian the most incredible feeling of accomplishment. He felt like an artist. He had never painted a masterpiece, or written a novel, but for a moment, just by looking at Yolanda's body in this paradise of water, Julian thought about what Picasso must've felt when he painted the Guernica, or Michelangelo when he finished his statue of David.

Yolanda was knee-deep in the turquoise sea as she splashed a little bit of water down her breast and stomach. Julian came close to her. She looked back toward him, and gently put her tush in the water. She stood up, and the sand that had been on her was now gone.

Julian took advantage of her bent position and stuck his penis in her. She moaned and the two made love in the sea. When she turned to face him, Julian carried her as she rode him. They laid down on the crease of the dry and wet sand, and as the calm wake gently beat against their naked bodies, they alternated positions. The two stared into each other's eyes as she orgasmed several times. When he could no longer resist, he came inside her.

Yolanda rolled her eyes as she felt Julian's warm sperm within. She was still riding him hard. A moment later, with an insatiable gasp, she came loudly one final time, almost as if the whole world needed to hear her. Then, she giggled, and Julian laughed. He was still inside her, no more semen left in his drained testicles, but his cock still hard enough to hold its place inside such a warm, comfortable paradise. She got off and laid down next to him on the beach.

Julian exhaled, and with a single laugh said, "I probably shouldn't have finished inside you."

Yolanda played with his hair. "That's okay. I'm on the pill."

Julian smiled and cuddled with her as they both rejoiced over the best sex of their lives.

CHAPTER 19

Loreto

JULIAN AND YOLANDA HAD SEX thirty-eight times over the course of two weeks. They broke every kind of barrier imaginable. The sea, every stateroom, the bridge, the stern, the bow, the galley, and even the tender hosted their physical acts of love. There were some things Julian considered too far, but enjoyed being with her nonetheless. She was a great gal, and her cooking was splendid. She made shrimp quesadillas aboard *The Cecilia* one night; Rubio even took note of the recipe and called them *Yolandadillas*.

On January 8, after weeks of passion and lust, Yolanda disembarked *The Cecilia*. They were anchored in Puerto Escondido, a staggering bay surrounded by large Cardona Cacti and pristine, primitive life.

"Are you sure you want to stay here?" Julian asked as Rubio lowered the tender.

"Yeah, I've got an uncle who's driving down from Loreto. He's picking me up. I've got to go back to school tomorrow."

They held each other, and Rubio started the tender. Julian gave Yolanda one last kiss on the lips. She boarded the tender and Rubio took off. Julian watched them reach the beach and Yolanda waved goodbye as she walked away from the sunset.

When Rubio got back on board, Julian was sitting off the bow with his legs dangling overboard. Rubio went into his stateroom and came back with a joint. He lit it and passed it to Julian. The two men enjoyed the reefer on that golden afternoon. Julian remembered the last time he had smoked marijuana, close to eight years ago, with the Dahlgreens at their home in Cabo. He went into a brief trance and remembered what a great couple the Dahlgreens were.

He talked with Rubio about them, and made them sound like crazy New York billionaires who loved to party and have a great time on the water. He thought about giving them a call, but his mind went back to wondering about Yolanda. He began to feel guilty about all of the unprotected sex he had had with her. It wasn't a practice that he participated in often, but something about Yolanda inspired skin to skin lovemaking. Julian would remember some of the sexual experiences he had shared with her and smile, but a little fear crept up. He told himself he would get checked for venereal diseases as soon as he could. Rubio made munchies for dinner, and they listened to early David Bowie albums well into the night.

Julian, Rubio, and Reyna continued to sail north on the Sea of Cortez. They anchored in every bay they could find, disembarked on every island possible, hiked natural trails, and enjoyed their time. Julian called Yolanda several times during the first weeks after they had been together, but soon realized that they had nothing in common. Julian also had a strange feeling that Yolanda was hiding something, possibly a boyfriend, because she was extremely awkward when they talked on the phone. He realized that their attraction was a mere physical one, so after some time, the calls stopped.

When *The Cecilia* anchored in Loreto, a small city founded by the Spanish in 1697, Julian got a full medical exam, which included blood work, x-rays, urine, and stool samples. He tested negative for venereal diseases, which gave him peace of mind, because the thought of HIV or herpes had been slightly haunting him since Yolanda. The doctor told him that he was in great shape, but advised him to drink less alcohol and add more fiber to his diet. When they bought provisions that afternoon, Julian asked Rubio to get a lot of fruit, leafy greens, and a large pack of condoms.

"Are you going on another sexcapade?"

Julian chuckled. "Just in case it happens, we need to have plenty of protection on board."

They spent months anchored in Loreto. The town had a mellow vibe that captivated Julian, who became very conscious of his health and well-being. Rubio would cook healthy meals, and Julian exercised daily. He went on long hikes with Reyna, and was constantly looking for ways to improve himself. Loreto was a special town for Julian because it was his parents' favorite place. He remembered his youth and how they came here often on their boat. At times, it was hard for him to deal with such severe emotions and he found himself giving in to nostalgia, which was different than how he had been dealing with grief throughout his life.

He would walk down the old streets and see the shadows of his parents. He often fantasized about writing their biography.

Maybe I would start their book something like, "Cecilia Samarín and Oliver Mayorca had both been journalists and eventually founded the Baja Geographic Society. They were adventurers, bold."

"Yea, they don't make them like that anymore," he told Rubio one evening when referencing his folks.

"They made you. *You sound like that,*" said Rubio.

"Well, maybe I'm the last of 'em," said Julian with a hiccup.

He began to feel slightly different about the way things had turned out. He still craved revenge on Axel, but knew obsessing about it could destroy him. Julian enjoyed afternoon walks in town; greeting the locals and exchanging a word with them gave him a sense of belonging. He found a small bookstore, Catacumba, that sold all kinds of gems, and he would spend hours picking through books, old Baja maps, antique almanacs about the Sea of Cortez, and Jesuit mission journals. One night, the owner sold Julian a sextant from the 1800s. It was in great condition, and Julian considered it an heirloom. To accompany this nautical instrument, Julian got a waterproof copy of *Traveling the Roxo by Way of the Sextant* by Alejandro Alberque.

When he returned to the ship after wandering the town, dinner was usually ready. He read in the evenings and would share what he had learned with Rubio. He read novels, short story collections, poetry, history, Baja legends, almanacs, and plenty of spiritual treasures that began to define his thinking. Julian wanted to leave behind the resentment and hate he felt for his cousin, so he pushed himself to be the better man.

Perhaps it was all of the books Julian had read over the past months that gave him a thirst for adventure. Books like *The Fountainhead*, *Treasure Island*, and *Pillars of the Earth*. Poetry compilations by Neruda and Whitman, short stories by Borges, great teachings by James Allen and Ralph Waldo Emerson, and Mexican historical novels by Enrique Serna.

Julian's soul became lit with passion, and he began looking for more out of life. Becoming sensitive to the people around him, he noticed that Loreto had so much more than what appeared at its surface. Its people had convictions, history, and heritage. Julian admired this, and he started to firmly believe in things like the law of attraction, a principle that became a driving force in his life.

"Yea, it's great that you're bettering yourself, Julian, but are you getting any charters? Our books are empty!" said Alberto Fontana over the phone.

"Not everything is money at this point," said Julian.

"Maybe not for you! But we're partners!"

"I've worked hard since I was twelve. Never took a vacation, went to the academy, graduated top of my class, straight to work, then the port captainship. I think I deserve a little break," Julian responded.

"Well, don't get too comfortable. I'm not gonna let you retire if that's what you're thinking. We're taking a lot of risks with this yacht; at least let's have it make us some money," Alberto said.

Julian understood the attorney's concern and he began formulating a plan. He wanted to revive the Baja Geographic Society, his parents' institution, but wasn't sure how to go about it. He remained in Loreto with an open mind.

CHAPTER 20

The Pistol & Rifle

URING ONE OF HIS WALKS in Loreto, Julian met a man by the name of Silvestre Greene, a well-known and respected Loretian who spoke of the nobility of the town, the good spirits of its inhabitants, and its natural wonders. He and Julian became friends, and Silvestre introduced Julian to an organization over which he presided, The Loreto Pistol & Rifle Club. It wasn't a usual hunting club; it functioned more like a hybrid between a Lions Club, Toastmasters, Rotary, and, of course, a shooting range. They held 7:00 a.m. meetings once a week, where members would discuss important issues related to their community. Topics ranged from trash collection to proposed developments to politics. Julian attended a couple of these meetings, and he respected how well-informed and involved these people were. Silvestre later explained to Julian that his family had been among the founders of The Pistol & Rifle, and that the Greenes could be traced back to Loreto almost since its inception. He mentioned that he was a descendent of a famous English buccaneer named Leopold Greene.

On Saturdays, the Pistol & Rifle would hold various activities for its members and their families. There was usually a hunting activity, depending on what was in season, and a group of men would head out into the wild in search of deer, quail, or pheasant. Twice a year, the club would raffle permits for peninsular bighorn sheep, a protected species. For those who stayed in the club's facilities, there were marksmanship competitions and activities. Part of the responsibility of being a member was that everyone had to teach at least one workshop a year for either kids or teens, so the kids would learn about gun safety and would hone their skills in either shotgun, .22 caliber pistol, archery, or long-range pistol.

One Saturday, Julian accompanied Silvestre on a deer hunt. They met at the club at 04:00, and drove up to the Sierra Giganta. They followed a trail, marked by washed-out orange ribbons that had been put up years prior by members of the club. Julian wasn't a member, so he wasn't carrying a rifle, only binoculars. When they sat to rest, Julian spotted a stag. Silvestre unloaded two rounds and registered the first kill of the group. This happened twice more, and all of the men were impressed with Julian's eye.

"I don't believe you've never hunted before," said Silvestre. "It seems to me you are a natural."

That night they camped in the wilderness. They made a bonfire, and Julian told some stories about his days at sea. The next day, they continued their hunt, but were unlucky. Sunday afternoon, Julian brought Rubio and Reyna over to the club's facilities and Rubio cooked the deer. He made deer stew, deer machaca burritos, and deer ravioli. Everybody loved the food and were fascinated with the new guy in town. Silvestre bragged about Julian's "eye." The men who hadn't gone on the hunt made Julian promise that he would go with them on future expeditions.

As the night progressed and the beer cans tinned empty, Julian opened up to Silvestre and told him how impressed he was with the organization.

"Well, we are very proud of it," said Silvestre. "It's the only one like it in the whole of Mexico." He continued, "This club started in 1790, twenty years before Mexico's independence. It used to be called the Loreto Militia. It began as an association of men that were fed up with the Spanish military.

During Mexico's fight for independence, we fought for our homeland and won. In the years after that, the association changed names a half-dozen times. We faced threats of all kinds, some of our members were even executed. In 1910, when the Mexican Revolution came along, we joined forces with the Peninsula Fighters and stocked up on weapons. After that, we changed our name to what it is today. And ever since then, we have continued to grow in numbers and influence."

Silvestre took a deep breath. "You see, our struggle here in South Baja has always been the same — a struggle for self-governance. Mexico City is too far, and we cannot allow them to dictate terms."

"I'll drink to that," said Julian, and the men finished their beers.

He became a member of the Loreto Pistol & Rifle Club, and over the next weeks, took advantage of membership perks as much as he could. Julian learned how to shoot, operate, clean, and store shotguns, along with various-caliber deer rifles. Since the Pistol & Rifle was such an old and prestigious organization, it had a preference on weapon permits. They helped Julian buy and secure permits for a couple of weapons: a Chiappa Triple Barrel shotgun, designed for hunting every kind of fowl imaginable, and a .308 caliber Browning BAR Mark II Lightweight Stalker, the quintessential medium-range deer hunter.

Julian became a dedicated sportsman, hunting as much as he could, camping out, and enjoying time outdoors. In his first season, he registered seven stag kills.

"That's gotta be some sort of record," he said jokingly one night.

Hunting totally transformed him. He would not shower for days before a hunt, and when he shot to kill, he would sometimes imagine the face of his enemies.

When the season changed, Julian even trained Reyna to fetch fowl. The Pistol & Rifle members were impressed, since they had never seen a pitbull be such a good retriever.

Sometimes Rubio would accompany him, but he wasn't a very good hunting companion. He would complain about the bugs and the heat, and Julian would also make him carry the game, so he would come up with excuses not to go. Reyna, on the other, hand loved going out.

Julian began to pay close attention to the stories around South Baja hunts. He heard the legends surrounding its islands, in particular the story about the wild goats of Cerralvo, and the endemic *Babisuris*, a ringtail cat, while believed to be extinct, was sometimes spotted. Julian's hunting instinct had been developed. He wanted a kill that was different. Silvestre suggested that he try his luck on Sancosme Island.

"People have spotted the albino deer there plenty of times, but there is no record of anyone ever hunting one down. Perhaps you could be the first," Silvestre told Julian.

They made plans to hunt the albino deer together, but never got around to it. When it was time for Julian to teach a class, he talked with Silvestre about teaching a freediving, underwater hunting, and spearfishing class. Silvestre loved the idea, so Julian got all of the necessary gear. He hadn't spearfished in years, but as soon as he started doing it again, it all came back to him. Three students signed up for his class. They caught some snook, and as Rubio made stew, Julian realized how much he missed being out on the water. He began to feel landlocked.

CHAPTER 21

The Bounding Main

JULIAN HAD ENJOYED HIS TIME in Loreto. He knew the bonds he had built with Silvestre and the members of The Pistol & Rifle Club were strong. Hunting was now on his list of passions, and for this, he would forever pledge to the PRC. Before sailing out of Loreto, Julian and Rubio built a clandestine gun rack for his rifles in the back of the master stateroom closet. The club threw Julian a going away party, and he promised that he would return soon.

The Cecilia headed east, with only the desire to escape the weight of land. Rubio was much happier at sea than he was on land. One afternoon, as Julian was on helm, Rubio was observing the horizon with a large grin on his face.

"What are you grinning about?" asked Julian.

"Ah, the bounding main," answered Rubio. "It has the power to heal, the power to set a person free. Only the bounding main."

Julian looked at the sea with its majestic beauty, smiled back at Rubio, and asked: "The bounding main?"

"It's an old name for the sea," said Rubio.

"Wow, about time you taught me something," Julian said.

Julian continued spearfishing for his food. A killer instinct had been born in him. One day, while he was submerged, he spotted a shark coming after him. He shot it through its side with his speargun, and the bleeding shark still came after him. Julian took out the knife he kept strapped to the outside of his right leg and stuck it below the shark's mouth.

"Nice mako," said a delighted Rubio when he saw the catch of the day.

Sometimes, when he didn't feel like spearfishing, he would swim out as far as he could to test his endurance. Reyna would sit astern and anxiously await her owner's return. When Julian came close, she would jump in the water and swim with him. Reyna was a happy dog, "a little boat rat," as Julian called her. She would stay in her bed for hours and even had a designated head that she used. Rubio cared for her and looked out for Julian. He prepared their meals with tenderness and advised Julian when required. The three of them were a family, a tight-knit group who loved and cared for one another.

CHAPTER 22

The Blue-Footed Booby

AFTER A WHILE AT SEA, little things began to get in the way of Julian and Rubio's relationship. Rubio resented that when Julian shaved, he purposely used the outside head and would leave all of his hair in the basin for Rubio to clean. Julian hated the disgusting crocodile sandals that Rubio always wore, especially the whiffing sound they made. Julian began taking his meals by himself on the bridge or out on the bow.

After nightfall, he would ask Rubio to turn off the music and dim the lights, and then he'd skipper the vessel by way of the sextant. He would pick through various books and almanacs to instruct himself. One day, he unfolded an old map and saw the tiny island of San Cosme, the place where people had spotted the albino deer. He had never noticed it on a map before, probably because of its small size and far-off location.

San Cosme is a fifteen-square-mile island, located in the exact middle of the Sea of Cortez, between Loreto and the mainland. It hadn't appeared on a map since 1881. The Mexican government didn't want anyone setting foot on the island because it was haunted, mainly by a plague of snakes. San Cosme is sometimes referred to as Rattleless Island, because it's home to a special mutation of rattlesnake that lacks a rattle. Preservationists say it's the only island where the rattle-less rattlesnake exists. The snake developed this mutation after generations of having little to eat but migratory birds, so along with its smaller size, it became faster and gained the ability to glide up trees.

Of course, Julian didn't know this because it wasn't in any of the books he had bought at Catacumbas.

On the horizon, San Cosme's inviting coast soon gives way to the mountain that makes up most of its terrain. Even though it's considered a desert, like most of the islands on the Sea of Cortez, San Cosme has varieties of cacti that aren't found in the rest of Baja, as well as flora that is more endemic to the Mexican mainland. Julian found it fascinating how large mangroves, mixed with desert plants, covered the edge of the island. They found a good spot to anchor for the night and Julian prepared his gear. He was certain that his hunt for an albino deer the next day was going to be successful.

The next morning, Julian was ready to disembark at 04:00. Rubio, on the other hand, slept in. Julian was angry that he had to wake him up, and Rubio insisted on not going.

"You don't have a choice, sailor."

"I always have choices."

Julian kicked the bed frame.

"Alright, alright, Skip," Rubio said.

They locked the boat and, with Reyna, they rode on the tender and beached like bloodthirsty conquerors. Julian, deer rifle in hand, wearing brown camo. Reyna ran all over the sand, scoping the terrain. Rubio tied the tender, hating every second of it.

"I can't believe you're wearing those piece of shit sandals on this hunt."

"I can go back to the yacht if you want."

"Smart-ass."

The tension grew between them as the sun reached high noon. The climb up the mountain was beginning to take its toll. When they stopped to rest, Julian reached into his backpack and realized there was only one canteen.

"Where's the rest of the water?" he asked.

"What rest of the water?"

"The canteens that I asked you to fill up last night."

"I filled them up and put them in the fridge."

"You left them in the fridge? I told you to put them in my backpack!"

"But you wanted them to be cold. I thought you saw me leave them there."

They yelled at each other back and forth.

"You know what? Go back to the yacht. And you better hurry so Reyna doesn't get dehydrated. You can stop at the stream she drank out of on the way up. She's gonna be super thirsty," said Julian.

"Yea, well, good luck on your hunt," said Rubio as he left.

Julian got even angrier over how happy Rubio was.

The hike up the mountain was strange. There was a strong silence all around the island that Julian found unnatural. The bushes and trees were closing in, and there was hardly a trail he could follow.

I need a machete, he thought as he moved heavy brush with his hand.

He found a creek and followed it up as far as he could, then sat in the shade to eat the grouper sandwich Rubio had made for him the night before. When he finished eating, he noticed there was a snake on the ground, very close to his foot. As he looked away, he saw another snake, a little larger with a fatter head closer to the water. Julian stood up on the sly. The vipers held their position.

The snakes gave Julian a general uneasiness, but his conviction to hunt down an albino deer didn't wane. The afternoon came around and Julian hadn't reached the summit. He climbed atop a giant boulder and took in the view for a couple of minutes. He could see *The Cecilia* anchored in the bay, and the bounding main behind her. When he was climbing down from the rock, he almost put his hand on a serpent that was wedged into one of the rock's crevices. He watched her slide down the rock. She was small with a large diamond head.

From then on, Julian was in a bad mood. He didn't like this island anymore; he wanted to return to his yacht, where it was safe, or at least free of snakes. He considered going back, but thought about Rubio and how happy he was going to be that his hunt had turned out futile. He marched on. By 16:20, Julian was very tired. He was almost out of water and had no more food. He took a breather, and when he leaned against a tree, he saw a majestic bird land on a trunk. A blue-footed booby with a black and white goose-like neck and orange eyes. Julian was in awe of the bird. He stared at it with great wonder, until something blurred behind it. Beyond the bird, out of a large cave, a tall four-legged creature exited.

He almost dropped to his knees. The deer wasn't albino, it was blue. He held the rifle with both hands, but when he thought about pulling it up to his face to take aim, he noticed he was shaking. The blue deer gazed at the horizon like a king upon his domain. It was the most monumental animal he had ever seen; it had posture, elegance, and an aura of purity. The blue deer turned around and looked straight into Julian's eyes. The man began to weep. He felt the animal's soul talking to him. It was a mixture of guilt and happiness. The blue deer turned around and walked back into the cave. Julian wiped the tears from his eyes and began his journey down the mountain.

Everything had changed. The silence that surrounded the island before had been replaced by strange bird chirps and the ricketing of wild flora in the evening wind. Julian's mind was running, but his body was tired. He got back to the bay and realized that the tender was still beached.

"Rubio!" he yelled. His heart thumped, anticipating that something was wrong.

"*Chingado*," he whispered.

A distant but loud bark.

"Reyna!" It was from atop the mountain.

He looked down and there were Rubio's tracks with that stupid crocodile imprinted on the sole of the sandals. The tracks led to the bush and disappeared, replaced by curved lines. Julian followed them, fearful of finding his friend in peril. The sun was setting when he arrived at a hilltop. He had no idea where to head next. He found a stretch of trail and saw Reyna wagging.

"Reyna!"

"Your friend is fine," said a calm voice.

Julian felt chills down his spine and turned around quickly.

A small man casually holding a bow and arrow pointed at the ground was standing two arms away.

Julian pointed his weapon at him.

"That won't be necessary," said the man as he turned around. "Follow me," he continued as he went through a stretched trail.

Julian followed the small man to a hut made of adobe, mud, and branches. When they entered, Julian saw Rubio on the ground, covered with a blanket, next to a small fire. He reached over to him and held his head; Rubio could barely open his eyes.

"He was bitten by a snake," said the man. "Twice, in the right leg."

Julian pulled back the blanket and saw Rubio's leg, bloated like a beached jellyfish. When he realized Rubio was wearing his ugly sandals, he took them off his feet and began to weep.

As Julian exited the hut to let some air dry his tears, the small man followed.

"I told you, he's going to be fine. I've given him medicine," he said.

"He has to be. He's the only family I've got." Julian hugged him.

The man went inside for a moment and came back out.

"Here, take this tea for your nerves. It will help."

Wicho was a member of a tribe known as the Huicholes, a people who made their way over to San Cosme Island after the arrival of the Spanish, over 400 years ago. They arrived in San Cosme with one mission: to protect the blue deer. Wicho explained how the blue deer was an important aspect of their faith, and when the Spanish arrived and heard of such a "demonic creature," they were keen on eradicating it from the face of the earth. The Huicholes couldn't allow this to happen, so a group of them sailed over to San Cosme with the last herd of blue deer.

"They made this island their sanctuary. Even the snakes protect the blue deer," said Wicho as Julian entered a trance-like state.

After generations, the Huicholes keep sending one of their members to live permanently on the island to protect the deer. There was no community, just solitude. Wicho congratulated Julian on not having raised his rifle against the deer.

"You see, the blue-footed booby and I work together. I was watching you the whole time. If you would've raised your rifle, you would've gotten stung by one of my poisonous arrows," Wicho said, "and I wouldn't have saved your friend."

That whole night, Julian was submerged in ancient wisdom. His eyes bulged with visions, his anxieties fled, his ears heard the earth, his brain understood, his soul was aroused, and his spirit was calmed. He was aware that seeing the blue deer meant he was ready.

The next day, a warm breeze awoke Julian. The hut was nice and cool, the fire was out, everybody was gone, and Julian felt rested. He stepped outside and Rubio was sitting on a rock overlooking the bay.

"It sure feels nice to be alive," said Rubio with a scratchy voice.

Julian hugged his first mate. "You have to ask for permission to die, sailor."

The pair looked for Wicho to thank him, but he was nowhere to be found. Reyna led the pair back to the beach.

"What the hell did he cure me with? Peyote?" asked Rubio as they rode back on the tender.

"I don't know, but he gave me some, too, and I was tripping," said Julian.

Rubio asked about his hunt. "Did you get your albino deer?"

"No, he was blue, and I couldn't kill him."

"*Blue?* Was this before, or after the peyote?"

"At this point, I don't think it makes a difference," said Julian.

When *The Cecilia* finally left the bay, a blue-footed booby flew off the deck.

CHAPTER 23

The Call

WHILE UNDERWAY, JULIAN ENTERED HIS quarters to answer his satellite phone.

"Hello?"

"Well goddamn it, I've been trying to reach you all day," said Alberto Fontana

"My old friend, I've got the craziest tales for you," Julian said.

"I bet you do," Alberto replied.

"It begins with a white deer, and it ends with a blue one, and Rubio getting bit by a rattlesnake without the rattle."

"Oh geez," said Alberto with a laugh.

They talked for twenty minutes.

"I'm glad the old bastard's alright. Can you imagine if they would've had to cut his leg off? Missing an eye and a leg? Ha! A true pirate! I'd have to get him a parrot to finish the ordeal!"

"No, we ought to get him a blue-footed booby instead!"

They laughed at Rubio's expense.

Then they got down to business, with Alberto asking a lot of questions about the condition of the yacht.

"She's tip-top," said Julian.

"And business? Any news?"

"I've got some ideas on reestablishing the Baja Geographic Society, taking people on adventures. I know some kickass spots."

Alberto interrupted. "Listen, I've got to kill a couple of birds with one stone. I need to take some time aboard the yacht. I'm embarking on a new venture that has to do with shipping, and a potential investor is flying in from Mexico City next week. I would like to wine and dine him aboard *The Cecilia*. Would it be possible for you to come pick us up in Ensenada a week from today?"

Julian had no intention of taking his yacht to the Pacific. It had been a long journey getting to the Sea of Cortez, and he didn't feel like going back now, especially in a rush.

"Listen," said Julian, "right now we're east of Loreto. By the time I go around the tip of the peninsula, and push her up north, I would need close to $30,000 in fuel, and with all of the hours I'm going to clock in, she's gonna need service as soon as we get there."

"Fuck Jules, I need to be aboard the yacht on Tuesday. I already told my investor that he was going to love my yacht. And after he leaves, I told Tatiana, my *otra*, we would spend a week aboard together," Fontana said.

Julian took a deep breath. "Why don't I pick you up in San Felipe? It's only a two-hour drive from Ensenada, and the gulf is much nicer for yachting than the Pacific, incomparable."

"Perfect. Let's do that. I'll coordinate my people out of San Felipe," said Alberto.

"How many people are coming on board, and what are you looking for as far as service?"

"Well, it's the potential investor and his people. I think he's bringing two others with him. Listen, Julian, I need top-notch service and accommodations. If this guy agrees to fund me, it could be a real game-changer for us," Alberto said.

"There will be regal attention to detail. Just deposit $7,500 for fuel and beverages."

"What? Are you crazy? You're cruising around in this boat for months. I helped you in this giant scheme, and all I ask for is a little taste of honey and you give me this $7,500 ridiculousness?" said Alberto.

"But it's costing *me* to go up there. I haven't cost you anything," said Julian.

"Listen, don't nickel and dime me now!"

"That's just cost," said Julian.

"You do this for me, and I'll open some big doors for us. This is a big thing—a port deal. I'm talking *billions*. Bite the bullet with me on this, let it ride, and it'll pay off."

"Okay, I'll pick you up on Tuesday," Julian said.

He and Rubio pulled into Santa Rosalía and began preparations the next day. They bought supplies, fueled her up, and ran a complete diagnostic on the yacht. Rubio created the menu for ten days, and Julian bought expensive liquor.

"These Mexico City folks aren't used to drinking trash. We've got to get the good stuff."

CHAPTER 24

"Open Book"

DURING THE 250 NAUTICAL MILES between Santa Rosalía and San Felipe, they enjoyed great weather, low winds, and a sea of glass. Julian realized his eye had become quite versed in Baja, as he could now recognize the small nuances in the scenery and coastal flora between South and North Baja. When *The Cecilia* arrived in San Felipe the evening prior to the scheduled meeting with Alberto Fontana, they docked at the marina and Julian and Rubio discussed hitting the town.

"Hey, I'm all for it," said Rubio.

"Especially now that you're fully recovered from the snake bite," said Julian.

"Yea, these scars are here to stay."

"Just another battle wound," said Julian.

They had carne asada tacos and went into a club named Rockodile to have drinks. The music was loud and all over the place. Even though it was a Monday night and there were hardly any people at the club, it was obnoxiously fun.

When they left Rockodile, they walked on the main strip. Neon lights and dark alleys saturated the night as street vendors sold spare cigarettes and gum. Rubio convinced Julian to enter the only strip club in town, a small den called Iguanas. Some of the girls in the club were pretty, but Julian didn't really like the vibe of the place.

"What's the matter?" asked Rubio as Julian sipped on a beer.

"Nothing. I just don't really like strip clubs."

There was a hardcore porno playing on a flat-screen by the bar, and Julian shrugged and looked away. The DJ introduced Candy, a short brunette with a purple wig. Rubio spent $100 on lap-dances from Candy. Julian waited by the bar, but asked the bartender to turn the porno off.

It was midnight when they left the club. As they headed back to the marina, Rubio asked a polka band that was standing by the statue of a mermaid to play his favorite song, the folk-ballad "Open Book."

Julian laughed as the bandleader and Rubio fought over who sang the loudest. Rubio had a horrendous voice, but he sang with so much gusto that he almost made listening bearable.

The lyrics went, "*They say of me that I am an open book in which many people write.*"

Julian was not fond of traditional music, but every once in a while on a good night, he enjoyed a nice polka song, especially when it was sung from the heart. They were sauced.

The thought of Alberto and the way he had said *billions* entered Julian's mind; he got excited in that alcohol-driven way.

While everything was loud around him, he smiled and whispered to himself, "Julian Mayorca, *billionaire*."

CHAPTER 25

Back in Business

THE NEXT MORNING, JULIAN WOKE up with a huge grin. All of the singing and street dancing from the night before had put him in a good mood. He was happy that he was going to receive his friend and partner aboard the yacht. He went for a jog on the boardwalk, and grinned as he passed the mermaid-shaped statue that smelled like dried urine under the hot sun. He thought of the lyrics to the song Rubio had sung and meditated on how his own life was like an open book, especially how all of the people that he knew, one way or another, helped shift it. He thought about Boyd and the days of the *Almost Heaven*.

When he returned to the yacht, Rubio was making breakfast. The two ate green chilaquiles with ham, and Julian jumped into the shower. Rubio made sure the kitchen was spotless, and once Julian was dressed, he inspected every stateroom. Julian wore blue shorts and a white polo. He asked Rubio to shower and wear similar clothes.

"Like a uniform, Skip?"

"Exactly like a uniform."

"How many people are we expecting, Skip?"

"Three guests."

"Are you hiring any deckhands for this charter?"

"Nah."

"I mean, the two of us with no guests are perfect for this ship, but add some passengers and we're basically outnumbered here," said Rubio.

"I'm not scared of the extra work, we can handle it. Plus, I don't like hiring just like that. I've got to trust them, you know?"

"Ay, ay, Skip."

When Alberto arrived, Julian and Rubio were waiting on the dock to greet him. He was wearing slacks and a button-up shirt, and the three men he was with were wearing suits.

"Mr. Fontana, what a pleasure to see you, welcome aboard your yacht," said Julian.

Alberto smiled as he loved flattery. He introduced a tall, slender man, the only one of the three who was wearing a light-colored suit.

"This is engineer Antonio Blancarte."

"What a pleasure to meet you, sir," said Julian as they shook hands. "Allow me to help you with your bag."

Blancarte handed over the Louis Vuitton weekender he was carrying.

The other two men followed, and the black Mercedes Benz that had dropped them off left the marina grounds. As they entered the yacht, Julian could feel the stress these men were carrying. Roberto Fierro, the taller man who wore thin gold spectacles, was Blancarte's accountant and the CFO of his corporation. The other man, robust sixty-two-year-old Giancarlo Blake, was vice president of operations and Blancarte's closest confidant. Julian treated them with the utmost respect, and Rubio followed suit.

Alberto was overtaxed with pressure. Julian noticed this and took it upon himself to ensure his guests relaxed. Rubio prepared a jar of Pimm's and Julian poured each man a glass. Just after 2:00 pm., they were seabound. It was a lovely afternoon with clear skies and hot sun. The water was a thick jasmine-blue mirror that reflected eternity. Before they came out on the bow, the guests went into their respective staterooms and changed into shorts and t-shirts.

Rubio prepared ceviche for snacking, and Julian recommended a bottle of Mogor Badan Chasselas. The men talked in the salon for hours. Julian was mostly up on the bridge and Rubio made sure they had plenty of drinks and appetizers. Julian skippered the vessel coast side to the nearby town of Puertecitos. It was a short cruise, but they never reached speeds of more than six knots an hour.

"Why are we going so slow?" asked Rubio up on the bridge.

"Well, we're not in a hurry, and we don't want to take them too far. These Mexico City folk don't really know the Sea of Cortez. It's all the same if we take them down twenty miles or 200. Not only do we save fuel, but Puertecitos is amazing," Julian said.

They arrived at Immaculate Bay well before sunset. The Third Heaven would barely begin to describe the paradise. The stretch of ocean was surrounded by rough mountains and rocks, and the horizon to the south was led by an archipelago of islands that rose through the water like the humps of a bathing dragon.

Rubio and Julian served dinner on the stern. The men were amazed by the paradise they had posted at.

"I was in Manarola, off the Italian coast last year, and nothing compares to this. This is incredible," said Blancarte.

"And tomorrow, we have a surprise for you," said Julian, as he placed a lobster roll and a seaweed salad dish on Blancarte's placemat.

"Well, as long as it involves these two getting a tan," he said, pointing to Roberto and Blake. "Look at how white their legs are."

Out on the stern, the men smoked Cuban cigars and drank Mil Mujeres brandy well into the night. Julian rested in the Captain's Quarters, but would continually check on his guests. From what he could pick up, Alberto was negotiating stock on a project that was going to take five to seven years to build. Julian overheard amounts like $50 million and $100 million being thrown around and began to piece together an idea of the deal Alberto was working on.

The Punta Colonet Port was expected to be the biggest project in Baja. Over the past ten years, Alberto had bought over 5,000 hectares of land on the south Pacific coast of Ensenada. He had then partnered up with his brother-in-law, the architect Xavier Cho, and they designed and budgeted for a massive port of entry to and from Asia. The idea was to build a shipping port that would compete with Long Beach, California.

"But Ensenada already has a port," said Blancarte.

"Yes, a little port; Punta Colonet will be twenty or thirty times bigger. The Ensenada port only services the locals, and it's expensive to use. In a global market, it's important to create cheaper alternatives to everything, including shipping."

He was talking about a $2 billion project that needed not just capital, but also partnering with the Mexican government, the North Baja government, and the local government in order for it to move forward. Alberto Fontana's plan was to get Blancarte to put in the first $25 million that would help move the deal forward.

"I've got deals lined up with everybody. I even have my brother-in-law's uncle, Sergio Cho, ready to move. Once he finds out that you are in, he'll put in $100 million of his own money. Plus, you know what Cho is trying to do already? Because of the mining rights he owns all over the San Quintin Valley near where my property is, he's working to separate San Quintin politically from the rest of Ensenada, creating its own city, making it North Baja's sixth municipality. That's the kind of clout we've got behind this," Alberto said as Julian poured everybody brandy.

"Why haven't you brought him in already?" Blake asked as Roberto petitioned Rubio for sparkling water.

"Well, I know Cho. He's the richest man in Mexico for a reason. He's a shark. I want to have financial leverage when we talk to him. I don't want to give him more than 10 percent for his $100 million. And in order to do that, we need to have the project further along in development. I thought of you, Blancarte. You've worked with the biggest names in shipping, all throughout Latin America. I consider you a good business man, with the right ethic, attitude, and track record. I look at you not just as a capital investor. I want to tap into your expertise as well. You and I could be great partners and make a fortune together. I am offering you 20 percent for your $25 million. I'm giving you ten times a better deal than we are going to offer Cho. And you know what that means? As soon as Cho puts in $100 million for 10 percent, we have valued our project at a billion dollars. Talk about equity on your investment," Alberto said as Julian and Rubio retired back inside.

"In that case, I'll give you $25 million and I'm going to withdraw $200 million in a year's time. Deal?" Blancarte laughed.

His men followed.

"Well, not quite like that."

That was the last thing Julian heard as he stepped out.

Hours later, when the men finally headed to their staterooms, Alberto invited Julian to talk up on the bridge.

"This is the biggest deal of my life, Julian," he said.

"I'm here for you, man, anything you need," Julian said.

"I'm too tense. I don't think I can do this."

"What do you mean?" Julian asked.

"I want this deal too much. I feel like I'm jinxing it."

"Well, with that kind of thinking, you're about to."

"I know, that's what I'm afraid of," Alberto said.

"Listen, from what I could pick up, it seemed to me that they want this. You have the home-field advantage, and you're aboard this beautiful yacht. Pressuring them is not what you need to do at this point; it's actually the exact opposite," he said as Alberto bit his thumb.

"But you don't even know the details of our deal."

"You're right, but I don't need to. I know social dynamics and you, my friend, are pitching way too hard," said Julian.

Alberto let his guard down.

"Why don't we do this? Let me take your guests out on the tender tomorrow. I have this amazing spot that'll make them flip head-over-heels. These men need to relax; they're more stressed than anyone I have ever met. They're barely beginning to unwind, and you keep pushing them back into money and business. I know you men are workaholics and deal junkies, but let the sea work its magic on you," he said. "Don't worry — I'll keep my servant's hat on and won't talk about anything that is even related to work. You need to give them a little room to think."

Julian paused for a second, and an idea struck him.

"So, if you raise the $100 million from Cho, you are still two billion short. How are you going to get the rest of the money?"

"That's the thing. That's where Cho's clout comes in. Cho is the kind of guy that has other people throw money at him. He's so rich, even the World Bank throws money at basically any project he funds. The plan is to raise another $100 million from the Mexican government, and $25 million from the North Baja state government. Not only that, since Cho has invested close to $20 million in lobbying and a legal framework to get the ball rolling on separating San Quintin from Ensenada and founding it as a new city, his first intention is going to be getting the local government to co-invest in this port deal," Alberto said excitedly..

"But how is a newly formed city going to have so much money?" asked Julian.

"It won't. We are going to borrow 80 percent of the money we need from the World Bank. Once they see Cho and the Mexican government backing this deal, it's a guarantee for them. And we'll have the newly formed municipal government carry the debt," Alberto said.

Julian's eyes opened wide. "Have you told Blancarte this information?"

"No. I can't. Blancarte has very strong political connections in Mexico City and if, for some reason, he decides to use that kind of information against us, it could destroy the project before it's even begun," Alberto said.

Julian thought things over. After some time, he asked, "What politicians are backing you on this?"

Alberto said he'd talked to quite a few of them, including North Baja Governor Juan Zena, but he hadn't struck any deals.

"And that's one of the reasons I need Blancarte's money, for *politico* clout."

"What about Gilberto Alarcón?" Julian asked.

"What about him?"

"Have you talked to him about this deal?"

"You know, I haven't talked to Gilberto in a couple of years. I mean, he's up in Canada. I don't think he'd be interested in this deal."

Julian observed Alberto closely. "Well, when I met him up in Vancouver at the party, he gave me the impression he appreciated you very much. And he seemed to me like the kind of guy you could use in a deal like this. For starters, he's got a direct line to the president of Mexico, and he's not an elected official like some of these other guys who can't make a move without the media jumping all over them. He's a diplomat. If he likes the deal, he could operate for you without creating any negative attention. Look, all I am saying is why don't you call him? And if you're able to get him on board, Blancarte will feel the safety of a strong and trustworthy political connection. And that could be the little push you need to close this guy for the $25 million."

Alberto Fontana nodded with a tired look on his face. "Let me sleep on it. If your idea makes sense in the morning, I'll call Gilberto."

Chapter 26

Volcano Beach

A FTER BREAKFAST, BLANCARTE AND HIS men laid out on the bow. Julian put Herb Alpert's *Whipped Cream & Other Delights* over the yacht speakers and went up to the bridge where Alberto was waiting to talk to him.

"You know, I've been thinking, Julian. The idea you gave me is not half-bad. I'm going to follow through and talk to Gilberto Alarcón. I'm going to tell him about this deal and make him an offer. He could definitely be the right political partner for this project."

Julian was proud that Alberto was thinking aggressively. "Exactly! The project needs a solid political operator from the start."

Rubio lowered the tender. Julian instructed him to replenish the cooler with beer, wines, mezcal, and water. He also asked him to prepare snacks and to lay out four big towels. Before they boarded the tender, Julian gave brief safety instructions to the men. He didn't make them wear vests, but he instructed them on how to put them on quickly and safely.

"Where are we going, Skip?" asked Blancarte.

"To the most amazing spot in the world."

When the men were aboard, Alberto came out on the deck with his phone to his ear.

He put his hand over the phone. "Hey, you guys go to the beach. I need to stay here," he said and walked back in.

None of the men seemed to mind. They actually looked relieved to have some alone time. Julian instructed Rubio to stay with Alberto.

"Also, let Reyna out of her room for a while. And have dinner ready at 17:00."

The ride on the tender was fantastic. The wake was soft enough to make things interesting, and the wind was blowing gently on their faces. Julian skippered gracefully. He read the men's emotions like clockwork. He'd seen it before. First, a little fear when leaving behind the yacht, then people get over it and begin to feel euphoric. This is when they feel like having a drink.

Blancarte enjoyed sipping on the Chasselas, and the other men drank beer. Julian made some conversation and made sure to keep a smile on his face. The men joked around about various topics, including their desire for women and past experiences. Julian paid little attention to their conversation. He sensed the men's emotions turn to a mix of fear and wonder when they first spotted Volcano Beach on the horizon. Blancarte seemed to gasp, though no sound came out. There was a moment of silence so strong, everyone could hear the ocean wind call them over the tender's motor as they rode the final stretch towards the beach.

Volcano Beach is literally a volcano whose crater sits just above sea level, creating a natural pool inside the volcano. Because of the sulfur and other active properties of the volcano, the water in the crater is steaming hot. Julian pulled the tender up to the rocks and jumped overboard with the small anchor. He wedged the anchor between boulders and helped the men disembark onto Volcano Beach.

As the men stood over the boulder with the sea behind them, facing a giant pond of hot water, Giancarlo Blake uttered, "This is incredible."

Julian led them around to one of the smaller pools that had formed between the edge of the crater and the giant pond. This particular pool was carved out in such a way, it made the water extra hot. It was Julian's favorite pool because it was outside but in the shade. The boiling white bubbles were big, and the men began getting in little by little. Within minutes, Blancarte, Giancarlo, and Fierro were soaking in the hot spring with their arms stretched dry over rocks.

Julian made sure they were comfortable and returned to the tender for the ice chest and towels. He catered to the men, who finished two bottles of wine and seven beers over the course of two hours. They alternated between sitting in the hot water and sitting outside on one of the rocks where they would only dip their feet. Roberto laid out in the sun for a little bit, and Giancarlo did breathing exercises while Blancarte spent longer periods of time in the hot spring. The men had a great time, chatting, laughing, letting loose. They never once mentioned money or business. They were like kids, rejoicing over being alive.

On the ride back to the yacht, Julian advised the men to drink plenty of water. They did, and hardly spoke. Their red faces and tired eyes had a distinct glow, one that evoked the feeling of having witnessed paradise lost. They boarded the yacht, showered, and changed. Julian stored the tender and Rubio finished setting the dinner table. Julian poured Rito rosé wine and the men insisted on waiting for Alberto, who could be seen and heard talking on the phone up on the tower. Julian went up to check on him, but Alberto was engulfed in conversation. He came back down and convinced the men to begin eating since he was still busy. Rubio served a delicious crab chowder, followed by stuffed snapper with apricot rice. As the men were complimenting Rubio's meal, Alberto came down with a huge smile on his face. The men cheered at his arrival.

"Even I almost missed you," said Blancarte.

"That was my compadre, Gilberto Alarcón," Alberto said. "We spent all day talking back and forth. We just negotiated my candidacy for Baja California's 4th congressional district next year. That is perfect, because in four years time, when San Quintin becomes its own city, I could be its first mayor and make sure our deal goes through," Alberto said.

Julian was very impressed to hear this, but remained quiet. Blancarte was the first to rise and congratulate him, and the other men followed. Julian poured Alberto some rosé.

"I don't want this shit. Pour us some tequila," he said.

Julian served shots of Casamigos and the men cheered.

Alberto didn't talk about business or politics for the rest of the evening. Whenever the men tried to get more information, he would shrug it off and change the subject. The men talked about their amazing experience at Volcano Beach and took turns describing the paradise Julian had taken them to.

"It's the most magical place I've ever been to, and I've set foot on every continent," said Blancarte.

That night, the businessmen went to sleep right after dusk. The hot spring, along with the sulfur and sun, mixed with alcohol and a great dinner, guaranteed they would sleep well. Julian and Alberto touched base up on the bridge while they smoked Cohibas and sipped Casamigos. Fontana thanked Julian for his advice, telling him how he had negotiated five percent of his total project with Gilberto Alarcón, on the grounds that Alarcón back him all the way to next summer's congressional race.

"Well, there's still a long way to go," said Julian.

"Yea, but my compadre is going to help me move all of the necessary institutional pieces. Why do you think I was on the phone with him for over four hours? He already committed to walking me through the whole process. Are you kidding me? For five percent? That's over $100 million," Alberto said. "And you know what he told me? That's why he's in Canada—the president personally sent him there to make relationships with the mining extraction companies that are looking to invest in not just Baja, but all of Mexico. You know what that means? A port deal like this is a game changer for foreign investment, particularly in mining. The guy is sold. And when I pitch Cho about foreign companies wanting to come into Mexico, he's going to want to be as close to them as possible. You know what they say—keep your friends close."

"And your enemies closer," interrupted Julian.

"Goddamnit Jules, you are a fucking genius!"

"Hey, I only suggested that you talk to him. You're the one that took it, ran with it, and made it happen. All I ask is that you don't forget about me when you get to the top," said Julian.

"When have I ever forgotten about you? We came up on this boat, didn't we?"

Yacht, Alberto, it's a yacht! Julian thought about correcting him as he puffed on a Cohiba. "We sure did, my friend. We sure did," he said instead.

After breakfast the next morning, Julian felt his left hand shake slightly. There was no pain, headache, or nausea, only an insatiable thirst. He gulped a beer and the shaking ceased. Rubio played Nick Drake's *Bryter Layter* over the yacht speakers, but when the song "Hazey Jane II" was playing, Blancarte, who was in the salon meeting with his men and Alberto, asked Rubio to turn the music off.

When they arrived at the marina, Julian maneuvered the yacht gracefully. When Blancarte, Giancarlo, and Fierro disembarked, Alberto had a big grin on his face. Julian thanked the men for being great guests, and insisted that if they ever needed a yacht charter, *The Cecilia* would be there for them. The three men got picked up by the same black Mercedes that had dropped them off, and Alberto stayed on board, waving to the men as they drove away.

"We did it, *Cabrónes!*" he said as he waved a check in front of Julian's face. "I closed that mother-f. You would've been so proud of me. He wanted to leave the yacht without committing to a deal. I told him that Gilberto Alarcón was operating on this from the inside, and if it wasn't his $25 million, I already had people in Canada waiting to throw money at this deal."

Julian grabbed the check from Alberto's hand. "Two hundred and fifty thousand. That's hardly the $25 million you were looking for."

"Give me that," Alberto said as he took the check from Julian's hand. "It's 1 percent of the money, Julian. We agreed that 1 percent was going to hold him. He has 30 days to deposit 10 percent, which is $2.5 million, and within 90 days, I'm gonna get the full $25 million."

"Well, good for you, Alberto. At least I know who's buying drinks tonight," Julian said as he put his arm around him.

That night, Alberto, Rubio, and Julian got extremely drunk in San

Felipe. They had dinner at the Tropicana Grill and Julian and Rubio rejoiced with Alberto over the deal.

The next morning, Alberto was ready to leave after breakfast.

"I need something from you, Julian. Gilberto called me this morning and he…" Alberto took a sip of his coffee, "informed me that this port deal cannot proceed until we have a plan of attack against a specific enemy — one that you share with us." He took another sip of his coffee.

"Axel," whispered Julian, almost unconsciously.

"That's right."

"But why would Gilberto worry so much about Axel now? What's going on?" Julian asked.

"Axel is working with huge financial backing. We don't know who it's coming from yet, but his interests at sea are moving tremendously. We need to stop him even if it begins with massive media attacks," Alberto said.

"What can I do?"

"Tell me something: who is behind Axel? Who does he work for?"

"Listen, Alberto, I trust you. I know you're onto something, but I'm the one who's out here on Baja waters. If I tell you something and he figures out that it came from me, it's over, he's gonna destroy me."

Alberto stared directly at him.

"Axel got me good, and as much as I try to get over it, that shit breaks my heart. Every day, that shit breaks my heart. I mean, we grew up together, *primos*, closer than brothers."

Alberto listened attentively. He knew Julian well enough to know that if he was excusing himself, he was going to tell him something good.

"Axel works for Samuel Bracho."

"What? Directly?"

"Straight line, answers to the man himself."

"This is huge."

"Yea, the day Axel threatened me with a shotgun to the head and forced me to sign resignation letters, it was Samuel Bracho calling the shots," said Julian.

There was silence for a moment.

"You know what? It's good that you're telling me this. I hate that piece of shit, too. I knew he screwed you out of the port captainship, but, Jesus, working for Samuel Bracho?"

"Yea."

"It's a war out here, Julian. This is Baja. It's not civilized around here. It's the Viet Cong every day and our enemies are using napalm. We can't let that piece of shit win. We're gonna get revenge on Axel. It's as they say — he might've won the battle, but we're gonna win the war, my friend," Alberto said.

The pair stood up and hugged goodbye.

"And don't you worry about Axel Cuevas. We'll get back at that scum. You see, *I'm* your brother now, not him. We've got a chance. Let's strike."

CHAPTER 27

The Beaver

SPENDING TIME WITH FONTANA MOTIVATED Julian to work harder. "I'm too young to retire; I've got to make some moves of my own," he told Rubio.

"What do you suggest we do?" Rubio asked.

"Let's pick up this charter business," said Julian.

"How do we do that?"

"Let's head down to South Baja first."

Julian spent the next few weeks thinking up plans and business models for his charter company. It was hard for him to think about marketing and such things because the jobs he'd always held were official or back-of-house. But he kept an open mind and even began reading business books.

Months later, on a fine Wednesday, early in the afternoon, Julian was relaxing on a lounge chair as palm trees swayed and the sea gently beat the shore. With his right hand, he played with the warm sand below and scratched his chest with his left. He gazed at *The Cecilia*, which was anchored in the emerald-colored bay in front of him. Rubio could be seen drying clothes on the stern. It was a very hot day, but the shade of the palm trees made Rambo's Palapa Bar the best possible place to be. Rambo came over and handed Julian a bloody Clamato. Julian drank it for breakfast.

Rambo's Palapa bar in Mulegé was a lonely little bar on the beach. To the east, it overlooked Emerald Bay, and to the west, there was a small sweetwater stream that led to a beachside desert oasis. Julian had found the place by luck several weeks earlier, and he had stayed there ever since, anchored in what could be considered one of the world's best-kept secrets. As his mind wandered about Alberto Fontana and his port deal, his mobile phone rang.

"Hello? Mr. Mayorca? said a young female voice.

"Yes," his voice scratched gently.

"Hi, this is Collette, from Jacoby & Jewels," she said.

"Jacoby & Jewels?"

"Yes, you left your watch in consignment with us a while back — your Rolex," she said.

Boyd's old watch, oh fuck. "Oh, right. Well, how you doing?" asked Julian.

"I'm doing great. I'm calling to tell you that we've sold your Rolex and we're ready to cut a check for you," Collette said.

Julian sat up. "That's great news. How much?"

"Well, we've sold it for $50,000, but we take a 20 percent commission, so $40,000 for you."

"Right on, Collette! You should call me more often," Julian said with excitement.

Collette joked around with Julian for a couple of minutes, and Julian asked her if she could deposit the money into his account. She apologized and said it was against company policy. Julian tried to persuade Collette, but she stood her ground. He realized that the reason behind making him pick up the check was so he'd spend some of it at the shop.

He didn't mind and told her, "Well, that's a good reason to go to Cabo."

Collette agreed.

The crisp sound of an engine rumbled through the air. He hung up the call and looked up with a smile on his face; a beautiful white and red seaplane was flying above him. It lapped Emerald Bay three times and then alighted on the water. It taxied over to the small dock next to Julian's tender. A couple got out and tied the seaplane as if it were a regular boat. Julian could see them from afar, pointing at the natural beauty of the place. He could tell they'd found it by luck, just as he had weeks earlier. Rambo walked by Julian on his way to greet the couple.

"Why don't you get them a round of whatever they want, on me," Julian said. "Tell them I said, 'That was quite a landing.'" Julian laid back down on the lawn chair, closed his eyes, and was about to fall into a nap when he heard a female voice close to him.

"Thanks for the drinks."

Julian sat up and his jaw dropped. "Denise?"

Right behind her was his old deckhand, Ernie Jordan. Julian stood up and hugged Denise.

"Oh my gosh," she said, "Captain Mayorca! How are you?"

"I'm doing great," answered Julian, as he went over and hugged Ernie. "What are you two doing here?"

"We were flying and saw this spot. It's so beautiful, we had to stop," said Denise.

"You were flying? I thought you two were sailors," said Julian.

"Well, we're pilots now, too," said Ernie, with a grin so large, the sun reflected on his white teeth.

Julian was so excited to see his old crew that he ordered Cadillac Margaritas from Rambo. Denise asked for a club soda instead, but Ernie and Julian sipped cocktails, and the three of them caught up. Denise did most of the talking, but Ernie filled in at the right moments. It turned out that Ernie and Denise had resigned their port captainship jobs less than two months after Axel Cuevas took office.

"It was so different," mumbled Denise

"Yea, they wouldn't even let us aboard *La Capitana*," said Ernie.

"Haven't you seen the papers?" Denise said. "They're saying he works for Samuel Bracho, even put him out of prison."

"Wow," said Julian, satisfied with the info he had shared with Alberto Fontana.

They later told Julian that the two of them had looked for jobs as deckhands and sailors, but hadn't found anything. They were unemployed for close to three months, until Ernie got a job as a mechanic for a Canadian man named Kyle Willis.

"He owns a couple of Zodiacs. He does some whale shark tours with them. And *The Beaver* is actually his," Ernie said, pointing at the seaplane.

Denise explained how after a month of working there, Ernie was able to get her a job with Kyle, doing mostly errands and paperwork.

"She became interested in the seaplane, and one day — you know Denise with her charm — she convinced Kyle to take her flying," Ernie said.

"That's all it took. One ride on *The Beaver*. The week after, I was taking flying lessons," said Denise.

"And then *I* was taking lessons. Because you know me, I can't fall too far behind," Ernie said as he winked at Julian and put his arm around Denise.

"Wow," said Julian. "Well, how long has it been since we all worked together?"

Denise looked at Ernie. "Three years," he blurted out.

"Three years. Three freaking years?" said Julian. "I can't believe it!"

"Yea, it has to be about three years. It takes two years to get your flying license. And I've had mine for about six months now," said Denise.

"I barely just got mine two weeks ago," Ernie said.

After talking a while, Denise asked Julian, "You wanna fly around for a little bit?"

"You better believe it!"

As they approached the dock, Julian said he had something to do aboard the yacht.

"This is your yacht?" asked Ernie.

"Do you two think you're the only ones with the cool toys?" Julian asked. "I'll be right back. I've got a surprise for you guys."

"How about you ride the tender and we'll meet you over there," said Denise.

Julian rode over to *The Cecilia* and tied the tender to the stern. He rushed inside.

"Put on some shoes, I've got a surprise for you," he told Rubio.

When they exited the salon, *The Beaver* was pulling up to the stern of the yacht. Denise, in the pilot's seat, waved, while Ernie threw Rubio a rope.

"There he is!" said Ernie.

Rubio held the rope, speechless and in awe of the whole situation.

Julian stepped on one of the floats and got into the plane. After a moment, Rubio followed. Ernie, as copilot, handed them headsets. Denise welcomed them aboard and turned serious as she taxied. Then, little by little, *The Beaver* began gaining speed and a moment later, they were airborne.

"Nothing beats the moment of takeoff," said Julian.

"Roger that," said Denise as she flew over Emerald Bay.

Weightlessness would best describe how Julian felt; enthusiasm had been birthed in him again. He couldn't remember the last time he'd been on a plane, and this was an experience unlike any other. *The Beaver* was a six-seater; the four seats behind him were empty, and the plane felt like an old-school, yet strong, aircraft.

"What year is this?" Julian asked over the mic.

"It's a 1962," answered Ernie.

The airplane's engine had a unique sound, like a clean relic.

"She's gorgeous," said Julian.

Below them were the mangroves of Mulegé, where dense vegetation replaced sandy beaches. Tones of green mixed with blues; the sun reflecting off the water caused the wake to appear mystical and ageless.

Rubio didn't say a word the whole time they were in flight; he just looked out of his little window. After a while, they left the coast and headed over the mountains.

When Denise made a turn, she said over the headphones, "And to your left, you can now see the great Pacific Ocean."

It was remarkable. They had seen the sea, the desert, the mountains, and now the Pacific, all within an hour of flying.

"This is incredible," said Julian.

"Yea, flying has changed our lives," said Ernie as he glanced back at Julian.

The Beaver landed back at Emerald Bay. Denise pulled up to the stern of the yacht.

"That was too much fun," said Julian.

"Just another day in paradise," said Denise.

"What are you guys planning on doing next? Why don't you come aboard the yacht? We'll prepare a late lunch-early dinner," said Julian.

The couple looked at each other and Denise said, "Well, we wanted to head back to La Paz. You know, Mr. Willis is waiting for us."

"Why don't you head back later? You have to try Rubio's cioppino. It's amazing," said Julian.

"The thing is, if we don't head back now, we won't be able to fly out until tomorrow. We're still not too comfortable flying this baby out at night," said Ernie.

"Well, I understand," said Julian. "But just so you know, there's plenty of room aboard my yacht for you guys."

Ernie and Denise exchanged a couple of words in that language that couples share.

Denise pointed over to the dock. "Let us make a call to La Paz. We're gonna dock it. Why don't you come meet us over there, and we'll let you know if we can stay or not."

"Why don't you just tie her up to the yacht?" Julian asked.

"Well, we could, but it's not safe. We rather dock it. There's a special piece that you need if you want to be able to tie the plane to a ship," said Ernie as he closed the door.

"Just pick us up over there," said Denise, as they taxied *The Beaver* to Rambo's dock.

Twenty minutes later, Julian was skippering the tender back to *The Cecilia* with Ernie and Denise as passengers.

The couple had managed to convince Kyle Willis to let them stay an extra day out in Mulegé, and Julian arranged with Rambo to allow them to dock *The Beaver* overnight. After they boarded the yacht, Julian gave them a detailed tour of the vessel.

"Wow!" said Ernie as he looked through the yacht.

"She's impressive. If you don't mind me asking, Skip, how much was she?" Denise asked.

"A true captain will never reveal the price of his lady, but she's a $5 million yacht that looks like a $10 million yacht. Truth is, I got a great deal on her," said Julian with a smirk. "But it's thanks to Rubio that she looks this good."

Rubio was cooking in the galley.

"He's the one that cleans, waxes, and makes sure she's spotless."

Rubio looked their way, spatula in hand. "Thanks, Skip. You flatter me."

"Oh, and we've got one other crew member you haven't met yet," said Julian.

Reyna came out, wagging her tail. Denise knelt down and petted her.

"Reyna's the real owner. We all just work for her," said Julian.

They laughed.

Over dinner, the old crew had a joyous time. They joked around about, reminisced, and laughed over the same jokes they used to laugh about years ago. To remember was to live again.

"Why did you really leave the port captainship?" Denise asked after they had drunk two bottles of Baron Balche Cero wine.

"Well, as you know, my cousin's a son of a bitch. I really had no choice," said Julian.

The couple insisted that Julian tell them more, but he wouldn't.

"So what's the deal with *The Beaver*? I love that thing. When can we go flying again?" Julian asked.

"Whenever you want," said Denise. She talked about how casual Kyle, the owner, was with them. "He loves us. We're like his kids. I mean, he *has* kids, but they don't care about him."

"How's his business doing?" asked Julian.

"Not too good. That's the reason we're out here. We're testing the plane because he made us an offer, The guy's eighty-two. He's getting real old, and the business isn't giving him much. He wants to sell the plane and the Zodiacs and retire. I mean, really retire this time."

"How much is he asking for the plane?" asked Julian.

"Well, since she's in practically mint condition, he's asking $450,000. But because he loves us, he told us that he wants *us* to buy it from him. We told him that we don't have that kind of money. So he told us he would sell it to us for $375,000, and all we had to do was pay 10 percent, and after that, make payments."

"Wow, that's a really good deal," said Julian.

"Yea, it is," Denise said, "except that we don't even have the $40,000 down payment," She looked at Ernie and the two of them laughed.

"How much could you really make with a small plane like that? I mean, if you really worked it," Julian asked.

"Well, we've done some numbers. We could do a really good tour for $500. Call it a ninety-minute tour, floats down, back within the hour. Up to six passengers. We do three trips, three days a week, and five trips on weekends, and we're in business. That's being optimistic, but to be honest with you, I know Ernie and I could do it. All we'd have to do is spend some money on marketing, and with Cabo alone, we could hit those numbers."

Julian was impressed with the way Denise was talking. He'd never heard her talk like a businesswoman. He liked this side of her, how she opened up, and he was excited about a potential opportunity.

"What about competition in Cabo?" he asked.

"That's where it gets tricky. There really is no competition. You see, Kyle warned us that the Mexican government is very difficult when it comes to dealing with recreational aircraft, especially because of the drug dealers — anything that's less than a jet, they trip like hell over it. Plus, there is no legal framework for the floatplane. So, because they don't know how to regulate it, they make your life a living hell," said Denise.

"I'm sure there's a way around it," Julian said. "I mean, isn't there like an *agencia*, but for planes?"

"Well, the floatplane can be underwritten with an *agencia*, but it would only cover it while on the water. Once it's airborne, it's on its own, legally speaking," said Denise.

"Well, couldn't you get some sort of permit?" asked Julian.

"Yea, but you have to get it directly from the Mexican Air Force, signed by the top guy himself. And good luck getting through to him," said Denise.

"What's his name?" asked Julian.

"General Agundez Velarde. You know him?" asked Denise.

"I've never heard of him," said Julian.

Rubio served chocolate mousse for dessert.

"I'm impressed, guys," Julian said. "You two, the way you've come around and reinvented yourselves, as pilots and business people," he smiled. "You know, I'm in a similar situation with this yacht. I have a partner — a minority partner, if you will, who owns 15 percent. I've promised him we're gonna make some money with the yacht, but...." Julian stopped talking. He stared blankly out the window.

"But, what?" asked Denise.

Julian looked at her and Ernie, who was leaning into the table.

"Why don't we partner up? I mean, you guys have the plane, I have the yacht, and we could work both angles. Think of that — air *and* sea."

"What? That would be amazing, Julian. Are you kidding? We would love that," Denise said.

Ernie nodded in silence with a big smile.

"If anyone can get a permit to use the seaplane, it's me. We still have contacts," Julian said with a grin.

"It's genius," said Denise.

"Yea, I mean, the four of us, our old crew. We could all work the yacht when we get a charter. You guys can work the plane whenever a client wants something more."

Julian leaned over and high-fived Denise and Ernie.

"And we could promote it together. Double down on social media as the ultimate adventure platform," she said with excitement.

"What do you think?" Julian asked Rubio.

He grabbed another bottle. "I think it's the best idea you've had since you bought this yacht, Skip."

Pop! went the cork.

PART II

The Business

CHAPTER 28

Percentages

SINCE THE NIGHT HE'D DREAMED up the Air & Sea project with Denise and Ernie, Julian felt revitalized. He approached things with a different attitude. A sense of purpose overtook him, and a passion for being reunited with his crew began to drive him. The Jordans flew back to La Paz the following morning and Julian arrived at Marina Palma a week later.

The Thursday Julian arrived, he went back to his house, but Rubio stayed on the yacht. The following morning, Julian had a meeting with Denise and Ernie.

"Kyle is eager to sell it to us," said Denise.

"We told him that we're starting our own business, and he was thrilled. But, we've gotta be frank with you, Julian. He did warn us that the Mexican government is a bitch to deal with when it comes to the floatplane," Ernie said.

"Well, nothing is easy. But the fact that there's no competition makes it something that could really pay off," said Julian.

"That's the same thing we're thinking," Denise said. "If anyone can do it, it's us. I mean, you have a lot of connections. I know you can call in some favors for our business."

"You're goddamn right I'm gonna call in some favors. I'm gonna call a whole list of favors. I'm not taking no for an answer. Our business needs to be a success."

"We're with you, Julian, 110 percent. We've worked with you before, we know how solid you are. I guess the only thing left to talk about is money," said Denise.

Ernie nodded.

"Can you invest the $40,000 we need to get the payment plan going with Kyle?" Denise asked.

Julian crossed his hands and took them to his face. "Well, how much money do you guys have to invest in the plane?"

"Not a lot," Ernie said. "We have a little under $10,000 saved up. But that's all we've got."

"One more thing. Kyle said that if we close the price at $400,000 he would throw in three of his Zodiac tenders," Denise said.

"Three of them? Are they in pretty good shape?" Julian asked.

"Yea. Two are 500s, and the other is an older Yachtline. I mean, it's a good deal. The guy pretty much wants to close his business. He also told us he would gladly hand over his client list. Like Denise said, the guy's basically retiring," said Ernie.

Julian took a deep breath. "Can I meet him? I would like to talk to him."

Denise and Ernie exchanged a glance.

"That's not a problem. But we haven't told him that we're going to have a partner. I mean, I am more than happy to introduce you to the guy, but once he knows that there's another person in on our deal, he might want to raise the price. Or, even worse, he might not want to do the whole installment thing. I mean, he's doing that because he loves us and really trusts us."

"Okay," said Julian. "After the $40,000, how much are the payments?"

"He wants $5,000 a month for six years. The guy already gets a pension from a company he started in Canada, and he's got savings, he just wants this money to live off of. And in Baja, $5,000 a month will go a long way," Ernie said.

Julian was very excited about the deal. He was already formulating a plan to make it work.

"Based on your experience, how much would we end up spending on maintenance?" he asked.

"Not much. His parts are old, but they're good," said Ernie.

Denise interrupted: "The point of the business is to scale, Julian. I took a class at South Baja University, and I learned that the most important thing when going into business is scalability. Are we able to scale?"

Julian thought this was very interesting, and Denise continued talking about the necessity of thinking long term.

"The seaplane is a good deal, but if we want to turn this into a real business, we are going to have to grow and get another aircraft in less than four years."

"Three years, probably," interrupted Ernie.

"I like that," Julian said.

"If we save 20 percent of everything we make, we'll be able to have a nice little bundle for emergencies, and we'll be able to buy another aircraft in a couple years if we play our cards right," Denise said.

Julian was ready to make a deal. "I'll put up the $40,000, but it has to come through my business account directly to his account."

"I don't think that's a problem. Once the money is deposited into his account, I don't think he'll care where it actually came from," Denise said.

"And you gotta tell him to give us ninety days to make the first $5,000 payment."

"I don't think that'll be a problem," Denise said.

"We've got to work hard to be able to pay the monthly $5,000 out of our business," Julian said.

"That's exactly our priority, Julian," Denise replied. "How about we talk about the split?"

Julian was ready. He'd been wanting to have this conversation, but wanted them to bring up percentages first.

"Well, there are two things to do here. One, lay out specific tasks. And, two, lay out our assets," he said. "You guys are bringing in the plane, the expertise, and work. I'm bringing in the cash, the yacht — which is at least $5 million — and myself as CEO," said Julian.

"So that means I would be V.P.," said Denise.

"And Ernie, you could be Director of Operations," Julian said.

Ernie nodded.

"I want this to be fair, because, you gotta remember, I'm also coming in with a partner, and he's more like a silent partner, but I have to notify him and pay him 15 percent of my share," Julian said.

"But why would he be a partner on the plane, too?" Denise asked.

"Well, because I'm going to spend $100,000 in three months to get this operation up and running. Other than the $40,000 I'm putting in for the plane, I'll need to put away $60,000 for operations, marketing, and expenses, $30,000 of which will come from me and I can probably get my partner to invest another $30,000. To be fair, I believe Agencia Mayorca needs to get 80 percent, then 10 percent for you, and 10 percent for you." Julian pointed at Ernie and Denise.

The couple looked at each other and Denise replied, "I appreciate the offer, Julian, but we're not willing to take less than 40 percent," she said.

"But you aren't putting in any of the cash," said Julian with a smile on his face. "I'm putting in all of the expensive toys."

"Yes, it's true, but we brought in a significant discount on the plane, and our work — I mean our pilot licenses, Ernie's mechanical skills — and the fact that we're a crew of pilot, copilot, first mate and sailor. Plus, I'm doing all of the marketing."

"Man, so, you're going to be doing everything, huh?"

"Well, yea."

They laughed.

"Also, the plane is only going to be a $40,000 out-of-pocket cost. After that, the $5,000 a month is going to pay for itself," said Denise.

Over the next hour, the three of them went over all of their tasks and responsibilities. They put a value to everything they were bringing to the table and negotiated every detail they could think of. In the end, Denise and Ernie committed to devoting all of their waking time to the company. The three partners also agreed that they weren't going to charge the company a salary for at least six months. Julian said he would prefer it if they waited until there were profits. Denise and Ernie agreed, but were concerned that the $10,000 they had to live off would last them a little more than three months. They finally settled on 70 percent to Agencia Mayorca and 30 percent for the Jordans. Julian agreed to it since he still had full ownership of the yacht, and he wanted to motivate the couple; he knew how hard working and loyal they were.

"With Ernie and Denise by my side, we can build the best charter business in Baja," Julian said on the phone with Alberto Fontana.

He explained the whole scheme.

"I need you to put up $30,000," said Julian.

"What? Why?" Alberto wanted to know.

"We're buying a plane! You're my partner. I need you vested in this," Julian said. "We need to spend on marketing, startup costs. And, listen, our new partner, Denise, she's good at all of this."

Julian could tell Alberto saw this project as a fun alternative to all of his other businesses, and he was convinced the project could be a thriving venture.

"So, when am I going to be able to fly on the plane?" Alberto asked.

"Next time you come into town, for sure," Julian said.

He asked Alberto to draft the necessary contracts to partner with the Jordans.

"What are you guys naming the company?" Alberto asked.

"Baja Air & Sea."

"I like the name. I'll send you my thirty."

CHAPTER 29

King Cobras

ALBERTO FONTANA REFERRED JULIAN TO an accountant he did a lot of business with out of La Paz, a gentleman by the name of Fabio Delgadillo. He set up a meeting between the two of them, and, two days later, Julian showed up at Fabio's bayfront property. He knew he had arrived because his name was on the office building. It was an impressive setup. There was a security checkpoint and plenty of parking. A handful of armored trucks, black Suburbans, white trucks, and silver cars had FABIO CONSORTIUM logos on them. The guards and drivers hung around in circles, smoking cigarettes.

The building's original name was *La Comisión* and even though it attempted to be modern, you couldn't call it that, exactly. Five stories spread out but well-kept, it was Mexican-modern influenced. Originally the building was a government-run medical center, then the Secretariat of Tourism. In 2006, Fabio negotiated with the then-governor of South Baja, Giovani Rodriguez, to purchase the multi-million-dollar property.

By the time Fabio was able to underwrite *La Comisión* to one of his many corporations and actually move in, the building was a whole different beast. Fabio had his people completely remodel it into a high-class boiler room. There was a fountain in the lobby and a reception area where beautiful people introduced themselves. Everybody was dressed business-formal, which was very unusual for La Paz, where shorts and flip-flops were perfectly acceptable in all business settings. The lobby was spacious and Julian was greeted by a lovely brunette.

"Captain Mayorca?" she said.

"Julian, please."

"Nice to meet you. I'm Elvia, one of Papa Fabio's junior executives."

"Papa Fabio?" Julian asked.

"Yea, he insists that all his employees call him Papa." She rolled her eyes in a cute way.

"Oh God," said Julian.

"No, thank goodness he doesn't make us call him God, because for the money he pays us, we probably would," Elvia laughed.

"I'm not calling him Papa."

"Have you met him?"

"No, this is our first meeting. I was referred by my good friend and attorney, Alberto Fontana."

"Oh, yes, Mr. Fontana, great friends of Papa Fabio. He's a good friend to all of us. He sends us perfumes and gifts every Christmas."

"Really?"

"Yes, to all the girls, at least."

"Classic Fontana. That's nice, though," said Julian with admiration for his friend.

"*I* think it's nice. Some of the girls don't like it, though. They think he's trying to get something else, if you know what I mean."

"Well, they're not wrong. Always trust your instinct," Julian said as he bit his lip slightly.

Elvia stared. "So you *haven't* met Papa Fabio?"

Julian shook his head.

"Oh, just wait then. You'll be calling him Papa before you know it," she laughed.

"Why do you say that?"

"Let's just say *he's charming.*" She handed Julian a tablet. "Can you please fill out all of this info? It's for our records."

"Sure." Julian tapped the screen and entered his business name, contact information, and answered a few questions.

Elvia served Julian a delicious cup of specialty coffee and offered him fruit. He declined the fruit and sipped on his coffee.

This place was buzzing with activity. Beyond the reception desk, Julian could see an army of accountants and executives typing away at their computers and laptops. Some made phone calls, others were at stand-up desks. A few small groups were in discussion, and at least six people were on video conferences of some sort.

Julian was escorted to Fabio's office penthouse overlooking the bay. The tall CPA welcomed him warmly.

"So you're a friend of the Ape's," said Fabio.

"The Ape?" said Julian.

"Yea, that's what we call Fontana around here — *the Ape*."

Julian laughed. "Why do you call him that?"

"Have you seen how hairy his back is?"

"I've never seen him shirtless."

"Well, it's not a pretty sight!"

Fabio advised Julian to establish a limited liability company instead of a corporation because an LLC didn't tax profits after they were distributed by the owners. They talked for almost two hours about business; Fabio was very cool and easy going. He had confidence and was personable. Eventually, they moved on to other topics, like fishing, boating, and golf.

"What do you mean you don't play golf?" Fabio asked.

"Well, I've dabbled. I mean, I have a nice swing." Julian mimed a golf swing.

"Let's go play sometime. I have, like, 100 rounds of free golf at Paraiso. It's a bitchin' course. Are you free tomorrow?"

"Sure, man, I'm down," said Julian.

"You have sticks?" asked Fabio.

"Sticks?"

"Sticks! You know, golf clubs. Do you have golf clubs?"

"Nah, man, I don't," Julian said.

"You like King Cobras?" Fabio went into a room at the other end of his office.

"Like the snake?" Julian asked. *Where is he going? This guy's too much.*

Fabio's workplace resembled a presidential office with a huge boardroom table and lots of different areas for people to work and have impromptu meetings.

What is he doing back there?

"No, King Cobra golf clubs," said Fabio as he came out with a brand new set of clubs and handed them to Julian.

"What is this?"

"These are for you, my friend. You look like you could use a good set of clubs. They're brand new, stiff shaft, perfect for a strong guy like yourself."

Julian picked up each club. King F-9 Speedback driver, all black King Forged Tec irons, Superlite Fairway woods, wedges, and a custom putter with the Mexican flag engraved on it.

"Oh, shit, not the putter." Fabio pulled it out of the bag, went to his desk, grabbed a different putter, and stuffed it in the golf bag.

"I can't take this, it's too much," Julian said.

"Nah, some guy paid me $10,000 that he owed me with pallets of King Cobras. I literally have a truckload of them."

"How did he get them?"

"I don't ask those questions?" he smiled.

"You're a smart man," said Julian.

"Not as smart as you, Captain Mayorca! You spend your days at sea on a luxury yacht. I spend my life in an office. You've got it figured it out. I'm just trying to hang out with you, so take my gift. I'll have my driver pick you up tomorrow at ten and we'll go hack it up at the expensive golf course!"

"Wow, you're too much, man, I swear!" Julian hugged Fabio.

"I have been called Extra!"

They laughed

"Here, take some golf balls. They have my logo on them."

Before leaving, Fabio said he would handle all of the startup's due diligence based on their conversation and the information and contracts Alberto Fontana had already sent him.

Julian tried to get an invoice from him.

"Fontana's already taking care of it," Fabio said.

This was the main reason Julian knew it was necessary to bring Fontana into the plane partnership — he was a stand-up guy who played fair and always came through.

"I don't know what he told you about me, but I'm sure glad he did," said Julian.

"You and I are going to make a lot of money together, Papa. I can sense it. You have a big dollar sign on your forehead. You're a winner; you smell like money. What cologne are you wearing? Carolina Herrera?" Fabio asked.

"No, it's Creed, Millésime Imperial," said Julian.

"*Millésime Imperial.* Nobody wears Creed in this town. You know who does?"

Julian smiled and shook his head.

"Winners do! You do Papa!" said Fabio.

Julian left Fabio's office with a new accountant, new golf clubs, a new friend, and a strange desire to call another grown man "Papa."

"Elvia was right. It's only a matter of time until I fall into his *Papa* game!" he whispered to himself as he laughed and loaded his new King Cobra golf clubs to his Land Rover.

CHAPTER 30

Baja Air & Sea, LLC

Less than a week later, when the Jordans gave Julian the go-ahead to deposit the money for the plane, they had already made significant progress in planning out a strategy for the business. With the help of Vivian, Denise's designer friend, they created a logo that had three round icons; one for Baja, one for air, and one for the sea. They made a plan to call Kyle's old clients and notify them of the management change. Denise started working on an online marketing and social media strategy, and Julian worked on securing the necessary permits and paperwork. Ernie's job was to oversee maintenance and service.

Julian made sure that Rubio earned an income from the new company.

"You are the only employee of two companies. How does that feel?" Julian asked.

"Why is that?" asked Rubio.

"Because each company needs to have an employee, and I'm not hiring anyone new."

Rubio didn't really understand the logic behind it.

"Look at it this way: you work for me from eight to five, then you get off and come work at my other company from 5 to 1 a.m. Legally you'll be working for me sixteen hours a day!" Julian laughed.

"Oh come on, Skip. I'm already here 24/7," said Rubio.

"Yeah, that's why it's not a big deal, don't worry about it. You're getting paid well, plus, you'll be saving up two pensions. Makes you look like you've got two jobs. It shows that you're responsible."

"But I am responsible, Skip. Always have been."

"Yea, but not like this," said Julian.

When Ernie and Denise came back from closing the deal with Kyle, Julian asked ,"Where's the plane?"

The couple laughed, and told him Kyle had allowed them to keep it in his water hanger on his property near Caimancito.

"Is he going to charge us for storing it?" asked Julian.

"He's going to charge $400 a month after the first two months. And that's another thing," Denise said. "He only let us skip payment on the first sixty days after the deposit. So sixty days from today, we owe him $5,400."

"Well, that just means that we've got less time to pop our cherry," said Julian.

They all laughed, but Julian thought he wanted to buy his own piece of land to store the seaplane.

"What about the Zodiacs?" he asked.

"They're there. We can use them whenever," said Ernie.

"Is he going to charge us for keeping them there?"

"No, not the Zodiacs."

"So let me get this straight. I just paid for something that its old owner is going to keep?" asked Julian.

"Don't worry. I've got keys to the place. He's got all of the tools and everything's there. It's not like we have to go out and buy new stuff," said Ernie.

Julian was a little suspicious about the whole thing.

"Julian, don't worry. The guy's Canadian. He's nice. Plus we already told him we have a partner. Next time we go flying, you can come meet him," said Denise.

She handed Julian the signed contract that released *The Beaver* from Mr. Kyle Willis' possession and to Baja Air & Sea, LLC.

Chapter 31

Startup

JULIAN SET UP A HOME office in his living room. He got two glass desks with swivel chairs and also turned his round breakfast table into a meeting table. Denise and Ernie would show up at 08:00, and Julian would already have a pot of Oaxaca coffee brewing. The three of them worked nonstop on launching the business. Julian's course of action was to focus first on the yacht, because he still felt unsafe about using the plane for business, especially because it needed to be flown covertly to avoid unwanted government attention. Julian had been unsuccessful in getting an appointment with Admiral Gomez, his *padrino,* and head of the Mexican Navy in South Baja.

Gomez was a former mentor of Julian's during his time at the Mexican Naval Academy and one of his biggest supporters when he was port captain. Julian had even gone to the base in person, but Gomez's secretary had told him that the admiral was out at sea and she didn't know when he would be returning. Julian saw Gomez as the only person who could help him legalize the use of the seaplane.

Denise worked on building the brand and identity of the company. When she began her online campaign, she realized that professional photographs were what made the difference in getting likes and engagement. She convinced Julian to buy a fancy camera and she began fooling around with it. Ernie was the most intrigued by the new toy. He carried it with him during his chores and would snap away in between. A look through Ernie's lens found beauty where most people wouldn't even glance. Denise encouraged his new hobby, as it proved useful. He eventually enrolled in a weekly photography class at the state college.

Baja Air & Sea's Facebook, Twitter, and Instagram accounts began steadily gaining followers. Other than the beautiful pictures, Denise attributed the accounts' success to the quality of her copywriting, posting consistency, and use of unique hashtags like #BajaLife, #BajaAir, and #BajaSea. She also wrote press release articles and got them published. Her approach was holistic in terms of brand, experience, and lifestyle. After calling every person on Kyle's client list, she also called tour companies and travel agents, and put Baja Air & Sea on their radar. She was proactive, professional, and smart. Julian supported her as much as he could.

Ernie would stay in the office until 09:00, and after a small recap with Julian, he would head back to Kyle's hangar at Caimancito, where he kept shop. He had been working on one of the Zodiac motors; there seemed to be a problem with the intake manifold. He had already replaced some parts, but still couldn't get it to run properly. While he worked on the Zodiac, he would run the airplane engine for a little bit, just to "keep her greased." Around noon, he would return to the office. Rubio served lunch at 13:00. They usually ate in the backyard, unless it was too hot, then they would have a family-style meal on the breakfast/meeting table. Rubio would then clean the house and make sure Reyna had her walk. Rubio was happy with this new routine. When he was done, he would head out to the yacht to cook dinner. When he got to the yacht at around 17:00, Ernie was usually there, making sure the yacht was spotless, the engines running well, and all of the gear organized.

Julian and Denise would arrive at the yacht around 18:30, usually in separate cars, because Julian would spend a lot of time with Fabio the CPA discussing finances and playing golf. The two of them had become friends, and Fabio supported Julian in his new venture. Fabio sometimes accompanied the B.A.S. crew on their evening cruises aboard *The Cecilia*, which usually consisted of anchoring in the middle of La Paz bay for dinner and catching the sunset.

Julian was in charge of legal and financial affairs. With Fabio, who was certain Baja Air & Sea was going to be a success, Julian set up a financial plan for his company. Via email, he corresponded with Margot at Alberto Fontana's office. She handled most of the paperwork, including contracts, and stored copies of everything important. She also handled certain bureaucratic tasks, like filing a copyright form with the Baja Air & Sea name and logo. Margot was a great asset, even if she was far away. It made Julian feel like he had a whole net of support, and he did. He was blessed to have such a great team willing to make something happen.

The night they finalized all of their company papers aboard the yacht, Fabio took a picture of Ernie, Denise, and Julian holding copies of the articles of organization. In the second set of photos Rubio held a pan. The four of them had huge smiles on their faces.

CHAPTER 32

Flocks of Seagulls

A MONTH HAD GONE BY since they'd established Baja Air & Sea, and they still hadn't gotten their first sale. Julian was beginning to get anxious.

"It's only a matter of time until we get clients, Skip. We have a great presence, and I've been following up with all of my contacts. We've done the necessary due diligence. I mean, all of the experts say that it can take up to six weeks to get your first client in a high-end business like ours," said Denise, as the two of them discussed strategy over coffee.

The fact that he still hadn't gotten ahold of Admiral Gomez was adding stress to the situation. Julian decided to take Reyna for a walk to let off some steam and think about solutions.

As he began to worry about money, he remembered that he still had a big check waiting for him at the jewelry store in Cabo.

He walked over to Manglito, the small beach near his house, where he often went to reflect and exercise. As he watched Reyna rush into the calm sea and chase sardines that gathered near shore, he reminded himself about the true meaning of life. He had to relax and take it easy. After all, he had the privilege of living in South Baja, in one of the most astonishingly beautiful places in the world. He promised himself he wouldn't become obsessed with business.

I believe in Denise's method. She's right. We've planted all the good seeds; we just have to be patient and proactive and clients will start showing up, he thought to himself as a wet Reyna ran up and down the beach, chasing flocks of seagulls.

When he returned to his home office, he told Denise he was going to Cabo for the weekend. He wanted to spend a couple of nights at a new hotel he had seen online called The Commune. Denise agreed that a couple nights away would help him relax.

"Yea, I also have to pick up some money from a Rolex I left in consignment a while back. They called me from the shop to let me know that they sold it," Julian said.

"Well, there you go. What better excuse to go to Cabo than that?" said Denise.

"Yea, well, I gotta collect my debts. Gotta have cash to put into the business."

"Everything's going to work out fine, Skip," she said.

CHAPTER 33

Nautical Expo

Julian drove to Cabo in his Land Rover through Todos Santos. The contrast of a South Baja desert with strong palm trees and the cool Pacific Ocean coast made Julian hopeful. He had Caesar Salad and shrimp for lunch at the Hotel California and drank a Cadillac Margarita. On his way out, the waiter gave him a shot of tequila on the house.

Ninety-seven minutes later, at exactly 16:41, he pulled into the motor lobby of The Commune Hotel in San José. Karla, a petite *morena* in tight khaki shorts, complimented his car and handed him a ticket. Linda, an Asian girl with a smile, asked to carry his weekender bag. Julian declined. Linda escorted Julian into the sanctuary of the lobby, a holy place of luxurious comfort. The smell of ocean, infused with crisp drying lavender strategically placed by the staff, gave Julian a peaceful easy feeling.

He checked into his room, and his breath almost left him when he opened the door. A panoramic uninterrupted ocean view and a royal suite of style and class to enjoy it in. There was a spacious terrace with a jacuzzi large enough to fit eight people. He opened a bottle of Champagne and poured himself a glass.

Julian took a deep nap, awoke, and went downstairs for dinner. He sat at the bar and drank Cadillac Margaritas while he dined. There was a group of about thirty people that sparked Julian's interest. They were the typical yachties in their seersucker shorts, polo shirts, and Top-Siders. Julian overheard them talking about "a boat show," but he didn't approach them because he hated the usual "my yacht's bigger than your yacht" yachtie talk.

"Is there a boat show in town?" Julian asked Gabriel, the concierge.

"Yes sir, the Nautical Expo is taking place all weekend at the Cabo Convention Center."

Julian asked Gabriel to purchase a ticket for him. The next day, he headed over to the expo. It was an incredible setup with different boats on display, along with stands that were selling the latest in marine technology. Julian was impressed with the Jetlev-Flyer, a jet pack that propelled water at high pressure back onto the surface, allowing the wearer to soar into the air. He was watching a video demo and talking to the salesman when he saw a beautiful blonde wearing a tight white skirt pass by. Julian couldn't help but turn his head.

"Not bad," said the salesman as he complimented the lovely blonde. Julian smiled.

As he walked around the expo, he realized it was more than a regular boat show; it was a convention dedicated to the more extreme side of the industry.

"The toys coming out today are truly incredible. It's the stuff we used to dream about when we were kids," said Patricio, a salesman for BladeFish, an underwater propulsion device, also known as a water sled.

"Take the BladeFish for instance, This small turbine can lead you in scuba diving trips like never before. You can now have the power and speed necessary to not only capture more, but to navigate underwater."

Julian nodded as he picked one up. "And it's not heavy at all."

"It's the smallest water sled in the market."

"Julian?" a friendly female voice interrupted.

It was the beautiful blonde in the white skirt he had spotted before. Now that he was facing her, she seemed more perfect — gorgeous, mesmerizing, stunning, with small freckles on her face and wavy hair that brushed against the skin near her olive-green eyes.

God, who is this? "Yea, I'm Julian."

The blonde let out a small laugh. "You don't remember me, huh?"

Julian smiled. "I'm afraid not."

"It's me, Regina. Regina Dahlgreen."

His jaw dropped.

"Oh my God, how are you? You are so grown up," Julian said as he handed the BladeFish back to Patricio.

"Come here, let me give you a hug," he said.

She reached in and gave him a good one. He caught the smell of her hair, triggering millions of endorphins in his brain.

"I was just thinking about your parents the other day. How are they? It's been so long since I've seen you guys."

Regina kept a smile on her face, but looked away.

"Excuse me, I don't mean to interrupt," said Patricio, "but here's my card. If you're interested in testing some of our equipment, don't hesitate to give me a call."

Julian put the card in his pocket.

CHAPTER 34

Dahlgreen

JULIAN REMEMBERED WITH GREAT AFFECTION the time he had spent with the Dahlgreens over the years. He was sipping on a beer while Regina drank iced tea on the Cabo Convention Center terrace that overlooked the sea.

"I still remember that day when I was out on the yacht with you guys, and your dad came out wearing your mom's thong," Julian said as he laughed out loud. "Your mom was so embarrassed, but Soren didn't care. He jumped into the water and swam around while your mother threw a fit."

"Yea, those were the days," said Regina. Her smile waned. She sat in silence, gazing at the sea.

Julian noticed. "Is something wrong?"

Regina sighed. "My dad's in jail, and my mom… my mom's dead."

The gentle breeze ceased. The air became thick with the heat.

"What? Oh my gosh, I'm so sorry…" he paused, but needed to know. "What happened?"

Regina took a gulp of iced tea. "About three years ago, we were in our house in the Hamptons. We were laying out in the sand out front when twenty FBI agents came running towards the beach and arrested my father. Over the following days I learned that they were accusing him of fraud. It turned out he had been operating a massive Ponzi scheme that could be traced back to the 1970s when he started his business. The newspapers called it 'one of the largest fraud cases in Wall Street history." We're talking over $35 billion worth of embezzlement.

"After that, my life became a nightmare. My mother felt guilty from the start, although she never confessed to anything. I always got the impression that she had something to do with his arrest. Whatever the case, the government seized everything, all of our wealth. The money in our accounts, gone. Our townhouse, our cars, our place in the Hamptons. They even took my horse. It was horrible.

"My mother and I moved in with her sister and she began drinking a lot. On the day of my father's sentencing, we learned that he had another family. So imagine finding out your father is getting sixty-five years in federal prison without parole, and, to top it off, he has a whole other family with a wife, son, and daughter. I think that's what did it.

"My mother would never leave my aunt's house. She was drinking all the time, concerned over the media destroying our family's name. None of her friends would talk to her. And then we started receiving threats from all kinds of people, saying that we owed them money. It was a nonstop nightmare. One day I went into her room and I found her with an empty bottle of oxycodone still in her hands and a quart of vodka she'd spilled all over herself.

"After her funeral," Regina continued, "it was one of those reality moments. I had to make big choices. And that's when it came to me — the government wasn't able to take our house here in Cabo, or our yacht and helicopter. My dad had set it up as Mexican corporation under my name, and they never went after my stuff here. So, my choice was either live disgraced in the states as the daughter of a thief, or move to Baja and try to make something happen."

Julian's eyes welled up. He placed his hand on Regina's.

"That's the saddest thing I've heard in a long time," he said. "I loved your parents very much, and in my memory, they will always exist as I knew them, among the best friends I ever had. Truly great people."

Regina looked at the sea. "I know it sounds weird, Julian, but I've made peace with it, and I've come to understand that their destiny is not my destiny, their lives will not define mine."

Julian nodded as his eyes became sad. Regina looked over and touched his shoulder.

"Maybe you could write to my father. I'm sure he would like that," she said.

"You know what, I will," Julian said.

The two sat in silence for a moment, and then Regina sighed and looked at Julian.

"And what about you? I've been trying to get ahold of you since I first got here, but nobody seems to know anything about the mysterious ex-port captain."

CHAPTER 35

The Love of His Life

JULIAN AND REGINA TALKED ALL afternoon. It was almost as if they were old friends. But they *were* old friends, only the last time he had seen her was eight years ago, when she was nineteen. And now, at twenty-eight, she was so beautiful and strong.

"So, what's next for you?" Julian asked.

"Well, I've kept my yacht, the *Dream On*, and my Eurocopter. I've recently started a business doing yacht charters and rides on the chopper."

"You're kidding," he said.

"No, that's why I'm here at the Expo. Scouting out all of the new technology and toys to see what I can offer," she said.

"What's the name of your company?"

"Baja Explorations," said Regina, and handed him a card.

"Well, I'm actually doing something similar," said Julian.

"Really?"

"Yea, I have my yacht, and we just bought a seaplane, so we partnered up with a couple of pilots."

"And what's the name of *your* company?" Regina asked.

"Baja Air & Sea."

Regina looked at him for a moment and smiled. "I have to be careful. That makes you my competitor."

Julian took a moment and grinned. "You and I are not competitors. We are friends, and if you ever need anything from me, like a second yacht, or a seaplane for a special tour or charter, just call me and we'll do business together."

Regina smiled.

"I like that. Same for you. If you ever need a helicopter or another yacht, don't hesitate to call."

"See! We're *collaborators*," Julian extended his hand.

"Sounds wordy, but deal," said Regina.

They shook hands.

"What are your plans for dinner?" Julian asked.

"I'm supposed to have a meeting, but let me check." Regina pulled out her phone and began texting.

"Well, I was thinking of having dinner at Nic-San tonight, if you aren't too busy," said Julian.

"Who else is going?"

"Nobody. Just me. And you, if you want to come," Julian answered.

"You were going to have dinner at Nic-San by yourself?"

"Yea," said Julian as he stared deeply into her eyes.

"I don't believe you," said Regina as her phone rang.

She picked up the call, and moments later had to excuse herself.

"You know what, Julian, I'm not gonna be able to cancel on my meeting. It's a client of mine. But I'll tell you what. I'll make it up to you. Why don't you meet me at my place tomorrow morning? We'll go out on the yacht."

Julian smiled. "Sure. At what time?"

"Eight o'clock. You remember where my house is, right?"

Julian nodded.

Regina gave him a kiss on the cheek and disappeared back into the expo floor.

Julian sat on the terrace in silence for half an hour. Regina's absence sunk in. He felt his heart beat faster, and he wanted to have her, but not necessarily in a sexual way. He felt like hugging her, kissing her, and holding her, but at the same time, he wanted to honor his friendship with the Dahlgreens by protecting her now that she was alone. He had crushed hard before, but this was different. As far as he was concerned, at that moment, Regina Dahlgreen was the love of his life.

CHAPTER 36

Espiritu del Cabo Cove

Julian made arrangements with Patricio, the BladeFish dealer, to come by The Commune at 07:30 to drop off a demo that he could take out on the water. He then drove to the Dahlgreen estate, located at 2401 Espiritu del Cabo Cove. He had to pass a guard to enter the gated community, and when he showed his ID, the guard told him that they were already waiting for him. Julian remembered the Dahlgreen estate perfectly, but he was impressed nonetheless.

From the outside, the house looked like a traditional one-story hacienda because of the large courtyard out front and the church-esque dome that towered over the main entrance.

"Welcome," said Regina, as she opened the front door. "I wasn't sure that you'd remember how to get here."

"I'm an explorer, Regina. I never forget how to get somewhere," said Julian.

"Excuse me, Oliver Cromwell," said Regina.

They laughed.

Juan, a deckhand, came out and took the BladeFish from Julian's hand.

"Yea, I brought that so we could test it," said Julian.

Once inside, the estate revealed the passion and craftsmanship that it had taken to be built. It was a feat of modern engineering, with glass windows overlooking a private cove and five stories that went down to an isolated beach.

Each floor was decorated according to a theme. The top floor, where the kitchen and dining areas were, had an Asian theme, with statues, gongs, tapestry, and ornaments like teapots, and swords.

"Let's take the stairs so I can give you the grand tour," said Regina.

The next floor down was the modern art floor.

"Very cool," said Julian, as he looked at a colorful painting of non-symmetrical squares.

"Yea, that's a Hans Hoffman," said Regina.

This was a fascinating floor. As he looked at the works of art that drew his attention the most, Regina dropped names. Julian would nod, pretending like he knew who they were. Philip Guston, Mark Rothko, Jasper Johns, Nancy Graves, among others. Julian didn't know who these artists were, only that it was all very expensive.

Modern art is cool and everything, but I don't remember the Dahlgreens having this many paintings.

The two floors below were the living and sleeping quarters. Two master suites, fifteen guest bedrooms, all decorated in luxury and comfort. Living rooms, a private movie theater, and a wine cellar with over 5,000 bottles. The floor at the very bottom was the "Beach Club." It consisted of an indoor/outdoor pool, a fire pit, barbecue, and sunning area that led to the private cove. But it didn't end there; the Dahlgreen's had built a dock to their yacht, the *Dream On*.

CHAPTER 37

Dream On

As Julian boarded the *Dream On*, Regina gave instructions to the servants that worked on her property. Julian was impressed with her management skills as he grappled with absorbing it all. The tragedy that had befallen her family would have defeated many, but here was someone who was dealing with it like a professional.

And bathing in all of this luxury, he thought as he stared at Regina with a smirk on his face.

"What do you think about a Cabo Pulmo dive?" she asked.

"Excellent. I'm your guest, Regina. You call the shots."

She smiled at him and went up to the bridge to notify the captain of their plans.

The *Dream On* was a superyacht. At 165 feet, she stood proud, with four decks of entertainment and luxury. A red Eurocopter sat on the top deck. The yacht had been completely customized for the Dahlgreens at Alpha Shipbuilders in Germany.

Julian had been on the yacht before, and it didn't cease to impress him. Even though it was one of the biggest yachts on the Sea of Cortez, it wasn't pretentious. Its design wasn't modern or disruptive; it was more of a classic exploration yacht, with clean lines, lots of space, and subtle elements of elegance, like the grey and red hues that mixed perfectly with the pearly tower, or the light blue tinted windows on the bridge.

They were sitting in the salon going about twelve knots on their way towards the East Cape when Julian asked what had been on his mind all morning.

"How did you manage to keep all this hidden during the prosecution?"

Regina looked towards the water. "I didn't. My dad did. He had put all this under a Mexican corporation and made me the owner. And since I was never investigated, or linked to any of his crimes, they couldn't touch me. Remember, I was born here in Cabo, a Mexican citizen, completely binational."

"That's right. When I first met your parents, they were living full time down here. Must have been the early '90s," said Julian.

"Yea, I never understood why, but I found out. It turned up during his trial. That's when my dad first got investigated by the SEC, and was lying low down here. I don't know how he fixed it at that time, but he was able to return to the states and be back in business for another twenty-plus years," said Regina.

Julian asked to go up to the bridge, where he met the captain, a Danish man named Christen. He was blown away by the technology and sophistication of this yacht.

"This yacht can really go anywhere in the world," said Julian.

"Yea, anywhere but the states," said Regina with a smile.

"I thought you said you were clean, never investigated. Why can't you go stateside?"

"You know why my dad's in jail?" said Regina, narrowing her eyes.

"You told me, he scammed a bunch of people, a giant Ponzi," said Julian.

"No, he scammed a bunch of *rich* people *with* power. Anyway, I can't afford another legal battle if they come after me."

When they got to Cabo Pulmo, the sun was almost at high noon and the wind was blowing gently through the bay. The turquoise water was still, and schools of fish could be seen swimming below. The aft deck on the yacht had a mechanism that would lift the top layer, revealing a dive shop beneath it where not only the scuba equipment was stored, it also had the prep benches and a whole bunch of aqua toys.

"We can't take the speargun, since this is a natural reserve," said Regina.

"Okay. Let's take the sled; let's see if it's worth all the hype," said Julian.

The pair jumped into the water. The ocean floor was twelve meters down, and their descent was smooth. They both knew the drill, stopping every couple of meters to unplug their ears, taking the necessary time for their bodies to adjust to being underwater. Once they were standing on the ocean floor, the pair took a moment to appreciate all the life happening around them. A tortoise was swimming uninterrupted, corals the size of small cars, and rock formations that looked like ancient architecture.

Julian turned on the BladeFish and signaled toward Regina to hang on to him. She hugged him from behind and the blade propelled the pair to swim fishlike through the seabed. Partaking in underwater speed was cool, but the experience of bonding with Regina was what Julian found thrilling. He could feel her body through their wetsuits; it was magical. Regina poked Julian's rib and Julian slowed down. She pointed towards a small rock formation. Out of it came a long eel that swam through the water with finesse. Through their journey, they spotted a large grouper, a dorado, and a school of snook.

When their oxygen was running low, they decided to head up to the surface. Once they cleared their ascent, they realized there was more wake tossing the surface than when they had gone in. Not only that, the *Dream On* was far, almost two miles away.

Julian looked at the yacht, and then looked at Regina. "Well, let's see if this BladeFish can take us back."

Regina hung on to Julian, but riding the BladeFish surface level wasn't as efficient. The wake kept hitting them in the face, and it was uncomfortable. Regina would let go and Julian had to keep stopping.

"Why don't you take the BladeFish, and bring the tender. I'll wait here," Julian said.

At first, Regina didn't want to, but Julian convinced her that he was going to be okay. Regina took the BladeFish back to the *Dream On* and instructed the crew to lower the tender and go get Julian, who was swimming towards the yacht, but was beginning to get tired with all of the scuba gear strapped to him. Even though the whole ordeal took less than twenty minutes, it felt like an eternity.

"I thought you'd forgotten about me back there," he told Regina when he was back aboard.

"I *had* actually, but the crew kept asking me about you. If it wasn't for them, you'd still be floating around," she said.

"Tough love," said Julian loud enough but under his breath.

They laughed.

"Are you getting hungry?" asked Regina.

"I can eat."

"All right, come with me," she said, as they walked to the top deck towards the helipad.

Regina boarded the pilot seat of the Eurocopter and asked Julian to get in and put on a headset.

Julian sat in the co-pilot's seat. "Where are we going, hotshot?"

"My chef's wife just had a baby. He was unable to come along today, so we have to go back into town for lunch," she said.

The crew released the safety straps and Regina turned on the helicopter. The blades started spinning, the floor shook, and the Eurocopter ascended smoothly over the yacht.

"Just in case you're worried over decompression sickness, we will only be flying at 1,500 feet, so it shouldn't be a problem. Anyway, if I pass out, you got this, right?" Regina looked over at Julian with a smirk.

Julian knew damn well that one shouldn't fly after diving, but he felt completely safe in the chopper with Regina, not only because of the low altitude, but because he was enchanted with her presence. She was like a drug to him, just being around her made him feel invincible. The flight over Cabo Pulmo and through the East Cape was phenomenal. The graceful tides below them, the enchanting sea, but more than anything, the company.

"You really got it going on, don't you?" Julian said over the headset.

"A girl's gotta do what she can to survive. I mean, I do have class, though."

They laughed.

Regina landed the Eurocopter in the courtyard in front of her estate. As she was shutting down the engine, Julian placed his hand on top of hers.

"Thank you for bringing me back safely," he said.

Regina smiled, and they got off the chopper.

Julian walked towards his Land Rover. "I'll drive. I know a great place."

CHAPTER 38

Zenith

Julian and Regina had lunch at Apostolis, a small Greek restaurant in San Jose. Over sustainable *totoaba* fish and olives, Regina talked about how she loved the sea, but explained how flying helicopters was her true passion. She told Julian how, after high school, when all of her friends were going to university, she had gone to the New York Helicopter Academy.

"Yea, my dad was really supportive. He wasn't like other dads that insisted I go into law, or finance, or to Yale, or Columbia. My dad never cared about any of that. When I told him that flying helicopters was what I wanted to do, he was so proud of me," she said.

"Yea, that sounds like your old man. Always so cool," said Julian.

"But my mom, she hated helicopters. So my dad told her I was interning at a Wall Street firm, just so she wouldn't lose her nerves."

Julian took a moment. "Tell me something, how's your helicopter regulated? Business speaking?"

"Oh, we're talking shop?"

They laughed for a second.

"It's just, I'm having a hard time regulating my seaplane, and any advice would help."

"If I told you the story of how I got that helicopter to Cabo, we'd be here another three hours," she said.

"I've got time for you."

"Okay, well, that heli was up at the shop in San Diego getting fixed when all hell broke loose. It sat in the shop for almost two years. When I finally caught on, Gary, the mechanic, didn't want to just let the bird go. He wanted money, a lot of it, like a million. He had done $87,000 worth of work. That and the storage, according to him, totaled a million-a million-plus. So I'm thinking, *This guy's trying to take advantage of me, knows the situation with my father, thinks he can squeeze money out of me or keep my bird, or worse, do both.*"

Regina took a sip of water.

"So, I said, 'I'll give you $100,000 and just let me get my bird back.' He says, 'Either give me a million or I'll tell the government that this helicopter belongs to your father and they'll take it.' I tell him, 'It's my bird, it's from a Mexican company.' He doesn't care. You know what I did?"

Julian shook his head.

"I moved to San Diego, and for three months, I studied everything about Gary and his shop. One day, he and a friend took my bird flying and ended up coming back late. They didn't store her in the hanger. They let her sleep outside. That's all it took. At this point, I already knew where they kept everything, so I wore all black, covered my face in a ski mask like in the movies, took the keys, jumped in my bird, and flew her all the way to Cabo myself."

"What? Oh my god, so you stole it?" Julian laughed.

"No, I mean it was always legally mine; I just can't stand being taken advantage of."

"And you flew her across the border, all the way to Cabo? How many stops is that?"

"Like, twenty-five."

They laughed.

"Gangsta," said Julian.

They laughed some more.

Julian was glad Regina was opening up to him. He liked hearing about her parents and her adventures, but the feeling that she trusted him was what made him happy.

Julian asked Regina to accompany him to Luxury Avenue so he

could stop at Jacoby & Jewels and pick up his check.

When they entered the store, Colette greeted them with enthusiasm. "Mr. Mayorca, I'm so glad to see you again," she said.

"So am I," said Julian.

"Feel free to browse through the store. And if anything interests you, I can give you a discount of up to 20 percent depending on the item," Collette said.

Julian's phone rang. It was a blocked number. He excused himself and stepped outside to take the call. Regina looked through the store.

"Well, if it isn't my long lost friend," said the deep voice on the other end. "Why have you taken so long to contact me?"

"My dear Admiral. You have no idea how grateful I am that you've called," Julian said.

"My secretary told me that you came to the base in person. I'm sorry I couldn't get back to you sooner," Admiral Gomez said.

"Don't worry about it. How you been?"

"Well, what can I say? Somebody's got us by the balls, but that's a whole different story; I don't want to get into it over the phone," said the Admiral.

"How's your family?" asked Julian.

"My wife's making my life a living hell. And my kids, well, they're my kids," he said.

Julian laughed.

"So what's new with you?" asked Gomez.

"Well, I'm back in South Baja and wanted to talk with you," said Julian.

"When can you come see me?"

"Whenever you have time," answered Julian.

"Come over to the base tomorrow morning, 0-800," said Admiral Gomez.

"Perfect, see you there."

When Julian walked back into the store, he noticed that Regina was trying on a blue Zenith Naval Aviation Pilot 20 watch.

"That looks good on you," he said.

"Yea," said Regina as she took it off.

It was a special edition watch with a blue strap and a golden insignia on the black face. Perfect Swiss engineering, elegant chronograph, with the day/date feature off center. Regina excused herself to go to the restroom, and Julian asked Collette to wrap up the watch and to cut his check for the remaining amount. After the watch, with its 20 percent discount, Collette gave Julian a check for $34,700. He concealed the watch and walked out of the store to meet Regina.

They walked around the mall for the whole afternoon. Regina bought a couple of swimsuits, and Julian bought a new pair of Top-Siders. Spending casual time and money with Regina thrilled Julian; it made him feel as if they were a real couple. He invited Regina for dinner, but she insisted on going back to her place first. Julian dropped her off at her estate and she agreed to meet him at The Chamuyo restaurant at 7:30.

Julian got to the restaurant ten minutes early. He arranged to be seated at the best table, close to the fountain. When Regina arrived, Julian was blown away. She was wearing a long blue skirt, a tight top, and heels. As she approached him, Julian's face practically melted from happiness. When she greeted him with a kiss on the cheek, he felt like the luckiest guy in the world.

"You are the most beautiful girl I have ever seen, Regina. I'm so proud of you," he said.

"Oh, stop it," she said.

Their conversation ranged from the mundane to the complications of the charter business in Baja. When Julian asked what bottle of wine they should get with dinner, she said she didn't drink.

"Alcohol always played a big role in my parents' lives, and I'm trying to break some of their patterns," she said.

Julian was impressed and ordered Malbec by the glass.

When they were halfway through sharing a *dulce de leche* dessert, Julian took out the Zenith Naval Pilot 20 watch and put it on her wrist.

"Oh my god, did you really get this for me?" Regina asked.

"I did," said Julian. "Just a little something for you to remember me by, especially now that we are colleagues in the same industry. Think of it as a gesture of good faith."

"Thank you so much," said Regina as she hugged him. "But we're *collaborators, remember?*"

They laughed.

Julian could tell she loved the timepiece, as she kept looking at it every few moments.

"Let's go out," said Regina. "It's old-fashioned karaoke night at El Campanario."

Julian laughed. "Karaoke? I've never done that in my life."

"Well, this is your chance. They only play classic songs — just perfect for an older guy like you," she said.

"What!" Julian threw a crumpled paper napkin at her face.

They laughed together.

CHAPTER 39

It's Only a Paper Moon

Julian was holding Regina's hand as they walked up the dark staircase towards Campanario Saloon. The buzz of holding her, mixed with the blue and green neon lights that led up to the bar, made Julian feel like he was entering a different dimension. Once inside, there were red booths facing a stage with an ocean view behind it. The darkness of the sea gave a profound resonance to the place. El Campanario was swanky, but there were only a handful of other people scattered throughout the bar. Julian and Regina decided to sit in a booth close to the stage. As they slid into their seats, Julian placed his arm around her. Regina browsed through the songbook.

"Okay, you first," she said.

"No, you go first. You're the expert here," replied Julian.

"You're in luck! They're only showcasing songs from the 1930s," said Regina.

"Why does that make me lucky? I hardly know any songs from the 1930s," said Julian.

"Don't pretend the '30s weren't your dancing days," joked Regina.

As Julian looked through the songbook, he said, "You go first. I need the extra motivation of seeing you up there before I can muster the courage to sing."

"What? Having your arm around me doesn't give you enough courage?" said Regina as she stared into his eyes.

Julian thought about kissing her. *Her puffy lips, and those eyes....*

God, those eyes.

But Regina let loose from Julian's arm. She stood up and walked towards the karaoke machine, typed some numbers in, and the track began.

"*Blue moon, you saw me standing alone, without a dream in my heart, without a love of my own,*" Regina sang in a strong, conquering voice.

With every word she sang, Julian became more enamored with her. "Blue Moon" had never made sense to him, but that night, at El Campanario Saloon, the song cut right through his heart. He was certain Regina knew the lyrics, since she was making eye contact with him during most of the song. When she finished, everybody, including the bartenders and waitstaff, clapped. Julian held her and kissed her forehead, congratulating her on her artistic sublimity.

"Don't even sit down. You're next," said Regina.

Julian walked over to the karaoke machine and typed in the numbers to his song. When the tune to "It's Only a Paper Moon" began playing, Julian said, "And since we're on the subject of moons, I want to dedicate this song to this lovely lady." He pointed to Regina.

"*It's only a paper moon, sailing over a cardboard sea, but it wouldn't be make-believe if you believed in me,*" Julian sang with style.

He didn't have a good voice, but the way he articulated the words, and the confidence he delivered them with, made Regina blush. Especially at the end, when Julian came up to the booth and held her hand while he sang:

"*Without your love, it's a honky-tonk parade, without your love, it's a melody played in a penny arcade... It's a Barnum and Bailey World, just as phony as it can be, but it wouldn't be make-believe if you believed in me.*"

Everybody clapped. Julian took a bow, and when he returned to the booth, Regina whispered in his ear, "I *do* believe in *you.*"

Julian and Regina spent another hour talking over the smooth jazz playing in the background of Campanario Saloon. When a drunk, fat man got up to sing Duke Ellington's "It Don't Mean a Thing (If It Ain't

Got That Swing)," Julian and Regina stepped out onto the terrace. The ocean breeze was strong, and Regina had chills all over her arms. Julian held her.

"It's crazy. I used to have the biggest crush on you."

"Well, I have the biggest crush on you *now*," said Julian as he went in for a kiss.

Regina turned her head slightly — the classic *cobra* kiss-evasion move.

He let go.

"The thing is, Julian, you don't understand. When I first came to Baja, I looked and looked for you. I even went to your office at the port captainship. But I didn't find you there. I found the new port captain, Axel Cuevas."

At the very mention of his name, Julian's heart sank. His face turned dead.

"He was very kind to me and helped me a lot during a time that I needed it the most. He was there for me, and we started dating over a year ago," she said.

At first, Julian was silent.

"Axel Cuevas? You know he's my cousin, right?" he said.

"What? No! He never told me. And I asked him about you. He said he knew nothing about where you were," said Regina.

"Yea, well, that's Axel for you."

For a moment, Julian thought about spilling his guts to the woman he loved and telling her about Axel's betrayal, but he decided to keep that information to himself.

"Do you love him?" Julian asked.

Silence. Only the breeze.

"There are many ways to love a person. But, yes, I do love him."

CHAPTER 40

The Warehouse

THE FOLLOWING MORNING, JULIAN DROVE back to La Paz with a broken heart. He had never felt love rise up in him like it had over the last few days with Regina. He kept thinking about the time they had spent together. Scuba diving, on the yacht, on the chopper, shopping, singing. And then, the worst news of his life.

Not only was she taken, she was taken by Axel Cuevas, the very same person who had taken his job, his life, and his family. The thought of Axel kissing Regina, touching her breasts, grabbing her legs, making love to her, infuriated Julian, so he tried to focus his mind on the upcoming meeting with Admiral Gomez.

When he entered the Mexican Navy Base, Julian didn't want to seem upset in front of the Admiral, so he summoned the best smile he could. Admiral Gomez was happy to see him.

"How are you, old boy?"

"I'm so glad to see you, Admiral," he said.

"You know, when I heard that you were looking for me, I got so excited. You know what I told my wife? He's back! The son of a bitch is back!"

"Yea, well, I'm back. And I'm in business now. I wanted to come to you because as the highest Naval authority, I wanted your blessing," said Julian.

"What's your business?" Gomez asked.

"I've bought a yacht, and I started a charter company," said Julian.

"That's great. What kind of yacht is it?" asked Gomez.

"She's a 90-foot, tri-deck, completely remodeled and looking mighty fine," said Julian, as he realized that he missed being aboard his yacht. "I want to invite you and your wife aboard for a dinner cruise or a little fishing so you can get to know her, because she's at your disposal."

"We would like that very much. Maria is going to be very happy to hear it," Gomez said.

"You know that you and your wife have been two of the most important people in my life. Everything you did for me when I was at the Academy Taking me in and teaching me the ropes I'm never going to forget that. You're my *padrino*. Regardless of what happens, you will always be my godfather," said Julian.

"You were our golden boy, Julian. And then we made you port captain. The youngest in Baja history," said Gomez with a look of nostalgia.

Julian knew the Admiral wanted to ask him why he had resigned, but Julian didn't want to head down that route, so he steered the conversation.

"Admiral, there's something I want to ask you."

"Go right ahead, son."

"Well, after I bought the yacht, I partnered up with a couple of pilots who own a seaplane. Our sole purpose is to offer sea and air adventure packages, so I have taken a financial interest in the plane. But I have a problem — there is no legal framework to fly it. In order to operate it at the commercial scale, I need a military permit from you," said Julian.

Gomez chuckled. "And you think I can print and sign a permit, just like that?"

"Well, not *just like that,* but I was hoping you would help me deal with the Mexican Air Force, and with whomever I need to. Because I need it in order to be in business," said Julian.

"You know, Julian, there *is* something I can do for you. But, I've got a small business venture of my own that maybe you can help me with," said the Admiral.

"I would love to hear it," said Julian.

Gomez smiled, stood up from his chair, and headed for the door. "Come with me."

Julian followed as they walked through the base. They passed by a squad of young sailors who saluted them. Julian appreciated the respect. Toward the far side of the base, they entered a large industrial warehouse. When Gomez turned the lights on, Julian could see an incredible amount of civilian boats, small yachts, tenders, jet skis, and all kinds of vessels.

"What's all this?" he asked.

"These are the things we have confiscated from people," said Gomez. "Mostly people engaged in illicit activity on our coasts. But there are also things here that were handed over to me by other government agencies, because of tax evasion and other crimes. The President of Mexico pushed a law that everything that is confiscated must be put to use. So, by definition, everything that floats and breaks the law in Baja is handed over to me."

Julian smiled a bit. He suspected he knew where Gomez was heading.

"And what, exactly, are you thinking about doing?" Julian asked.

"Well, there's a grey line here between what the law says and what I can actually do with all of this stuff, I can use it for official Navy business, but let's be honest, how the heck am I supposed to use WaveRunners on official Navy business? I can sell the vessels, but the money has to go back to the Mexican Government, and nobody wins when that happens. Or I can lease the vessels to established companies on a per-day premium that I set. So, my offer is this: You take a look around our inventory, see what we have, and whenever a client of yours wants, something that you don't have, you come and pick it up. And here's the deal, officially: I'll give you a very low premium," said Gomez, winking.

"And unofficially?" said Julian with a smile.

"Well, unofficially, you kick back a percentage directly to me. And everybody wins," said Gomez.

Julian looked around the warehouse. The amount of vessels was overwhelming.

"Do you have an inventory for all this stuff?"

"Yes, I do. I'll send it over to you. And, Julian, I just want to say, whoever leases the vessels must get approved by a committee that they've put in place. And they are requiring that lessees be established companies with no ties to Mexican Navy officials. So, our timing is perfect on this," said Gomez.

Julian smiled as he looked around the warehouse. "Well, let's do it, Admiral. You've got yourself a deal!" He stretched out his hand.

Gomez shook it. "I'll take care of the legal work for your seaplane. Just send me all the information, and I'll meet with General Agundez Velarde and ask him to sign off on permits."

CHAPTER 41

Yakov

ERNIE JORDAN WAS THE MOST excited about the vessels they had negotiated with Admiral Gomez.

"So when can we go see them?" he asked.

"Well, I've sent him all of our company's information, along with *The Beaver*'s, so as soon as he has our permits ready, I'm going to invite him aboard the yacht for a little cruise," said Julian.

Denise was bothered by Julian's dealings with Gomez.

"I just wish you would've consulted with me before submitting our company to the scrutiny of being a Navy contractor," she said.

"You know, Denise, I completely understand. But it happened so fast. I asked him to help me with permits for *The Beaver*, and he turned it around on me and offered me an opportunity. Don't worry, Admiral Gomez is like family to me; he's a no-bullshit kind of guy."

Denise still didn't seem convinced, so Julian printed out the inventory Gomez had emailed him and brought it to her.

"Just look at this inventory, they've got master crafts, Sea-Doos, jet skis, cigarette boats. I mean, come on!" said Julian.

Denise smirked; it was her way of giving in. Ernie, however, couldn't hold his excitement. He looked meticulously through the list, salivating at using all of the toys.

"How was your weekend in Cabo?" asked Denise.

Before Julian could answer, thoughts of Regina ran through his mind. The love, frustration, and a million conflicting feelings rushed back in.

"It was good. There was a Nautical Expo in town, and I ran into an old friend. We had a good time, and I also bought one of these," said Julian as he showed them the BladeFish.

"It's actually a pretty cool underwater toy. But at surface level, not so much," said Julian.

Ernie grabbed the BladeFish, took it outside, and rinsed it down with a hose. Rubio came in with Reyna, who rushed over to Julian. As Julian petted her, Rubio asked quietly, "Did you get laid?"

Julian smiled. "No, unfortunately not."

Rubio smiled and gave him a hug. He cooked shrimp burritos for lunch.

Julian was glad to be back in La Paz. The past couple of days had been dreamy with Regina, but he realized that this was his reality: his crew, his friends, his family. As Julian looked around his home office — Rubio cooking, Ernie giving Reyna a bath outside, Denise on the computer — he acknowledged that his main responsibility was to this group of people, his crew. As Julian was drifting in thought, Denise called him over.

"Check this out, Skip."

Julian leaned over her shoulder and looked at her laptop screen. There was an email.

Hi, need to book a 10-12 day charter up the Baja coast. Are you available? - Yakov.

Julian got excited over this potential client.

"Write back to him," he said, and he began dictating the email to Denise.

Dear Yakov, thank you for contacting us. We are the premium yacht charter company in Baja, and are fully equipped to handle whatever needs you may have. Please let us know your departure date, the number of passengers, and any particular activities or destinations in Baja that you are interested in so we can send a quote and proceed. Sincerely, Capt. Julian Mayorca.

Denise sent the email. Minutes later, Yakov responded: *We are only two passengers, and we are interested in cruising your virgin coasts. Total discretion is required. Can you help?*

Julian found this very interesting, and again dictated the email to Denise.

Privacy is the #1 priority for us, and since we know the peninsula better than anyone, we are going to take you through the inner coast of the Sea of Cortez to the most pristine destinations you can imagine... Please let us know the details of your voyage, so we can make proper accommodations. Sincerely, Capt. Julian Mayorca.

Within sixty seconds of Denise hitting send, Julian's house phone rang.

"Baja Air & Sea," answered Denise. "Yes, just a moment, please," she said, as she walked over to Julian. "It's Yakov," she handed the phone over.

"This is Captain Julian Mayorca."

"Good day, Captain. I am Yakov," said a voice with a strong Russian accent.

"Good day to you, Mr. Yakov. How can I be of service?" said Julian.

"Well, like I said on email, we are looking to charter your yacht. We have seen pictures on internet, and we think it's nice," said Yakov.

"Sounds great, when do you want to book your charter for?" Julian asked.

"Well, we will arrive in La Paz on Wednesday, and we would like to get underway as soon as possible," said Yakov.

"Okay, Wednesday it is. And are you looking to go anywhere in particular?" said Julian.

"No. We just want to explore the most virgin coasts of your peninsula, and if it works out for us, we might be looking for a long-term relationship with you and your crew. But like I said, you need to keep every detail of our trip private," Yakov said.

"That's not a problem, Yakov. We have dealt with a lot of celebrities and important people who value their privacy," said Julian.

Denise looked at him with doubt.

"Good. What about your rate?'" Yakov asked.

"Well, our standard rate is $3,000 a day, and you said you needed the yacht for twelve days. That comes out to $36,000," said Julian.

There was a brief pause on the line. Julian looked at Denise, who appeared nervous. Julian feared that he had highballed him a little bit, and expected Yakov to negotiate.

"Okay. Where do we send money?" said Yakov.

Julian gave him their account info and the two men agreed that they would meet at the Marina Palma on Wednesday at 1400 hours.

"All right, we've closed our first deal!" said Julian excitedly after hanging up the phone.

He and Denise hugged. Ernie and Rubio began asking questions about the client.

"I don't know exactly who he is, but he sounds Russian. Either way, we are booked for twelve days beginning on Wednesday," said Julian.

"Should I get provisions?" asked Rubio.

"You know what, let's wait until the money comes through, let's see how serious…" but before he could finish the sentence, he got a chirp on his smartphone. It was a notification from his bank that there had been an international wire transfer for $36,000 into his business account.

"Guys, the money has come in!" said Julian with a smile. "These guys are serious. And we have officially popped our cherry."

They all screamed and cheered. Before Julian dispatched everyone to their pre-charter responsibilities, he told them: "One more thing: these clients are huge on privacy. I don't know why yet, but it's important that you don't mention anything to anyone. Don't tell anybody that we're going out to sea, and don't tell anybody that we even have a client. Understood?"

They all agreed to keep their mouths shut.

CHAPTER 42

The Calm Before the Storm

B Y NOON WEDNESDAY, THE WHOLE crew was aboard *The Cecilia*. The yacht looked impeccable; there wasn't an inch that wasn't polished, nor a stain anywhere. The galley was filled with fresh produce, the cabinets stocked with wines and liquor, and the staterooms smelled like fresh citrus zest. Denise made sure the whole crew was wearing the white Baja Air & Sea polo shirts that she had gotten embroidered.

"The only crew member missing is Reyna," said Julian, realizing he had never been out to sea on the yacht without her.

"She's better off with your neighbor and her kids," said Ernie.

"Yea, but I'm still gonna miss her," said Julian.

Rubio prepared some tapas in anticipation of the guests' arrival and Denise chilled a bottle of vodka. Julian put *Harpstrings* by Christian Bach over the speakers and sat astern, enjoying the classical music. It was a beautiful, sunny, calm day, with a gentle breeze flowing.

Yakov and another man arrived shortly before 14:00. Yakov was built like a boulder, strong and tall.

"This is my brother," said Yakov.

The brother nodded. He was older, much shorter, and a little fat. The pair entered the salon and sat down on the couch. Julian greeted them and gave them basic safety instructions regarding life vests.

"Perfect, let's go, man. We need to be out of here!" said an eager Yakov.

Julian didn't understand their rush, but he turned on the engines and headed out to sea.

Once they were out of the Bay of La Paz, the men snacked on some tapas and drank the vodka that Denise had put out for them. They were having intense conversations in Russian, and even though none of the crew could understand it, they could sense it was something important.

Yakov gave Julian instructions to "just keep going north," and Julian did.

The first day, they anchored for dinner close to Coyote Bay. Yakov and his brother dined astern, waited on by Denise and served by Rubio. The men didn't care to make small talk with anyone. They were set on their discussions and the crew didn't intervene.

Over the next three days, it was much of the same: Yakov and his brother talking nonstop in Russian, the crew invisible to them. The excitement the crew had been anticipating was wearing off. The men didn't want to stop, didn't want to fish, didn't want to swim; they just wanted to keep going north. The crew's only entertainment was trying to guess what they were up to.

"They're spies," said Rubio.

"No, they work for a mining company," said Denise.

Julian agreed with her. "Whenever they *do* get down, all they do is grab the dirt and look at it, how it dissolves in their hands."

"Yea, they're miners. I've worked for miners, that's exactly how they look. But, in my defense, a lot of miners *are* spies!" said Rubio.

They all laughed at his logic.

On the fourth day of their journey north, they passed the town of Loreto. Julian asked if they were interested in stopping in the town. Yakov said no.

When Julian was alone at the helm, he would look at the sea and think about Regina Dahlgreen. He felt so connected to her, as if his life and her life were mirrors of each other. On the fifth day, as he skippered and thought about his beloved, he began to see a clear picture of what was going to happen to Axel Cuevas, the snake between him and his girl.

I need to kill him.

As he thought about how he was going to do it, he felt the sea gain strength. The wake became choppier and the sky above closed in. Within minutes, heavy rain was beating down and the sea was rocking *The Cecilia* hard.

Denise came up to the bridge. "What's going on, Skip?"

"It all closed in on us real quick, the storm came out of nowhere," he said.

Julian began to navigate as best as he could, but the waves kept tossing and turning the yacht. Then the waves became larger. The yacht would rise and fall, while at the same time rock as the waves hit hard from indirect angles. As the yacht hit a wave, Julian heard a loud noise, followed by screams coming from inside.

"Denise, go check what that was," he said.

She went below deck and returned.

"It's the guest. He broke a bottle and began yelling. He just shut himself in his stateroom and won't come out. He's in there screaming," Denise said when she returned.

"Yakov?" Julian asked.

"No, the brother," said Denise.

A sigh. "All right, hold the stern," said Julian.

Denise took control of the vessel.

Julian entered the salon. As he stumbled his way around the broken glass that Rubio was trying to gather without cutting himself, Ernie came up to him.

"I don't know what happened, Skip; they were arguing and it became heated, then the brother grabbed a bottle and threw it at Yakov, who ducked. Then he continued to yell at him, and Yakov just stood there listening. When we tried to calm him down, he began yelling at us in Russian and ran into his stateroom."

Julian didn't know what to make of it. What seemed strange to him was that Yakov would take such abuse from his brother. Julian walked up to the door of the master stateroom. Yakov was standing outside, trying to talk to his brother through the door.

"What's going on?" he asked.

"I don't know. It's been a real rough time for him, and I think this storm really upset him," said Yakov.

"Mind if I talk to him?" Julian asked as he held onto the doorknob.

"You can try. I don't know if he would like to talk," said Yakov.

Julian knocked on the door, and there was no answer. He knocked again, and still no answer. Julian tried to open the door, but it was locked. He took the key out of his pocket and unlocked it.

He let himself in and shut the door behind him.

CHAPTER 43

The Crimean

THE YACHT KEPT ROCKING AS Julian entered the master stateroom. The brother was kneeling by the window. He appeared to be weeping, but he had his eyes closed and his hands to his chest. He was mumbling something to himself.

"Are you okay?'" Julian asked.

He turned around and Julian realized that he was praying.

"I'm sorry, Captain. I've been irresponsible aboard your ship. It's just that when the storm hit, I realized how far I've come, and yet, I am still as vulnerable as I was back home."

"What's going on, sir? I understand your need for privacy, but you've been aboard my yacht for five days and I don't even know your name," said Julian.

"My name is Oleg, Captain, and I'm sorry if I've been disrespectful," he said just as the ship hit a big wave that made him jump to his feet.

"They say a storm defines a man. You seem like a tense man. Perhaps you need to relax," said Julian.

"I can't relax, Captain. I am a most wanted man, even nature wants me dead. Perhaps it would be best if I jumped overboard, maybe then the storm would calm," said Oleg.

"Listen, whatever it is that you're going through, I'm sure it seems like the end of the world to you, but let me tell you something, it's not. Even this storm, yea, it seems nasty, but it too will pass," Julian said.

Oleg looked at Julian attentively for a moment. "Can you keep a secret, Captain?"

"I most certainly can. I wouldn't be in this industry if I couldn't."

"I used to be the Prime Minister of my country. I was head of the Republic of Crimea. I used to have everything under my control. But the annexation, man. The fucking annexation allegiance fucking betrayed me," said Oleg as he reached in his side bag and took out a blue, red, and white presidential band.

Months back, Julian had heard something on the news about the annexation of Crimea by Russia, but in general, he didn't have a clue about the situation.

Over the next hour, while the storm tossed them around the room, Oleg told Julian that he had always been in favor of Crimea leaving the Ukraine and becoming part of the Russian Federation.

"Since the beginning, that was my agenda, but as soon as it became a political reality, they betrayed me and pinned me as the enemy. My political enemies crucified me, and Putin, the son of a bitch wants me dead," said Oleg. "I fought for him, you know? But now, I have to run, exiled forever. They said that I was anti-Russia, working for the Americans. Me? I'm ex-KGB. My whole life I have fought for the annexation of Crimea. But the bastards raided my home, took everything away from me. My family, they are in exile, too. They are living in Switzerland now, where they are safe. But me, not even in Switzerland I am safe. Putin wants me dead," Oleg said as he started crying in anger.

Julian felt for the man.

"You know, what you just did Oleg, opening up to me, that took courage. I want you to know that I am here to help you. I understand how you must feel. As a matter of fact, I was a victim of a political betrayal here in Baja. Not quite at your scale, but it hurt like hell," Julian said.

"So, that's why you left the port captainship!" said Oleg.

"How did you know that?"

"Yakov was my head of intelligence, the only man who has stuck with me through thick and thin. We researched you good before we decided to come to you," Oleg said as the first smile since Julian had met him escaped from his lips.

"Well, I'm impressed. And, look, Oleg, the storm has calmed. Everything is going to be alright."

CHAPTER 44

Operation Greg

WHEN EVERYBODY WAS CLEANING UP after dinner the next evening, Oleg asked to speak to Julian in private.

"Here's the thing, Captain, I need your help in something," he said as they reached the bridge.

"Anything, Oleg," said Julian.

"I want to purchase a piece of land here, where we can live. I want it to be isolated from everything. Can you help me?" he asked.

Julian thought hard about the implications. "You know that it's going to be expensive getting beachfront property anywhere in Baja, plus there are a lot of hurdles to go through."

"Money is no problem. I have plenty of it. And the hurdles — that's why we came to you, because if anybody can help us get through them, it's you," said Oleg.

Julian smiled as he understood that being hired by Oleg had been a careful, methodical act, not some simple business transaction.

"How did you find me?" said Julian.

"Well, at first online. Then we scrutinized all of the information we could find about you, and there was something in you that we liked. We figured you were the man we were looking for," said Oleg.

Julian thought about how all of the marketing and PR work Denise had been doing on social media had already paid off.

"And, another thing. You are going to be our only contact here in Baja. I want to cut a deal with you, so that whenever we need anything, we just give you a call, because we can't trust anybody," said Oleg.

"Like a personal concierge?" Julian asked.

"Yes, but an extremely well-paid one," said Oleg.

Julian agreed to help Oleg, but as they shook on it, Julian asked, "Why Baja?"

Oleg smiled. "Well, it's the farthest away from Putin and Russia, without cold weather. Plus, I had an uncle who came here once as part of a political envoy back in the USSR days, and he always said that it was the most amazing place he had ever been to. Ever since I was a little boy, I've wanted to come here. So I figured this was my chance."

That night, when Oleg and Yakov went to their respective state-rooms, Julian called a meeting with his crew. He told them about Oleg and all of the info he had revealed to him. He also told them about the deal Oleg had offered.

Everyone gave their opinion, but in consensus, they were all supportive of Julian's decision.

"This is an operation that we must be careful about. We must treat this client with extreme privacy, and he's going to require a lot of special attention, so whenever we talk about Oleg and Yakov, we need to use a code name," said Julian.

"How about Goldfinger?" said Rubio.

"I don't know if a James Bond reference is our best bet," answered Julian.

"How about Mr. O?" said Ernie.

"Well, using the first letter of his name is not that covert, and for some reason, Mr. Orgasm comes to mind," Julian said.

They all laughed.

"Why don't we call him Greg? And everything dealing with them can be known as Operation Greg," said Denise.

"Wait, who's Greg?" asked Ernie.

"Both of them," said Denise.

"Shouldn't each of them get their own code name?" said Ernie.

"No, I like it, they're both Greg. We fool anybody into thinking they're just one person. Gotta stay one step ahead of the enemy, huh Chief?" said Rubio.

They all laughed.

"I like it, Operation Greg!" said Julian.

During the next couple of days, Operation Greg took on a real meaning. Oleg went to look at property with Julian five different times. The first time, the beach was too rocky, and Oleg didn't like that. They kept yachting north and to a beach that had too much cacti. Oleg was underwhelmed. They kept exploring, but all of the beaches had something that Oleg didn't like.

"And how are you going to live, Oleg? You're going to need to build a house," said Julian.

"Yes, Yakov and I will build," he said.

"What about materials. How are you going to get building materials out here?" said Julian.

"You will bring materials for me," said Yakov.

Julian was beginning to feel saturated with the expectations of his new client, but he remained silent.

CHAPTER 45

Mercenary Point Ranch

On day eleven of their journey, Julian was beginning to feel frustrated with Operation Greg. He didn't know what the Crimeans wanted, or what expectations they had about living in the Baja wilderness. When they anchored at Mercenary Point, Julian had no hope that Oleg was going to like the beach, but as soon as they saw it, the Crimeans were astonished. The sand was thin like heaven's dust, and the water had a golden spark to it. Beachside, there were palm trees, and to their surprise, there was a small cabin.

"This is the land I want," said Oleg.

"Okay, you guys make yourselves invisible while I go talk to the owner," said Julian as he walked toward the cabin.

Jacinto, an older man wearing denim shorts and an old T-shirt, came to the door.

After Julian introduced himself, he told the man: "We are interested in buying your property. Are you selling by any chance?"

"No, this land has been in my family since the *Revolucíon*," he said. "General Agustín gave it to my father personally."

"I understand, sir, but I was hoping that we could talk to you about the possibility…." Julian realized Jacinto was not interested, so an idea struck him.

"Look, how about this—we've been out on the sea looking at property for days, and this particular property we loved. How about you let us invite you to lunch aboard our yacht, and we can talk about an offer, no commitment," said Julian.

As he stepped on the sand and looked out towards the sea where *The Cecilia* was anchored, Jacinto looked a little more interested.

"I've never been on a luxury yacht before."

"Well, now is your chance," said Julian with a smile.

"No commitment, right?" said Jacinto.

"Yea, no commitment, we just want to talk over lunch," said Julian.

"At what time?" Jacinto asked.

"How about I send the tender to come and get you in an hour?" said Julian.

"Okay, fine," said Jacinto.

They shook hands

"What do you like to eat?"

"*Carne asada*," said Jacinto.

Ernie picked up Jacinto and brought him on board. The table was set up astern, and Denise brought the men beer. Jacinto was very happy about being aboard, and Julian offered to give him a tour of the yacht. The Crimeans had agreed to stay in their staterooms so they would not be seen, and everybody treated Jacinto with Baja California warmth.

When Jacinto entered the galley, he yelled out, "Well, if it isn't gorgeous Rubio!"

Rubio looked up from his cooking, and a smile came to his face.

"Jazz, my man, how are you?"

The two men hugged and talked to each other like old friends. It turned out that Rubio and Jacinto knew each other from twenty years prior, when they worked for the phosphorus mine.

"Yea, I was the head cook at the mine, and Jazz was one of the union leaders back then," said Rubio.

"This is great, why don't you join us for lunch, Rubio?" said Julian.

Rubio grilled steaks as Julian and Jazz stood around drinking beer and chatting. The three of them shared jokes, stories, and generally shot the shit about life in Baja. Instead of sitting down properly to eat lunch,

Rubio handed them warm tortillas and cut steak. Guacamole and salsa were laid out, so they ate taco-stand style, casually standing by the grill, eating one taco after another. For dessert, they went up to the bridge and drank mezcal. After a while, Jazz became very comfortable, and he started talking about his kids and grandkids. Julian could sense the nostalgia, as Jazz said that he never got to see them.

"Yea, they all live in Cabo, and I hardly make it out there anymore," said Jazz.

"Why not?" asked Julian.

"Well, after my wife died, they never come to visit, and, to be honest, my pension barely covers the cost of living," said Jazz.

"So, you live out here by yourself?" Rubio asked.

"Yea," answered Jazz.

After a moment, Julian sized the man and asked him about his spread of land.

"Twenty hectares. Five of them are beachfront," said Jazz with pride.

"That's a lot of land for somebody to maintain by himself," said Julian.

"Yea, I don't really bother with it anymore. I just stay in my cabin most of the time."

"Jazz, what would you do with a million dollars?" Julian asked.

"Heck, I don't know. I've never been a greedy man. I guess I would go visit my kids, maybe help them start a business so they can make something for themselves."

"What if I told you that I could do that for you. I am willing to pay you a million dollars for your spread of land, plus another $100,000 for your cabin," said Julian.

"But where would I live?" said Jazz.

"You can get a great place for a third of that and live closer to your kids. Plus, you would still have enough money to help them start a business," said Julian.

"But what if I spend all the money? Then I'm going to be left poor and old, and I'm not even going to have my plot and cabin to live in. My *compadre* sold his land ten years ago, and in two years, he had spent all of the money. When he died, he didn't even have a pot to piss in," said Jazz.

"Look, I understand your concerns, but there are financial measures we can help you out with. For one, put some of the money away in a fund that pays you a salary and dividends each month, so you don't have access to it whenever you want. Tools like that guarantee you'll make the best use of your money," Julian said.

Jazz mulled it over.

"Look, why don't you go back to your cabin and sleep on it. Tomorrow morning, I'll go over and have coffee with you, and we'll talk then."

Jazz agreed, and the three men continued drinking mezcal and telling stories. When Ernie gave Jazz a ride back to his cabin, Julian went into Greg's stateroom.

"So, what did he say? Is he selling now?" Oleg asked.

"Well, I've offered him *two* million dollars for his property, plus one hundred thousand for the cabin. He said he was going to sleep on it," said Julian.

"How much land are we talking about it?" said Oleg.

"Twenty hectares," said Julian.

"Good," said Oleg.

"So, just in case the deal goes through tomorrow, how do you plan on paying for it?" said Julian.

"Well, we have a little over a million in cash with us, then we could wire the rest of the money," said Yakov.

"How are you gonna wire it from here?" asked Julian

Oleg stood up, looked at him square in the face. "I have my satellite phone. One phone call! That's all it takes, one call and I can get anything done."

Julian cleared his throat. "Nice."

"But here's the thing, we can't have the property in our name," said Yakov as he put his arm around Julian. "We need to put the land under someone we can trust."

Julian felt the pressure of what Yakov was really saying.

The next day, Julian went to have coffee with Jazz, who was glad to see him.

"You know, Julian, I hardly slept a wink," he said. "You made me think about my future. I have always been poor, I have never resented it. Nor have I ever coveted wealth. But to think that at the end of my life, I can have some money to help my kids and put my grandkids through school, that really motivates me," he said.

"And it should," Julian said. "You deserve the comfort of money, and I'm going to help you manage it correctly so that you have enough to last you the rest of your life."

After a moment, Julian stuck out his hand. "Do we have a deal?"

"One *millón*, plus a hundred thousand," said Jazz as he shook Julian's hand.

"But there's a catch. You have to leave your house today and take whatever you want with you," said Julian.

"What about my truck?"

"I'll give you fifteen thousand for that truck, and another five thousand if you leave all of your pots and pans, and take only your clothes with you," said Julian.

"And where am I going to sleep?" Jazz asked.

"I'll tell you what. You clear your house today, and you come back to La Paz with me on my yacht, and we finalize the sale at my accountant's office over there," said Julian.

"Why the hurry?" said Jazz.

"It's not a hurry. It's just that I like you, and I want you to cruise down to La Paz with me. It's going to be real fun."

Jazz thought about it for a moment. "Okay. I'll close the deal with you on one condition."

"What is it?" Julian asked.

"When we get down to La Paz, I can invite my kids and their families, and we can have a day aboard the yacht."

"You got it," said Julian.

As Jazz prepared the few belongings that he had, Julian went back to the yacht. He met with Oleg and Yakov, and told them that the deal was closed.

"It's going to be a little over $2.1," said Julian, his voice steady.

The men were ecstatic.

"We have a place!" said Yakov.

"Man, we are so blessed to have found you, Julian," said Oleg.

"We would like to stay here tonight, if possible," said Yakov.

"I have already talked to him, but we have to be smooth. I don't think he should see you guys. People here talk a lot, and we don't want him talking about selling his land to a couple of Russians," said Julian.

The men agreed.

"So, first thing's first, let me see the money," said Julian.

Yakov handed over a duffel bag.

"There's one million exact in there. I make a phone call and you get the rest via wire," he said.

"Okay, here's what we're going to do. Get all of your stuff ready, and we'll leave it out in the salon. I'm going to put the money in my room, and I'm going to go get Jazz. When I come back with him, I'm going to take him into the room where the money is going to be, and I'm going to let him count it. I'm going to shut the door, and when that happens, you have to get out of here, and Ernie will take you to the beach," Julian said.

As the Crimeans got their stuff ready, Julian took the money into his quarters. Lucky for him, it was all in bundles of $10,000. He counted $500,000 and put it in an old Jansport backpack he found lying around. He put the other $500,000 in the safe. He went out to the galley and told Rubio that Greg was staying in the cabin they had just purchased.

"Fill up a couple of bags' worth of supplies and food. Be sure to include liquor and everything, so they can take that with them," he told Rubio.

He went back to check on the Crimeans, who had all of their stuff packed.

"Are you ready?" said Julian.

"Yea, just a couple of things. We're going to need supplies," said Yakov.

"I've already told Rubio to pack up food and liquor for you guys, plus there's a small store, about fifteen kilometers east, down the dirt road, where you'll be able to buy almost everything," said Julian.

"I don't think I'll be going to the store, but in case of extreme emergency, it's good to have options," said Oleg.

"Just dress like gringos and pay in small bills," said Julian.

"Maybe Yakov could go once to check it out," said Oleg.

Yakov nodded in a *no big deal* kinda way.

"I've also arranged for the man to sell us his truck for an extra $20,000. It seems like it's in good condition," said Julian.

"Julian, you are a goddamn genius," said Oleg, putting his arm around him. "I only need a couple more things. I need a rifle. Just in case anything goes down, I want to have some way to protect myself and maybe hunt a little," said Oleg.

Julian thought about the rifle and shotgun he had stored.

"Well, right now, I could sell you a .308 Winchester rifle, or a triple-barrel shotgun. What do you prefer?"

"You mean you have these weapons here?" asked Oleg.

"Yea, I also have a handgun. What, do you think I ride around unarmed?" said Julian.

"Julian, you are a badass mother, you know that?" said Oleg, laughing.

Julian asked Ernie to bring up his rifle and shotgun. When Oleg saw them, he was set on the rifle.

"One last thing; whenever you talk to us, use the codename, Greg, okay?"

"Wait, who's Greg? Me or him?" Oleg asked.

"Both of you."

"Okay," they said in a casual unison.

When the Crimeans' gear and supplies were in the salon, Julian assembled his crew along with the guests for a briefing.

"Guys, these gentlemen, who we refer to as Greg, are staying here on this piece of property we've helped acquire for them. These gentlemen are more than our clients, they are our responsibility. We have a binding and fiduciary commitment with them, making us responsible for their safety during their stay here in Baja. Greg is a priority for us. So, having said that, you are well aware of the need for privacy. Any questions?

They all shook their heads.

"Jazz, the seller of the Mercenary Point Ranch, will come aboard. He will ride with us down to La Paz, where we will close the sale of his ranch, so when he comes aboard, it's important that we act as if Greg was never here, is that understood?" Julian asked.

"Yes, Captain!"

"Okay. We need to work together. Jazz's entrance and Greg's exit need to be timed perfectly. I'm going to go on the tender and get Jazz. When we come aboard, I want you to receive him like the valuable guest that he is. Rubio, hand him a beer, but keep the small talk to a minimum. Then, I'm going to lead him to the Captain's Quarters, where I have his money. We are going to be in there for about fifteen minutes, so when I shut the door, Rubio, you need to load Greg's stuff into the tender. Denise, I need you to go and get Greg out of their stateroom. Greg will then board the tender. Ernie, you skipper the tender and make sure everything is fine. Are there any questions?"

"What about keys to the place?" Yakov asked.

"I will get keys from Jazz, and I'll leave them here on the bar. When you exit the stateroom, be sure to pick them up and take them with you," said Julian.

Before Julian boarded the tender, he gave Oleg and Yakov big hugs. "I'll call you when I get to La Paz, and we'll settle things then."

When Julian got to Mercenary Point, Jazz was waiting for him.

"I thought you had forgotten about me," he said.

"Not at all, my man. Just making all of the necessary accommodations to host you on our ship, the way you deserve to be hosted, as a guest of honor," said Julian.

As Jazz boarded the tender, Julian asked him, "Got all of your stuff?"

"This is it," said Jazz. He pointed to a small bag.

When they boarded the ship, the crew greeted him with enthusiasm. Rubio handed beers to both men, and Julian set the keys to the ranch on the bar.

"Jazz, why don't you come with me for a second; I have something for you," said Julian.

He led Jazz into the Captain's Quarters and pulled out the backpack with the money.

"This is the way it's going to work: I'm going to give you $500,000 as a signing bonus. With this money, I advise you to buy a place to live. Give some money to your kids. Do you have any idea what kind of business you want to help them start?" Julian asked.

"Well, my daughter-in-law makes really good burritos. I was thinking about talking with them about opening a burrito shack in Cabo," said Jazz.

"That's a great idea. Let me know if you need any help with the business planning. I have a great accountant. The remaining $620,000, I will help you put it in the bank so that you get money every month."

"Like a pension?' said Jazz.

"Exactly like a pension. I have really good friends at Banco Santander, and you can even put some money away for your grandkids so they can go to college," said Julian.

"I like that," said Jazz as he finished his beer. "Thank you, Julian. You know what? Why don't we go get some tequila and celebrate?"

But before Jazz could reach for the door, Julian said, "Why don't you count your money? I'm gonna go get a receipt."

"I don't need to count it," said Jazz.

"It's half a million dollars. You should count it and never take it for granted."

The seriousness of the statement got to him.

"I'll be right back with that tequila," Julian said and stepped outside.

Out the window, Julian spotted Greg riding the tender with Ernie towards Mercenary Point.

"Denise, quick, make a receipt showing we gave him $500,000 in cash, and write down that we agreed to a price of $1,120,000, which includes the cabin, everything in the cabin, and his truck."

Denise printed two copies of a makeshift receipt on company stationery, and Julian brought them into the master stateroom. Both Jazz and he signed it. Julian put his copy in the safe. Moments later, when Ernie was back, Rubio entered the stateroom with a bottle of Cazadores tequila. The three of them began drinking, eventually making their way to the bow, where they continued to have a good time while Denise skippered south towards La Paz.

CHAPTER 46

Cashmen

THE RIDE SOUTH WAS SMOOTH. Jazz was thrilled about moving closer to his kids and having the money to look out for them. Julian was ecstatic about having made his first million. Neither his partners nor the Crimeans knew how much he was making for having brokered the deal, since he had doubled the price of land between Jazz and Greg. When all the transactions were finished, they were set to collect at least $1.2 million profit from the property flip and services rendered for the journey. Julian knew the money was going to be a real game-changer for the business.

In between shooting the shit and drinking with Rubio and Jazz, Julian would think about the possibilities the money brought.

Maybe I'll pay off The Beaver, he thought between sips of Cazadores.

When the yacht got to La Paz, Jazz and Rubio spent another night aboard, drinking and reminiscing about old times.

The next day, Rubio drove Julian and Jazz to their meeting with Fabio, the CPA. When they got to the office, Julian asked Rubio to wait in the lobby.

"My pleasure, Skip. With all these beautiful ladies everywhere, free snacks, strong coffee, are you kidding me? I'm gonna use their nice head, too." Rubio walked off.

Once inside, Julian, Jazz, and Fabio finalized the sale of the property. They put it under Baja Air & Sea LLC. Instead of liquidating the debt with Jazz, Fabio convinced both parties to pay Jazz monthly installments of $3,000 for the next seventeen years.

"Therefore, you can be sure that you won't spend your money and your capital is directly attached to the success of Baja Air & Sea LLC," said Fabio.

"No offense, I trust you and everything, but what security do I have if they stop paying me?" said Jazz.

"Well, you can take your land back if they default — half of it anyway," said Fabio.

"Couldn't I just put it in the bank? Doesn't it just earn interest?"

"You could, but banks are tricky little fuckers. They report everything to the government and the taxman will come after you hard. The way I'm proposing, it's clean, minimal taxes," said Fabio.

"Simple, I get $3,000 every month for 18 years?" Jazz asked.

"Seventeen years and three months to be exact."

"On the first of the month? Every month? No excuses?"

"You can come here and pick up the money directly if you prefer."

"Deal!" Jazz extended his hand.

Fabio held it. "So, now that we've got the $620,000 they owe you figured, I heard you've got $500,000 in cash?"

Jazz nodded as he picked up the backpack and held it to his chest.

"I would not be a good accountant if I allowed you to walk out of here with that much cash," Fabio said. You're too easy of a target, an enormous liability."

"What do you mean?" Jazz clenched the dirty Jansport backpack.

"It can get stolen, lost, spent at the slot machines, or given away. Do you understand that $500,000 in cash is life-changing money?"

Jazz nodded, completely sure of himself.

"It's too much of an asset to wander around aimlessly with. I don't want you to come back a week later with no money. So, my question is, what do you want to do with it?"

"Well, I want to buy a place in Cabo, something nice, but not too fancy."

"Okay, let's set aside $250,000 for your house. That's with everything, including closing costs, water, power, and taxes for at least two years," Fabio said as he wrote the amount on his tablet. "Let's add another $25,000 for furniture, appliances, and all the other stuff. So, at $275,000, you need to look for a house that you can buy for $200,000 cash."

"Ah! So that's how accountants work! I had always wondered, you know when I heard *accountant* or *CPA* in a movie. I never knew what they did," said Jazz.

"That's right. I'm your new best friend." Fabio smiled.

"You trust this guy?" Jazz looked at Julian.

Julian nodded. "That's why they call him Papa," he smirked.

"Okay, what are we gonna do next, Papa?"

"I'm gonna hold on to that money for you. Don't worry, you'll get contracts and a bond from Papa for whatever amount as security. The reason for this, again, is taxes. Hacienda is an angry fat Mexican taxman who is not your friend, and cash is the instrument with the highest tax rate. So depositing cash in the bank would cost you thirty percent."

"$150,000," said Jazz quickly.

"Correct. The moment you deposit $500,000 in cash, it becomes $350,000."

"Fuck that!" said Jazz.

"Exactly!"

"How are we going to avoid this?" Jazz asked.

"Go look at houses or maybe a condo. Find a place suitable for yourself. The moment you find the perfect home, all you have to do is call me. I'll deal directly with the seller, realtor, or whoever, and arrange payments and deposits."

"Cool, what about if I want to buy furniture and all that?"

"For all of the big purchases, I will either make electronic financial arrangements with the stores through other accounts and jockey the cash myself, or, if they're into cash, I'll arrange a cashman to deliver the money or accompany you to make purchases."

"Cashman?" Jazz interrupted.

"Yea, cashmen are people in my employment who are armed, usually ex-Mexican military. They are trained to carry large amounts of cash in bulletproof cars or armored trucks if necessary. But not only big amounts; you need a couple grand, can't come pick it up here? Call me. They've got GPS trackers on them at all times and are also bonded and insured for millions. They can either accompany you to make purchases or deliver whatever amount necessary."

"Okay, cashman, what's the catch? What makes you so much better than a bank?"

"Look, Mr. Jacinto, I like you. Come back in six months, once you have a place, you're settled. I'm gonna take care of you. We'll make money with the rest of your money; we'll make money together. The $3,000 a month you'll be getting from Baja Air & Sea, that'll be just gravy. If you have $200,000 in cash, there's money to be made. We'll buy some stocks, finance some projects. Julian mentioned maybe opening a restaurant, putting your grandkids through school. All that takes work, planning, and commitment. We'll figure out the best options for you, Papa, I promise. But I want you settled in before we start firing off this ammo."

Jazz smiled. "You're good, Papa. How much do you charge?"

"I'll take the first ten installments of your payments directly from Julian, so you won't get your first payment until early next year."

"Thirty thousand is too much. I'll do fifteen."

"I don't make any commissions off of you. I work 100 percent on your side, especially at buying and selling the high-ticket items. I'll be taking care of you for the next seventeen years, if not more."

"Look, man," Jazz said. "I'll pay you $20,000, but we're doing one payment from Julian to you, one payment from Julian for me, and we're done in fourteen months."

"Okay, Mr. Jacinto, you've got a deal," said Fabio.

Jazz stretched out his hand. They shook.

When Fabio went outside to talk to his junior executive, Julian asked Jazz if his family was going to come aboard the yacht.

"They can't today, Skip. Let's leave it for another time."

"Hey, you like Dodge Rams?" Fabio interrupted as he walked back in.

"What, the trucks?" said Jazz.

"Yea, why don't you let my cashman take you to the dealership so you can pick one out for yourself. Next year's model just arrived."

"Really, like a brand new truck?"

"Yea, you need a car, And this is the one thing I'm gonna let you splurge on. Do you have a bank account?"

"Yea, at Banamex. It's where I get my pension every month."

"How much do you get from your pension?"

"$800."

"Okay, leave that there, leave that account only for your pension. First thing I'm gonna need you to do, shit, you don't even need a cashman. Rubio can take you. Go to the HSBC bank; take your ID. Miriam, the manager, will be waiting for you. It'll be quick — just sign some papers. You won't even have to deposit any money there. I'm going to transfer your money electronically into this new account on the last day of every month, unless you prefer to come pick it up here?"

"No, electronic transfer is fine," said Jazz.

"I'm going to register you as a consultant so you get a better tax margin and it doesn't mess with your pension. After the bank, go get a smartphone. My cousin owns a shop at Plaza San Diego. I'll let him know you're coming so he can have everything ready. Then go to the Dodge Ram dealership and ask for Octavio. He'll be waiting. Just choose a truck and leave. I'll handle it."

"Sounds great. Anything else, Papa?"

"Yeah, give me the backpack." Fabio stretched out his hand.

"What, this old thing?" Jazz held the backpack tight.

"Look, it's gonna take us a few hours to draft contracts. You can either wait or leave the money here with Papa, where it's safe."

Jazz handed the backpack with the money to Fabio.

Fabio pulled $5,000 out of the bag. "Here, this is for you to indulge a little bit. Go shopping for clothes, have dinner, buy food. Buy gifts, buy nice presents for your kids, grandkids, in-laws. Now is the time to redeem yourself, Papa. When you come back, Romina, my junior, who will be your account executive, will have everything ready for you to sign."

"Excellent!"

"I'll ask her to find you a short-term rental in Cabo. Here, write down your kids' address so she can find something nearby for a month or two, until you find a place to buy."

Jazz grew serious. "I'm scared. I feel like it's one of those moments, you know? *Is it too good to be true?* You know what they say about things being too good to be true. Maybe I should just take back my money and run? I fear that I'm gonna walk out of here, and I'm gonna get scammed, one way or another, and you're all in on it!"

"Shoot, even Rubio is in on it?" said Fabio sarcastically.

"Even Rubio!"

Julian and Fabio laughed.

"I mean, It's good that he's not here because he would've been offended!"

"He's outside, do you want me to call him?" said Julian as a jest.

"Oh, he's outside!" Fabio repeated in a funny, loud whisper.

"I just don't want to get fucked, and I feel all lubed up, you know?" Jazz groaned.

They all laughed.

"Mr. Jacinto, let me tell you something. I love money. I absolutely adore it; it is the ultimate goal in life for me. First of all, do you understand how much respect I have for you? You walk in here with your $1.2 million and no liabilities. Shit, you're my hero. Half a million in cash? You just made it to a higher level. And you're in luck, because you came to Papa. I'm your moneyman, you get that? When you think of money, all you have to do is think of me. Pick up the phone and call Papa. I'm your personal credit card. I'll tell you what you can afford, I'll negotiate prices and arrange payments. Papa's got you! So take this card and answer my question: are *you* ready for the next level in your life?"

Jazz ripped Fabio's business card out of his hand. "Fuck it, let it ride." He looked at Julian. "Call Rubio. We're getting a new Dodge!"

They all laughed.

CHAPTER 47

A Real CFO

JAZZ AND RUBIO LEFT ON a high note. They were off to run errands, buy a phone, sunglasses, clothes, and a truck. Julian stayed behind with Fabio at his office.

"You see what I did?" said Fabio

"What did you do?

"I just got Baja Air & Sea a $620,000 interest-free loan," Fabio smiled.

"I was wondering what you were doing. I just remained quiet and went with it." Julian smiled.

"So, you consented."

"What?"

"When you remain quiet, you consent. But it doesn't matter. Look, you already gave Jazz $500,000 in cash. That's a huge burden for a guy like him. He might not know it, but it is. Now, if you give him the other $620,000 you owe him, he's gonna have $1.12 million liquid. We can't allow that!

As an accountant, it is my fiduciary responsibility to do some vetting; I decide who gets to work for money, and who deserves money working for them. It's better this way. Trust me—keep your money. Your $620,000 can become $5 million in ten years with a solid investment portfolio. Shit—in my hands, with the investments I'm currently working with, we can make $10 million in the time it takes us to pay him, plus we would be making that money with his same $620,000 that we borrowed for nothing. Let's pay Jazz $3,000 a month for seventeen-plus years. Who cares? That's free money!"

"I like your style!" A smirk from Julian. "I mean it's a good deal for Jazz, too. We're taking care of his money."

"Exactly! You see, we'll know if he finds a good place soon, and if he's responsible, and comes to see me in a couple months with a good head on his shoulders," Fabio said, "I'll let him play— shit, I'll let him play with fifty to a hundred thousand. Like I told him, let him buy some stocks, get some returns. But I gotta make sure he's somewhat *established* first, before he can start playing hardball."

"No, I dig it… I signed the papers." Julian grinned.

"You consented!" shouted Fabio.

"I consented," said Julian. "There's something else I should tell you."

"What is it?"

"So I'm doing work for this international firm and large deposits are coming in from Switzerland," said Julian.

"Oh yeah, how much?"

"About $1.5 million."

"Into your business account?"

Julian nodded.

"Wow, has any of it come in?"

"Yeah, $36,000, but I'm invoicing him for $1.5 million as soon as I leave this office."

"So, you'll have $1.5 million out of which $620,000 is the *interest free loan* we just got. What other monthly debts do you have?"

"We've got the *Beaver* seaplane, and some rent. But I'll get Denise to straighten it out with Elvia, our account manager," said Julian.

"No, I've got it all right here in your file — your yacht expenses, dock fees, everything's really well organized. Might as well plug in Jazz's monthly $3,000." Fabio began typing.

"Wow, how did you get all that info?" Julian interrupted.

"Denise sent it to us." Fabio looked Julian in the eye for a moment, then went back to his computer. "Dang!" a huge smile. "Did not expect that!"

"What?"

"You pay Rubio very well."

"Yeah, he's spoiled. Fucker saves all his money, too," Julian said. "Never spends a dime, has the same crummy apartment he got from public housing twenty-five years ago and his old truck, plus he collects disability because of his eye. He's my retirement plan! If shit hits the fan, I'll just work for Rubio."

They laughed.

"By the way, I've got another $500,000 in cash," Julian confessed with a sigh of relief.

"You've got *what*?" Fabio asked.

"I've got another $500,000."

"Yours?"

"Yeah."

"Where?"

"My yacht."

"Let's go get it, my cashman."

"Negative. You're not gonna get your greedy little hands on my cash until you tell me exactly how we're gonna play ball," Julian interrupted.

Fabio smirked. "Okay, this is the deal: that money, is it yours, or is it the company's?"

"Well, that's my dilemma?' said Julian.

"Run it by me?"

"What?

"Run your dilemma by me. How did you make the money?"

"Well, I middle-manned it. My clients wanted to underwrite that particular parcel to my company for privacy reasons, and I told them it was worth two million, but I'm only paying Jazz *one*."

"Classic hustle," Fabio said with a huge smile.

"Well, I saw an open door."

"And, correct me if I'm wrong, you ran, *not walked* through that door of opportunity."

"Of course. There's a window of time for decisions like that."

"You're a top businessman, Julian. Do you know that?"

"I'm no *top* businessman, no. You said so yourself — it's just a hustle."

"Yea, but hustles are the very top of the pyramid in this global scheme called capital." Fabio was vibrant in his delivery. "You are the 1 percent, Julian."

"Get the hell out of here!" he laughed. "What does that even mean?"

"Let me run it by you. You used the yacht, which is the company's biggest asset, your business partners as crew, their marketing expertise to get the clients, and even though you billed your clients separately for services rendered, there's a whole million that you're making from them out of thin air, to put it one way."

"That sounds about right."

Fabio turned serious. He tapped the fingertips of his left hand loudly on the wooden table while staring dead-eyed at Julian. "Okay, you have two choices: keep the $500,000 you have in cash for yourself. Doesn't mean you couldn't come to me as an individual and make that capital grow with investment accounts. Truth is, if you only notify your business partners about the other $500,000 that's scheduled to come in as a deposit, that would still be more than enough profit; they would be more than happy. Fontana can get some return on investment, Denise and Ernie can finally get paid good. It would be enough for everyone."

"Even Fontana?" Julian interrupted.

"Like I said, you know my loyalty is with Fontana, but half a million on the books is gravy, especially if I'm able to kick $100,000 back to him from there. He's satisfied, your other partners can split another $100,000, and they would be ecstatic. You would still have a $300,000 profit on the books that came from the flip. Plus, the other couple hundred thousand from actual services rendered. Obviously, it wouldn't look like profit; we already have a million justifications for keeping our tax rate low. So, if you want, keep the $500,000 for yourself. I would not care."

Julian exhaled. "What's my second option?"

"Full disclosure. Tell your business partners exactly how much you're making and keep things transparent. I mean, you have to think about the cost of money. If you were to bring me $500,000 in cash right now, I could guarantee you a 12 percent annual return on the money."

"Guaranteed?"

"One-hundred percent. And I'd still be making money from it. Shit, twelve percent is super conservative, that's just to make a point… Any *pendejo* that calls himself an investment banker can get you 12 percent annually. You don't even have to pick a lot of stocks, just blue-chips and mutual funds. So, at 12 percent a year, you can get $60,000 profit easily. This is after taxes and everything — clean."

"Really? Wow."

"So, you have to think: Can you make more than $60,000 your first year if you put that $500,000 bag into your business?"

"Probably," said Julian.

"This is ending the year with $560,000, so you have to take into…"

"I've got some investment accounts in the states. I know how principal works," Julian interrupted.

"Okay, okay, okay," Fabio smiled. "Now, let's think about the global amounts. You have the $1.5 million that's coming in, plus your $500,000 in cash. That's $2 million. With that much, I can make you $240,000 in return every year for the rest of your life. So the proposal is very very simple: if you leave the $2 million in the account, you need to make $20,000 a month in profit for it to be worth it. And for that to even out with wages, debts, rents, and most fixed costs, you need to generate at least $35,000 a month income, give or take. Can you do that?"

"Well, Denise insisted that we get *Greg*, our new client, on a $36,000 monthly retainer."

"More power to you, then. Listen, I'm not going to make up your mind. I want you to come to me and tell me what you want to do with the $500,000 — if you want to keep it or if you want it on the books. Either way, it's not a dilemma for me and there's complete privacy between us, but it seems to me that you could have a real CFO in that Denise lady. I can tell just by looking at her spreadsheets. You should involve her more on the financials. She gets it."

CHAPTER 48

Smiles

AFTER HIS MEETING WITH FABIO, Julian took Denise out for coffee. They went to a trendy new roaster by the marina called Cactus Taza.

"I talked to Fabio. He thought your idea about getting Greg on a monthly retainer was spot-on."

"Yeah, it's all about cash flow," she said.

"He liked your spreadsheets."

"Really?" she blushed. "That's so cool. Papa Fabio is a baller."

"He is. I don't know how he does it."

"Well, how do you think he does it?"

"I mean, for starters, he's a lot more than a CPA, and his Consortium is a lot more than an accounting firm."

"That's for sure," interrupted Denise.

"He's an investment banker who's gone rogue, in a way."

"What do you mean? Rogue how?"

"Well, the Mexican banking system is shit, complete shit, right?"

Denise nodded.

"So this guy circumvents the whole thing, doesn't give a damn, uses banks how and when he wants. But he actually delivers huge returns to his clients, which is insane. I mean, he's a financial genius."

"No, I know. Everyone I talk to highly respects him."

"The thing is, the Mexico stock market is a good old boys club. Worse than you can begin to imagine. And these guys make a killing and don't share any with the rest of the country. I'm being real when I say that the Mexico City guys who control the stock market literally all went to high school together. They're beyond billionaires, and they're that tight knit. You need people like Fabio to break down these financial walls," said Julian.

"Yeah, I saw a video online not that long ago where he was a guest speaker at an international tax summit organized by the United Nations. Can you believe it?" Denise said.

"Sure. He probably got the president of Serbia and the prime minister of Zimbabwe to call him Papa."

They laughed.

"On a serious note, I want you to come to our next meeting — with Fabio and I."

"Sure, Skip. Is everything alright?"

"Yeah, but you know, a large investment is about to come in. I want you on the frontlines of the financials."

"Okay, great, but do you want to tell me more about this large investment?"

"It's Greg, the money, the monthly retainer, the rifle, a commission for finding the property, legal fees, closing fees. Let's bill him for everything — the truck, pots and pans, all of it."

"Oh, okay, got it. I thought you meant somebody was going to invest in our company. Greg's not trying to be a partner is he? Buy stock?"

"No, no, not at all. By 'investment' I meant income, revenue. I'm working on organizing my thinking. Fabio calls it software, but it's the mind frame and the words you cast that end up becoming."

"So how much money is coming in?" Denise asked.

"Based on the conversations I've had with Greg and Fabio, the expectation is $1.5 million."

"What?"

"I need you to invoice Greg for $1.5 million. Just put 'services rendered,' and we can break it down internally, no need to be super specific with them."

"But what about the $500,000 in cash that you already gave Jazz? The one I gave you a makeshift receipt for"

"Just do the invoice for $1.5 million and they'll only send $1 million. They'll discount the cash themselves."

"10-4, Skip." Denise already had her laptop out.

Julian talked to Greg later that afternoon and told them that they had finalized the deal.

"So, I need the $1.2 million that's still owed for the property at Mercenary Point Ranch, plus our commission, legal costs, closing fees, and monthly retainer. We're going to close off your bill at $1.5 million," said Julian.

"Listen, Julian, we agree with the price, but we are going to be needing things from you. Remember 100 percent privacy. And we need you to be available to us all the time," said Yakov.

"That's exactly what the monthly retainer is for; we're at your beck and call," said Julian.

Two days later, the money hadn't come in, but Julian wasn't worried. He knew it was bound to come in at any minute; he felt it closing in. He had good sense for that money. He showered and threw on his best garb, keeping his outfit casual but sharp. He packed the $500,000 in a Tumi weekender bag, grabbed the makeshift receipt that Denise had made for him, put it in his pocket, and also grabbed Boyd's Smith & Wesson .45 caliber handgun. Julian concealed the weapon and then drove down the Malecón. That evening he checked in to the Costa Baja hotel and got a massage. He needed to think about how to handle the money.

When he came back into his room, he checked his bank account and a wire transfer for $1.5 million had been deposited.

"Boom!" he said to himself with a huge smile. That night he had room service for dinner and fell asleep watching television.

The next morning, he summoned Ernie and Denise to the hotel restaurant.

"A $1.5 million deposit just landed into our account," Julian said, showing them the balance.

"That's incredible!" said Ernie as he got up and hugged Julian.

"But I thought you said they were only going to send one million because they'd already paid Jazz $500,000 in cash," Denise said.

"Yeah, I said that because I was unsure about how it was going to go down. But here it is." Julian smirked. "And that's not all of it."

The Jordans stared, perplexed.

"I've got another $500,000 in cash."

"What? Where?" Ernie couldn't hold his excitement.

Julian gently kicked the Tumi weekender bag. "Right here." Another tap with his foot.

"Wow, I love you, Skip," said Ernie as he peeked inside the bag.

"Where is all this money coming from?" said Denise.

Julian explained how he'd doubled the actual price of the Mercenary Point Ranch. His business partners couldn't believe it.

"How did you get away with that?" Denise wondered.

"Well, I just took a risk. I figured this was our chance, and they didn't say anything."

"You are a genius, Julian," said Ernie.

"Plus, I mean the guy was president of Crimea. I'm sure he escaped with quite a bit of money. His deposits are coming in from Switzerland," said Julian.

"Yeah, I've been doing some research online and they're accusing him of taking over $800 million out of the country," said Denise.

"Man, don't tell me that. We should have charged him five million for the parcel," said Julian as they all laughed.

"I'm going to be transparent with you guys. When the money came in, I had a bit of a dilemma. I was torn between keeping some of it for myself or leaving it for the company. In the end, I realized I had plenty of justification for investing in you guys. After all, we're a crew and even though I upsold some property to make a lick, we all contributed."

"It's a lot more than a lick," Ernie interrupted.

"My point exactly. I made this company money because I really believe in you and I want you to know that we're in it together. We are partners and I want what's best for you. I want our company to have these funds available not to spend frivolously, but to grow. Denise, I've seen how your business mind works and I like it. I'm a hustler and a captain, but you, you are like a high-profile, high-performing executive, and I want you to believe that Baja Air & Sea is a multimillion-dollar company!"

"Cheers," said Ernie with water.

"What's this?" said Julian. "Bring us mimosas," he told the waitress.

When the drinks came and they finally cheered, Denise didn't say anything, but Julian knew she was proud of him.

"You're smart, not because you left the money in the business," said Ernie, "but because you invested in *her*," he pointed to his wife.

She was all smiles. Her eyes glazed with pride.

"So, both of you, take this bag and go to Fabio's office right now. Figure it all out."

"What about you? Aren't you coming?" Ernie asked.

"No. Here, take my gun," Julian said softly as he handed Ernie the Smith & Weson under the table. "I've already talked to Fabio. From this point on, we're gonna let Denise take the lead with the financials. She's the new CFO."

"Thank you, sir. I guarantee that you won't be disappointed." Denise nodded, blushing with an ear-to-ear smile.

"I don't expect to be. You'll just have a lot more work to do."

"I love the work!"

"What are you going to do, Skip?" said Ernie.

"Me? I've got a golf lesson!" Julian smiled.

CHAPTER 49

Caimancito Hangar

A MONTH AFTER THEIR $2 million gain, they got a special permit signed by Air Force General Agundez Velarde for seaplane use, thanks to Admiral Gomez. Julian used some of the money to liquidate the debt on *The Beaver* from Kyle Willis, who was impressed by how quickly they paid it off and offered to sell them his plot of land with the seaplane hangar.

The parcel, known as Caimancito, was a special piece of real estate. Feathered in exotic palms from eight of the world's deserts, It had a wide seawater stream that led directly to a virgin inlet from La Paz bay. Three pristine hectares of South Baja California prime. There was the casita, which was small but very well-kept with a modern design. It had a walk around porch, a manicured desert garden with raked sands, and a variety of custom details.

Kyle was private about his home; he wouldn't even invite Denise and Ernie inside—they could do whatever they wanted all over Caimancito, but would never go inside the casita. The hanger where the floatplane was stored was commonly referred to as Building X. There was a ramp that led from the stream directly inside where *The Beaver* could be kept on dry ground. Inside Building X, a perfect little workshop for Ernie had been carved out. There were tools and spare parts for the plane and enough room to store and work on the Zodiac tenders.

The third structure on the site was a small two-story watch house known as the Commodore Tower. It wasn't really a tower, and it wasn't that high, but it was a special nook that appeared both playful and serious. It had a small footprint behind a very large Canary Island date palm. The tower rested near the property line, with the neighbor's hill behind it. The hill offered shade during critical hours and, with the windows open, the tower was cooled by a natural breeze. It was the only part of the property with a little green lawn around it. Kyle had built the Commodore Tower for his grandkids with the loving care of a man who works with his hands. The children only came once.

Julian loved the idea of the Commodore Tower as his office. It had white and blue Mykonos-inspired round edges with that hint of sustainable desert architecture. The ground floor consisted of two rooms carefully offset with a small open area at the entrance. Each room was eleven-by-twelve feet and shared a common bathroom. The second story was a big open studio that covered the whole floor with a separate area for a closet and the master bathroom. Up the stairs, there was a rooftop deck that provided uninterrupted bay views. Caimancito Hanger wasn't a private cove, but it was secluded enough to feel that way.

Denise, Ernie, Julian, and Kyle were standing on the rooftop deck of the Commodore Tower looking out to the bay.

"We can't dock the yacht here, but we can ride a Zodiac to the marina," said Ernie. "I've done it, it's cool as hell. Go and come back to work via dinghy — it's great."

"Yeah, let's get a jet ski," said Julian in jest.

"Heck yeah! Better yet, we can anchor around the bend and use tender. Bet it would take less than twelve minutes," said Ernie.

"Sounds like you made up your mind. You need this property," interrupted Kyle.

"You still haven't given us a price, Mr. Willis," said Denise.

The old man stiffened up. "Look, the property is worth at least $1 million, and that's low-balling it. If I wanted to work on selling it, I could probably get $1.6 million without getting greedy, maybe two million."

"Do you know how many buyers there are for two million?" Julian asked. "None!"

"Look, Mr. Mayorca, I'm going to be real with all of you." Kyle looked at Denise and Ernie. "I want to leave my casita to you two."

"Really?" said Denise

"Yes, when I die, this house that I live in will become yours."

"Wow, Mr. Willis. What can I say?" Denise looked at Ernie.

"Thank you!" he said.

"We're flattered. We love you, Mr. Willis," said Denise.

"You two have been like my children these last years. You're so hardworking, you remind me of myself when I was your age. I was a real go-getter. I want to do something nice for you."

The Jordans hugged Kyle, a little tear in their eyes.

"So, let's do this." Kyle wiped his right eye. "Buy the whole property for $800,000—the land, the hanger, and this Commodore Tower. It includes the rights to use the stream and access to the bay, which is a federal area."

"Okay, so you gifted my partners the casita *when* you pass? And you're selling us the rest for what you consider a hefty discount?" Julian asked.

"To put it in your terms, Captain, correct — at a *hefty* discount," said Kyle.

"Why not just give them the whole parcel, everything? You don't need the money!" said Julian.

Kyle laughed. "Well, that's not how things are done."

"Haven't you learned? This is Mexico, we do things differently! Give it to the Jordans! That would be a transcendent act. Build a legacy for yourself!" said Julian.

Kyle was laughing. "Oh, Mr. Mayorca, you are as brave as they say. You're funny, too."

"What's so funny? Being generous? I'll tell you what — you give the Jordans this plot and I'll commission the best artist to build a statue of you."

Kyle laughed. The Jordans laughed, too, but they were nervous.

"Imagine…" Julian raised his hand towards the water. "Kyle Willis, Benefactor."

"Oh, Mr. Mayorca, you should do standup comedy." he calmed down. "Seven-fifty."

"Seven-fifty what?" said Julian.

"I'll sell you Caimancito for $750,000 and the Jordans get my casita when I pass."

"$500,000, but you leave all your tools, equipment, parts, workshop — pretty much everything on your property except the casita and your truck. As-is!" said Julian, stretching out his hand.

"$700,000 if you still build a statue of me," said Kyle.

"I'm not building a statue!" Julian laughed. "Look, I'll give you $550,000 and I'll let you build your own statue."

"You pay me $650,000 cash right now, I'll take it!"

"$600,000, no statue, on credit, interest-free direct financing," said Julian.

Kyle shook his head. "This is elder abuse! You're betting that I'm going to die before you finish paying me!"

Everybody laughed.

"$630,000," said Kyle.

"$620,000, and we go visit our wealth manager right now," said Julian.

"$625,000, just because you said *wealth manager*." Kyle stretched out his hand.

They all laughed.

"No statue?" said Julian.

"No statue," said Kyle.

Julian shook his hand. They hugged and laughed.

After discussing it with Fabio, they paid Kyle 10 percent down and committed to pay him the rest in $4,000 monthly installments for eleven years. Kyle agreed to the selling price, but wrote into the deal that he would be allowed to live in the casita he had lived in for the last twenty years, rent-free, for the rest of his life, and that afterward it would go to Denise and Ernie Jordan.

The Caimancito property wasn't a big property, but it had a lot of potential. Julian loved it because he could tell it had been built with care. Kyle's vision was reflected in the workmanship, but Julian understood that Kyle wasn't the one to take such a vision to a higher level; he was. It took fourteen days for them to fully move into their Commodore Tower office. Julian claimed the second floor loft, Denise had the better of the two ground floor suites, and they turned the other room into a boardroom. She hired Vivian, a designer who ran a creative agency out of La Paz called Vloom, to help with the feng shui.

In the open area at the entrance, they put a thin glass desk and a rock fountain.

"But we don't have a receptionist," said Denise.

"But you will," said Vivian.

They opted for clean, almost minimalistic decor. Julian got a vintage orange sofa and hung framed maps of Baja California on the walls. The rooftop deck was Moroccon style with cabanas, drapes, plush sun pillows, and space for a bar.

"We're going to need a pool," said Julian as they were having a rooftop chat.

"Are you thinking about throwing parties?" Vivian asked.

"No, but just in case, get a nice sound system."

Vivian took notes.

High-speed internet took another week to install.

"Satellite internet is the only way to go in a place like ours!" said Julian.

"Plus, we can put the VPN to anywhere and unlock different content based on our supposed location," said Ernie.

After they had set up their office in the Commodore Tower, Greg began requesting building materials. Julian commissioned Ernie to quote the cost and he would then double or sometimes triple the price. To transport the supplies, Julian contracted with Admiral Gomez to use a Sabreline 36 trawler for cheap. He then upcharged all possible fees and forwarded the invoice to Greg, who arranged to have the money wired. Ernie would then travel up the coast, usually with Rubio. He didn't like

Denise staying behind alone with Julian, but he never said anything.

But Julian was only interested in one woman, Regina Dahlgreen. He thought about her all the time. He remembered her eyes, her lips, the way she moved her hair, her voice, her scent, and her hands. He wanted her in his life, even if she was in a relationship with Axel. He felt like he had to do something.

But what if I go through all of it, only to be rejected by this queen I have fallen in love with? he would think to himself.

Fear and doubt began to sink in, but Julian couldn't allow the doubt to win. He had to be certain that Regina was interested in him. He took out his phone and sent her a text message.

Hey, I just moved into a new office, next time you're in La Paz, you should come visit and we can catch up! wrote Julian. He hit send, and read the message over 10 times, wondering if she had gotten it, or if she could have changed her number.

Oh shit! Why did I put an exclamation mark! WTF is that?

By the time he got her, *Sound's good, Mr. Paper Moon,* reply, Julian had gone through a range of emotions. When he read the text, he was proud she had called him *Mr. Paper Moon.* In his eyes, the nickname signified that the time they spent together had meant something to her, too. He smiled. He began texting her at least once a day to share a joke, a comment, or a thought. She would always text him back within the hour, and the two began a period of light flirting.

CHAPTER 50

Project Baja

DENISE CONTINUED HER AGGRESSIVE SOCIAL media campaign promoting *The Beaver* and *The Cecilia* through all available channels. She joined skydiving networks and yachting vacation threads. Ernie upgraded his camera gear, acquiring professional lenses, rigs, tripods, and reflectors that helped him stage his shots. Photography showed a sensitive side that Julian didn't know his deckhand had. Denise would then post photos of the vessels and short videos of their cruises and flights. Their Instagram account was attracting more followers. Denise was a machine, professional, thorough, and committed. The million dollars Julian had made for the company had given her the motivation she needed. One morning, as the two were having coffee, Denise told Julian she had been contacted by Wally Sanz, a producer based out of Los Angeles.

Wally was doing a special for Netflix about wingsuit flying. In his email, he wrote that he had been down to La Paz on vacation and wanted to return and use it as a film location.

"He already said *The Beaver* is fine, but he needs a helicopter," said Denise.

"Why does he need a helicopter?" Julian asked.

"Because he wants to film the wingsuiters from there," said Denise.

"Wingsuiters?" asked Julian.

"Yeah, those are the guys that wear the weird-looking suits and glide through the air."

Denise showed Julian a couple of YouTube videos of people wing-suit flying.

"That's amazing," said Julian as he watched clips of people flying close to rocks and steep cliffs.

"Yeah, the point of wingsuiting is to fly as close as you can to objects and to elongate the flight trajectory as much as possible," Denise explained.

Julian asked Denise to get Wally on the phone. They put the call on speaker and the three talked about the logistics.

"Oh, you guys are gonna love this. It's going to be a new high for the industry. I can't tell you more details. 'Project Baja' is under wraps, certain things still gotta get approved by the platform," Wally said.

"Privacy is the core of our business model," said Julian.

"So, what kind of helicopter do you have available?" asked Wally.

"A red Eurocopter, unlike any you've ever seen," said Julian.

"Great, see you Saturday," Wally said.

"A red Eurocopter?" asked Denise after the call.

"Yeah, my friend Regina has one. We'll join forces," said Julian.

"What? She knows about this?"

"No"

"Then why did you commit?" said Denise.

"Listen, sometimes I just go by instinct."

PART III

Tandem

CHAPTER 51

Los Barriles Bunker

REGINA AND AXEL HAD STAYED in at his Los Barriles place. Axel called the small house "The Bunker," because it was his hideaway from every day life. It wasn't underground or made out of concrete. But the hills and palm trees that surrounded it gave it an air of privacy and escape.

A breeze came into the room from the south window. Axel rolled over on the bed and kissed Regina from behind. Her back arched and she moaned as she always did when he touched a certain spot near her sacrum.

The bed was still laced with last night's dreams. Regina recognized in herself a desire for greatness. She did not feel innocent or naive, but feared that others saw her that way. Life had taught her to never let her guard down. She knew that her father's legacy could be a curse if she let it. But her purpose in Baja was clear—she wanted to become a respected person.

She wanted to pull strings, to deal in the affairs of men. As a young woman, she knew she had to work harder than anybody else. She was wrapped in these thoughts when the phone rang. Axel, wearing only boxers, got out of bed and answered. He stepped outside as he always did to take the call.

Regina knew Axel was involved in things outside the official realm of the port captainship, but she didn't care. It didn't bother her and she never asked. She figured this was because of a pattern in her life — a pattern of rich men who disregarded the law and used power to get what they wanted.

Maybe it's part of my father's curse, she thought as she got out of bed and into the shower.

As Regina washed away the salt and sweat, she wondered if the fact that she didn't care about her boyfriend's illegal activities meant she didn't love him. She wondered if loving meant worrying about the other person's safety and integrity.

As she dried off in the bathroom, Axel jumped in the shower.

"I gotta rush back to La Paz. I've got a meeting with the secretary of tourism. The man is such a tool, I swear only idiots make it in politics," Axel said.

"No wonder you got so far ahead then," Regina said with a smile.

"Oh, *and* she's smart."

They both laughed.

"Hey, listen, we're throwing a party aboard the *Dream On* on Saturday," Axel said. "I've invited the mayor of La Paz."

"Is the yacht gonna have to be moved to La Paz? Or can she come to Cabo?"

"Her driver can bring her, and maybe we can ride back north on the yacht," Axel said.

"That's fine, honey. I'll have my chef put together the menu," she said.

She hated it when Axel acted like the *Dream On* was his yacht, when it was all hers.

"You should wear the skirt I got you for the party," said Axel as water splashed his face.

"Yeah, perfect," she answered, thinking about all of the permits Axel had secured and political favors he'd done for her Baja Explorations business.

I guess that gives him some entitlement over me, Regina thought.

Axel left when a government suburban came and got him. They kissed, and he squeezed her butt gently. She bit his lip and thought about how it gave her a little power over him. She had some toast and looked at the time. The Zenith watch Julian had given her showed 10:25. She stepped outside and got into her Toyota Land Cruiser.

Regina took the off-road shortcut to San José. She was going through a dusty straight when her phone rang. It was Julian.

"What a surprise. I thought you had forgotten about me," she answered.

"I *had* actually. I was just wondering whose number this was," he said.

After a casual conversation and some mild flirting, Julian brought up the Netflix show.

"Listen, some Hollywood producers are coming in and we need a helicopter with a pilot. And, of course, I thought of you." Regina was stoked that Julian was giving her a business opportunity and agreed to be a part of the team. After they discussed pricing, routes, and logistics, Regina agreed to have the Eurocopter in La Paz no later than Friday evening.

At her home office, Regina was preparing a budget and flight plan when a call came in from Axel. He wanted to consult with her about what alcohol to buy for Saturday's party. A warm shiver ran down her spine when she realized she had a scheduling conflict between Axel's party and Julian's production. She thought about canceling her commitment with Julian, but then remembered that she really needed the money. She had the yacht, the mansion, and the helicopter, but the couple million dollars in her Mexico account were drying up quickly, especially with a $120,000 monthly cost of running her estate alongside her yacht and helicopter business. And not only that, she wanted to see Julian; she wanted to talk to him. She liked Julian and hoped to get more business from him. She didn't want to let him down on the first attempt. Then she thought about canceling on Axel, but that was a stupid idea. She knew that wasn't an option. Axel was a power player. If he didn't get his way, he had ways of hurting her, and she knew he had no problem using his position to get his way.

Her chef put together a great menu for Axel's party: ceviche, grilled tuna, quesadillas, and a full array of sashimi. Regina thought about the catch-22 of her boyfriend's parties. They were filled with the most distinguished of people: politicians, businessmen, millionaires, celebrities, and even diplomats, but they never paid. Axel didn't pay, either. He would send over the liquor, some of the ingredients to prepare the courses, and would give her a couple of port captainship fuel vouchers. But it wasn't like she made any money on her boyfriend's cruises. Still, she saw her time with Axel as an investment. Not only had he helped her get in business, she also got the occasional client from these parties.

"Screw it," she whispered as her mind wandered into the future. "I'm doing both."

She made the arrangements for Axel's party on the condition that the yacht be scheduled to embark out of La Paz.

"That works even better," said Axel over the phone.

Later that day, he sent over the alcohol.

CHAPTER 52

Flyers

FROM THE SKY, LA PAZ Bay looked like a whale's tail. Regina was piloting her helicopter. It was spotlessly clean with detailed trims, embroidered Ds on the headrest, and seating for six passengers. Regina spoke to Julian over the CB radio. Julian was in the copilot's seat. They had just finished testing the flight plan.

"All right, so make sure you're out of the way enough with the helicopter. I don't want the skydivers getting all chopped up in the rotor blade," said Julian.

"Roger that. I wouldn't want to get any blood on my bird anyway," said Regina.

"Real humanitarian," said Julian.

They laughed it off.

Denise, who was piloting *The Beaver*, sensed the playfulness between Regina and Julian over the airwaves. She smiled as they flew over Punta Prieta towards Balandra.

Balandra Bay is one of the best beaches in the world. Its famous mushroom rock is considered an icon, juts up from gentle waters creeping into its salt lagoon. Stretching over thirty hectares, Balandra's deepest point is at under five meters, so most of it is a walkable, swimmable paradise with almost no wake.

"And we're back to our location," said Julian over the CB.

"Ah, Balandra, couldn't have picked a better spot," said Regina as she landed on the gravel parking lot south of the bay.

Julian had negotiated a fee with the municipal police for closing off access to the salt lagoon, so men in uniform were waving off onlookers. He had also arranged for firemen and paramedics to be on call, and had contracted a lifeguard fleet to be alert beachside. It already looked like a big production, and there weren't even any cameras out yet. Denise alighted *The Beaver* in the center of the lagoon. She taxied to the shore and stepped onto the sand.

"Great landing," said one of the young lifeguards, who looked at Denise as if she were Wonder Woman.

Ernie secured the plane to the back of Julian's Land Rover.

"You don't *land* on the sea, you *alight*," Denise said as she walked toward the parking lot.

A little **after 9 a.m.,** a convoy of two sixteen-passenger vans, a trailer, and a utility wagon rolled past the police and parked opposite the fire truck. Julian walked over to Wally, the producer, and the pair shook hands.

"We're all ready for you," said Julian.

Three "flyers," as they were called, walked over to *The Beaver*. They were followed by a cameraman and his assistant. The cameraman captured them strolling toward the plane. He made them smile as he compared them to astronauts on their way to Venus. Scott, the tallest of the three, complimented Denise's tan. She smiled it off, as she could tell that he really wanted to compliment her legs. She welcomed them aboard the plane. After unhinging the steel rope, Ernie walked the plane off the beach and jumped into the copilot's seat with wet shorts. Denise turned on *The Beaver* and taxied to the center of the salt lagoon.

The director of photography, two cameramen, and two assistants walked towards the shiny red Eurocopter. The rotor and the handsome blade on its tail were already spinning.

"Watch your heads," Regina cautioned. "I don't want to lose anybody yet."

The men strapped themselves in. She pulled on the collective and the chopper lifted off.

"Gentlemen, we are airborne," she said as she fiddled the pedals and moved the cyclic with precision.

The men prepared their cameras and began capturing video of the earth and sea below.

Other than the cameramen on *The Beaver* and on the chopper, there were seven more cameras on the ground. Three photographers were set up in the surrounding mountains alongside the salt lagoon, and three more were set up on the beach. A small camera crew was also set up in one of the Zodiacs in the middle of the bay.

"Got yourself one heck of a show," said Julian.

"Yeah, and wait until you see the climax," said Wally, as the two of them sat in a shaded tent set up as their basecamp.

"You think you've got enough cameras?" said Julian.

"Not only that, all of the flyers are wearing GoPros. It's gonna be beautiful," said Wally.

The Beaver reached 10,000 feet and began to shake a little.

"It's an air bubble," Denise said over the speaker. "When the ground is too hot, the cold air above it condenses and creates pockets."

The flyers didn't care. They were focused, attentive, and ready for action. When the plane plateaued at 12,000 feet, they lined up. Ernie got out of the copilot's seat and opened the cabin door.

"Uno, dos, tres," said Dan Frazier, the first flyer, as he jumped out of the plane and into the blue sky.

"No guts, no glory," said Sergio Meza, the second flyer, who did a backflip out of the plane.

"I dedicate this jump to the most beautiful pilot in the world," said Scott, the third flyer, who looked at Denise, winked, and spread his wings over the sea-level mountains.

Scott caught up with Sergio and the two of them flew side by side.

Together they caught up to Dan, who was already some ways ahead of them. Wingsuit-gliding was the closest thing to flying nude. The men flew with such natural ability that to the cameras, it seemed like they had been born with wings.

"Oh my, look at that," said Wally.

They looked up at the three men who seemed like birds in sun-struck beauty coming into Balandra Bay. The three were holding hands, flying inches from the rocks and trees of Indio Mountain, west of the salt lagoon. Controlling every single move with the precision of hawks on a high-speed hunt, together, they stretched their wings like heaven's own sons.

On the ground, Julian looked at Wally, who was having the time of his life.

"Here they come," Wally said.

The flyers let go of each other and descended close to the water of the salt lagoon. Nobody opened a parachute. The three flew over it smoothly, arched their backs, extended their wings, and began to break over the water. With their speed decreasing by the second, Dan and Sergio hit their chests against the water and alighted. Scott brought himself completely to a halt, tilted back to stand, and took six steps on the water before coming to a full stop. He stood casually in the shallow end and walked to shore.

"Oh, my God! He walked on water, he walked on water! Did you see that?" yelled Wally as he hugged his host.

Julian hopped on a Zodiac and went to get Dan and Sergio, who were calm, lying face up, floating on the water. He helped them board the tender.

"That was an amazing feat," said Julian as he skippered back to shore.

With no cameras on them, the two men just smiled in silence, acknowledging that they had been topped by Scott.

CHAPTER 53

Wrap Party

JULIAN HAD A SMALL PRODUCTION-WRAP party aboard *The Cecilia* for the cast and crew of *Project Baja*. After they stored and sent off their equipment with the post-production unit, the crew took turns loading onto the Zodiacs and unloading aboard the yacht, which was anchored northwest of the lagoon. Rubio had food and drinks laid out, and Reyna was joyful around the guests. Ernie and Denise had to go store *The Beaver*, and Julian's only desire was to spend more time with Regina. He begged her to come to the party with him, but she said she couldn't.

"Come on, at least come aboard the yacht until Denise and Ernie return," he said.

"How long do you think they'll be?" said Regina.

"Like, not even five minutes," Julian faked desperation.

Regina laughed. "Fine, but afterward, you're coming with me on a helicopter ride."

"Why is everything with you a negotiation?" said Julian.

"I've got somewhere to be. Deal or no deal?"

"Where do you have to be?"

She touched his face, looked into his eyes, tilted her head, barely winked, and exhaled.

Julian was melting for her. "Baby, with those eyes, I'd follow you to the end of the world."

She blushed. "Let's go."

He grabbed her arm and walked her to the tender.

Aboard *The Cecilia*, Wally was intoxicated, not just on mezcal, but on the rush of knowing that they had just made history.

"You walked on the water," he told Scott, with his heavy arm around him. "Do you know what that means?"

"That I'm the best wingsuiter out there?"

"No, that you are Jesus ef'n Christ," said the producer.

Everybody laughed. Wally made a toast.

Julian put his arm around Regina as Wally told a story about skydiving back in the 1980s.

When Ernie and Denise got back to the yacht, Regina told Julian: "That's our ride."

Ernie, who suspected that Scott was crushing on Denise, insisted he stay aboard the yacht.

Denise took Julian and Regina back to shore.

When they got to the beach, Julian told Denise to look after everything while he was gone with Regina. Julian didn't know where they were going, but he was hoping they were going away for good, like teenage lovers with nothing holding them down.

The Eurocopter stood on the gravel parking lot, awaiting its pilot. Julian dismissed the municipal police officer who was still guarding Balandra Bay, thanked him, and gave him instructions to re-open the location for public use. Regina smiled as Julian hopped aboard the chopper. Moments later, the rotor blades began to spin and they ascended into the air. Below them, shiny sea, above them, golden sky, around them, French engineering. Julian was sure that this was their moment; he thought that maybe they were going back to Regina's yacht to make passionate love.

"What's the plan, hotshot?" he asked.

"I've got a party to attend and you're coming with me."

"Wow. Am I your date?"

"No, you're not my date, you're my hostage," said Regina.

At that precise moment, Julian realized what was happening.

"Is Axel Cuevas going to be there?" he asked.

"Of course, he's the one that planned this whole party," said Regina.

Julian's face dropped.

"Relax *Jules*, everything's going to be alright. You're with *me*."

They were flying over the sea. Unparalleled South Baja beauty.

My mother used to call me Jules. He sighed and looked ahead.

CHAPTER 54

The Host (Part I)

AXEL CUEVAS LOVED HOSTING PARTIES. He was an entertainer, a man who splurged on details and charmed his guests. People enjoyed his parties. Axel always had the best wines, the best food, and, of course, the yacht. *The Dream On*, considered the most elegant party platform on the Sea of Cortez, solidified his social standing, and strengthened his leadership. Everybody wanted to attend his parties. Axel was a man who wore many masks. He was an expert in making it seem like he was relaxed and easygoing, even a little careless. But on the inside, he was a shrewd, calculating man. His guests weren't only handpicked, they were curated. For Axel, everything was business; pleasure was just another part of the master plan. He never welcomed attendees unless he had something to gain from them.

That Saturday, Axel Cuevas's guest of honor was the mayor of La Paz, Bárbara Pérez, a 50-year-old lesbian who had come to power the year prior. As port captain, Axel kept a close relationship with most civic leaders. Barbara, however, had been too wrapped up in her own affairs and they hadn't had the chance to engage properly. Axel was interested in knowing her political ambitions; it was obvious she wanted to be governor; everybody who gets into politics in Baja dreams of being governor. He wanted to know more about her, her flaws, her goals, and how he might do business with her.

Barbara was a tough lady. She held her head high and believed in the message she was spreading: social justice, boosting tourism, and public safety.

"They all work hand-in-hand," she said.

"Mrs. Mayor, I invited you aboard the yacht today to talk about *that* point exactly."

The mayor looked at him with the dread of an uninvited conversation.

"Forgive me, but I'm not going to waste your time. I want you to have fun today, I really do, but what I am selling is a special forces and weapons training program for police officers," Axel said as sea wind blew through his soft and well-kept hair.

"It's a program designed in Israel by the toughest minds in defense," he continued.

Barbara liked what she was hearing.

"And how much is this little program?" she asked.

"There is the training program and the training and weapons program, where we also exchange your department's weapons for new ones and, obviously, give them training on newer technology and advanced weaponry."

Barbara looked at him with an air of greed.

"Our plans begin at $200,000. We offer financing and there can be up to a 10 percent kickback to you." A wink. He lowered his voice. "Personally."

Barbara looked at him. "I think you and I are going to get along, Mr. Cuevas, but I don't get into any business for less than 50 percent."

Axel smiled. He was ready to negotiate.

"You can have the markup if you help me push it through the committees in ninety days or less."

Silence. A look from her, a smirk. He had her. Hook, line, sinker.

"Come by my office Monday morning. We'll get it done," Barbara said.

Now he was ready to let her enjoy the rest of the day aboard the *Dream On*. This defense training program was a powerful sell. It included more than just weapons; it included seminars, tactical gear, team building, metrics, skill analytics, and future projections for the city's forces. Axel's direct boss was the fugitive, Samuel Bracho, who, with the help of key people, was building back his fortune, gaining an inch of ground with every dollar, strengthening his position in the big leagues of power—the only game he knew how to play.

It's more profitable for everyone if you get the weapons package; plus, the officers will benefit a lot more, Axel thought as he rehearsed what he was going to tell the mayor at their meeting.

He took a deep breath and looked at the sea in front of him. It was going to be a good day. He put six bottles of Veuve Clicquot on ice.

CHAPTER 55

Barbacóa

SAMUEL BRACHO WASN'T JUST A recovering billionaire, he was a legend. He began making real money in the 1980s as a Mexican middleman for Pablo Escobar. During those times, he was able to negotiate the sole distribution of cocaine for two U.S. cities, Las Vegas and Phoenix. When he worked the streets, he was very careful, moved quickly, and was extremely frugal. He never sparked violence and always made smart moves. When he celebrated his thirty-third birthday at the Flamingo in Vegas, his fortune already consisted of $100 million.

After the fall of the Colombian cartel structure, Bracho left the cocaine trade and began making power investments in Mexico. He began mining in the state of Chihuahua. When the then-governor denied his bribe, Bracho ignored him, opening a mine west of Copper Canyon. An illegal mine, a pirate mine. A cave without mining rights, land ownership, or even permission.

The nineties became a new era for him; he was rich, he had survived the Escobar days, and he felt entitled, like it was time for the world to hear about the new *patrón*. Once his mining interests were solidified, he reached out to his friends in Vegas and established a network of slot machine lounges throughout Mexico. Grimy storefronts began popping up in Matamoros, Juárez, Tijuana, Obregon, and Guadalajara, storefronts that operated slot machine lounges behind velvet curtains. These "coin-swallowers," as they were known, weren't regulated and most were there without Bracho having to grease a politician's hand.

They were completely off the radar, illegal, pirate casinos. Bracho always said that if push-came-to-shove, he would bribe a politician, but he preferred blackmail, intimidation, or even killing them off to grow his empire.

"It's cheaper to kill someone than to pay them off for life, especially a *político*" was one of his mantras.

In 1997, he stole a herd of cattle from Arturo Mehling, a businessman who at the time kept pressuring the government to look into Bracho. That herd of fifty ended up becoming the backbone of another of his enterprises. Bracho opened his first slaughterhouse in Mexicali before the 1998 holiday season. Without having to pay certification or meet any health department standards, the pirate slaughterhouse was able to sell steaks for half the price of competitors. By the early 2000s, Samuel Bracho was a billionaire, supplying meat to not just Mexico, but the United States, Canada, and South America. Eventually a majority of his businesses aligned and became legal companies, but that was after he'd made hundreds of millions of dollars and left a trail of blood.

Throughout the years, Bracho made a lot of enemies, but none was more meticulous, more calculating, more strategic and obsessed with getting back at him than Arturo Mehling. For him, it became about a lot more than fifty heads of cattle. The cowboy-turned-industrialist believed in solid business practices and was absolutely disgusted by corruption. So, in 2005, Mehling bought the acclaimed *Gazeta* newspaper, a Baja California institution known, feared, and respected for its hardline reporting and strong stance against corruption. Mehling acquired *Gazeta* in a covert operation. Nobody knew the identity of the buyer, who'd used a blind trust and that was the way Mehling wanted to keep it.

When Mehling, under the pen name Pablo Heraldo, began publishing weekly editorials demanding the government step in and stop Samuel Bracho, whom he called the worst criminal in Mexico's history, things started to change. In 2007, Mexican President Felipe Calderon began a case against Bracho, who was already captain in a half-dozen industries, including agriculture and adult entertainment. His political clout had grown. He was godfather to Andres Ruiz-Garza, the twelfth son of then-mayor of Tijuana, Don Aldo Ruiz's.

Bracho's *compadre* Don Aldo ran Tijuana out of his house in the old racetrack, a palace of debauchery that was his prized possession. He kept a private zoo, an indoor shooting range, and a personal entrance to the Ardiente Casino he had built on the property. In the old days, the racetrack had been owned by John Alessio, the man credited with inventing the exacta, trifecta, quinella, and five-ten betting formulas. In those days, Ardiente Racetrack represented the pinnacle of West Coast glamour. But now it was run by a gangster who killed off the horses and replaced them with dogs that chased cloth rabbits. Don Aldo had inherited the racetrack from his father, Rodolfo Ruiz, who had been Secretary General under President Echeverría in the 1970s. Richard Nixon, a sworn enemy of Alessio, pressured the Mexican government to withdraw his federal gaming concessions. Ruiz took the opportunity to usurp the racetrack from Alessio and eventually gave it to his son to operate.

Over the years, Don Aldo turned the racetrack grounds into a canidrome and a casino. In addition to being mayor, he was the legal gambling tycoon of Tijuana, a millionaire by inheritance, a billionaire by hard work and unfair advantage, and a gangster by preference. Don Aldo had studied at Princeton but chose to leave the banking life and become a criminal. Don Aldo and Samuel Bracho together became the biggest threat to the Mexican establishment since Pancho Villa and Zapata. They were billionaire gangsters with no respect for the law and an unquenchable thirst for power.

Don Aldo had a larger-than-life persona; he was a celebrity of sorts. He had won the mayoral election the year prior because of his extreme antics — driving a Rolls Royce through the city's *barrios* while showcasing his wild animals and his supermodel wife. The mainstream media fed on this stuff. His fame grew across all of Mexico as a twisted Robin Hood; it even spread internationally through blog posts and viral videos. People worshipped him for his generosity towards the poor. Every Halloween, Don Aldo would throw the biggest monster-mash that led to a Dia de Los Muertos altar pageant. On Christmas, he would give gifts to the city's children, and on Easter, he would host the anticipated TJ easter-egg hunt, where he gave away flatscreen TVs, Playstations, GoPros, perfumes, and paintball guns. While the daddies drank beer and the mommies pissed away their factory paychecks on slot machines, the kids, and the city of Tijuana, were held captive by Don Aldo and his gifts.

Samuel Bracho's relationship with Don Aldo began when Bracho decided to enter the Tijuana marketplace with his slot-machine lounges. He was met with resistance from the city's only legal casino owner. Don Aldo researched Bracho and couldn't find anything — no arrests, no lawsuits, not even any associates worth mentioning. Don Aldo called his men in Mexico City and they painted an evil picture of Bracho.

"He's heartless. He'll kill a man just to prove a point. He doesn't give a fuck about whatever comes his way," were some of their remarks.

Don Aldo heard stories about the time he blew up a police station in Matamoros.

"Why isn't any of this in the media?" he asked.

"He sends newspapers a lot of money when he does something big. Pays them to not cover it. That's how he maintains his secret persona."

When Don Aldo hung up the phone, he knew he had to meet Bracho. Over the next couple of months, he sent Bracho invitations to his various events.

Samuel Bracho wasn't going to just show up to one of Don Aldo's parties. After months of no reply, Don Aldo did what his father used to do when he wanted to get noticed by someone of status. He sent Samuel Bracho a top-of-the-line bulletproof Mercedes Benz G500 SUV, black exterior with a tan cowhide interior.

"If this doesn't get him to come talk to me, maybe I'll send him my wife," Don Aldo was heard saying.

A week later, Bracho was touring Don Aldo's Ardiente Casino.

Aside from his known business antics, Samuel Bracho led a very private life. He had no real friends, few confidants, and well-paid goons handled his muscle work. But all of that changed when he met Don Aldo.

"What's the point of being a casino magnate if you can't splurge a little," he joked as he showed him the golden lobby and large fountains that trademarked his Ardiente Casino.

Samuel Bracho took a liking to Don Aldo. He saw qualities in him that he hadn't seen in any other person — real charisma and aristocratic power. The two began having lunch weekly. At first, their conversations were just small talk. Bracho liked that Don Aldo was larger-than-life, someone who knew how to spend his money, how to eat well, drink fine wines, and surround himself with gorgeous women. He was strong, funny, and bold. The two were polar opposites, but something drew them to one another.

Don Aldo respected the fact that Bracho was a conservative man, somebody who enjoyed secrecy and had made his own money. He was a vault; nobody could ever get any information out of him. He trusted no one and had that, *I'm not here to make friends* attitude. Don Aldo, however, could sense that Bracho had developed a fondness for him. Bracho would laugh at his jokes and ask questions about his business. He became particularly interested in the dog races at the Ardiente. On Wednesdays, the two of them began watching the dogs from Don Aldo's booth. The races became a bonding activity, as they both had a love for dogs. Bracho had a Doberman named Julio and a Belgian shepherd named Flem. He considered the dogs his only family. Don Aldo, not one to be topped, almost always had a herd of dogs around. The alpha male was a Bouvier des Flanders named Tom Tom.

Even though nobody knew where Samuel Bracho had come from nor the details of his life, he was still haunted by some of the secrets he kept. He had been born in the Mexican state of Durango. His father was a local chieftain who worked as a sheriff, and his mother was only fourteen when he was born. His father never recognized Samuel as his own child, and his mother grew up hating him. She called him *bastardo* and the devil's son. Samuel Bracho was an outcast since his first day. When he was four years old, he learned that his mother had been raped by his father. He considered this his curse, and became an unusually quiet boy. He didn't talk until he was ten. He knew how to, but being the smart boy that he was, he knew nobody wanted to hear him, nobody cared. When he was twelve, his mother caught a bad case of influenza and died on Christmas day.

On New Year's Eve of that year, Samuel Bracho went to 1334 Sierra Merced in Durango City and burned down a two-story house. He incinerated his father, his father's wife Lorena Conde, and their four kids: Laura, Paco, Carlos, and two-year-old Nina. From there, Bracho walked 200 miles to Mazatlán.

Samuel Bracho never married. Throughout his life, he had had intense relationships with several women, and even though he never really loved them, he had tried unsuccessfully to have kids with six of them. When the doctor told him he was sterile, he killed him to protect his reputation as an alpha male. His only soft spots were his dogs and his passion for reading. During his lonely childhood, his only companions were his dogs and books. His favorite subject was history. On his loneliest days, he had convinced himself that he, like Genghis Khan, Ho Chi Min, and Bolivar, had a great destiny ahead. He secretly compared himself with these men. He never told anybody about his love affair with history, so when Don Aldo told him the story about Zhuge Liang waiting for his enemies at the gates of the city by himself, Bracho knew that he had found a friend for life.

It became Don Aldo's goal to make Samuel Bracho feel at home in Tijuana.

"This is the most powerful city in Baja," he would tell him. "It's so close to the United States that you can almost smell it." .

Since he knew Samuel Bracho had a way of moving from city to city, Don Aldo felt it was his job to make him grow roots in Tijuana. Bracho began to enjoy a bit of the cosmopolitan lifestyle. Urban living started to have meaning; for the first time in his life, he was *in*. He liked Tijuana and Don Aldo introduced him to the well-to-do, making him feel accepted, almost like a real member of the community, something he had never felt before.

"You have to remember, this is a city founded by bandits, racketeers, bootleggers, filibusters. This city will clothe you; this city wants you here," Don Aldo told Bracho.

As time progressed, Bracho began going to hip restaurants, attending equestrian events in Tijuana on Saturdays, and bullfights on Sundays.

In 2002, he purchased a 2,500-acre *rancho* in El Porvenir and began keeping horses. By 2003, at fifty years old, he had planted a fifty-acre vineyard on the property. For the first time, he began thinking about retirement.

That same year, when he was hosting a *barbacóa* at his ranch, Don Aldo approached him with a business proposition.

"You know how it is. If people want to make something happen in Tijuana, they talk to me. But this opportunity, this particular one, I need someone like you for a partner," Don Aldo said.

Bracho was intrigued. "What's the deal?"

"Building a tunnel unlike any other. A strategic tunnel into the U.S."

"Tunnel? What are you moving, powder or people?" asked Bracho.

"Oh, we're not moving anything. The business model is to charge people to use the tunnel. I already know all the people, *they* do all the moving," said Don Aldo.

"Like a toll road?" said Bracho.

"Exactly."

The two were shaking hands over Scotch an hour later.

CHAPTER 56

Campo Casino

DON ALDO AND SAMUEL BRACHO built their tunnel about forty minutes east of Tijuana in the town of Tecate. The engineering behind the project was in contention with some of the finest work in the world. Strong Cemex concrete, a railway cart system for transportation of goods, pedestrian services like lighting and air conditioning, and even break rooms with water and provisions.

Stateside, Don Aldo and Bracho became partners with Walker Vigil, the chairman of the Campo Band of Kumeyaay. Even though Campo was technically in the United States, the poverty, the smell of dirt and no running water, the health needs, and the corruption, made it feel more like inland Mexico. This 800-acre parcel was given to the descendants of a people that roamed free and borderless for 10,000 years; now, they were held in the inland Sierra with nothing to drink but alcohol.

Chairman Vigil had left the reservation in his teens and lived with a foster family in San Diego who were very good to him. At twenty-six, when he graduated from Berkeley Law School, he began working for the firm Goodrich, Lobi, and Graham. After being in law for almost twenty years, he had a soul-search that led him back to the reservation. He was upset to see the wretched state in which his people were living and began getting involved in tribal politics. When he was forty-five years old, he became chairman.

During his first three years as chairman, he did a lot to help the people. He helped clothe and feed them, he even brought in teachers to educate the young and guest speakers to inspire them. But he still felt like it wasn't enough and realized he needed money to really change the situation. He went to Washington, DC, to become part of the Council of Tribes. He was disappointed with the bureaucracy and was unable to get help from them. For four days straight, he tried to meet with the Secretary of Indian Affairs, but he kept getting ignored. Vigil made friends with the assistant to the secretary, a nice lady by the name of Meredith. Vigil told her it was his dream to defeat the poverty and the misfortune that befell his tribe. He expressed his wishes to build a casino on the reservation.

"Then we will have the money to host cultural events, have schools, and grant scholarships to my people," he told Meredith.

On the fifth day, she told him that she could arrange a meeting for him with the head of the National Indian Gaming Commission.

Timothy Slang was the head of the commission. The two met for lunch at Washington Astorsia's restaurant. After much politicking and roundabouts, Mr. Slang made it very clear.

"You want a casino? Get me $50 million in cash and we can get you one."

Walker Vigil left Washington disappointed.

A month later, on his 49th birthday, he received a Brown Paso Fino Stallion as a gift. He had never seen such a beautiful horse; he named him Cuco. Three days later, he was meeting with Don Aldo and Samuel Bracho at the Ardiente Casino in Tijuana.

"We understand that your reservation is in need of services," Don Aldo said as Bracho sat next to him, paying close attention.

Even though Vigil hated the way Don Aldo pronounced the word *reservación*, he sat in silence and listened.

"We want to help you, but we need something from you."

Don Aldo asked Vigil about his main concerns for his people; they talked for an hour. When Don Aldo offered Vigil $10 million to let them build a "secret building" underground at Campo, Vigil told the men that what they really needed was a casino on their reservation. The idea of operating a casino in California struck a chord with Bracho and Don Aldo, especially if they could rock the cradle from the shadows.

After weeks of negotiation, Don Aldo and Samuel Bracho partnered up and arranged the delivery of $75 million in cash to Vigil's Campo house. Six months later, Campo Casino had permits and the work began.

"It's much easier to build our port of entry and exit at a place that's well transited and controlled by us. It's almost as if we're laundering the money as soon as it comes in," Bracho said as he looked over the building plans with Don Aldo.

When Campo Casino opened its doors to the public, the tunnel had already been running for a month.

The tunnel became the pride of their work. Every day, new customers came in. People walked in and out of the United States via a casino.

"That's the way it should be," said Bracho, who didn't even have a proper visa. "The United States should be welcoming people through a casino floor, not sending them away."

Samuel Bracho supervised the tunnel. He sealed his lips and held information against all of his clients to keep the operation secret. They had an American player, a "friend" of Don Aldo from Princeton, who was involved high up in customs receiving millions in hush money.

Samuel Bracho's fame and persona kept growing. He became more confident in himself, at ease. He even grew a little careless and showy with his money. But the tunnel became a huge success. People from China and Africa could comfortably smuggle into the U.S. contraband from South America and far away islands. Everything had a price, and by 2005, the tunnel was generating $1 million a day.

The Campo Casino, which was managed by Vigil under the silent partnership with Don Aldo, became a giant entertainment center with a shopping mall, a 27-hole golf course, and a luxury hotel. The *compadres* had hit a home run that solidified their wealth and their standing in the community. In 2006, Don Aldo won the mayorship of Tijuana.

CHAPTER 57

La Máscara Party

THE YEAR THAT DON ALDO became mayor of Tijuana, the United States Consulate in Baja was planning to move out of their historic building near the racetrack into a modern facility. When Don Aldo got ahold of this information, he arranged for the city to donate the parcel of land known as *Pechuga* near the Otay border for the new building.

The Americans built their new facilities to the highest standard in modern safety and technology. The old consulate building was put up for sale through the US State Department. Don Aldo ended up buying the old consulate building for $3.5 million through a phantom company. This was a secret project for him, so he hired California Brainhaus, a San Diego based internet of things inspired design firm to turn the building into the first fully functional smart home in Baja.

He remodeled the building and put in over two million dollars of electric, fiber-optic, and wireless technology. Thirteen months after he had purchased the building from Uncle Sam, he sold it to Bracho.

Bracho paid $7.2 million for the old US consulate in Tijuana. He spent a year renovating it and invested another $5 million in turning the four stories into his personal castle. From the pool on the rooftop, he enjoyed Tijuana Country Club views to one side, and to the other, gorgeous views of Don Aldo's Ardiente Casino. Bracho built his living quarters on the top level, and a residence for his dogs and bodyguards on the third floor. He flew in his business managers and engineers to build him a top-of-the-line business center on the second floor. To finish off his new home, he revived a regional garden and planted a lush lawn that opened up to the first floor indoor/outdoor terrace, where he built a reception hall complete with a dance floor and a large bar to host and entertain.

"What do you need all this open space for?" Don Aldo asked.

"To throw parties!" said Bracho.

"You, throwing parties? Ha!"

"You know, I've never thrown a party in my life, and I've been thinking…"

"Oh how times have changed. I'm proud of you. I'll give you Anuar's number. He's the gay dude who throws the best parties."

Three months after he moved into his consulate house, Bracho threw a masquerade ball. The invitation for the October party was embroidered in gold leaf and referred to the event as *La Máscara Party*.

Axel Cuevas attended that party. "It's the most epic Halloween fiesta I've ever been to," he was heard telling his friends later. Even though Axel wasn't on the party's guest list, he managed to get in because of his date, the reigning Miss North Baja, Angela Margolis. A slender brunette with puffy lips and green eyes, Angela was a graceful queen, elegant as a swan, and absolutely amazing company.

Axel Cuevas had met Angela during a photoshoot for Yatista Magazine aboard the *Zunset*, an eighty-five-foot Italian-made Amer Yacht that Axel was skippering out of Ensenada at the time. The yacht belonged to the Emerson Yacht Company, an international brokerage and charter service that held interests in the seven seas. While the yacht was in Ensenada, Axel, who worked full time for Emerson and only had to report once a month to Swiss headquarters, did whatever he wanted aboard. He threw parties, hosted poker nights, produced wet T-shirt contests, and was part of photoshoots. He even allowed Scorpion Dan, a narco-folk singer, to shoot his music video aboard the *Zunset*. He was part of all of this because he had one main goal: getting girls. He was a player with no scruples. He'd promise girls eternal love, wealth, and glamour just to get into their pants for one night.

Growing up, Axel Cuevas wasn't necessarily the black sheep of his family; he was simply two steps behind his cousin Julian Mayorca. The golden boy, who had lost his parents but had inherited well. Axel never knew exactly how much money Aunt Cecilia and Uncle Oliver had left Julian, but he knew it was plenty; he had overheard his own parents talking about it several times over the years. Through their teens, his cousin Julian had plenty of swagger and people looked up to him; everybody considered him a standup guy. He kept steady girlfriends and carried himself with natural ease. Axel, on the other hand, had been awkward and less sure of himself and his abilities. He was only two years younger than Julian, but it might as well have been a decade. Even though his parents never said it, he felt pressure to be more like his cousin. When Julian took up sailing, Axel picked it up, and by the time Julian began skippering his Winkle Brig, he would invite Axel to first mate. If they anchored out overnight, Julian would take time and teach Axel about knots, currents, and the stars. When Julian went into the Mexican Naval Academy, the only thing Axel wanted to do was to be a sailor like his cousin, but when he got into the Academy, Julian didn't have time for him. It wasn't that he didn't care, but he was so focused on getting to the top that he disregarded his cousin. Even though Axel and his family had always helped Julian out, he never felt like he owed them anything, and because of the grief and trauma associated with the loss of his parents, Julian became cold and indifferent, especially during those years.

Axel resented this, and something changed inside of him slowly; hate brewed. Throughout the years, Axel's mind got warped, and he became obsessed with being better than Julian. Axel worked out more, went out more, socialized, tried to make more and richer friends and be liked by all. He figured that if he was more popular, that if he got more girls than his cousin, he would be better than Julian Mayorca. Axel wasn't like one of those guys in Baja whose dream in life is to become a gangster or a narco; his intro into the underworld came because he went to a party.

The day before *La Máscara Party*, Axel had called his mother. During their talk, she told him that his cousin Julian was excelling as port captain, and because of that, he was running for president of the Baja California Port Captains Association. After Axel hung up the call, he invited Angela, Miss North Baja, over for dinner aboard the *Zunset*.

"What are you doing tomorrow?" he asked her.

"Well, I got invited to this really cool party. It's at the old US consulate in Tijuana. Apparently, it's somebody's mansion now. It's masquerade themed," she said.

"Damn, I want to go," said Axel.

"They're being really strict with the guest list," said Angela.

"Oh, so it's like that," said Axel.

"Don't look at me like that. I'm taking one of my girlfriends," she said.

"Look, I understand that you want to go alone with your girlfriends and look hot. You don't want one guy sticking to you, even though that guy is me," he said.

"You really are that careless. I'd heard stories about you, Axel Cuevas," Angela said with a playful tone.

"Well, let's be real, we both know that we can get some of *this* whenever we want," said Axel as he squeezed her bubble butt.

"You really are a man-hoe," she play-slapped him.

He smiled as he kissed her and seduced her into being her +1 for the next day's party.

La Máscara was one of those parties that people talk about their whole lives. Axel drove his older BMW convertible. There was no parking for blocks, so he and Angela ended up parking by the Ardiente fountain and had to walk on the Boulevard. The façade of the building had that imposing diplomatic feel to it, while still being the fortress it had once been under the Americans. The place stood high and a multitude of people outside its gates begged to get in. It was almost like a demonstration; word had gotten out and everybody in Baja wanted to come to the party. People were wearing Venetian masks, Katrina skeleton paint, and some wore Mexican wrestling masks with silver suits or tuxedos.

Axel and Angela snaked through the masses and reached the front gate. The doorman was a large brown man who recognized Angela and told her that her friends were already inside. The first floor was a portal into a different era. It had a style that was stolen from a 1980s Manchester club, but topped off with Mexican artwork. "Serious" by Donna Allen was playing as Axel led Angela through the dance floor. She let go of his hand, so he reached back and kissed her on the cheek.

"Do your thing, girl. I'll see you around."

She laughed. "Have fun, hottie."

Axel walked straight to the bar.

"What you got?" he asked, almost comically.

"The specialty drink for tonight is the Miami," answered the bartender.

"A what?"

"Grey Goose poured over rocks with Perrier, topped with a freshly squeezed orange."

"Nice, that sounds delicious," said Axel.

"It is." The bartender mixed one up for him.

Gorgeous women wearing masks were everywhere. Some had loose short dresses on, others long red ones, some had big hair and little masks, others huge masks and little hair. The party was beginning to heat up as the people let loose and the DJ took the music upbeat with heavier sounds. Axel was wearing a skinny tux with a small navy blue mask that made his best feature, his blue eyes, stand out. He was feeling confident as he approached a firecracker brunette with hips that swayed to the sounds of electro-jazz. Axel came up behind her and began moving with her. She turned around and faced him. She began dancing aggressively at him. They moved to the swing of the music, they drank, and she smoked a cigarette as they chatted outside in the garden. She said that her name was Mariana. Axel introduced himself as "Axe."

"Hey, I heard that there's a VIP area up there," said Mariana as she pointed to the rooftop terrace.

Axel held her hand as they ran up flights of stairs and through dim hallways. Coming into the third floor, Axel spotted a security guard on the opposite side of the hall. He pulled Mariana into a corner, and put his face in front of hers. She kissed him. They quietly laughed and kissed some more as Axel grabbed her firm ass. When they heard the guard take a phone call, they ran out and up the stairs, making it onto the fourth floor, where a smaller crowd was gathered. As they entered the light-blue-lit open space, with artwork by Lucero Acero hanging from the walls and ceiling, Axel spoke into her ear over the bass rhythm and soft salsa beats.

"What's the meaning of VIP?" he whispered.

"Very Important People," answered Mariana.

"No, wrong. Very Impressive *Pussy*." He puckered up and kissed her forehead with a loud *ppppua*.

He smiled, let go of Mariana's hand, and walked to the opposite end of the bar.

He ordered another Miami and noticed a group of well-dressed guys chatting on the terrace. He approached them and asked if they could spare a cigarette. As he smoked one, he made his way into their conversation. "What do you do?" asked one of the men.

"I'm a yacht captain for the Emerson Company," he replied. "I charter an eighty footer out of Ensenada."

The moment he mentioned the word "yacht," the look on the men's faces changed. They introduced themselves as Charlie, Horacio, Irving, and Karlo. The five let loose, chatting about everything from movies to girls. They humble-bragged about vacations they had recently taken or restaurants they had tried. Five Miamis later, Axel was alone talking to Horacio, a well-dressed investment banker.

"You know whose place this is, right?" asked Horacio.

"Yeah, it's the old US consulate," answered Axel.

"Yeah, but you know who owns it now, right?"

"Who? Don Aldo?" said Axel.

"No, Don Aldo sold it to Samuel Bracho," said Horacio.

"Who's Samuel Bracho?" asked Axel

"The most important man in the underworld," said Horacio.

"Well, does Mr. Bracho like yachts?" said Axel.

They laughed, cheered, and drank some more.

Horacio asked Axel to follow him to the north corner of the terrace. There, a geodesic sphere-like surface bubbled out of the fourth floor onto the terrace. To one side, it was surrounded by tall planted pines, but to the other, it had a complete sky and side view to the city. It was like an observatory.

"They call this the Igloo, but I call it the planetarium," said Horacio as they went through the small stairs and past the guard.

"I come here with the boss all the time," he said as they entered the igloo.

It was the most amazing office Axel had ever seen: Thick plexiglass with an octagon bubble structure that overlooked a digital center below, filled with incredible artwork and high end technology.

"From here, the boss controls all of his businesses, practically his whole operation," said Horacio with a drunken swagger.

Axel took it all in.

"Loose lips sink ships, Mr. H," a thick voice was heard from every-where.

The hairs on Axel's neck stood up as he watched Horacio's face turn from brown to pale to white.

"M... M, M... Mr. Bracho," Horacio stammered.

Samuel Bracho sat comfortably in the large leather chair behind his desk. His pants were down, and there was a skinny blonde girl sucking his penis.

"I've asked Clara not to stop. I hope this doesn't make you uncom-fortable, H, since, I mean, you just stroll into my private chambers whenever you want."

"Sir, I'm so sorry... but... but, you said that I could come in when-ever," said Horacio.

"Are you whining? Jesus, H, the last thing I want to hear while I'm cumming is your whining, fuck."

"I'm sorry, sir,"

"Shut the hell up, I'm almost done," said Bracho.

He finished. Clara swallowed and licked his penis sperm-clean. Samuel Bracho smiled and pointed at Horacio.

"You know what, you should get a blowjob."

He pointed at Clara, who nodded.

"Oh, that's okay, Boss. I don't want a blowjob," answered Horatio.

"You don't want a blowjob? What kind of man doesn't want a blow-job?" said Bracho in disbelief.

As Bracho stood up to buckle his pants, Clara, with her delicious high-pitched voice said: "I could give *him* a blowjob."

Bracho and Horacio turned their heads to Axel.

"*You* want a blowjob?" asked Bracho.

"I… *sure*," said Axel.

"Get a blowjob, come, sit in my chair. She's great," said Bracho.

He put his pants down and let Clara suck his penis.

Bracho went over to Horacio and pulled a cigar out of his pocket. He lit it as he turned on a ventilation system that cooled down the room.

"Don't lose your hard-on because of a little breeze," he said as he and Horatio laughed.

"With a mouth like that, I couldn't lose my hard-on if I was sitting on a glacier in the goddamn Artic. You were right, Boss. She is good," said Axel.

Everybody laughed as Clara sucked Axel, who sipped on a Miami and sat in a billionaire's chair overlooking city lights.

CHAPTER 58

I Would Buy a Yacht

EVER SINCE THAT BLOWJOB, BRACHO took a liking to Axel. He would often invite him over for lunch and Axel would end up staying for two or three days in his mansion. They would party, drink, but mostly what guided them was their pursuit of female genitalia. That year, between the two of them, they slept with over 300 women. This led to a bond so strong that even Bracho would pun:

"It's like we've had sex, but have never touched each other. We're milk brothers."

They were a tag team; they shared girls and worked them into various cycles, their main rule being: in by Friday, out by Tuesday. Sometimes Bracho would shag them first, sometimes Axel, it didn't matter. They talked about it openly. Bracho was into orgies, but Axel didn't even like threesomes.

"I'm old school, Boss," Axel told Bracho one day after having gone through a cycle of six girls over three days.

"Don't get me wrong, I mean, I can fuck three women in one day. I just like to take my time with each one; I like to give them all my love."

"Oh, Axel, when are you going to understand that love is exponential," said Bracho with a grin on his face and a drink in his hand. "We've got a good thing going here. You're my lucky charm."

"I'll drink to that," said Axel.

"I'm serious. You keep bringing me girls — girls like these — and I will open up a new world for you. What do you say to that?"

"You've got yourself a deal."

They hugged.

What Samuel Bracho liked about Axel Cuevas was his taste in girls and sense of humor. Axel not only had taste, he had skill. He knew how to pick up women that most men would be scared to death to talk to. He didn't pick up the usual riff-raff or party-girls. Axel went after cherries. Good girls from well-to-do families, girls who were members of the Campestre Country Club, the Britannia Racquet Club, or the Porvenir Hippicus Club. Girls who had attended American or Catholic schools. The ladies they went after *did* have a certain profile — usually in their twenties and thirties, but sometimes up to their late forties. They had never really worked or had responsibilities. Rich girls who mostly had allowances set by their daddies, mommies, husbands, or foreign trusts. Some of them were very wealthy, others not as much. It didn't matter if they had money, it only mattered if they were hot and had class.

"You see, I grew up with these girls, I can spot them, and honestly, these girls, I'd put them up against any of the hottest girls in the world," said Axel

"Well, you can't beat a soft ass that smells good," chuckled Bracho.

Since Axel was still officially working for the Emerson Company, one of their favorite double-date locations became the *Zunset*, which was docked at the Marina Coral in Ensenada. Bracho had never been on a yacht before the *Zunset*, and ever since the first time they took her out, he was hooked. He began to grow sea legs, he learned to enjoy and partake in the life aboard. Axel got Samuel to charter the yacht for three months and it was at his disposal 24/7.

After the three months, they had taken the *Zunset* all the way south, around the tip of Baja, back to the gulf, and were docked in San Felipe. By then, as expected, Samuel Bracho had become completely enamored with the Sea of Cortez.

"Wow, I had no idea this much beauty existed," he said one night.

Axel continued serving Bracho in many ways. Other than his wingman, yacht captain, and friend, he became his confidant, someone whom he trusted. One day, after they had returned to Tijuana, Axel was hanging out at the Igloo at Bracho's house when the boss received a payment of $30 million in cash. Since he was just sitting there, Bracho put Axel to work.

"Hey, start counting, buddy, you want to eat off the fat of the land? Start counting!" he told him.

Days later, when they were $18.2 million deep in hundred dollar bills, the twenty dollar bills came. After they had made sure that not a dollar was missing, Axel asked where the money came from.

"It's for some gold I mined and sold to the Acapulco Family," he told him.

"What are you going to do with this much cash?" asked Axel.

"Well, to be honest, all this paper is a pain in the ass. I'd rather do transfers. But these guys, well, let's just be happy they paid me with cash and not with lead," said Bracho.

"Well, if it's too much hassle, I'll take some cash off your hands," said Axel as they began stacking the money into a room-size safe.

"Oh yeah, and what would you do with it?"

"*Me*? I would buy a yacht," said Axel.

CHAPTER 59

"Argentine Diplomats"

Axel Cuevas' lifelong dream was to own a yacht. So when Bracho asked to help him buy one, he quit his job with Emerson Yachting Company, turned in the *Zunset*, and began working for Bracho's enterprise full-time.

"I don't want a small yacht, I want a big yacht, with a helicopter and everything," he said.

"Yeah, but those yachts cost $100 million, easy," said Axel.

"I don't care. Don't you want to skipper a real yacht? Or do you want to continue with your play-things?" said Bracho in his usual strong, yet joking, voice.

"Well, we're gonna have to travel to find it," said Axel, almost emulating his boss.

He learned a lot by observing Samuel Bracho, a mastermind businessman who looked after his affairs daily. He had computers running data all of the time, always up to date on the good and, especially, the bad news. He had screens showing his deposits and withdrawals, his profits and losses. He had operations with people all over the world, moving his money, and he, himself, smooth, in Tijuana. Bracho worked out of his office by himself—just his phone and his army of money. Axel considered himself lucky for being in his office alone with him often.

"I've got to stay here in my war room," said Bracho one afternoon. "You go..."

"What do you mean?" said Axel.

"Go find the best yacht for me."

The great commission fell upon him.

Axel personally shopped for Bracho's yacht. He went to Newport, Miami, Dubai, even Croatia. In the end, he bought a 220-foot yacht from Germanwork Shipyard, outside Hamburg. The yacht had been built by order of Prince Omar El-Kettana from Qatar, who put a $30 million down payment on the yacht, but when it was time to pay the remaining $100 million, he backed out. The shipyard sold the masterpiece that now included a black and white Airbus H155 helicopter and a custom-built helipad for $165 million. The yacht was completely designed by Guffen Haus to be the centerpiece of European magazines and the dream of American TV shows. A black and white motif blended seamlessly through the interior of the vessel in a rhythm, not unlike piano keys and curves. With eight staterooms, a saltwater pool astern, and all of the toys to guarantee greatness, the ship was a captain's delight.

Working for Bracho, purchasing a yacht, traveling well, managing the remodeling jobs for the yacht, and being connected began to change Axel. It wasn't that he was different, but he started to behave and act more refined, more calculating, more mature.

At first, it surprised him how well he could manage these affairs; then, he became sure of himself, like a man who finally sees his path in life. Axel Cuevas planned his career around Samuel Bracho. It was in St. Pauli, in Hamburg, a morning after partying all night with German girls, that he had what the Germans call a *tagtraum* or daydream about Samuel Bracho and *their* own relationship. He envisioned himself as a player in a perverse board game designed by his boss. With this, he realized that if he played the game well enough, he could have the life he desired.

The first rule of business that Samuel Bracho gave Axel Cuevas was privacy.

"Everything I do, I do in private, 'let not one hand know what the other is doing.'"

Axel handled everything regarding the yacht with tight lips. On the one hand, it was hard for him to not brag, and stay quiet. But, on the other hand, it was easy, because everyone treated him as the yacht owner. Axel got invited to dinners and parties, and he, being Mexican, was considered exotic, and became the life of the parties he was invited to. Axel was sharper than ever, more acute, more savvy. He used all of his time making contacts, gaining access to the world's elite, experiencing how they lived, how they spent money, how they partied.

When asked about the yacht, Axel would say he was the yacht captain and the business manager of the group responsible for making the purchase, but because he had that millionaire air to him, nobody believed him. Maybe it was because of the smirk on his face as he said it, or the way that he carried himself with security and gusto, like one might imagine a gunslinging wrangler dressed in fine clothes. When they delivered the yacht, Samuel Bracho flew to Europe and partook in the christening ceremony.

Six months later, the yacht, named *Durango,* was delivered in Cabo San Lucas under a Liberian single star flag. Nobody knew who the owner was, but it was operated by a Mexican *agencia* by the name of Baja Costas. Julian Mayorca, who was president of the Baja California Port Captains Association, received a call from Senator Rafael Mosto. The senator asked Julian for a personal favor; he asked him to give *The Durango* a letter where he excused them of all formalities throughout their stay in the Baja California Peninsula. When Julian asked who was aboard, the senator said, "Argentine diplomats. They have black passports anyway. The letter would simply help inform the locals of their status."

Julian, who believed in the economy of favors, agreed and signed off on *The Durango's* paperwork for the senator. He didn't even ask who was skippering the yacht; if he had, he would've realized that his cousin, Axel Cuevas, was in over his head.

That spring, *The Durango* set sail up the Sea of Cortez.

CHAPTER 60

"Baja Libre"

WORKING FOR BRACHO REQUIRED STRATEGY, patience, and a lot of left hand. Axel Cuevas became an expert at handling information and management for Bracho. He understood that his boss' life didn't revolve around *The Durango*, but for Axel, the yacht became his obsession.

"I don't really think the boss understands, this is one of the nicest yachts in the world," he told his first mate one morning.

In reality, the size and scope of the yacht frightened Axel. It was a saltwater behemoth; it needed a staff of thirty people just for it to function properly. Even though Axel didn't have the skills to captain such a yacht, he hired well and never showed his shortcomings. He compensated with authority and everybody considered him a tough captain. Even his crew didn't get a chance to judge his sea skills, because he didn't have to move the yacht much, since the Boss had ordered it to be anchored behind Isla Encantada indefinitely.

Samuel Bracho seemed to have a plan for *The Durango*, but kept it to himself. What actually became Bracho's obsession was his helicopter. He loved being in the air. The freedom and thrill of going over everybody and everything was a perfect combination for him. The helicopter pilot was Augusto Reyes, a retired Mexican Air Force colonel who had been recommended to him by Don Aldo. At that time, Bracho had commenced drilling on Isla Encantada for what appeared to be copper. The yacht was basically high-end lodging that Bracho used for himself, his acquaintances, and escorts when he visited the mine.

Bracho would fly his helicopter from *The Durango* to his Porvenir Ranch, where his bulletproof Mercedes G wagon was waiting to take him to his fortress in Tijuana. The yacht became a statement of will for Samuel Bracho; he took Don Aldo there one weekend. They had some girls, but they mostly talked about business. While aboard, Don Aldo told Bracho that he had the intention of becoming governor of North Baja California. For Don Aldo, being governor was something he had coveted since he first moved to Tijuana, 30 years earlier. Under the influence of the wines and the time spent aboard the yacht, Don Aldo asked Bracho for a favor. He asked if he could bring a group of people who called themselves the "The Baja Libre Association" aboard his yacht.

"They're a group of political operators. Not rich, but radical. And they are cooking something big," said Don Aldo.

Two weeks later, six people were invited aboard *The Durango*. Samuel Bracho asked everybody to meet at Porvenir Ranch at noon, from there, he arranged for his helicopter to fly them out to the yacht. The guests arrived aboard the Durango to a cool breeze and a cloudy day. Nevertheless, the calm of the sea and the beauty of the yacht captivated them. For dinner, Axel hired Luis Lozano, one of the best chefs from Ensenada, to cater to them. They drank Fragmentos white wine and Vino de la Reina red.

Samuel Bracho didn't really know what this Baja Libre Association was all about. The guys were so serious; they walked around and acted with certain airs that bothered Bracho.

"They don't belong on a yacht like this; they look like communists," Bracho told Axel Cuevas.

"They must've not gotten the memo that says: *no denim on yachts*," said Axel.

When it was time for dinner, Don Aldo said a few words thanking everybody. When he was finished, a fair-skinned twenty-eight-year-old named Geronimo Hernandez responded.

"Don Aldo, it is us that must thank you. You know what our association stands for. And although we are many different individuals, with many different beliefs, at our core, we are united by an ideal, a revolutionary ideal, that you, yourself agree with: the independence of the Baja California peninsula from Mexico. I mean, it only makes sense. For too long, our peninsula has suffered at the hands of these Mexico City folk. They take our wealth and give us rotten crumbs in return. We are fed up. We want our own republic, one that stands up to the corrupt Mexican ways, one that actually cares about its citizens, and one that grows sustainably and guarantees if not success, then the ability to better develop ourselves as human beings. We are tired of them taking possibilities from us. Everything that the Mexican government has done throughout its history has been to take, take, and take from Baja California, leaving us with nothing but a weak currency, crumbling infrastructure, and poverty that shouldn't exist in a land as abundant as ours. Yes, we are tired, but we are many."

Everybody clapped and continued their five-course meal.

The guests spent the evening discussing politics and smoking tobacco on the lower deck. Don Aldo sat quietly listening to the men, while Samuel Bracho and Axel Cuevas observed from above. Geronimo wouldn't really let anybody else speak, and even though he was the youngest member of the group, everybody respected him.

"Look at this kid, everybody treats him like he's a messiah," said Bracho to Axel. "Did you hear what he said?"

"Yeah, that they want to separate Baja from the rest of Mexico," answered Axel.

"Forget it, I'd have to be a fool to get involved with something as big and stupid," Bracho said.

"I mean, in principle, it makes sense, but how would you execute it? You'd need an army," said Axel.

"Let me tell you something: these kids, they just want to replace the old with the new, and if they get their way, they'll be just as bad as or worse than the current politicians," said Bracho. "But, I wonder why my *compadre* is getting in bed with these guys?" They sat and listened to the conversation below.

"So, how many people do you have in your association?" asked Don Aldo.

"Over 50,000 registered members. Not only have we worked hard to get those members, but we have worked in secret, having managed to not gain the attention of Mexican intelligence. We use secret lines of communication and operate in complete shadows. Some of our key members have backgrounds in covert ops, and we have already infiltrated every local government in both states of Baja. We are ready to strike at any moment," Geronimo said.

"That's great, but why don't you hold off on your independence?" said Don Aldo. "It's easy to talk about strategy, but none of you are mentioning the obvious; the fact that the Mexican government will fight this with firepower and blood." Don Aldo took a sip of water and cleared his throat. "War doesn't scare me, wrong strategy does. So, I brought you here today because I see your power, I feel your numbers, and I am in a position to make something happen for you guys. As you know, there will be elections this summer, and I have been summoned by my party to run for governor of North Baja. I haven't accepted the candidacy because, you see, I like pursuing things that are certain. So, I brought you here today because I would like to propose something that can benefit us both."

"A new country! That would benefit us both," interrupted Geronimo.

The men laughed.

"Yes, well, I'm thinking about a paved way there. One that doesn't involve so much bloodshed," said Don Aldo.

"Well, what do you suggest?" Geronimo asked.

"Let me use your infrastructure. Help me mobilize those 50,000 people so I can win the gubernatorial race and I will help your cause by beginning the process of independence from the inside.".

The discussion between Don Aldo and Geronimo went on for hours.

Even though there were six other people there, nobody talked to Don Aldo except Geronimo. It was like they were all subordinate to him. Samuel Bracho and Axel Cuevas would pop in and out of the room.

"How do you plan to sink the ship you're going to be skippering?" asked Geronimo

"The ship of government can be sailed to shore; it doesn't need to sink. There are measures that we can take. We solidify our economic independence from Mexico City, we lower taxes, increase tourism, orchestrate certain crises, accentuate others," said Don Aldo.

At a quarter past midnight, Geronimo and his people pledged their support for Don Aldo, who guaranteed Baja Libre 150 government jobs that Geronimo could handpick.

"We will mobilize our apparatus for you," Geronimo said as he shook hands with Don Aldo.

The next morning before they flew out, Geronimo went up to the bridge and personally thanked Samuel Bracho and Axel Cuevas for hosting them.

CHAPTER 61

Continuum

That summer, Don Aldo Ruiz won the North Baja gubernatorial election by under 30,000 votes. In South Baja, Julian Mayorca had been port captain for five years. The day that Don Aldo took office in Mexicali, Julian acquired *La Capitana* for official port captain duties in La Paz. They were at opposite ends of the peninsula having the best day of their lives. On Julian's end, *La Capitana* was a beautiful yacht; on Don Aldo's, the ship of government began its sail with a new captain. Life was in balance.

In the shadows of the new governor, Samuel Bracho was growing the cult of his persona. After all, he was Don Aldo's *compadre*. His captain, Axel Cuevas, had been asked to take the yacht down to San Basilio Cove. Once there, Bracho threw a party that Don Aldo didn't attend. He tried not to make a big deal of it, but when he tried reaching his *compadre*, he was unable. When Bracho got back to Tijuana, Don Aldo's secretary reached him and notified him that his *compadre*, the governor, wanted to see him the following morning at a clandestine ranch in Cantamar.

When Bracho got to the meeting, Don Aldo laid out some newspapers where they had made the front pages together. In the most recent one, there was a photo of them wearing tuxedos at a reception. *Gazeta* printed an article titled "Compadres" in which it described the relationship between Don Aldo and Samuel Bracho and even suggested their ownership of the Campo Casino.

"You gotta be careful; they can't pin us together," said Don Aldo.

"Who wrote this?" asked Bracho.

"He calls himself Pablo Heraldo. It's a pen name. I've done some research and nobody knows exactly who he is. See, I've got people inside this organization. My government has spent millions on advertising our programs and our image in this paper. But even after all of the money I've spent, I still can't find out who this Pablo is," said Don Aldo.

"Well, we need to go shake down these *Gazeta* fools and find answers," said Bracho.

"Out of the question. I cannot have them implicating me in violence, especially after an article that denounces me. It's going to seem like retaliation," said Don Aldo.

"Well, that's exactly what we want it to seem like so they don't mess with us anymore," said Bracho.

"What's the matter with you? How did you become so rich if you're so dumb? Have you lost your edge?" asked Don Aldo.

That first sign of disrespect and Bracho was heated.

"Don't you get it? We can't play at that level, not now!" continued Don Aldo.

"Sounds good *compadre*." Bracho's right eye began to twitch.

That whole night he tried to get his emotions in check. *Insulted by Don Aldo.* He tried to convince himself that it meant nothing, that it was best to let it go. But, no, that old devil from the Sierra was still inside him. Three days later, the *Gazeta* building was burned to the ground.

The burning of the *Gazeta* building took the lives of three employees: Margarita, a staff writer for the society pages; Raquel the cleaning lady; and Alfonso, the head of marketing. Arturo Mehling, writing as Pablo Heraldo, continued his investigation into Samuel Bracho until he got the attention of the Mexican president. Thirty days after the newspaper headquarters burned down, Bracho got a call from Don Aldo.

"I know what we need to do. We're finally putting this Gazeta thing behind us. Come meet me at my office in Mexicali tomorrow at 9 a.m.," said Don Aldo. "And, Sam, drive, don't fly. We don't need the extra attention."

"You got it, *compadre*," said Bracho.

Bracho asked his driver and one bodyguard to accompany him to the North Baja capital. The Mercedes Benz G500 drove east from Tijuana past Tecate and into the Rumorosa. The winding downhill highway covered with boulders was a spectacular vision over the sunrise. As Rafael, the driver, took an elongated left turn, they realized that the valley wasn't a clear space like it normally was. It was filled with over 400 men in uniform, their cars, trucks, and even a tank. The Mexican Army, Federales, state police, municipal police, customs, Red Cross, and even members of Interpol. The G500 came to a halt. A staredown of one facing hundreds, all of the government guns pointed at the Mercedes Benz, the silence made stronger by the winds of the salty plains.

Rafael, the driver, looked over. "What do we do, boss?"

"Just hold steady," said Bracho.

"I'm ready to die right here, sir. It's been a good run," said Sumo, his bodyguard in the backseat, as he pulled out his .45 Winchester Magnum.

"Good boy," said Bracho as his phone rang.

It was Don Aldo.

Bracho, with the tension of a man who doesn't want to make any sudden movements, asked Rafael to put the call on speaker. The driver pressed a button on the steering wheel.

"*Compadre*, I'm a little caught up, right now. I can't see very well past the third row of Federales, but I do believe their cars say 'State Police.' I wonder why that is. Aren't you governor? Doesn't that make you head of the state police?" asked Bracho.

"*Compadre*, I'm sorry to do this to you, but there was no other way. The order came straight from the president of Mexico. I mean, the guy personally sent men for you," said Don Aldo over the car speakers.

"Oh yeah?" Bracho asked casually. "What do they got on me?"

"Everything, but they want to put you up for a big one. They are saying you will be charged with terrorism."

"Terra... *what*? Do I smell like an Arab to you? Fuck that."

"Samuel, I told you, don't retaliate, don't do it. And what did you do? You burned down a goddamn building. This isn't the old times, we can't play that loud anymore."

"What was I supposed to do? Not care? That's not my style. Unlike you, daddy didn't give me a head start. I made my first *peso* the hard way."

"All you had to do was listen to me. Anyway, this is where we're at. Do the right thing. If you just turn yourself in, I promise you, I will get you out in three years," said Don Aldo.

"Yea, right, just like you are handing it to me now, *compadre*. I should've known better," Bracho said. He reached over and hung up the phone.

"Ralf, flip this bitch. Sumo, don't start shooting! Wait until you absolutely have to!"

Ralf made a U-turn, and the Federales streamlined after them.

The problem with trying to escape from the police on that particular day was that they were not only ready for them, they were craving action, wishing for it. The Federales caught up and flanked them on each side. Sumo lowered his window, the six inches the level-three bullet-proof glass allowed him to, and began shooting at the blue Federale Interceptor. He emptied a whole magazine into the cruiser and ended up killing an officer.

After that, the two remaining Federales backed away, and the G500 kept driving up the winding road. After less than three minutes of silence, Bracho and his men heard the helicopter above them. In a matter of seconds, Bracho heard two large thumps and looked over to his driver, who had lost consciousness, blood flowed down his face. The problem with bulletproof cars is that they hardly ever have bulletproof roofs. Bullets killed his two men. The car lost control and crashed into a boulder. When Bracho regained consciousness, he was in the custody of the Mexican Army.

The *Gazeta* covered the story as a success, praising the government and their allies for their tough stance against terror. Even though the army had killed Rafael the driver, Sumo the bodyguard, and Bracho's men had killed at least one Federale, the article said that Samuel Bracho had surrendered peacefully and that he was being transported to a maximum security prison.

CHAPTER 62

La Rumba

Two weeks after Bracho's arrest, when everybody who worked for him still didn't know what to do, Axel Cuevas got a phone call.

"Sons of bitches. They think they can take me out? Kill two of my men? They don't know who they're dealing with." It was Bracho. "We need to go strong against them."

"Where you at, boss?" asked Axel.

"I'm at Tres Marias Island. It's shit out here. This prison's crazy. There are pythons and killer bugs. Hey, at least it's better than Almoloya; at least I'm not in a bloody hole for twenty-three hours a day. But, listen, I don't have time for chit-chat. I've put together a deal to get out of here. These guys play dirty, but it's all I've got right now," said Bracho. "I need you to take The Durango past Manzanillo. When you reach the Michoacan Coast, a man by the name of Ronaldo will call you. I want you to do as he says. We're trading the yacht for my freedom," he said before the call cut off.

For two days, Axel Cuevas waited for another call or message from Bracho. On the third day, he decided to embark on the journey towards Michoacan. The crew aboard The Durango were anxious. The staff had revolved nonstop for years. They had a yacht on their hands that deserved to be handled by an admiral; instead, they had an unqualified lot—people hired through friends of friends. Although some were experienced seamen, a handful hadn't even worked aboard a *panga* before coming on board the megayacht. The first mate was Nato Alvarez, a

289

twenty-two-year-old virgin straight out of the academy. It wasn't that they were a bad crew; they were simply an odd crew that didn't fit well together.

Even during downtime, Axel never took time to form relationships with any of them. He spent his whole time bossing them around. He would give orders to whoever was around. If it was the first mate, he'd have him check the engine room for strange sounds, or if it was a deck-hand, he'd get him to polish the already shiny rails. Nobody liked being near Axel, and even though they had been together for years, they didn't really get along. Axel had unknowingly created a horrible work culture filled with his own mistakes and resentment from the crew. Nevertheless, good pay kept them loyal and aboard.

The voyage towards Manzanillo was smooth. Axel was lucky with the weather, which gave the false impression he was a good captain. He had even convinced himself that he could skipper the yacht to the end of the world. Who could blame him? The Durango gave everyone the impression that she could captain herself.

When they spotted Manzanillo Bay, they steered clear and continued navigating southeast through the night. The next day, they pulled closer to the coast and discovered a lush paradise, a thick jungle that weighed heavily on the eyes and on the soul.

Michoacan had a vibe to it, a strange sensation that emanated from its coasts. Turns out, the vibe that was felt by Axel and his crew off the Michoacan Coast was a vibe the local people call *la rumba* — a complex feeling, one that poets and mystics identify as the spiritual weight of having ancient ancestors guard the land with fire and blood. A land-casting of sorts. The winds that rolled off the coast felt heavy because Michoacan is protected by curses. It's a place that at one point had thriving kingdoms that were later swallowed by the jungle, a place so filled with bloodlust and magic that entire towns, people, and even forty-three students are still missing.

Axel decided to anchor the yacht in a small bay called Pariente. There was a humid breeze that evening, and something came over him.

He told his crew they were going to barbecue on the yacht terrace. Everybody was surprised, from Danny, the chef, to Humberto, the deckhand. The crew pulled together their efforts and threw a nice party.

Even though Axel felt tired, he was happy and relieved that they had made it to Michoacan. Danny cooked the steaks they had in the freezer. Lola, the yacht stewart, put on hit tunes; they were all grooving in the magic of the night. Axel felt like a real leader, somebody who, in times of adversity, had accomplished a feat, skippering this magnificent yacht.

He gave a toast and thanked them all, assuring them that this was a new stage in their lives as sailors. That night, Axel started making out with Lola on the stern. She was a brunette with freckles, a perfect little butt, and toned legs. Axel took her back to his quarters, and once there, she undressed him.

When Axel put a condom on, Lola looked back with snakey eyes of lust.

Axel chuckled and brought out some coconut oil.

That night, Axel let Lola sleep in his bed. At 03:33, he got up, put on his shorts, and went to the galley for a glass of water. When he returned to his stateroom, his phone was vibrating on the nightstand. Even though it was a private number, something about the way the phone hummed made him answer.

"Listen, the Michoacanos just called me. They are coming for you guys." It was Bracho.

"What?" said Axel in a tone that mixed disbelief with desperation.

"Look out to sea."

Axel went up to the deck and spotted two small lights coming towards him.

"Yeah, two boats coming my way," he said.

"Axel, listen to me. You've got to get rid of those guys."

"Let me wake the crew up; we'll fight them off."

"You're not listening to me! I need to get rid of the crew! They know too much!"

Axel grasped what that implied.

"The Michoacanos and I have a deal. I'm only calling *you* because you're my bro and I need you. So, right now, don't think just listen to me. Lower the tender and get outta there! Quick!"

Axel put on the only T-shirt he could find, grabbed his wallet, put on his Tag Heuer watch, and lowered the tender. When he was about to jump ship, he felt the lights getting close and for a split-second he second-guessed Bracho.

I can't let these people die, he thought. *I'm their captain!*

A warm breeze came from the coast. *The Durango* started rocking. The sea became choppier and the tender began pulling away from him. Axel stood there in desperation, holding the small boat with only a rope. He felt chills go up his spine as he jumped ship, turned on the tender, and sped away to sea.

CHAPTER 63

Bisonte

THIRTY MINUTES AFTER HE HAD abandoned his crew, Axel Cuevas's heart was still pumping with adrenaline. His mind was a collage—things, actions, and memories kept flaring up. He remembered Lola, the yacht steward with whom he'd had passionate sex just hours before. His memory of her legs, her scent, her passion for life and adventure met with a disturbing image of savage mercenaries jumping aboard *The Durango* and slaying her in cold blood.

Had they killed her right there in bed? Or had the mercenaries lined everybody up pirate-style and executed them one by one?

He thought the second option made more sense, because killing twelve people in their respective staterooms would be just too messy. The thought of it caused him to panic. He sensed them coming after him. He sped up the tender, going full throttle into the dark blue.

The reality of the massacre that occurred aboard *The Durango* was much more meticulous. The two small boats that approached were actually Zodiacs. Between the two of them, they were carrying twelve men, seven on the larger one and five on the smaller one. When they were close enough to *The Durango*, they turned off their lights. The smaller boat flanked starboard and the larger one port side. The men, who worked for the Knights of Michoacan, all happened to be trained by American special forces. They were agile, professional, and in shape, but that didn't make them any less bloodthirsty. The sicario who they called El Flaco threw a rope from the bigger Zodiac onto the yacht and climbed up swiftly, like a carnivorous squid. He secured ladders on both sides of the vessel and within six minutes, ten of the men, in full combat gear, were aboard. The alpha team, led by Bisonte, made its way up to the bridge. The beta team, led by a tall man with long hair known as Osfran, made their way below deck. The men all aligned themselves behind a specific crew member. Bisonte was behind Nato, the first mate, and Osfran was behind Danny, the chef. At 3:59 a.m., the ten men, like a perfectly synchronized swim team, pulled thick plastic bags over each of their victims and suffocated them, all in less than four minutes without a single drop of blood.

The sicarios had received an order for killing a crew of twelve, plus the captain. They looked for the remaining three like hounds off their leashes. Osfran found Humberto hiding inside one of the cabinets in the galley, scared, with his trousers wet and his eyes red. Osfran took pleasure in ripping his eyes out and cutting off his penis.

"It's good luck to take the cock from a victim while they are alive and scared," he told the other men while they assembled the victims astern.

The captain and the woman were still unaccounted for. Lola felt Bisonte enter the room.

"There's my captain," she said with a crackle in her voice, hoping for a second round of pleasure. When she realized it wasn't Axel, but a blood lusting savage, she saw the angel of death and fainted.

Bisonte felt like a true gentleman — where other men would have raped this sexy woman, he simply put a bag over her head and killed her like the average crew member that she was. No special treatment for being a woman. He had a daughter who had been to college and considered herself a feminist; maybe he had learned a thing or two from her, or maybe the angel of death's affairs was serious business for him. When Bisonte reached the stern carrying Lola's body, the other eleven naked bodies were already stacked up. Next to them was a pile of their clothes, followed by a pile of whatever jewelry and accessories they had on them. The sicarios worked like a slaughterhouse assembly line. One chopped up the legs and another pulled out each toe. The arms were broken at the elbow, and the hands were separated from the limbs. Then, each finger was pulled. Osfran separated the heads from the torsos. And Bisonte jumped in at the last stage, pulling out the teeth from the heads.

To these guys, all of the organs had value: hearts, kidneys, tissue, livers — anything like that they vacuum-sealed and put on ice. They would dispose of the rest with the help of the birds who, like mad piranhas, ate human flesh.

"That weirdo from the university called. *I want more pineal glands,* he told me. Bastard's in luck. He's gonna pay good," said Bisonte.

Only El Flaco stayed behind to guard the ship. Confident in the job they had done, he used the opportunity to nap on the deck. The Zodiacs returned with a cleaning crew two hours later. The cleaners gathered all of the personal items from the yacht that belonged to the deceased and separated them with meticulous perfection. When they were done, there wasn't a shred of evidence that Axel and his crew had been aboard the vessel. The cleaners were replaced with a maritime crew of six people, led by Captain Sandro Quintero, who, out of habit, raised a pirate flag.

CHAPTER 64

Adrift

THE SUN HAD FINALLY RISEN as Axel Cuevas felt his stomach give in. He was still going full throttle towards an unknown destination. All the adrenaline pumping through his body had finally taken its toll. It was as if he wasn't even conscious. He was in a twisted trance of guilt and sunlight. He didn't know where he was going; he didn't even know where he *was*. Over the last couple of hours, he had gone fast towards the horizon, not thinking about where—just far, away from the yacht.

The wake was beating hard against the tender, and there wasn't any land in sight. He checked for his phone but didn't find it, not realizing he had dropped it upon jumping ship. The tender was a twenty-five-foot Sport Runner. It was classy, but not very well-equipped. It had a long wooden bow and a deep-blue painted hull that blended well with the ocean. But it didn't have any shade. It had a thick leather couch that began heating up with sun, and to top it off, Axel had shit himself.

In an act of thoughtless desperation, he jumped into the water to rinse himself from the shame and defecation. As soon as he did, he noticed the tender drifting away. He swam to it and held on. When he got back aboard, he broke down and wept. His mind went everywhere — the fear of drifting into the unknown, his guilt over leaving behind a full crew of sailors, and his vulnerability and desperation made him feel the loneliness of the abyss.

Should I get on the CB radio and yell Mayday! Mayday! Mayday! Better not. These guys are probably listening.

He felt confused and betrayed by Bracho. He knew how his boss operated. He knew it was likely Bracho had ordered the hit with him aboard and had decided to spare his life at the very end.

Why else did he call me at the last second?

Axel undressed, washed his shorts in the saltwater, and put them out to dry. He sat naked on the helm and followed his compass north. He was sure that if he at least went north, he would hit land. He kept going until the red fuel reserve light came on. In the rush of his escape, the thought of fuel had never crossed his mind. When he realized the obviousness of his mistake, he thought himself a lesser captain, a hack, somebody who was unprepared for real challenges. He even thought about his cousin, Julian Mayorca, the great yachtsman, someone who would never get into such a situation—and even if he did, at least he would've had plenty of fuel. Axel spent all of that day naked and terrified, searching for migratory birds so he could somehow follow their trajectory and find land.

That evening, when his clothes were somewhat dry, he dressed and began looking for anything that could help facilitate his life. There was a small storage space underneath the dashboard. He opened it and found a first aid kit, a flashlight, and a flare gun. Even though the storage space was small, it ran deep, almost to the bow of the tender. He took the flashlight and pointed it at the deep end; there seemed to be nothing there. At sunset that day, after not having found land, hungry and desperate, he had no choice. Axel picked up the CB radio and turned the dial to channel sixteen.

"Mayday... help... *ayuda*," he said over the radio.

He continued this until his voice was hoarse and never heard anything but static. Around 21:00, the night began to get really cold, wet and windy. Axel opened the emergency blanket that was inside the first aid kit. It was one of those thin mylar sheets that come wrapped up in a tiny square. He rolled inside what felt like tin foil and tried to control his shaking.

Axel took out the flashlight, but there was nothing to shine it on;

nothing below, nada above. He held it against his chest, hoping the extra light would help warm him. When he summoned some strength, he shot a round from the flare gun. Like a shooting star, it passed by unnoticed. The flare's tail left a void where his salvation was; a deep hole filled his stomach. The hunger made the cold feel damp, the fear caused the rocking of the boat to sharpen. Axel was trapped. He didn't believe in himself and didn't know if he believed in God. He was feeling hypothermia reach his bones, but at the same time, his skin was burning from the hours of exposure in the sun. Right when he began to cry, when he wailed for his mother and begged forgiveness from his father, a feeling similar to vertigo came upon Axel, and thus began his first night adrift.

CHAPTER 65

Dead Fish

THE DAYS AND THE NIGHTS, the dead and alive; water for drinking, fish are my friend, was the first thing Axel carved into the wood of the tender. To accomplish this, he used a star-tipped screwdriver that he found underneath the seat. There, he also found a gallon of water, an actual blanket, and sunblock. After a month at sea, every item he had in his possession took on a whole new value. He would rearrange the items and look at them, almost as if expecting they would flare to life.

He had a special connection with the sunblock bottle; the shape of it appeared to be a little person and it reminded him of his earlier self, one that was insecure and tormented by false expectations. His parents had always been good to him, making him a bit of a spoiled boy. But the December of his seventh birthday, his cousin, Julian Mayorca, lost both of his parents and moved in with them. That's when everything changed. From that moment on, his parents focused on Julian, on making it easier for him.

Through the years, Julian excelled at the things Axel failed at and his parents adored him. These days, Axel didn't really think much about his cousin, but in this particular situation, he missed Julian. He wished he was out here with him on the sea so they could both help each other out like when they were kids on the Winkle Brig.

The tender drifted aimlessly with the current, straying further from the coast. With the rain came the utter disappointment, the fear of finishing last and never collecting another paycheck. Axel was cold, wet, hungry, naked, lonely, done to his bitter end. He gave up. Wanted to die. He threw himself into the sea, to die, to drift forever like a small particle in a non-metaphorical ocean. He was so weak that he fainted while clinging to the tender rope. The deep fear of dying kept him alive. When he awoke, it was daylight, and a vomitous smell was putrefying the still air all around him. He climbed back aboard and all he could see was dead fish. Hundreds of thousands of fish floating belly-up in the hot sun, decaying at an uncanny rate. Tuna, mackerel, dolphins, sharks, whales—it was a sea of glass and upon it was only death.

The pestilence, the triggers, the sole nature of that place burned a hole so deep into Axel, it shook his primal bone and his fear turned into desperation. The adrenaline of being alive kicked in. He wanted to breathe fresh air again and climb a mountain; he wanted a hot meal after a cold meal and to read the occasional novel. He wanted to have a woman, not *women* like before, but a single woman to love. Axel used the screwdriver to remove planks from the top of the tender. He made a mast and used the blankets to sail. That night, he made a little headway.

Redemption was not guaranteed, it was earned, Axel took on a stronger attitude and began to build his way out. Doing little things, like collecting nighttime dew, turned into big things like converting the tender into a somewhat-functioning sailboat. When he escaped the pestilence, he made a spear and caught live fish. He was aware of his mortality, but grateful for life. But he still struggled every inch of the way and through every moment of solitude. Axel spent 101 nights at sea. On the 102th day since the murders, he was devastated, lost for breath and hopeless. Out like gentle whispers from the deepest place within him came a call to God.

"Help... Please... I can't... Jesus... help.... Jesus...."

A whimper that begged for another chance at life, one that pleaded for a moment of grace.

After all of the knocking, that was the key that did the unlocking.

Axel was still curled into a ball, keeping himself warm with only the tears he cried unto God, when two patrol boats flanked the tender. Shocked, paralyzed by guilt and untrusting of gullible instincts, he didn't notice the three officers aboard who were wearing Port of Balboa yellow jackets.

CHAPTER 66

OB-08

A XEL HAD NO IDEA WHERE he was. He drifted in and out of consciousness, in and out of places. The beep that woke him up wasn't
one of the hospital beeps that he had become accustomed to; it was
a more personal beep, one that came from an analog wristwatch. The
man sitting next to him was in his late fifties, fit, clean-shaven with a
mustache. He smelled of nautical cologne and had dark, penetrating
eyes.

"It is not I that condemns, but heaven and sea," the man read from
a file. "These are the things that were carved on the tender where we
found you."

"Oh, hallelujah, how long was I out?" Axel asked, grateful.

"What's your name, son?"

"Axel Cuevas."

"Who do you work for?" asked the man.

"I have no boss," he answered.

"Was it your money that you were carrying?" he asked.

"I have no money," answered Axel.

The man with the dark eyes left the room and returned immediately
with armed officers who unplugged Axel from the machines and IV he
was hooked up to. They put him in handcuffs and a blindfold before
they took him away. Shortly, he found himself in a strange prison where
there wasn't any noise. From the inside, it felt like a container. Hollow, nondescript, in the outskirts of nowhere. He yelled and screamed,

kicked the doors and cursed loudly. Nothing; no food, no people, not even a sound on the other side of the container. For three days this went on, until the doors opened at high noon, and two officers brought water. The man with the dark eyes watched the prisoner drink like an animal.

"Who do you work for, Mr. Axel Cuevas?"

"I don't work for anyone."

"Why did you have so much money?" he asked.

"I don't know anything about any money," said Axel.

The man signaled with his head. The two officers held Axel's limbs as the boss covered his face with a rag and splashed his face with water. This practice tested a person's loyalty to the core. Made them question their very existence. Waterboarding was the devil's way of obtaining truth. Axel endured the maddening desperation, fixed for survival like a mad dog, fighting the inevitable peril of rabies. He screamed, he vomited into his own vocal cords, and pleaded. The feeling of drowning was like the virtual reality of death. After ninety seconds, Axel was sobbing.

"I work for Samuel Bracho. But he killed my men, my whole crew."

"And what about the $20 million hidden in the tender?" the man asked.

"Mister, please, I swear I know nothing about the money. The tender, I lowered it in a panic, because I knew that hitmen were coming after us. I swear I would tell you. I have nothing to hide. My name is Axel Cuevas and I am from Baja California," he said in an almost rant.

"Let him go," the man with the dark eyes said in a cool tone like the first note of a jazz album.

The man gave Axel, who was still sitting on the floor, a towel.

"Meet me outside when you're ready. We'll talk," he said as he walked out with his men.

It took Axel almost seven minutes to pull himself together. When he finally ran his hands through his hair to make it look slick with waterboarded water, he realized he was ready to face himself. He walked out into an empty lot on the far end of a shipping port. It was a beautiful sunny day in Panama. In the distance, he could see thousands of blue and orange containers, some headed to San Francisco, some to China, others to the UK, or Australia.

Crates, ships, traffic, movement, all at a distance, but where he was standing, only solitude. The man with the dark eyes was waiting for him at the edge of the industrial lot.

"What's next for you Mr. Cuevas? Your crew dead, your boss in prison, you missing with $20 million that you are not going to get back. What's next?"

Axel looked at the man, looked out to the bay, his hair still wet with the water of death. He sighed in relief at the air, the sun, and the ground.

"To tell you the truth, all I want at this point is a bowl of soup," he said.

"Very well," a smirk.

The man waved his hand towards the far end of the lot where a grey Mitsubishi Montero sped towards them and stopped three meters away. The man opened the passenger door and Axel stepped in. The man sat in the back seat.

"Let's go to OB-08," said the man.

OB-08 was the codename for the guest quarters at the Port of Balboa, the Pacific entry to the Panama Canal. The man who was playing host was Pascual Pizante, Balboa's port captain.

Mr. Pizante was a man dedicated to methodology and principle. A natural son of General Ezra Pizante, who was one of the founders of the state of Israel, and Simona Elizondo, a Nicaraguan aristocrat whose family was defeated by the same *Sandinismo* Ezra Pizante had come to covertly support on official Mossad business. Every day, Pascual Pizante had lunch at OB-08 at 13:00, a three-course meal, well served. Soup always extra hot, protein and fresh vegetables, and a small dessert.

Today, he had planned to sit with Mr. Cuevas and talk to him. Axel ate like a junkie smoking a laced cigarette. Desperate, the warmth of the soup loosened his stomach. Pascual let him indulge; he enjoyed watching this man gain his life back. Pascual had staff serving him at all times; he had inherited his mother's sense of style and class. He was a man of refined taste, but with vast intellectual capacity and leadership to back it up. While he ate, he enjoyed soft music in the background, usually big band or Tito Puente.

"Tell me about Samuel Bracho," said Pascual as they finished their meal.

"The guy's a billionaire, unstoppable, always making moves," said Axel.

"When you say unstoppable, what exactly do you mean?"

"Look, when Samuel Bracho wants something, he goes and gets it, actually pulls the trigger. Doesn't ask for permission, doesn't say sorry. That's the way he's always been," said Axel.

"Yeah, but that's exactly why he's in prison now," said Pizante.

"True, but the bastard already negotiated his way out," said Axel.

"How?"

"The yacht, *The Durango.*"

"The yacht that you were skippering?" asked Pizante.

"Yeah, he paid the Knights of Michoacan with the yacht, for them to get him out," said Axel.

"What prison is he in?"

"Tres Marias."

Pascual looked calmly at Axel, giving him the test of trust. "I'll tell you what, Axel Cuevas, you keep playing ball with me, telling me what I ask, and I'll give you your life back. But for now, you're my prisoner. Do you understand?"

Axel nodded.

"Good. I know what I need from you, but you just have to sit tight. You will stay in this house for as long as I need you; this is your prison and Dagoberto is your guard."

Dagoberto, the unbreakable first sergeant in charge of running OB-08, stared Axel down.

"Is that clear?"

"Yes, sir," Axel's voice cracked slightly.

"Captain, call me Captain. I will be back tomorrow for breakfast.

There is a small patio out back, there is some food in the pantry, and a library. No television, no phones. You must not try to escape, must not try to communicate with anyone. And if you break my rules, I or Dagoberto will kill you in a second. Is that clear?"

"Yes, Captain," said Axel.

CHAPTER 67

Pizante

PASCUAL PIZANTE WAS AN INSTITUTION of a man. After graduating alongside the Latin American military elite from the Chorrillos Military School in Peru, he had enrolled in the IDF and, because of his father's legacy, he shortly got invited to join Mossad. He cut his sea legs in the British Navy, and had been close to the power in Panama since the Noriega days. After the fall of the dictator, Pascual avoided being persecuted because of his background with the IDF. He spent some time fighting in Guatemala, disguised as a Jesuit, later fighting in Chiapas under Subcomandante Marcos.

Pascual was a jarhead, a military junky, armed forces, power structure, chain of command, handgun, knife, and rifle kind of guy. When he returned to Panama, his friend Pablo Orcí had become president. He gave him the job of Commander of the Panama National Guard, "the army that couldn't call itself an army." He was only on the job for eighteen months and the CIA got him out. He was asked to resign, but did not. With the budget to pressure Orcí, the Americans installed Sandoval Largó, a West Point graduate, in the commandant's office. Pizante was honorably discharged.

As Commander of the National Guard, he had built a personal relationship with Nev Rodman, the Israeli ambassador to Panama. After his resignation, Pascual got a contract as a security consultant to the embassy. When the Balboa port captain job opened, Nev moved all of his machinery to appoint a friendly. Some even say that Pascual Pizante had taken the job as Balboa port captain as a direct request from the prime minister of Israel, Yonatan Baron, who had been a professor of Pascual's during his Ph.D. studies at the Hebrew University of Jerusalem.

The Panama Canal is controlled by the Panama Canal Authority. It's a symbol of national pride, but also a closely watched political organization. The Port of Balboa itself is controlled by a small council who appoints a port captain, a strategic position that's been granted a lot of liberties. The captainship has ground-and-sea power and calls for strong management and a ride-or-die staff.

Pascual Pizante was a master at his job, not only in dealing with daily affairs, but in creating strategies of all sorts. From the logistics of running a port to media attacks on opponents to delivering information to rival shipping companies, Pizante created wars between parties that he deemed worthy of each other with calculation and for great gain. By the time he began having breakfast with Axel Cuevas, he had been port captain for fifteen years. He knew every trick, king, queen, one-eyed-jack, and every joker in the business.

Samuel Bracho didn't know it yet, but he was already a person of interest to an obsessed man — but not to just any obsessed man, one with tremendous scope. Pizante was a man in whose sights you didn't want to be in. A meticulous, calculating, and Machiavellian man, nothing got past him; his background included everything from private investigating, to Israeli Intelligence, to the British Navy, Panamanian Public Forces, and paramilitary operations. He knew how to execute complicated tasks with precision and impact. The $85 million he already had in the bank that nobody, especially not Melinda, his wife, knew about, helped him attain a certain confidence, but it didn't blind him.

Money didn't distract him, nothing did. He was not only a frugal man, he was a military man, disciplined, one who understood the importance of waking up early, staying fit, and enforcing power. This was a man who was so ingrained in the business of running a port that the $85 million he had in his account only meant he had been doing a good job. If there ever was a man who figured out the job of port captain as well as Solomon figured out the job of king, Pizante was that man. Never involved in a corruption case, never a scandal. Public funds never went missing, criminals got caught, violence was prosecuted. And the canal kept working; the canal kept giving to everyone who deserved a piece.

The first night Axel Cuevas spent as a prisoner of Pizante's was one for reflection. He showered with warm water, shaved his beard, trimmed his hair, and slept in a bed. He had his first dream of dead fish, an ocean of glass, a raft, and death all around him. He woke up early and showered again. In the closet he found medium-sized shorts, medium sized gray t-shirts, and socks, and even though Axel had always been a size L, he had slimmed down enough and looked frail, almost boyish in medium clothing.

At 07:15, Pizante always broke his fast in the same fashion: two "grilled" eggs as he called them — over-easy with a tiny bit of olive oil on a covered pan — a piece of sausage, toast with jam, and coffee.

"Have breakfast like a king, lunch like a prince, and dinner like a pauper," he would tell his men.

When they were finished having breakfast, one of the guards gave Axel a pair of sneakers. Pizante watched Axel put them on like a hawk watches a mouse exiting its cave.

"I've checked with my people... Your boss ain't getting out; he just got transferred to Almoloya, Mexico's underground maximum security prison, and it's nowhere near water. Turns out the Knights of Michoacan betrayed him. What did you say he paid them?"

"Well, we paid $150 million for the yacht. I went to Hamburg and bought it myself. And I know for a fact that he exchanged it for his freedom."

"Yeah, but the Knights screwed him, the Knights screw everyone," Pizante said, almost as if making a mental note to himself.

A shocked Axel didn't know what to say, so he did the right thing and remained quiet.

"I'll tell you what. You and I are going to do business; I'm interested in something that you have, but I will not tell you what it is quite yet. Not because it's a secret, but because you wouldn't understand. From here on out, after we have breakfast, you will come work for me. I must teach you something if you are going to be able to help me."

Axel's mind was all over the place.

"There are a couple of rules if you are going to work for me. Never speak without being spoken to, unless you have information that can change the game, then you tell it to me immediately in private. You will be observing certain things we do. Everything I set you up with is a test, and come dinner time, we will debrief, so you must remember important details. Other than that, be on your toes. I have you close to me for now because there is something I can gain from you, and that can change at any moment, always remember that," Pizante held up his index finger. "Is that understood?"

"Yes, Captain," Axel replied.

When they rode in a car together, Pizante made Axel sit in the front seat; he sat right behind him.

"You will be my acolyte and I will be your lord, do you understand?"

"Yes sir," answered Axel.

"You will do every single little thing I ask. You will shine my shoes, wax my boat, and catch fish for me if I want."

Axel was visually worried, not knowing what the expectations of his lord were.

Pizante noticed, winked, and changed his tone to a softer one. "I'll tell you something, you be patient and we'll get your boss out of jail."

That somehow relaxed Axel. "Yes, Port Captain."

For five years, Axel Cuevas worked under Pizante. He was a tough boss, a strong captain who expected excellence in every word, in every action, and in every thought. He didn't let Axel contact his family or anybody in South Baja for the first year. His mother, Luisa, almost fainted when she heard his voice. Gene, his dad, cried with joy. He told them that he had enrolled in the Merchant Marine and had two more years to go on his contract. Even though Luisa Cuevas found joy in hearing her son's voice, she didn't believe his story. She was sure Axel was in prison somewhere.

The relationship between Pizante and Axel Cuevas consisted of a flow of information. Axel felt like Pizante was mentoring him, showing him tricks of the trade, hustles, side-hacks. On one side, he was a prisoner, but on the other, he had all-access to the port captain's operation. He felt like he was being groomed. Pizante had an air about him, a patience; when he spoke, Axel listened. He learned and challenged his own perspective.

Pizante often picked Axel's brain about his past, about Baja California, about life in general, as if he was checking him for something. It wasn't until three-and-a-half years in that Pizante let Axel in on part of his plan.

"I want control of Baja California ports. If we can get control of the peninsula, we can capitalize on the flow north. There are interests, international interests, that want Baja," said Pizante.

Axel nodded, then smiled, "Let's go. I'm ready to go home, Captain," he said.

Pizante had him just where he wanted.

"Let me explain something to you: being port captain is a fun job. It's not like the armed forces, it's more civil, and clean in a way. But you have to be smart, you have to do your job right. For instance, when we found you, stranded in the ocean, lost, the moment they brought you in, the moment I took a look at you, I knew there was more to this story.

I saw the tender that you were in, that beautiful wooden boat, but something was off. I handled it, filed papers, medical for you, everything I had to do. Then I had a special unit tear the vessel apart. And lodged in a panel between the engine room and deck, what do I find? Twenty million dollars. I love that. I love my job."

Axel looked at Pizante and felt the bit of fear he usually felt when he knew the captain was about to make a point.

"I want to free Samuel Bracho from Almoloya," said Pizante.

Axel felt a throbbing pain, confusion. *Why does he want Bracho free?* But Pizante had a plan.

"I want to free Bracho because I want to free Baja California."

"Free Baja?"

"Separate the peninsula from Mexico. Create civil war, and in the end, build a new country."

Axel understood that this was bigger than Pizante. "Anything you need, Captain," he said.

"What I need is your loyalty."

That dark stare that he felt on that first day they met.

"I've shown you a lot over the years, I've taught you about this job. Being port captain has a lot to give, a lot of money to be made. I taught you all this for a reason."

Axel nodded.

"You told me about your cousin, Julian Mayorca, the guy who has my job in South Baja."

Axel's face lit up.

"We're going to make him go away, and you're going to fill that position; take his job, become port captain of La Paz, and preside over the Baja Port Captains Association," said Pizante.

Axel felt his spine twitch with rage. He couldn't speak. He was scared of Pizante.

"I know what you're thinking, Axel, and I tried, I did. Through my contacts, we even offered him money — lots of it. He doesn't play ball. He's a proud son of a bitch. So we must get rid of him by other means."

Axel felt empty, but he scrambled to rescue the bits of decency he still carried somewhere within him.

"With all due respect, sir, why do you need me in that particular position, why so close to home?"

Pascual paused a second. "You know, Axel, I've mastered this job, 'Balboa port captain,'" he made a motion with his hand, and pride came to his eyes. "It's not only this job, it's much bigger. I'm also on the International Council on Ports and Harbors, a network of port captains from around the world, and I need you to be my representative in Baja California."

Axel looked seriously at Pizante.

"Sir, but how can I hurt my cousin, somebody who is like my brother?" said Axel.

"Your brother? Has he once tried to contact you while you've been out here? Has he used his position to look out for you, or your parents, or anything?"

Axel shook his head.

"It makes perfect sense. We don't have to kill him, just force him to resign. We take a million dollars and we put it in the governor's pocket so he appoints you. Within a day, you are port captain."

Axel worried.

"I've got it all worked out. In one swift move, we free Samuel Bracho, we put you in the port captainship, you get rich, and we gain Baja for our cause."

"What if it goes wrong and we end up killing him?" said Axel.

Pascual smirked. "Don't you worry about your cousin. He's going to be better off. There's a war coming, Mr. Cuevas, and we're on the winning end."

That night, Axel couldn't sleep. His whole life had been completely turned around again. Full circle. Back to Baja to take his cousin's job. He was scared, he didn't want to kill Julian.

I don't mind hurting him though, he thought.

He knew he couldn't kill Julian. He justified it. *If I kill and take my cousin's job, it would look very suspicious. In order to not kill him, I just have to make him resign like Pascual said.*

He felt some relief, convincing himself that no matter what happened, he would not kill his cousin. As he lay in bed wondering about Pizante's plan, he thought about the task before him. In a moment of clarity, he felt the breeze of survival.

I've come this far and survived; now, I get a good job, some power, my own connections, and with this, Samuel Bracho will be indebted to me, he began drifting into sleep. *Plus I get to go back to Baja, back to the paradise road and marina,* he drifted, gone as the fly that smashes into Morpheus' web.

CHAPTER 68

The Old Mansion

PLAN BRACHO WAS ORCHESTRATED BY the same mastermind who helped Subcomandante Marcos with the occupation of San Cristobal de las Casas in Chiapas in 1994 and numerous other political stagings, protests, and coups throughout Latin America. This time, Pizante spent fourteen months piecing together every aspect of Bracho's exile, from the Almoloya escape through a series of false flags, tunnels, briberies, and general confusion, followed up with a media storm about his escape making an international mess with the intention of creating the perception that the Mexican government was inefficient and corrupt. Pizante set up residence for Bracho at the Old Mansion up Luciano Road in Santa Rosalia in South Baja.

The history of the mansion went back to 1870, when a Frenchman by the name of Cummings, following rumors of precious metals, found copper coming out of the ground in the middle of the Baja peninsula. From there on, the development and exploitation of Santa Rosalia began. Cummings went back to France to raise capital for a mining operation he began calling *Boléo*, which means "shined," as in "shoe-shined"—folkloric Baja slang for the hills of Santa Rosalia that shone with copper. One bank became interested in the scheme and decided to fund the *El Boléo* operation. That bank was House Rothchild.

Through the better part of a century, the Boléo mine thrived alongside the town, giving its owners riches on riches and the workers an uphill social struggle. The company built the town of Santa Rosalia to resemble a small French village, Eiffel church and all. In 1885, House Rothchild, very pleased with the return on investment, sent a representative to scope out the expansion of their business.

Philip Lelouch, a second cousin of the bank president, was sent to set up residence in Santa Rosalia. Philip was incredibly smart, sophisticated, cunning, talented, and the perfect combination of witty and firm. He was also eccentric and queer. He dressed professionally but wore colors that were campy and a little too fashion-forward for a man of his time. Philip had style, was cosmopolitan and was backed by the head bankers of the world.

When he arrived in Santa Rosalia, there was nothing but men working the mine and a dusty old town. He began his business in seriousness, analyzed all of the possibilities, and saw the industrial potential of Baja. Eventually, he got rid of Mr. Cummings and he became president of El Boléo Mining Company. During his tenure, he spearheaded the building of a shipyard, a port, a marina, and the crown jewel of his forty-year stint in Baja, his mansion.

The Old Mansion was built on a hill that overlooked the town with the mine operations at a distance. When the dark cloud of industry didn't betray nature, Isla Tortuga on the Sea of Cortez was visible. The mansion was perfect for its place and time. It had a touch of ambition and class, with a style that was almost decadent. White pillars, deep pink exterior walls, three pools, sunbathing rooms, croquet lawn, six bedrooms, and lavish bathrooms.

Philip opened his house to guests and friends. He didn't let that interrupt his drive for wealth. The mine continued to grow; he built roads in and out of the town, installed cobblestone on the streets, and tried to befriend the workforce. That was his biggest battle. The town was 99 percent Mexican, brought in from the mainland or other parts of Baja. The 1 percent who were French, owned 99 percent of the resources and wealth. Whatever was left after profits was reinvested in the town, never in its workers or their needs.

Still, Philip tried to make amends. He would often tour the work facilities and tried to better the working conditions by opening a medical center. He even commissioned a modernist church that was brought in from France. Philip also selected his favorite workers to come hang out with him. He'd give them alcohol and make passes at them. He got away with it because he was the *patrón*. This created a unique culture within the company and town.

As Philip's empire grew, he discovered magnesium mines nearby and began exploiting them. He used his own ships to export the minerals directly to San Francisco, where he got paid big dollars. As time went by, his taste became more eccentric, more demanding, and he began bringing in boys in their late teens and early twenties from mainland Mexico. He loved his boys; their sex, sucking their manhoods, and kissing their backs.

Philip Lelouch was a prince of the new world. He would host exotic parties, orgies, and cultural nights that included theater and readings of plays. He would invite people from San Francisco, Los Angeles, and old friends from Europe to come hang with him and "the natives," as he called the boys that he loved so much. At one of his parties, Gen Amand, an aspiring shipping broker who was recently involved with the creation of French Indochina, invited Philip on a venture.

Never one to say no to a profit, Philip began renting the port at El Boléo for the influx of opium from Indochina into Baja. From there, he would send it to San Francisco by boat, to Los Angeles by land, or to mainland Mexico, where he had cut a deal with the Mexican Army to supply them during the *Revolución*.

Some of the opium began to stay behind in San Rosalia. At first, very little, for Philip's own consumption. A bohemian at heart, always wanting to experiment, try more, feel more. He began sharing his opium with his boys. At first, no pain, just the incredible lightness of being. Then the path to addiction, withdrawal, cramps, anger, rejection. The boys began to crave, began to suffer. Philip tightened his grip, exiling from his town and from his world those who crossed the line.

This went on for years, leaving Philip thin, frail, spent. Business decayed, but World War I and its treaties brought plenty of business to the banking house behind him. Philip kept the company going, always pushing for more out of his men and his resources. In September 1928, Philip met Luciano, a 20-year-old from La Paz. Philip wanted Luciano, he lusted over him like sailors lust over mermaids. He became a testament to his virility, but Luciano never wanted him in return. Philip tried everything, giving him love, wealth, drugs, alcohol, but Luciano didn't want him.

One day, Luciano finally gave Philip permission to penetrate him. That night, after their passion was consumed, Luciano hung himself in the town square. Philip mourned, cried, and even named the street that led up to his mansion in his honor, Luciano Road. After this, the people of El Boléo began to see the *patrón's* weaknesses as clear as day. On the foggy Friday morning of February 25, 1929, Philip Lelouch was found dead, floating in his mansion's pool. The world without Philip Lelouch began a new era, even for the most powerful banking house in the world.

The following year, House Rothschild sold the mine, dismembered their operations in Baja, but kept the mansion in its private real estate inventory. For almost eighty years, the Old Mansion sat in still silence, decaying with time and natural forces. By the time Pascual Pizante began making inquiries into secret holdings in the Baja Peninsula, the mansion was a thing of legend and local tall tales.

CHAPTER 69

Sunseeker

IN THE DARKNESS OF HIS cell, his thoughts became the dark rooms of the inferno. Solitary confinement was the only option in Almoloya. Prisoners are underground, fed through a slot at the top of their door. They were allowed one hour of sun per week, under strict supervision. At a certain time in the early morning, a single ray of sun passed through a hole in Bracho's cell. It was only for about twelve minutes, but for that time, Bracho would put his face against the sun, feeling its warmth, seeking its light. Waiting another twenty-four hours of darkness, just for that fleeting moment of vitamin D. On the day that Pizante executed Plan Bracho, the only thing in Bracho's mind was the desire for sunlight.

Samuel Bracho had no idea he was leaving Almoloya that early morning. The guard who liberated him kept treating him like a maggot, bound, and with a cover over his head. Bracho thought it was standard procedure; he was already psychologically broken. For that reason, Pizante made his escape not only a surprise for Bracho, but an extension of the system, to be carried out as if he were still a prisoner.

Bracho was awoken at 2:20 a.m. with a kick from the guards. He was escorted outside and thrown in the backseat of a car, still bound, head covered like a blind bat. They took him on a forty-minute car ride, during which he could sense the valleys and streets of central Mexico only through his nose and ears. The men transferred him with the same hostility unto a Bell 500. He went on a three-hour helicopter ride. Throughout the whole procedure, Bracho assumed he was simply being transferred for a court date, further sentencing, or another prison.

When the helicopter landed on a beach near Zihuatanejo, the smell of the ocean seemed familiar to Bracho. A smile flowered on his rag-covered face. The helicopter team put Bracho on the ground, unshackled him, removed the blindfold, and quickly evacuated, airborne in under three minutes. Bracho looked around, his hands unbound, the sunlight, the sand, the fresh breathable air, freedom, life, five years of imprisonment, over. But why? How? The rush of emotions, one thing to the next.

He looked out, and at a distance, in the open water, at the crest of the bay, he saw two yachts. A sixty-two-foot Sunseeker Manhattan and an eighty-foot Azimut Carat. From the yachts, a small tender was making its way towards him. It was Pascual Pizante skippering the tender, coming in slowly as a hunter approaches a stag while the rest of the venison pant for the water. He beached the tender over Zihuatanejo wake and walked over to Samuel Bracho.

Pizante extended his hands as if they were being formally introduced.

"Samuel Bracho, I am Captain Pascual Pizante. As you have probably noticed, you are a free man, and I wanted you to hear it from me. I was the person who made it possible."

Bracho smiled and shook his hand. "Well, thank you." He went in for a hug and Pascual allowed it. A tear of joy followed by a moan. Bracho was free and grateful.

"What do you want from me?" Bracho asked.

"To start a war," said Pizante.

A laugh. "Then I'm your man."

"Before we get in the tender and discuss the plans that we have considered, I need you to know something, Mr. Bracho. Axel Cuevas was number two in this operation. It was also because of him that we are doing this for you,"

"Goddamn playboy. He's behind this, too?" interrupted Bracho.

"Yes, and I have been training him for years for this very moment.

We liberated you because there are certain interests that need your attention. Things are different now. You don't have what you used to have."

"But I have accounts that nobody knows about, cash hidden, resources," said Bracho.

"Yes, we know that, and we'll talk about everything. You are no longer alone Mr. Bracho. Pizante is behind you."

They made their way to the tender and Pizante skippered it over to the Sunseeker where he pulled up astern. Axel Cuevas, wearing navy shorts and a polo shirt, was almost unrecognizable with a grown, but well trimmed, reddish beard.

"There he is," said Bracho as he smiled and stepped aboard.

Axel Cuevas did a second take when he saw his old boss.

"What? No love?" said Bracho as he noticed a stone-cold Axel.

"You called me two minutes before they were going to kill me. You were about to have me dead," said Axel.

"Bullshit, you wanna know what happened? Do you really want to know? For two days — for two whole goddamn days — I was trying to get a phone call to you. Couldn't get it to save my life. And as soon as I could, I called you."

"At 3:30 in the morning? You finally got a phone to call me?"

"This is prison; there's a method for everything. The guard who let me use his phone, Miguel, his shift began at 3:00. As soon as he was clear, I called you, I swear. You're my brother!"

Axel sighed; he let it go.

Pizante, who had been a passive observer, got back on the tender.

"You guys go ahead and catch up. Let's meet at the next stop." Pizante turned the tender around and headed towards the Azimut Carat, a much more slender, bigger yacht.

The two yachts had been acquired as a loss by a Pizante middleman, who confiscated the idle yachts from the Marina Flamenco in Panama. Part of his plan was to take them to Baja and sell them on the black market. Pizante didn't worry until somebody claimed them stolen, but these yachts never would be, because each owner owed at least five years of dock fees.

The logic of the procedure was simple. From Zihuatanejo to Mazat-lán. There, they were going to pick up weapons and personnel that would be assigned to both Samuel Bracho and Axel Cuevas. Pizante had his own small team aboard the Azimut and plenty of cash in the safe. They gave the yachts some horsepower on the ride up to Mazatlán. While Axel was on helm of his own yacht, he told Bracho his intention to take his cousin's job, and become port captain of La Paz.

"But I need you to play the part, Boss. When we come into La Paz, you have to be the one to make the offer. We know he's going to be running a drill at sea; we know he's going to come aboard the yacht. But the ultimatum can't come from me. He needs to know that you're behind me and that we're having mercy on his life," said Axel.

"So, this guy, Pizante, frees me from prison and wants to install you as port captain in La Paz? What does he gain from all of this?"

"Don't know for sure, but he is backed by some heavy money, deep intelligence; Pizante is up to something big, and he expects us to play ball with him," said Axel.

"Yeah, I'll play ball, but I don't like to be played regardless of who it is."

"Yeah, but this guy saved my life and he freed you. We owe him."

Axel told Bracho about how he had been adrift after escaping the murders, detailing the part of his rescue in Panama, the torture, and later the years serving under Pizante.

"You know why he kept me around? Because of the $20 million he found in the tender, money that I knew nothing about," he took a deep look at Bracho. "I had to convince him that you were my boss and that we could make more if we got you out of prison."

Bracho smirked, half-believing his story. "He found that? I had al-most forgotten about those twenty sticks," said Bracho. "Yeah, the damn Knights of Michoacan fucked me." He winced with hatred. "But you know something? They're sitting on $100 million of my money, and they don't even know it."

"What do you mean, boss?" said Axel.

"I hid $100 million aboard that yacht — cash — in *The Durango*." Bracho wet his lips in anger. "I'm gonna find that yacht, and I'm going to take it back without them even knowing."

"You don't think that they found it already?"

"There's no way. It's in a secret compartment that they don't know how to access. I mean, you didn't even know about it, and you skippered the damn thing!" Bracho laughed.

Axel was shocked. He had negotiated the purchase of *The Durango*, supervised remodeling jobs, spent most of his time aboard the yacht, and he'd never known about the secret compartments or the money.

What a captain! he thought, feeling like a boy at a poker table.

Axel and Bracho knew they had a difficult road ahead of them, but for the rest of the ride, they relaxed. Friends, with the wind to their faces, looking ahead to the horizon and new days.

Pizante knew perfectly well what he was doing. Letting two old friends reunite. He needed them to know that he trusted them enough to give them their freedom, their space, and their own time.

Mazatlán at night was an intimidating feeling. The city lights, the music from the discos, and the overall vibe of vice and decay. Axel and Bracho didn't disembark from the Sunseeker. Pizante and the crew from the Azimut handled everything. People came, people went, money changed hands. Four new passengers joined Axel and Bracho, two highly trained agents: Zev who was slightly dark-skinned, and Navit, who was stocky and white. Zev was assigned to Axel and Navit was assigned to Bracho.

Pizante made it clear that even though these were highly trained guards, "they're gonna report back to me."

"So he's my new prison guard, is that right?"

"Not at all Mr. Bracho. They work for you. They're here to help. You do understand that there's a long road ahead of us? And they are simply an insurance policy. Plus they're cool people, isn't that right boys?"

Zev and Navit introduced themselves and were friendly and helpful around the yacht.

Pizante handed them a small arsenal, a couple of shotguns and pistols. "Something to keep safe," he told them.

When they were about to depart, Pizante brought a couple of ladies from Mazatlán aboard. Priscila and Cynthia, two gorgeous girls who looked like perfect 10s: tall, slender, well-kept, glossy skin, pearly eyes, sexy as can be. They came from the neighboring town of El Rosario, where the women are so beautiful, it makes men grow roots and wings at the same time.

Samuel Bracho had a play day with both women in the master stateroom. When he began to worry if he, after five years in solitary, was going to sexually deliver, Cynthia, the one with the bigger ass, slipped him half a pill.

"Cialis, baby. It makes you hard like a rhino." Both the girls laughed.

True to her word, the rhino roamed the plantation of desire, like an African horn chasing the hunt.

Zev talked with Axel up on the bridge; he was open and honest. "It's like Captain Pizante said, I'm just an insurance policy; I'm here to help you pass the information upstream," he said.

"Yeah, but if something goes wrong, you can kill me any minute," said Axel.

"It's not like that. I'm on your side," said Zev.

Turned out that Zev was a strategist, a great listener, and somebody who was going to help Axel overcome the obstacles ahead.

Bracho's guard, Navit, felt at home in the galley. He cooked a delicious fish stew for dinner; everybody had a good night.

CHAPTER 70

The Mayorca Play

THE SUN CREEPING UP, TWO yachts going over thirty knots; it almost seemed like they were racing on the Sea of Cortez. The Sunseeker was ahead by a good distance. Pizante made sure of it. The reasoning behind bringing two yachts was simple; he couldn't afford to be on the same yacht as a fugitive. Just in case anything happened, he needed to have negotiating leverage or at least be able to flee. They had been going all night. Slow and steady, but with the sunrise came the need for speed, the desire to feel the rush of adrenaline through morning veins.

"With this speed, we will be in La Paz in three hours," said Pizante over the CB radio.

"Let's press on, press on," answered Axel as Zev came up to the bridge with a cup of coffee for his captain.

"Remember, I'll inform you of Julian Mayorca's whereabouts when we're a little closer. Did you already talk to Bracho and the boys about today's plan? Over," asked Pizante far-side of the radio.

"Yes, sir, we're on, aboard, and ready. Over."

The initial feeling of guilt had subsided. After all, he hadn't seen his cousin in over seven years. Adulthood had taken them on different roads. Axel had one of those moments of blissful wisdom that one feels above deck on the open ocean. He wondered if adulthood really had taken him and his cousin on different paths, or if they had bluntly chosen the lives they were living. Axel realized it was a matter of physics. Two opposing forces, two opposing lives, so much energy behind them, causing them to merge; the only possible outcome was a collision.

"Oh, one more thing," said Pizante over the CB.

"Go right ahead," answered Axel.

"No is not an option. We need him to stand down or die."

Axel felt that pain of fear. "But, sir, he's family, we went over this. I can't kill him and take his job. It would look bad" he answered.

"Yes, I know, but in case he gets too stubborn, Zev and Navit are ready to execute him and the whole crew."

Axel gasped.

"Don't worry about it. Get him to sign the resignation letter and we won't have to kill him. But remember, if we do, you can always play the victim and still get the job vowing to avenge his death," said Pizante.

"Sir, let me handle it, no bloodshed. It's better that way for all of us," he said.

"Sounds good, but you better get that resignation, or I'm calling plan B," said the commander.

Zev, who was in the seat next to him, touched his shoulder. "I understand where he's coming from. He just wants assurance. But don't worry, Axel, I'll help you make it so there's no blood."

"Thanks, Zev," said Axel, holding back so many things that he wanted to say.

Axel asked Zev to hold the wheel. "Just make sure that the compass stays in that angle."

"You got it, Skip," said Zev as he took the helm with a smile.

Axel rushed below deck and knocked on the master stateroom. Cynthia answered the door, still with that post-coitus glow.

"Hi, honey, daddy's still sleeping," she said.

"Okay, girls, wake up. I need to talk to him. Put on your swimsuits and get a fucking tan. Shower, get out of here!" he said.

The girls hissed and scrambled out of the room and into the one next door.

"Jesus, Axel, what happened to that magic touch you used to have?" Bracho asked as he turned and smiled.

Axel opened the blinds. "I'm not kidding boss, you and I need to work some things out."

He would've never talked to him that way in the past; they both knew it, but times had changed, positions shifted.

"Bring me some water!" he yelled, and Navit quickly entered with a glass of water and some Ibuprofen. Axel was surprised at how that action seemed so natural, almost as if they had been in their respective roles for years, decades even. But, no, it was their first morning together, and Bracho had marked his territory. Navit exited the room with the same swiftness he had come in with.

"How did you?" asked Axel, pointing at the door.

"Oh, Navit? He's cool. I let him fuck Cynthia last night; turns out that meant a lot for him."

"Wow," said Axel.

At that moment, a smile came to Axel's face. He felt the certainty that the both of them, together, were capable of incredible deeds. He realized that Bracho's innate power, the way it just came out of him, was the reason behind Pizante's move into Baja California.

"Today, we're going to pull a move. Julian Mayorca, my cousin, is port captain in La Paz," said Axel.

"Yeah, I remember you talked about him. Shit, he's still there? What is he, a lifer?"

"Yeah, well, not for long. Today we need to make him understand that he needs to resign."

"How do you suggest we do that?" said Bracho, sitting up on his bed, arms crossed over his naked torso.

"We need to make him feel death, but we can't kill him. Do you understand?"

Bracho smirked, "Why are you telling *me* for? What exactly is it that you want me to do?"

At that moment, Axel felt a certain inspiration, that inner voice that sparks and moves humanity in new ways, making things clear to him.

"According to our intel, when we approach La Paz, Mayorca will be running a drill at sea; when he finds out that it's me aboard the Sun-seeker, I'll invite him over," Axel paused. Like a director staging a play, he saw through the grid, and the blocking revealed itself to him, clear as the morning.

"When I bring him into the main salon, you and Navit can be waiting for him. He has a gun, the shotgun, and you... you threaten him." said Axel as he took his hands to his face in almost a prayer-like manner.

Showtime is when the magic comes together, every player to his part, every beat, every scene. Action, emotion, reaction, and stimulus. Like a supporting actor, Samuel Bracho rehearsed with his director. He got into character and found a light green cashmere sweater in the closet. He put it on over his bare skin and kept looking through the drawers.

"Yeah, you're threatening him because he knows who you are. He's got to see the power behind me and respect that," said Axel. "But you can't kill!"

Bracho laughed. "Relax. If anything, Navit will kill him, not me."

In one of the bedside drawers, he found some spectacles. He put them on and was shocked by how much better he could see.

"Huh, funny. All that time in prison, and I never realized my eyesight was bad. Then I put on these glasses, and boom! I see clearer."

The glasses were round and the lenses darkened as exposure to light became greater, turning them into complete shades if the sun was bright enough.

If the salon was going to be his stage, then the whole yacht was his theater. Axel made sure Zev stayed on the bridge. To his surprise, he was a good helmsman.

"You think Pizante would hire somebody with no sealegs to work in ports?" said Zev.

He made his way to the bow.

"Girls, you're perfect right there, tanning on the bow like supermodels," Axel told the girls.

They laughed.

"Listen, we are going to handle some business when we get to La

Paz. The port captain is going to board. When that happens, I need you girls to stay up here at all times. Is that clear?"

The girls agreed, not too convincingly.

"I'll tell you what, we'll give you each $100, but if the port captain sees you, talks to you, or approaches you, *do not engage*. Is that better?"

"That's right, honey, now you're talking our language, but we charge upfront," said Priscila.

"Nope, this is acting, not tricking. You get paid afterward."

They nodded.

"I'd pay you to look hot, but you're already doing it," said Axel, almost missing earlier times when getting girls and hopping parties was all there was to his life.

Zev was happy when he was on helm. "I love holding the wheel, wow, the speed, the wind. This sea is amazing," he said with wonder.

"You know, for a couple of goons, you and Navit are something else," said Axel.

"It's because we've seen war." He gave Axel the deep stare of bloodshed and gunpowder. "We've lived it, we *were* it, and we don't like it."

"I love to hear that. I think you and I can get along," said Axel. "Listen, the Mayorca Play," he paused. "First, we'll wait for them to make contact. Once they do, you will take the radio call. When they ask you to identify yourself, decline to reveal the shipmaster's identity. Tell them businessmen on leisure kind of thing, but notify them that the captain of this vessel is Axel Cuevas. If they don't know who I am, just tell them that Julian Mayorca is my cousin." A dramatic beat. "If Julian gets on the radio, then I will too. But if I know Julian, he'll want to come aboard the second he hears my name."

Navit cooked egg sandwiches in the galley. Bracho ate like a madman. It was eerie how the glasses fit him so perfectly.

"Okay, so I just hold the shotgun," said Navit as he cooked the eggs. Bracho laughed.

"You don't have to hit him," said Axel.

"Yeah, you do, if you want to beat him, break him down psychologically. You have to give him a little heat, let him know who's in charge," said Bracho.

"The laws of physics are in your favor, Mr. Cuevas," said a voice so powerful that for a split second, it made everyone feel for their lives. It was Pizante.

"How did you get on board?" asked Axel.

Pizante smirked.

"Those are the kind of things you still haven't learned from me, Mr. Cuevas. After all of these years… The laws of physics are in your favor." He smiled and took out an envelope from his back pocket. "We need Mayorca to sign this letter, both copies. If he signs it, he can live, is that understood?"

"Yes, Captain," said Axel.

Bracho continued eating and Navit looked to Pizante, like they were saying to each other, *if he doesn't sign, his body will be thrown out to the water, ready to be eaten by sharks.*

"Also, as soon as we finish, we need to evacuate these yachts. Broker's picking them up in forty-eight hours."

Pizante left the exact same way he had come in. The tender aboard the Azimut had two 350 Yamaha outboard motors. Miguel, his personal deckhand, pulled up next to the Sunseeker, through the wake. Pizante at sixty-one years old, made the jump gracefully from ship to ship. Axel went up to the deck to see him head back to his yacht.

"Impressive," yelled Zev from the bridge, smiling.

Aboard the Azimut, a whole different operation was underway. The war room was happening in the salon. Pizante was making sure media outlets were being fed stories about Samuel Bracho and his escape. Not just any stories, the right stories that benefited their operation. Some made Bracho out to be a folk hero who defied the Mexican government.

In others, he was a bloodthirsty outlaw who was going to kill anything in sight. Pizante had learned many years prior that tactical media was just as important in modern warfare as the execution of armed conflict. Pizante had contacts, ties, informants in media institutions all over the Americas. In the war room, he was also planning their arrival in South Baja, the logistics of their pickup point, and their transfer to the Old Mansion in Santa Rosalia.

The clock was ticking like the metronome of opening night. The stakes were high, the wind was cooling, the sun was strong. Julian Mayorca could be seen coming in on the tender. He was on the CB radio, talking with his crew, something about going fishing. From the Azimut, Pizante listened in; he had asked Zev and Navit to open their audio channels so he could listen to the exchange. Axel was still on the bridge, waiting for his lead actor to come closer and at least appreciate the beautiful women laying out in the sun.

Scene one, *Cousins*. Julian Mayorca and Axel Cuevas hug. They hadn't seen each other in seven years, family, at one point closer than brothers, about to collide, making time for small talk. Scene two, *The Salon*. It was hot in there. Julian comes in, gets a shotgun butt to the head by Navit. Samuel Bracho holds court, like the adversary he so comfortably is; good actor, good casting. Axel, the director of this tragedy, holding his hands to his mouth, clenching.

Praying to his God, asking for the life of his cousin. *Please don't kill him, please don't kill him.*

By the time Julian had signed the letters and was walking back out the deck, *alive*, Axel went into a trance, almost like a decompression.

Scene three. *Power Shift*. Mayorca goes back on the tender, silent, he goes fishing with his crew aboard *La Capitana*, they caught two dorados that day. The Sunseeker and the Azimut dock at a private cove. Three suburbans pick up Bracho and his people and drive them to the Old Mansion in Santa Rosalia. For the rest of that day, Axel Cuevas felt high, like if he had swallowed drops of clonazepam. He was all smiles, the great and bloodless benefactor.

CHAPTER 71

The Conversion

As Pascual Pizante spent more time in Baja, his relationship with Samuel Bracho strengthened. The two men became close; it was Pizante's psychology that made the relationship possible. He knew the time Bracho had spent in prison had broken him down, mentally, if only enough to show a crack where a strong foundation used to be. Pizante took advantage of Bracho's vulnerabilities.

The exploitation of Samuel Bracho's image didn't stop. He became a pop culture figure throughout Mexico and the southwestern United States. Somebody like Zorro or Pancho Villa, a person who embodied the dream of the outlaw; a bandit fighting the corrupt powers. The media couldn't get enough of "Bad Bracho." Everybody had something to say about him; all had suspicions and theories of his whereabouts. Some said he was a Hacienda holder, growing tobacco in Nicaragua, others that he was an informant to Cuba. Some even went as far as saying that Bracho had been seen in Los Angeles. But infamy wasn't the only thing Pizante wanted out of Bracho. He wanted inside information to strengthen his cause, which was to weaken the Mexican federal government. Pizante would spend weeks in Santa Rosalia at a time, planning, strategizing, working and getting in with Samuel Bracho, who constantly listened to Pizante's rants against the Mexican government.

"A bunch of thieves, a bunch of crooks, a bunch of inefficient politicians that don't deserve a crumb of power," he would say.

"Hey, I agree with you, those sons of bitches never did anything for me except lock me up without even a goddamn trial. And you know what? These politicians, they befriend you, they do business with you, and then they leave you out to hang for the vultures. At least it's what my *compadre*, goddamn Don Aldo, did with me," said Bracho as they sipped iced tea on the Old Mansion terrace.

Pizante made Bracho spill the beans about Don Aldo, about the Campo Casino, and everything their relationship involved. Pizante chewed on that information for weeks. When he went back to Panama, he had his sources look into Don Aldo. Two months later, when he returned to Baja, he told Samuel Bracho in person.

"Your *compadre* stole all of your wealth, he took over your whole financial operation, most of your foreign trusts and accounts. Almost everything."

Bracho was speechless

"Your house, hacked, your car, hacked. Don Aldo had full access to all of your computers, recordings of your voice, passwords, your car was tapped, your house was, too. He kept everything. He was spying on you the whole time."

The rage settled in Bracho's face, like when a wrinkle forms on a forehead, or a mole erupts on the skin.

Pizante gained Bracho's trust when he swore to him that they would avenge Don Aldo's betrayal. "We will get back at him in due time. And we'll make a lot of money in the meantime. But I need you to march under me," said Pascual.

Bracho agreed, and little by little, he became Pizante's drill sergeant, enforcing everything the commander wanted, not realizing he had become completely brainwashed by this figure, like a new convert who worships his redeemer.

The Host (Part II)

A<small>XEL</small> C<small>UEVAS</small> <small>POURED</small> C<small>HAMPAGNE</small> <small>FOR</small> Barbara Perez and her aides. The mayor of La Paz and her entourage were on the bow of the *Dream On* overlooking Isla Partida. They were discussing the new water park in La Paz. Axel smiled, looking as if he was interested in what they were saying, but in reality, his mind was in other places.

So many days behind him now—port captain for four years, a seniorship since the time he took the job from his cousin, ripping it from his hands and using the power as a platform to grow. His personal fortune, at over $5 million in cash and real estate, was growing a million-plus a year. And that was only what *he* got, the cherry on top. So much was happening in his position. There was money to be made every day. The port alone left a fortune, but he had other jobs, he had been trained to do more, deliver more, and the interests around him didn't just belong to him. He was simply a piece of a machine.

Samuel Bracho was shielded from Interpol, he couldn't be touched; Pascual Pizante, who operated his empire with diligence, made sure of it. Even though Pizante was rich and powerful, he needed Bracho on the ground, operating from behind another veil. Bracho was a man who knew how to work and get his hands dirty. Eventually, Bracho and Pizante formed an alliance as strong as the cement and gravel that mix into concrete. The Pizante-Bracho axis ran a complex operation, one that Axel Cuevas wasn't even fully in on. He did know that he had two jobs to do apart from his port captaincy duties; one, selling special forces defense programs to all of the federal, state, and municipal police forces in Mexico, a business that generated $12 million the year prior in government contracts.

Axel mostly did sales; weapon deliveries were shipped by Pizante himself. All the orders, like a military chain of command, came from Pizante through Bracho. Axel's second job consisted of recuperating whatever he could from Samuel Bracho's estate, or at least the parts he had stashed away over the years. Pulling out of businesses, liquidating assets, tough dealings that required a lot of loose cash to grease palms and not leave paper trails. Axel Cuevas did for Bracho what nobody else could do. He had position, status, and cash flow. He had built relationships all over Mexico, with police chiefs, mayors, governors, and congressmen. He was sleek, tough, and visionary. Axel was well-trained, first by Bracho, then by Pascual.

He laughed at the joke Barbara made about seawolves as he looked at the ocean from the beautiful yacht. The only thing missing at that moment was his lady, Regina Dahlgreen.

She's supposed to be here by now, wondered Axel as he looked at his Royal Oak Off Shore, watch. The time was 16:40.

He longed for her sweet smell, which was poison to him. She was a woman who had captured his heart. Regina had come to replace all the emptiness he hid within. She was an anchor, important to his whole operation. Regina was a trustworthy person; she inspired that in others. Her reliability was something she had inherited from her father. Perhaps it was her olive eyes, or her smile, but she evoked strong feelings in men, in Mexican men in particular. She had been told that her vibrant personality made others feel alive. She knew that she was a girl whose presence was missed when she left the room.

Axel had never met a girl like Regina before, a sensual yet serious, light-hearted, and complete woman. He imagined that's how a queen or somebody who was royalty would be. He looked back at his younger days when chasing tail was all he wanted. He did not yearn for the past. He was in love with this girl in a whole different way; he respected her and wanted to be with her. She possessed him to not look for sex outside of their relationship. Axel felt a sacred bond with her. Around Regina, he felt strong and guarded, like a sheltered soul in an ocean of loneliness.

The flow of his thoughts was interrupted by the sound of rotor blades, motor, and wind being split up into particles, a necessary disruption that happens when a helicopter arrives on the scene.

"Who's that?" asked the mayor.

The bird had entered their airspace.

"That's her," answered Axel.

He took them up to the bridge to observe the landing.

CHAPTER 73

Fixer

REGINA DAHLGREEN LIKED TO FIX broken things. In high school, her friends would always come to her for advice, particularly when they had fought with somebody. She was a mediator; she liked to get in between people and help make amends. She had learned these kinds of things from her father.

"If you spot a problem, go out of your way to fix it. Take ownership, build relationships, make things happen, business is about creating value, constantly," she remembered him saying.

But it wasn't just his words that turned her into a "fixer," It was her father's flaws. Ever since she was little, she could spot them. That pungent smell of marijuana that was always around the house when she was a baby, the way he would get too excited when talking on the phone, and, later, the guilty eyes that Soren could hide from the whole world, but never from his daughter. In the end, it was the feeling of being a fugitive, a refugee — a feeling that she carried deep in her heart. This feeling stirred her desire to be a fixer.

She knew there was something between Axel and Julian. Since the time she had reunited with Julian, she had been poking around, asking questions, trying to get intel on the muss between the old and new port captains. But everywhere she turned, people told her: "Cousins, probably still working together."

When she told Axel that she had run into Julian at the Nautical Expo, he was thrilled.

"I love Julian, did I ever tell you that we're cousins?" he said

"No, you didn't, not even when I asked you about him," Regina answered.

"Well, you found him. I know nothing about him or his whereabouts. What is he up to, anyway?"

"He started a yachting company and partnered up with a couple of pilots who have a seaplane, doing something similar to what I'm doing with the *Dream On*," said Regina.

"What *we're* doing. Don't forget, we're partners," said Axel, giving her a kiss on the lips.

That night they made love.

The morning that Regina mentioned to her boyfriend that she had worked a deal with Julian on the same day as Axel's party, he took the time to be transparent.

"There was some beef between him and I, but I'd like to put it behind us. I'll tell you what, bring him to the party afterward. He might not want to go if you tell him, because of hurt feelings. But if you have to kidnap him, bring him. I would love to settle things with him and have you help me."

She had done just that—tricked Julian into coming with her aboard her helicopter to meet with Axel. She wasn't obeying orders; she genuinely wanted her boyfriend and her old friend to spend time together with her and somehow resemble a family.

On this particular day, as Regina was flying her Eurocopter, she felt something strange for Julian. It was definitely love, but it was more the love that one feels for a father than the love that corresponds to romance. Julian made her feel tender, comfortable, safe, somehow protected. But Axel, who was waiting aboard the yacht, was exciting. And though Julian had dark features and was generally handsome, Axel Cuevas was hot, sexy, stylish, and beautiful to look at. Still, riding this close to Julian on the helicopter gave her that itch of the coxal that one feels when temperatures rise.

She liked him, his presence, his voice. There was something honest about Julian that Axel didn't have. Axel had that need to be recognized, and

Julian possessed such grace that he didn't need to belong. Regina enjoyed Julian's company, but knew that he kept certain compartments of himself closed permanently. She wanted him to open up; she wanted to heal those parts of her with the antidote that Julian carried in his own wounds.

Regina was in a bind.

She felt that Axel was somebody who was always playing a game of cat-and-mouse. She had noticed that about him early in their relationship. He was sneaky, up to something, always hiding layers of himself — not layers of hurt like Julian, but layers of secrets, business, and intentions. She didn't judge Axel; she enjoyed entering the arena with him, playing with him sometimes, gaining an edge, raising the stakes, then releasing the tension.

"Julian, I have to ask you something before we get to the party," she said as she handled the chopper with natural ability. "Axel says he wants to put everything behind him, but what happened between you and him?"

Julian chuckled. "Do you really think that five years ago, I just gave him my job?"

"No, I don't. What happened?"

"Oh, Regina, you're falling right into his plan. What were you thinking by bringing me here? You are playing a part in something bigger!"

"What's going on between you?"

Julian looked at her hair, the way it shone in the light sun, and out of instinct, he moved his lips up to his nose. "If he hasn't told you, then I can't tell you."

"Oh, it's like that. Well, one of you two is going to tell me," she said with a more aggressive tone.

"Well, isn't *he* your *boyfriend*?" said Julian.

Regina took a moment, and adjusted her tone. "Yeah, and you are a friend. Family, for me *and* him. I want the two of you in my life, without having it be awkward, " she said.

Julian looked at her and smirked. "Okay, Captain."

She was holding the collective, and he gently slid his hand on top of hers. She let him keep it there for a moment, but when she reached for the controls, it fell off.

CHAPTER 74

Lovebirds

A s he was riding copilot in Regina Dahlgren's Eurocopter, Julian Mayorca remembered the day his cousin betrayed him. For Julian, it wasn't about Samuel Bracho or political moves, it was about family losing all meaning, all hope. Looking right with a sigh, the bounding sea; looking left, the endless beauty of Regina Dahlgreen. Olive eyes and peachy skin, glimmering as a mirage of his own fantasies. The desire for this girl was unlike anything else for Julian. He thought about the day they had spent together in Cabo. He remembered the private cove where she kept her yacht, and that thought somehow led back to Axel and how he and Samuel Bracho had a goon hit him with a shotgun to get him to resign.

So much shit, he thought as he turned and looked at his girl, who was not his girl, but the girl of his enemy, who was also the same person who had put him through *so much shit*, and whose party they were arriving at. *At least it's her yacht and not Axel's*, thought Julian as they spotted the *Dream On*.

A chopper landing on the yacht during a party gathered a gallery of onlookers, who could not ignore this gorgeous feat of engineering. Regina rushed down from the helicopter to help the deckhands tie the bird down, working with gusto and authority. It was recognizable to everybody that she was a passionate person, in love with her work and good at it. As the rotor blades stopped spinning and the wind ceased to blow sideways, the party gravitated back towards the bow; but from the bridge, where Axel Cuevas was standing, Julian and Regina looked like a couple of lovebirds on their way to paradise, only touching ground to pick fruit.

CHAPTER 75

Highball

As Regina got down from the helicopter, Julian looked at her beautiful butt through the white shorts she was wearing. He was ready to follow her the world over. He clicked off his seatbelt and stepped down from the bird. Just then, he realized there was a gallery of people staring at them. The yacht turned into a microscope, and he was the molecule being observed.

In the corner of his eye, from up on the bridge, he spotted his cousin. Axel, wearing sunglasses, slightly took them off to make eye contact with him, just eye contact, no nod, no smile, Julian looking up, Axel looking down like a crow atop a boating tree.

Julian walked toward the party that was happening on the upper deck. He felt like a celebrity on the red carpet, everybody wanting to be greeted by the man who arrived via chopper. The ones he didn't know nodded; the ones he did reached out for a handshake, a hug, a kiss on the cheek from the ladies.

"I'm gonna go change," said Regina

"Where's the bar?"

"That way," Regina pointed as she headed below deck.

Julian began his pilgrimage, but with every little chit-chat and every forced hello, the bar seemed further away, like a carrot to be chased in the afterlife's tunnel. Julian feared that the next person he greeted was going to be his cousin. He had already made up his mind to face Axel, but he'd much rather do it with a drink or two inside him.

"Scotch-rocks and Scotch and soda in a highball glass, both doubles," said Julian when he finally reached that magical place.

Pedro was the gatekeeper, a bartender ready to pour the grace of God. Julian drank the whiskey on the rocks and took the highball with him. He went out towards the bow to get the fresh air that's only available on luxury yachts. At a distance, Julian could hear the music rising. It was Poolside doing a cover of the Neil Young song, "Harvest Moon."

He took a nice swig. The sun was at an angle where one cloud in the sky blocked its shine.

"Welcome to my party," said Axel.

Julian turned around with the natural grace of someone who's forgiving but still holding a grudge.

"*Primo*," said Julian, who reached out and gave Axel a hug of Judas.

"What the hell are you doing here, Julian?" said Axel with that unfunny sense of humor he possessed.

"Well, I just came in for a highball." Julian raised his glass, half smirk on his lips.

Axel took a second. "Relax, I wanted you to come today." A perfect smile. "What do you think? That Regina's just going to bring some guy on her chopper and fly him into *my* party without my consent? What kind of man would I be if I allowed that to happen?"

Julian felt the weight of the world on his shoulders. "Well, I'm here now!" He finished his highball like a sleazy detective.

"Julian, *primo*, I want to make amends," began Axel. "You see, things have changed, when I last saw you at my parent's house. I tried telling you; things aren't really black and white for me." Axel took a break, as if expecting Julian to say something. "You have no idea how hard it was for me to convince them not to kill you. That was a battle that I fought and won, so don't come at me like some little girl that doesn't understand that."

Julian looked at him, all seriousness in his eyes. "Oh, you're my savior, and all of this time, I was thinking that you were the one who betrayed me."

"You saw the people who are behind me, what I'm involved in. It's no joke," said Axel.

"Why do you do this Axel? Why do you choose to go down this path?" Julian asked.

"What path? What the hell are you talking about?" Axel said.

"Look, she brought me here by surprise. You, you tell me you wanted me to come. Me being set up, it's a pattern with you."

"No, but…"

"Let me finish. I'm not being disrespectful. And if we're gonna have a heart to heart, we're gonna have it the right way," said Julian, holding his hand up with authority.

From the bridge, Zev and another bodyguard took a peek below; they saw the boss talking intensely with a darker gentleman.

"Mayorca," Zev whispered to the bodyguard from afar.

"The path of darkness is very lonely, Axel. You hurt me bad, you hurt your parents, Gene and Luisa, and what? You're gonna hurt Regina, too?"

Axel forced a smile to his lips. "I would never hurt that girl. She means the world to me. In fact, when she told me she was going to work with you before my party, I insisted that she bring you on board, I told her that we needed to patch things up — cousin stuff. And, of course, she helped me get you here," Axel could sense Julian's concern. "Relax, Julian. I'm not gonna hurt you, I'm not gonna hurt her, and I'll even prove it to you, okay?"

Julian eased up, remembering their childhood together for a brief second.

"I actually wanted to see you because I need to talk to you about something," said Axel as he grabbed Julian's arm gently and walked alongside the rail, like a politician talking to a new ally.

"When Regina told me that you had your own company, I looked you up." Axel pulled a smartphone out of his pocket. "You have a good social media profile, impressive," He showed him Baja Air & Sea's Instagram, with 100,000 followers.

Axel put the phone back in his pocket.

"But I looked beyond the surface. I had some friends pull up your company papers." Axel looked at Julian to see his reaction of fear-filled surprise. "You know, as port captain, I have to make sure everything is in regulation. And I ran across something very interesting,"

Julian held his breath, *How deep did Axel's investigation go? Was he going to trace his company down to the 'acquisition' of the Almost Heaven?* Within, panic. His expression, stoic.

"It turns out that your partner, attorney Alberto Fontana, is a mutual friend, somebody who's becoming of a lot of interest to my organization."

"Fontana?"

"Yes, we know he has plans to build a port at Punta Colonet. We know he got $50 million from Antonio Blancarte, and that Sergio Cho is getting in on it. Long story short, my people and I, we want in," he looked to the horizon. "I talked to Fontana last week, and he responded with an email, telling me that there wasn't any room for us on this deal. I've decided to give him three more days to change his mind, and I need *you* to talk to him." Axel looked at Julian, "I figured, if anybody can warn him about my people, you can."

Axel took a beat. "Honestly, I don't want to carry any more weight on my conscience, so speak to him; tell him to take our money for his own good."

Julian stared blankly, processing the deal that Alberto Fontana had been working on for years, buying land in Punta Colonet, all of the prospecting, due diligence, permits, loans, policy, politicking, networking, fundraising, engineering — work that had gone into that project for years, and these entitled mobsters just wanted to muscle in and take a piece.

Julian looked at Axel with the same disgust as he felt for him. "Yeah, I'll talk to him, but I've got to get another highball," he shook the empty glass.

Axel sighed, nodded gently, and began to walk away. "Let's keep talking. Enjoy your evening. It's gonna get better."

Julian made his way to the bar, where Pedro was delivering Ten Commandments Scotch whiskey. He had a shot while he waited for his double highball. A gentleman by the rail was smoking a cigarillo. Julian asked him for one and smoked it with his Scotch. He couldn't believe it, the audacity, the attitude, the complete disregard for business or respect.

Axel had balls as big as the *Dream On*.

Regina walked onto the deck with a smile and her usual air of elegance. The sight of her eased Julian's mind for a second. He took a swig of his highball. She approached him.

"So did you and Axe kiss and make up?" she asked.

"Almost," said Julian.

"Good, because he really wanted to see you. He cares a lot about you, you know? He's very interested in what you're doing, with the yacht and plane," she said.

At that moment, Julian saw beyond her beauty. He saw a frightened twenty-eight-year-old girl who wanted to fix problems that were well beyond her.

"Listen, your boyfriend is not who you think he is," said Julian.

"What?" said Regina, not finishing her words, distracted by the music behind her that began to fade as the conversations around them got louder.

"You still have a lot to learn, Regina," said Julian.

She smiled with a look that said *you have no idea*.

From the speakers came Axel's clear voice: "Good evening. Welcome aboard the *Dream On*, Baja Explorations' luxury yacht."

Everybody clapped. Axel stood in the center of the crowd. "Of course, none of this would be possible without Regina Dahlgreen." Her name was followed by a cheer. "The girl who flies a helicopter onto a yacht without a blink. Wow! You're a star," said Axel, looking at Regina.

"Come here," he continued.

Regina walked gracefully towards her man.

They were a beautiful couple, good looking, sporty, attractive. Even Julian couldn't stop staring at them, feeling contempt. Jealousy, anger, and sadness rising inside of him, but no action. He just stood silently. Internally, he was screaming to himself: *That's my girl, that's my job, you're an asshole!* Lacking the courage and the death wish to say it out loud. The thought of saying that and sounding like a bitch made him laugh to himself.

Axel continued, "I wanted to invite you all tonight, because it's a very special night for us. I wanted you to all be here," he let go of Regina and pulled a small box out of his pocket. "It's hard for a guy not to fall in love with you."

She smiled like the sun setting over an island. He kissed her on the lips. No question, no answer, but Regina had a ring on her finger. The yacht went wild: cheers, laughter, joy. From the back, Julian stared at the couple with emptiness in his dark eyes.

CHAPTER 76

AeroBaja

REALITY HAD BLURRED. EMOTIONS AND thoughts had become one. Memories, hopes, dreams, disillusions—all blended into a giant goo called life. Julian woke up aboard *The Cecilia*. The master stateroom smelled like the Scottish Highlands, where Ten Commandments whiskey was malted into single barrels of heaven-turned-hell.

Highball after highball, he drank himself into oblivion. Vague memories of a dark-skinned man skippering a tender, communicating via CB with Denise and *The Cecilia*, getting their coordinates. Julian getting dropped off on his yacht after being breached, poked, and used by Axel Cuevas and, somehow, hurt by Regina Dahlgreen.

"Uff… Engaged?" said Julian to himself. That raspy hungover tone of loneliness. He held his hands to his head and almost wept.

All of the thoughts began racing back to him: Alberto Fontana, Axel Cuevas, the threats, intimidation, and, worst of all, that insatiable thirst for power that could be felt around Axel. Julian was a sensible man and his cousin's actions damaged him deeply. He went into the galley, chugged a glass of water, unplugged his phone from the charger, and dialed Alberto.

"We need to have a serious conversation about Axel Cuevas," he said.

"Goddamn it, I was wondering where his next move was going to come from," said Alberto.

"He got to me yesterday, wants in on Punta Colonet."

"Damn it, Julian! What did he say?"

"Well, he said a lot of things, but mostly that you've got three days or else."

"Or else, what?"

Julian could feel that he was getting under Alberto's skin.

"Listen, I hate to be the messenger, but the way he came at me. We gotta talk, and not by phone either. I want to help you."

Five minutes later, Alberto had bought a same-day plane ticket for Julian, who got cleaned up and boarded AeroBaja's flagship La Paz-Tijuana route at 13:15. The plane was an old MD-81; the seats were stained red, and it smelled like a sweaty saloon. There were some steel elements to the aircraft that made it look particularly dated. Takeoff was loud and rowdy, things rumbled around and the flight attendants had a negative attitude.

When they reached peak altitude, the flight attendant announced that smoking was allowed from row 19 to row 27. Julian couldn't believe it. Well into the era of Facebook, and AeroBaja was still allowing smoking on board. During the two hour and two minute flight, Julian, who was seated in row 16 of a rather empty plane, witnessed five people light up. When the flight arrived in Tijuana, Julian went straight to the curbside where Alberto was waiting for him in his Land Rover Discovery. This time, however, Fontana had a driver and a bodyguard riding shotgun. He was also escorted by a black suburban.

"What's with all the security?" asked Julian.

"We're in the big leagues now," said Alberto.

Julian got in the back seat, next to his business partner. One of the bodyguards closed the door behind him. The Discovery took off.

CHAPTER 77

Caesar Salad

Caesar's on Revolucion Avenue is the go-to place in Tijuana, an eating and drinking establishment that was founded during American Prohibition. A classic restaurant with a mahogany long bar, serene ambience, and good service. Pictures on the wall of the golden days, when Tijuana was nothing but a casino, a resort town where Chaplin, Garbo, Hayworth, and even Capone would weekend and party. Alberto and Julian had a table set up in the private room, guards outside the door, a bottle of rosé on ice, two glasses poured and paired with Evangelina sparkling water. Beto, the waiter, prepared table side salads.

"The history of the Caesar salad begins here in TJ," said Beto.

"We don't care about the history of the Caesar salad. Just serve it already. And bring us the food. Leave us alone, we've got to talk," said Fontana, not angry, but serious.

"Yes sir." Beto left.

"You don't understand, Julian. These guys push themselves *in*. *Pinche* Cuevas. The son of a bitch. He wants to put in $25 million. I never wanted him to come in, but you know how he is. *Persuasive*. So I tell him, send me the deal in writing, and I read it." Alberto scoffed. "It says that after month three, I would have to begin paying him back a million dollars a month."

"To hell with that!" interrupted Julian.

"That's right!" continued Alberto. "But, you see, I looked right through them, and the son of a bitch. The son of a bitch. That's how they do it! They go in and they start milking you, milking you, until they break you, then they get violent, and bully the life out of you, and break your fucking business and ruin your life while they're at it," said Alberto.

"Well, they already got violent. They came looking for me to get to you, asked me to remind you that *he's* the guy that took my job at gunpoint while Samuel Bracho bitch-slapped me. I mean, I don't want to be here any more than you do, but what do we do?" said Julian.

"Well, I'm not letting them into this deal, no way. Everybody would pull out. Sergio Cho would pull out, Blancarte would sue, they will corrupt the whole deal. Goddamn savages," said Alberto.

"Do you think they found out you led the media offensive against him?" said Julian.

"I don't know."

The waiter came into the room, took their salad plates, set down Beef Wellington for Fontana and Escolar for Julian.

"I've given it a lot of thought, Julian, and I wanted to let you know in person. I'm having a meeting tomorrow with Don Aldo Ruiz, ex-Governor of North Baja."

"What are you gonna talk to Don Aldo about?" said Julian.

Alberto sipped from his wine glass. "Protection, Julian. We need protection."

"You know what I hate? I hate the fact that you didn't come to me first. Why do I have to hear all of this from Axel? Why couldn't you come to me?"

"Jesus, Julian. Wake up! This is the real world and it's happening 1,000 miles per hour."

"That's the thing — not for them. Not for Axel, Bracho, and whoever else. They're always one step ahead. It's not coming '1,000 miles per hour' for them; they've got everything perfectly planned," said Julian.

Over the following hour, they went through a lot of scenarios, some of them futile, some of them practical. After dinner, when they were down to their last bottle of Gran Ricardo red wine, Julian began to feel zealous; he had peace in the midst of this war. They agreed that Julian was going to stay the night, and that the two were going to recap for lunch, after Alberto's morning meeting with Don Aldo. Alberto picked up the tab and Julian gave him time to leave with his entourage.

Moments later, Julian casually made his way to the bar. He had a quarter bottle of mezcal with some people who were on a culinary tour.

"We're just here to have the Caesar Salad," said a chubby brunette.

"Where are you from?" asked Julian.

"From Wisconsin."

"You came here all the way from Wisconsin for a salad?" he asked.

"Not just a salad," she said with a wink.

Two hours later, they were sharing the corner room at the OneBunk Hotel down the street.

CHAPTER 78

Tandem

As an engagement present, all Regina Dahlgreen wanted from Axel was for him to go skydiving with her.

"You've got to trust me. If you and I are going to get married, I need to know that you trust me," she told Axel, naked under her in the master stateroom aboard the *Dream On.*

"Yeah, but to jump off a plane with you is a whole different thing."

"No, we're not just jumping together, we're jumping tandem," said Regina.

"*Tandem*?" he repeated.

"Yeah, you're going to be strapped to me because *I* control *you*," she said playfully.

"Jesus!" Axel laughed and embraced her passion.

Over the past year, Regina had spent every Tuesday morning with her friends at Cabo Skydive. Great guys who had an old twin engine Cessna that they used to take skydivers out. They loved working on jumps with Regina, especially Elias, one of the younger trainers. Only twenty-five and an excellent skydiver, he had been in the U.S. Army, but had been discharged. Regina enjoyed skydiving with him. He taught her tricks of the trade and was passionate about the craft. He even showed her how to lead somebody on a dive and was the first person to fly tandem under Regina's control. Even though she had always kept a couple of parachutes aboard her helicopter, she had never jumped from it because she didn't trust anybody else to fly it. But six weeks prior, Elias introduced her to Casper Jones, a retired U.S. Navy helicopter pilot who lived in the East Cape. Regina took him up on her bird, and when she let him have the controls, she knew she had met the only other person in South Baja who could maneuver her Eurocopter. She hired him part-time to copilot and to service the helicopter.

On the Tuesday morning that she arranged to bring Axel on his first skydive, he received a phone call that upset the day's course of events.

"Hello," answered Axel as he exited the shower.

"I hope you're not getting too comfortable," said Pascual Pizante.

"What a pleasant surprise, commander," said Axel, who was secretly nervous whenever Pizante broke rank and called him directly.

"I hope you know what you're doing regarding this port deal, Axel. We need to be *in* on the ground floor of this project."

"I know, sir. What do you think I'm doing?"

"Not working on it enough. Bracho is already telling me that you're being too weak."

"But, sir, I have a plan… I know these guys, I'm gonna persuade them," interrupted Axel.

"Well, you better speed it up. I'm getting restless."

"I will not let you down, sir," were the last words Axel told Pizante before hanging up.

When Regina and Axel rendezvoused, he was feeling angry, eager to know what was happening with Julian and the ultimatum he had given him about Alberto Fontana and the port deal. The three days had been up two days ago. He dialed Julian's number, no answer. Regina could tell he was distressed.

"What's wrong, honey?" she asked as they drove toward the landing strip off Cabo del Sol.

"*Nada*, just this work thing I've got to deal with," he said while shaking his head, grabbing the wheel with one hand, and fiddling with his phone with the other.

"Do me a favor, clear your mind. Focus on me, on this adventure, on the moment," she told him.

"Yeah, you're right; this might be our last day on this earth."

"Don't think like that, Axel, don't even joke like that. Skydiving is serious, and the law of attraction is just as strong as the law of gravity," said Regina.

"I'm just kidding, I'm not scared, I've been through worse," he said.

"Yeah, I bet you have, but it's nothing compared to what I'm going to put you through in our marriage."

A laugh. The tension easing.

"Oh, the things we'll do for a piece of ass," he said.

"Yeah, a piece of ass with a helicopter." She slapped him on the arm.

As they drove past the mountains, they spotted the red Eurocopter. It was waiting for them on the small dirt landing strip where Cabo Skydive held their operations. Casper Jones was running his checklist while sitting in the pilot's seat. As they pulled up, Elias, the trainer, jumped out of the helicopter to greet them.

"Welcome to the best day of your life, Mr. Cuevas," he said.

"Or the last," said Axel.

The helicopter rose and they became airborne.

Metal cutting through air like an instrument of death. Complex transactions of emotional, monetary, and physical value. Loss, constant loss, going through Axel's head.

"Hey," a break in continuity, "where are you today?" said Regina.

"I'm here, I'm ready to do this," he said.

"You better be, because once we're on our dive, you need to focus. You know the whole mentality of this is *live in the moment, be in the moment*. It may sound cliché, but it's true. And if you're not here, I'd rather not do this," she said.

Then a thought came to her and she began playing with the engagement ring he had put on her finger three days earlier.

That gesture struck a chord with Axel. He got up and put on the jumpsuit Elias had laid out for him.

Regina put on her parachute and Elias strapped the harness on Axel's chest.

"It's important that you listen to her entirely. She is trained to act on a different number of scenarios. You just enjoy it and don't get too stiff," he said.

Regina had finished prepping. She looked like a warrior, ready to descend on her target.

"Okay, we're at 10,000," yelled Casper from the cockpit.

Regina stretched and hyped herself up, doing a war call of sorts.

Axel wasn't sure who he was looking at. She looked like some sort of beast putting together a ritual. Elias strapped Regina to Axel's back. He double-checked her chute and gave her the okay sign.

"Try not to get in my way," she yelled in Axel's ear, but it felt like a whisper over the white noise of adrenaline.

"Let's try to hang on the rail," she said.

The two of them crawled like a spider onto the bottom rail. Then Regina held him like a pro wrestler and dove backward for a free fall of thousands of feet. They spun, they twisted, almost as if their weight wasn't flesh. Axel, scared, thinking control was being lost, began to panic, tried to extend his arms, but Regina pushed them in, fear rising, but then she let go.

"Now, fly!" she said.

Axel, birdlike, extended his arms like featherless wings and felt the air, finally living in the moment, where nothing else mattered.

The earth zooming in like an HD spycam, pulling them fast but not hard. Soft, like the air they were leaving behind every nanosecond, but firm like the runway below catching up to them.

"Pull!" Regina yelled with a yank of the chord.

A halt of freedom, but a rush of blood to the dome. Floating like a leaf that falls from a tall tree, little by little approaching the X.

"Wow, my God, no wonder you do this so much," said Axel as they touched solid ground.

"You passed the test Mr. Cuevas. You're an alright guy. I don't care what they say about you," she said.

"And *I* love you, I don't care how crazy you are. I will never try to change you," he said.

They kissed and shed their jumpsuits like snakes in the summer.

When the helicopter returned to the airstrip, only an open parachute and tire marks remained of the tandem skydivers.

PART IV

Payoff

CHAPTER 79

Learjet

JULIAN HAD BEEN STUCK IN Tijuana for four days. It was already Wednesday. He didn't know what to do, so he listened to audiobooks and took long showers. The night before, he had taken a walk in the Tijuana beach neighborhood called Playas; he even sat up against the U.S. border fence, 100 yards from where it sinks into the Pacific Ocean. As he looked towards San Diego, he experienced a desire to leave it all behind and just move stateside. No more Axel, Fontana, or Regina.

But what about my yacht? And the Sea of Cortez?

To be back on the water was the only thing he truly desired. Alberto Fontana wasn't picking up his phone, so he wasn't answering, either, when Axel Cuevas rang. Alberto had sent a driver who was on standby in case Julian needed to move. He was meditating on all of this, letting water run on his head in his hotel room shower.

When he got out and began to dry, his phone rang.

"Pack your bags, we're getting out of here," said Alberto.

"Where we going?"

"Taking you back to La Paz. Don Aldo let us take his jet."

Julian put on his cleanest jeans and the new Dr. Martens boots he'd bought in a Tijuana hipster boutique. He stretched his less-wrinkled shirt, put everything in a small carry-on, and headed out. The driver was already waiting for him. Without saying a word, he opened the backseat door. Julian jumped in, put on his headphones, and listened to classical music, a meditation of sorts that he'd been practicing to still his mind.

The suburban pulled up to the private flight terminal at the Tijuana International Airport. When the driver stopped the car, Julian felt it all come back to him. His problem, Axel Cuevas and Samuel Bracho wanting in, Alberto Fontana pushing them out. What did he get out of all this? Was it even worth it? He thought about his yacht, *The Cecilia*. And his great, great crew, Denise, Ernie, Rubio.

Maybe that was his prize. At this point, he was willing to accept that. The driver opened his door. He was at the airstrip. A sleek white and red Learjet, with the airstairs down, waiting for him. Seconds later, Alberto's Discovery came speeding. Alberto bolted out the front door.

"They're all animals. It's the goddamn Viet Cong out here," he said, touching Julian's arm before climbing into the Learjet.

The Ardiente Casino logo was stylishly etched on the side of the plane and the back of the seats. The pilot was locked and loaded in the cockpit, and only Alberto and Julian were on board. The interior of the jet was completely remodeled, with seating for eight passengers: three in a forward sideways couch and four small couches placed astern, facing each other.

The copilot was the last to board. He closed the door and Alberto and Julian sat down face to face.

The copilot, who introduced himself as Marcelo, told them there were no servers aboard, but there was a fully stocked bar. He asked them to fasten their seatbelts for takeoff. "We're looking to get into LPZ at right under ninety minutes. Enjoy the flight," he said as he went into the cockpit.

Takeoff. The rush of leaving the ground behind. Alberto made the sign of the cross. Gaining speed, gaining altitude, and for two minutes, silence, as the engines fought gravity.

"We're playing hardball, Julian. "

He interrupted a holy trance.

"Don Aldo is in. He doubled down. When he heard that Samuel Bracho was behind Axel, his eyes lit up. You should've seen him."

Julian took a second. "How do you see Don Aldo involved in all of this?"

"Well, this is the thing, I met with Don Aldo this morning. He wanted to talk to Axel personally, so I got him on the phone and told him we would send the Learjet to pick him up." Alberto unclipped his seatbelt. "Axel Cuevas is coming back to Tijuana with me today. We're only touching base in La Paz to drop you off, and I'm flying back with him. Axel and I are having dinner with Don Aldo tonight." He made two whiskey rocks, gave one to Julian, and sat back down.

"I don't get it," said Julian, who wouldn't touch his drink.

For the next several minutes, Alberto explained what he and Don Aldo had come up with.

"Don Aldo says that Axel used *you* to get to *me*, and that now they want to use *me* to get to *him*," he said, taking a swig of his whiskey.

"It's like checkers," Julian said.

"It's like *chess*! Don Aldo is waiting for them to come for him. I mean, he knows that Samuel Bracho knows what everybody knows — that Don Aldo stole a lot of Bracho's money after sending him to prison. Don Aldo is a very methodical guy. He sits back and collects data, views all aspects, then makes a decision and strikes." Alberto sat back in his seat.

"What do you think is going to happen now? After the three of you sit down for dinner?" asked Julian.

"Well, Don Aldo said that what he really wants to know is who is bankrolling Axel and Bracho, that's the answer to everything."

"What does Don Aldo get out of helping you?" asked Julian.

"Well, he's going to have to come in as a partner in the Punta Colonet Port," said Alberto with disappointment. "Don't look at me like that, Julian. I had to choose between Satan and his brother. At least I know Don Aldo and he didn't try to muscle his way in. I invited him. Better than fucking Bracho, and what? Cuevas, the extortionist, the prick. I'd rather see him dead than to do business with him!"

"Well, you're going to do business with him tonight, at the dinner table. What do you think is going to happen? The three of you are going to make a deal and who's going to lose? Who has the most to lose, Alberto? You do!" said Julian.

"Damn it, Julian! You don't think I know that? I'm just trying to stay alive. I'm playing hard, trying to make a hundred, two hundred million for myself. You think that's easy?"

Julian was serene, businesslike. "Don't you think I should be at that meeting?"

"With Bracho and Axel?"

"Yeah."

"Nah."

"Why?"

"You don't want to be that close to the fire."

"I'm already burning, but you know what? Don Aldo is going to stick it to you; that's his nature."

"Yeah, and what about Axel? I know what he did to you. Don't you want to get back at him?"

"Yes, I do, but," Julian sighed.

"*Ahhh* what? Do you want him pushing you around, bullying you forever? I don't know, maybe you like being his bitch?"

"We're the good guys, Alberto! We always have been. We can't play by their rules; we don't know their game!" Julian took a second, breathed in the altitude, and took a swig from his water bottle.

"It's not about good or bad, Julian. I mean, I don't make my decisions like that. I just can't let these guys come into my business like bloody cowboys, guns blazing. I have to try to retain some control of the situation. And, yes, deep down, I know the same thing is going to happen with Don Aldo, but if somebody's gonna fuck me, I'd rather choose who. Besides, Don Aldo knew my father," Alberto said as he poured himself another drink.

Julian made his way to the WC, urinated, washed his hands, and splashed some water on his face.

"What a day, what a day," he said to himself in the mirror.

At that moment, he heard a voice within him that calmly said "*be still.*"

"Thank you, God", Julian whispered.

He came out of the WC with peace and stillness.

"There's one more thing," Alberto said.

Julian sat down and clipped his seatbelt.

"Don Aldo asked me if I could help him find Bracho's old yacht, *The Durango*." Alberto paused and observed Julian's reaction.

Nothing.

"As it turns out, Axel Cuevas used to be that yacht's captain."

Another pause, another blank stare from Julian.

"Don Aldo's been on the tail of the ship for five years. Last somebody saw it was in Bahia de las Palmas, about three months ago."

"Bahia de las Palmas, near the East Cape?" asked Julian.

"Yeah."

"Why does Don Aldo want to find this yacht?"

"Well, I think there's something aboard that interests him. He wouldn't exactly tell me."

Julian nodded. "How do we know that the yacht isn't on its way to China right now?"

"That yacht is so hot, if it ever set foot thirteen miles off shore, in international waters, the Americans would move in on it faster than they did on *The Dock Holiday*," Alberto said.

"How do you suggest I go about finding the yacht?"

"Well it's a 220-foot yacht. People are going to remember if they saw it. We think they're hiding it, not knowing what to do with it."

"Do you think Axel or Bracho know its whereabouts?" Julian asked.

"We don't think so. Word on the street is that the Knights of Michoacan took the yacht as payment from Bracho. Don Aldo's intelligence tells him that they slaughtered the whole crew."

Julian took a moment to collect his thoughts. "I'll do it. Somebody who allows his crew to die like that? Bracho is a freaking animal." Julian shook his head. "If this yacht's in Baja California, I'm finding it."

"I knew we could count on you. Don Aldo is not as bad as they make him. It's good that I'm working directly with him while you're on the water. You're an ace up our sleeve," said Alberto.

Julian grinned and the copilot's voice came on the speakers, notifying them about their descent into La Paz.

Wheels down, hot runway surrounded by desert, air stairs down. The copilot thanked Julian. Alberto stayed aboard. Somebody rushing to the Learjet with sandwiches. When they were standing at the sill, Alberto reminded Julian of the love and passion that motivated him.

"You know how I am Julian. I have to play big. I've got to make it. I'm not gonna lose this one. This port is going to change Baja."

And walking towards them, Axel Cuevas, dressed like a model, alone, no bodyguards, no one, just him — a public servant hoping not to be seen by anyone, approaching the plane like a seasoned jetsetter.

"Are you two faggots gonna kiss goodbye, or is Julian flying back with us to Tijuana?" he asked.

"Is that all you got? A homophobic slur? You're weaker than I thought." Julian smirked. "No, I'm staying in paradise, tired of TJ. I got you your man, man." He pointed to Alberto. "And you know what? I hope it all works out for you, for the both of you." He gave Alberto a hug and shook the copilot's hand.

"Good to see you, Axel. I hope you don't need anything from me anytime soon," Julian said as he walked by him.

"I don't need you. I choose to use you," Axel said.

Julian took off his sunglasses and stared directly into his cousin's eyes. "That's right, and it's gonna stop!"

Axel looked into those mad eyes filled with a pain that belonged to Julian. For a second, he sensed it, the fear of being alive. Axel walked up the airstairs with a bad feeling in his gut. "Close this thing. It's hot!"

Julian walked across the tarmac and into the main hall. The Learjet taxied behind him.

CHAPTER 80

Side Piece

JULIAN WALKED INTO THE LA Paz Airport through the small door near the private terminal. The air conditioned hall smelled of Pine-Sol. Through the glass, sweaty tourists and locals scrambled through little stores and restaurants, waiting for their planes to colder destinations. He walked out the front doors into a warm, light breeze and a shaded area where people waited to get picked up or hire a taxi.

"Hey!"

Like the trumpet of Zion, the most beautiful sound entered Julian's ear, traveled through his vessels and put an immediate smile on his face. It was Regina Dahlgreen. She followed up her greeting with a slight touch on his arm.

He looked at her and sighed in deep relief. He hugged her so naturally that she felt his tenderness and even a hint of vulnerability. She was attracted to the feeling, flattered by it. Julian was obviously crushing on Regina. Her sensitivity was catching it.

"Wow, you smell good," he said.

"Ha, well, you're in a good mood," Regina said with a smile of her own.

"You put me in a good mood," he said with a whiff of pride. "What are you doing here?"

"Well, I came to drop off Axel and I went inside to use the restroom," she laughed.

The Learjet flew behind them. "There he goes," he pointed up.

"What are you doing?" she asked.

"I'm just flying in. I had to skip town for a couple of days," he said, wondering if she knew about what was happening with Axel and Alberto Fontana.

"Cool. Were you gonna get a taxi? Because I can give you a ride if you need one," she said.

Julian smirked on top of his smile and they walked toward Regina's Land Cruiser.

The ocean doesn't comprehend the complexities of earth, and neither do I... I am an ocean man, temporarily cast on soil, thought an inspired Julian as they were in Regina's car, traveling fast down semi-isolated roads, passing El Centenario, heading back to La Paz.

"Are you hungry? Because I know a great little spot around here."

"Not really hungry," she said, "but I'll have an iced tea with you."

"I'm starving. You're gonna love this place," said Julian as he gave her directions through a beachside road.

Playa Coyote restaurant was a large open room, decorated at the whims of the owner, Kendra, an orange-toasted white woman in her sixties. Photographs of her and her friends hung on the walls — on a fishing boat, somebody holding up a dorado, another one with a marlin, a shark jaw displayed like a trophy. Fishnet on the ceiling made the place look authentic, kinda tacky, but kinda cool. The terrace led to a small private cape that Julian referred to as the Cape of Little Hope.

"Yeah, this is a place where you bring your side piece," Julian said as he munched on tostadas and guacamole.

"Your what?" asked Regina.

"Side piece, you know? Like the person you see on the side, the one you don't want to be seen with," said Julian.

Regina laughed. "Is that why you brought me here?" she said, faux-offended.

Julian nodded. "Come here..." he lowered his voice.

"What?" she almost didn't hear him.

"Come closer..." lowering his voice even more.

Regina scooted closer.

"No." He shook his head. "I'm in the booth, you're on a chair in front of me. I've got an ocean view. Come, sit by my side." He touched the empty space next to him.

Regina was hesitant. She sighed, stood up and sat next to him.

"Hey!" he whispered.

"What?"

"You're so gorgeous."

She laughed.

The waiter set a dozen rock oysters in the middle of the table and a red seafood stew in front of Julian. He began slurping down oysters.

"You're not gonna get fresher oysters than these," he said. "These guys pick them from the little rock out there. I've seen them," said Julian as he sprayed a dash of lime on an oyster and took it down. "The freshness of the entire ocean in a single bite."

"Wow, now you're making me want one," said Regina.

"Go ahead, you're going to love them."

She sprayed lime over the shellfish.

He stared at her.

"Stop," she whispered.

Julian winked.

"You need to stop." She smiled.

"I can't. I'm into you big, even when I'm not with you, you're on my mind. I want you bad. Be my queen."

"Well, you need to stop. I am not *your queen*. Eat."

He ate.

"Can I get a glass of red wine, please?"

The waiter nodded from across the floor.

When it arrived, Julian poured a bit into his stew.

"Julian, what business are Axel and you up to?" Regina asked.

Awkward silence.

"None of yours." He smiled and put his face close to hers.

Regina's smile faded and she pulled away. "Not funny, Julian. I need to know what I'm getting into."

Julian scoffed.

Regina turned stoic.

Julian cleared his throat. "Listen, what he and I have going on is not business. It's extortion from his end at best. I'd rather not deal with him ever again."

"What did he do?"

"How do you think he got to be port captain?"

"Oh, please!"

"Come on. It's *Axel*, the most corrupt piece of shit in Baja, and that's saying a lot! Don't act like you don't realize who you're engaged to."

"Are you serious?"

A long sigh. "He took my job five years ago. He came in by sea. I went aboard this yacht he was skippering, this Sunseeker, and Samuel Bracho put a shotgun to my head. They threatened me and told me to either resign or die alongside my crew."

"Jesus, Axel did that?"

"Yeah, and if he's capable of doing that to me, imagine what he can do to hurt you," Julian said.

"He would never hurt me."

"That's what they all say."

Just then, a trio of musicians came up to their table.

"A little bit of *música* for the *señorita, Capit*án?" It was the accordionist who did the talking.

"*Ándale!*" Julian gave him a crisp twenty-dollar-bill.

The trio included a harpist and a guitarist. They played a Spanish version of "Chapel of Dreams."

"*It is heaven to know just what happiness means. It is found at the door in the chapel of dreams...*" The trio sang like angels.

Regina's eyes teared up. Julian grabbed her hand under the table. He closed in on her right ear. "I love you."

Regina shook her head. The tear she was holding back rolled down her cheek.

"I need you," a playful whisper. "Allow yourself to be with a better man, no regrets." Long pause. Regina's hand still connected to Julian's.

"And to think," said Julian, close to her neck.

She moved her hair to the other side. "To think what?"

Julian put his left arm around her. "When you first came to Baja, you went to the captainship looking for me, right?"

Regina nodded, becoming comfortable in Julian's arm.

"If he hadn't taken my job, you and I would've met then, and who knows. You and I could've been married already." His voice almost cracked.

"And *what*? You and I get married? *Then what*?"

Julian blushed. "A couple of kids?"

She laughed. "*Kids*? You're *that* traditional?"

He rubbed the back of her head with his left thumb.

"Run away with me." He kissed the right side of her neck softly.

"What?" she said, curious.

"I'm in love with you. Let's go somewhere together, anywhere you want, my treat. And, if you like it, we can stay there forever."

"Where would we go?" she asked.

"Wherever. New Zealand," Julian said.

"What? I love New Zealand!" She got excited.

"You see! It's meant to be."

"Seriously, who do you know in New Zealand? Do you know the Stewarts? Carly and Lawrence? They were friends of my parents."

"No, but I know Frodo, Gandalf, and a sexy elf lady who would be glad to see me," he said.

"You are a tool, you know that? An absolute tool."

They both laughed.

He moved his face closer to hers.

She blushed.

He smiled and stared at her lips.

She moved away from him and stood up.

"*Que pasa?*" he asked.

"*Que pasa contigo?*"

Julian chuckled.

Regina straightened her shorts and fanned her face with her hand. "Whew," she smiled.

"It doesn't have to end here. This can be a beginning — not an end."

"Julian, I can't." Her smile waned. "Perhaps you're right. Perhaps you and I could've ended up together in a parallel reality, but this isn't it."

A dense pause.

"You know what hurts?"

"Don't do this, Julian. Don't go down that route."

"What? You don't even know what I'm going to say."

Regina crossed her arms.

"The expectation, that's what hurts," he said. "Death of expectations we build in our heads."

"Your expectations are your own. I had none coming in here, *zero*. Except for a good conversation, and a chill time," said Regina.

"Well, I hope one of us got their expectations fulfilled."

"Now you're just being passive-aggressive," said Regina.

"Passive-aggressive?" Julian scoffed. "I'm heartbroken. I said I love you, and it means nothing to you."

"No, it doesn't mean *nothing*. It means the world to me. But what? You're fifteen years older than me and…"

"First of all, wow, I can't believe you went there. Being ageist is super uncool, especially in this decade." He smiled a little. "Second, I am *not* fifteen years older than you. Axel is only two years younger than me — and I'm a huge upgrade."

"It's not an age thing, Julian, it really isn't. I mean, it crosses my mind, but that's not it. It's this cat-and-mouse game between you and Axel that I'm starting to find terrifying."

"This isn't a cat-and-mouse game, this is a fucking tiger," Julian stabbed his thumb against his chest. "Against a desert coyote at best!" He pointed out towards the sand. "We represent entirely different principles, completely different karma."

Regina looked away.

"What do you think is going to happen? Do you think Axel is going to end well? Do you really think he's going to give you the stability you seek and provide for you with honor and dignity? *Which is more important than money, by the way.* Be real. And the people he's involved with? *Vamos,* Regina. You need to go after the things that really matter, not flash and glitz. All of that *will* fade."

Regina kept shaking her head.

"You need to stay with me if you know what's good for you," Julian said. "I don't know how else I can transmit this passion I feel for you. But the truth is, it really comes down to your choice."

"Yeah, it is my choice, and my choice is… I don't know, but I'm leaving. I think you need to get your own ride out of here," Regina said.

"Oh, it's like that?" he smirked.

She turned around and walked out of the restaurant.

Julian took a moment too long in chasing after her. When he stepped outside, her Land Cruiser had already left the parking lot. His carry-on, however, was casually placed on a corner, waiting for him. Even after she'd stormed out, she still worried about him having his belongings. That was a good feeling. He went back in and paid the bill. He asked the owner to call him a cab. On the ride home, he reflected on being a side piece.

CHAPTER 81

"Nowadays"

TWENTY HOURS HAD PASSED SINCE Regina Dahlgreen had left Julian stranded at Coyotes de la Playa. Even though Regina had left, he felt satisfied with the moment they shared. He was happy that he had woken up in his own bed at home. After making himself breakfast and cleaning around the house, Julian was ready to begin his tasks. He called a company meeting. They met aboard *The Cecilia* at 14:00. Denise, Ernie, and Rubio were all there, joined by Julian and Reyna. It was a lovely afternoon. Julian let them all speak first. Denise had the business report for the flyers event. To think that only a week had passed since the paragliders filmed over Balandra Bay mesmerized Julian. They had made a $7,000 profit.

"And you already paid Regina?

"Yes sir," said Denise.

"Seven racks, not bad," said Julian.

"Ernie, how's Operation Greg?" he asked.

"Well, I just came back two days ago. They're good, they aren't going to need anything for another twenty or thirty days. They're almost done with the deck that they're building," said Ernie.

"Yeah, we billed them $125,000 for fees, just this past quarter," interrupted Denise.

"Great. Do we have any business for the yacht or plane for the next couple of days?" Julian asked.

"Nothing booked yet. I'm sending my bots to do some magic on social every day, but right now, we're open," said Regina.

"Your *bots to do some magic on social*? What does that mean?" said Julian.

"Oh, sorry. Ha! It's slang. I'm going to use some technology to get likes and engagement on Twitter, Facebook, and Insta," she said.

"Is that how the kids talk nowadays?" said Julian.

Denise smiled.

"What's going on on your end Rubio?" said Julian

"We could use some fresh produce, fruit, fish," said Rubio.

"Okay, give him some money to stock up," he said.

Denise nodded.

"Ernie, how's our lady on the water?" he asked.

"She's running great. Really behaved well last week when we took her out to the event. She's clean; I mean, Rubio cleaned her a couple days ago," said Ernie.

"Yeah, and I waxed her, too," said Rubio. He brought out some snacks — mixed nuts, dried fruit, cheese — and set it on the table.

Julian was silent for a moment.

"I need you guys to know something that I've been holding from you for some time," he went on and told his crew about the day Axel Cuevas betrayed him and Axel's involvement with Samuel Bracho. He reminded the Jordans that they had been aboard *La Capitana* that day while he was being threatened in the vessel in front. He opened up like never before. "Axel betrayed me."

"So that's why you quit the port captainship!" said Denise.

"I had to, And ever since, I've been running from my cousin, who still finds ways to get to me. Here's the thing, just last week, he used me to get to Alberto Fontana, our partner," said Julian.

Rubio already knew parts of the story, but he was still shocked by what he was hearing.

"Fontana is involved with building a port in Punta Colonet. Big business, talking billions. Axel and his mobster influences want in, and when they found out Alberto was a partner of ours, he pressured me to get to him. As part of his strategy, Alberto had to get backup from Don Aldo Ruiz in Tijuana, and now, Don Aldo has requested our help," said Julian.

"He requested our help to get back at Axel?" asked Denise.

"That's right," answered Julian.

"What does he need?" she asked.

"Before Samuel Bracho was locked in prison, he owned a 220-foot megayacht called *The Durango*. Deal is, he traded it with the Knights of Michoacan, and they ended up betraying him. Now Don Aldo is interested in the whereabouts of that yacht."

"What does he want us to do about it?" asked Ernie.

"He needs us to find the yacht. It disappeared from the map. They want to make sure it's not in Baja, because it was last reported three months ago around Bahia de las Palmas, but nothing is sure." Julian paused. "I'm sharing all this information because we are a team. I don't know what's so important about that yacht, but if it's a way of getting back at them, I really want to do it. I'm gonna need your help, because Axel and Bracho on the loose, nothing is safe — our livelihood, our company, our family, even our way of life is going to be stripped from us. We already saw how this man impacted all of our lives once before, and we know he's bound to do it again," said Julian.

"We're with you, man 100 percent," said Ernie.

Denise nodded.

"You want me to slice those bastards?" said Rubio as he pulled out a knife from his apron.

They all laughed and forgot their troubles for a second.

Julian asked them to stay put, but said he, Ernie, and Rubio would probably have to leave port soon, leaving Denise to stay behind and operate the business.

"No way that you guys are leaving without me," she said. "If we're going out to sea on a mission, I'm going."

"But who's going to look after our business?" he asked.

"Julian, I'm totally wireless. We've installed satellite internet aboard *The Cecilia*. I can respond to emails and everything while at sea," said

Denise.

"But the plane?" said Julian.

"The plane is going to be fine," said Denise.

Julian looked at Ernie. "Don't look at me, she's your business partner too," he said.

Julian took a minute. "You're right. You are a great first mate and I'm glad you're on board," he said as he shook her hand.

CHAPTER 82

Puff

RUBIO OPENED A BOTTLE OF wine while the crew continued to chat on deck. Julian stepped outside to make a call.

Admiral Gomez was heading back to the Mexican Navy base when his phone rang.

"Admiral," Julian said, "I need to see you, something big is happening."

"Meet me at my office in ninety minutes," Admiral Gomez said.

When Julian arrived, Admiral Gomez was smoking a long Habano cigar.

"Guess who's at it again?" Julian said.

"Who?" a puff on his cigar.

"My cousin."

"Axel Cuevas?" another puff.

"Yeah." Julian went through the whole story, hoping to get some guidance from the only man he fully trusted in matters of power.

"Don Aldo Ruiz is no joke, Julian. I mean, you have Samuel Bracho on one side, and Don Aldo on the other. Fuck," his cigar finished, the Admiral put it out on the ashtray.

"I know, that's why I'm coming to you," Julian said. "I've been commissioned to find *The Durango*."

"Commissioned by who? Fontana?" Admiral Gomez asked.

Julian did a half nod. "Higher."

"Oh shit, who?"

"Don Aldo Ruiz."

Admiral Gomez's eyes lit up. "What do you know about *The Durango?*"

"Not a lot, except that it's a big yacht, used to belong to Bracho, disappeared, and apparently it's of value to Don Aldo to find it." He paused a moment. "It was last seen here, in South Baja, three months ago, around Bahia de las Palmas. Do you know anything about that?"

"Well, about six weeks ago, a helicopter comes back from a mission and the pilot tells me he spotted the biggest yacht he's ever seen on the southeastern side of Isla del Carmen. Black hull, grey deck, modern design, all of the description matches *The Durango.* Just a month prior, I had received a memo about the yacht, stating it's red-flag status accompanied with orders from the secretary of the Navy and Interpol that if any authority sees this vessel, to seize it, notify them, and hold it. So, I give the order and we return with manpower, and the yacht is gone. We looked for it for miles along from where it was, and *nothing.* The following day I did a tour of the area myself, *nada,*" said Admiral Gomez.

"What did the pilot say?" asked Julian.

"He stuck to his guns. We even drug tested him, trying to make a point, but nothing, the guy was clean."

"Where was it spotted?" Julian asked.

"On the southeast bay of Isla del Carmen," said Gomez.

"The island where the old salt mine used to be?"

"That's the one!" answered Gomez.

"Did you guys go into the town and ask about the yacht, look at the marina?" asked Julian.

"That town is empty, the marina is abandoned, the island's a goddamn ghost mine. *Vacía.* My men shot a wild bighorn lamb; apparently, it's some sort of breeding ground. There's a small shack on the north bay that serves as the guest quarters for whenever a hunter comes in, which is not often, since hunting one of these lambs costs between $45,000 and $100,000. We didn't care, me and my men. We hunted one, cooked it, ate it. Delicious. We didn't see a goddamn soul or a trace of *The Durango*.

"What about Loreto? It's only fifteen kilometers west. Did you guys check Loreto?" asked Julian.

Gomez just stared back.

"I'm sorry, I'm just asking," said Julian.

"What do you think we do here?" Gomez said.

"Secure our seas from any and all enemies, both foreign and domestic," said Julian.

"There you go, you remember."

"Once a cadet, always a cadet."

Silence.

"Julian, let me ask you something. If you find this yacht, and you disclose its whereabouts to Aldo Ruiz, what does that solve?"

"We think it will lead us back to Samuel Bracho. I think that it can be used to hurt Axel."

"Hurt Axel? That's your goal? Let me tell you..." Admiral Gomez took a step back and looked from side to side. "Why don't we kill him? Why don't we just get rid of the scum?"

Space. Heartbeats. Sounds that often go unnoticed.

"No. I... I can't. My aunt and uncle... I just can't do that to them."

"Good, because that's not the way I roll. But I would've helped you if that's what you needed," Gomez said with a wink.

When they shook hands goodbye, Admiral Gomez held on to Julian's hand. "One more thing. If you find that yacht, if you see that yacht, or even if you hear anything about it, call me first. We'll corroborate. You got that?"

"Of course, *padrino*."

CHAPTER 83

Sense of Density

"*Sail, sail, sail, oh Cecilia, sail to the land of the sun, rise, rise, rise like tomorrow, you aren't just one*," sang Ernie to the melody of his ukelele, a recent gift from his wife to celebrate their seventh anniversary.

Julian and Rubio stood beside him near the grill on the yacht, sipping on whiskey sodas. Reyna, the queen of the boat, rubbing herself on Julian's leg. Denise was inside on her laptop. The song, the night, the stars; the crew was back on the water, on their way to Loreto, where Julian was going to lead the expedition to find *The Durango*.

He smoked a cigar while the boys joked and drank into the night. He took his habano and Reyna up to the tower, which overlooked Agua Verde Bay. He thought deeply about the events of the past week: Alberto Fontana, Regina Dahlgreen, her engagement, Axel Cuevas, Samuel Bracho, Don Aldo, The Learjet, Admiral Gomez, *The Durango*, Isla del Carmen, his charter business, and, of course, *The Cecilia*.

The only thing that makes it all worth it. He puffed and observed his crew.

Up there on the tower, he made amends with himself, the peace of mind that comes with choosing not to be a victim. He knew he had to fight for himself, for his legacy. He didn't want to decay; he needed to overcome, he needed to focus, and give a solid blow to his cousin and his enterprise of criminals.

The next day, they spotted Isla del Carmen, a daunting 37,000 hectares of dense ecosystem.

"It's too big of an island to just circumnavigate it senselessly," said Julian.

"Let's go into Loreto first. I have an idea," he told them.

With smooth sailing the whole way, they headed into Loreto. At the marina, Rubio stayed aboard while Ernie, Denise, and Julian had steak salads for dinner at El Nido. Afterward, the three walked the boardwalk with Reyna.

"What are we doing here, boss?" asked Denise.

"I have some friends in this town. I need to make some inquiries, poke around a bit before we head out to the island," he said.

Denise looked at him with some doubt.

Julian could sense something that he didn't like. "Listen, you've got to trust me. I've got to find out what the story is, and in Baja, there's always a story," he said.

The next morning, Julian went to the Pistol & Rifle Club's 7:00 a.m. meeting. The facilities looked good; the shooting range was improved, and there were some new tables.

"Julian Mayorca!" said Silvestre Greene enthusiastically.

They hugged.

"How are you doing, my main man?" said Julian.

Club members surrounded Julian. Most remembered him well and were glad to see him.

"What are you doing here?" one member asked.

"Well, I came to renew my membership," he said.

They all laughed.

They served coffee and sweet bread at the meeting. Julian helped himself while he listened attentively to the discussion. It was about the sign at the front of Loreto. Some residents wanted it removed because it didn't go well with the architecture of the rest of the town.

When the session had adjourned, Julian paid his membership dues and asked Silvestre Green to let him borrow something to shoot with. "Let's go out to the range and fire a couple."

Silvestre Greene took out the .357 long barrel revolver that was in his locker. They shot at fifteen, twenty-five, and fifty yards. Julian shot better at twenty-five yards, but Silvestre crushed it at fifty.

"Did you ever get your albino deer?" Silvestre asked as he fired a shot.

Julian looked at him and remembered his failed hunt. "Man, San Cosme Island is crazy. I'm never going back *there!*" he said.

Silvestre laughed and fired another shot.

"Speaking of islands, do you ever go hunting for bighorn sheep over at Isla del Carmen, just across the bay?" asked Julian.

"I got invited once." He fired a shot. "Didn't have a chance to go. Somebody tries to go every year, but the permits are super expensive — I'm talking $100,000 — and these guys are tough negotiators. They don't want just anybody to hunt bighorn. I haven't heard of anybody from Loreto going out there recently, or successfully for that matter."

"I've gotta ask you something. I don't want it to sound strange, but I'm conducting an investigation. Do you know anything about a large yacht that was anchored off Isla del Carmen recently?" asked Julian.

Silvestre patiently cleaned his gun. "No, I don't. Why?"

"Well, I'm looking for a missing yacht. A megayacht — luxurious, top of the line. Used to belong to Samuel Bracho, called *The Durango.* Anyway, the yacht is missing, and just six weeks ago, a ship matching its description was spotted off isla del Carmen. But, when the Mexican Navy returned, the yacht was no longer there. The fleet covered the whole area, but the yacht was never spotted again," said Julian.

"Interesting," said Silvestre as he finished cleaning his pistol.

When he had put it in its case and checked it back into his locker, he told Julian:

"I have a friend who I think you might be interested in talking to. I'll look for him when I get to my office. I'll call you if something comes up."

Julian walked out of the club, feeling strong. Shooting the pistol had refreshed him and lent positivity to the day. He walked down to the old bookstore, Catacumbas. The smell of history translated into damp pages and fed by low light created a hunger within him. He gazed through endless books, eventually buying *Man's Search for Ultimate Meaning* by Viktor Frankl. He went to the Café Exquisito for lunch and read well into the afternoon.

That day, Julian decided to be free. In Frankl's words, he wasn't going to be a slave to circumstances; he was going to make the ultimate decision of picking his own attitude. He walked to the beach, stripped off his shirt, emptied his pockets into his shoes, and went for a swim. Refreshing himself in the warm waters of Loreto Bay, unique for their density.

When he came back and put his shirt on, he checked his phone and saw he'd missed a call from Silvestre Greene.

"Yeah, I have a friend you should talk to. Come over to my place for dinner at eight. You remember where I live?" Silvestre asked..

"Yes, I do. I'll be there," said Julian.

He hailed a cab back to the marina, showered aboard *The Cecilia*, took a nap, and changed. Before heading out, he poured himself a highball, after the first sip, he looked up and his whole crew was surrounding him, like mad dogs awaiting instruction.

"I'm having dinner with someone who might help our case. I can't tell you anything yet, but when I know exactly what we're going to do, I'll be clear with you guys, okay?"

They all nodded.

CHAPTER 84

Bocamía

SILVESTRE GREENE HAD A LOVELY house. It wasn't big or design-er-influenced; it was simple architecture, perfect for the heat. It had big trees that cooled it down and the kind of open spaces that wise men favor. The dinner table was served. Gabriela, his wife, had cooked shrimp chile rellenos, clam pasta, and tomato salad. Silvestre sat at the head of the table. To his right sat a man with skin browned from years in the sun.

Silvestre introduced him as Willy Becker.

He wore a worn-down white dress shirt and khaki pants that were small but looked loose on his slender figure, barely held on with the assistance of an old belt. The strangest thing about Willy was that he wasn't wearing any shoes.

Julian wanted to ask: *You get invited to someone's house for dinner. What made you decide to go barefoot? I mean, I'm open-minded and all, but you've got some messed up feet.* He kept it to himself.

Willy Becker's feet were dirty and worn down from walking around barefoot through Loreto for thirty-plus years.

Willy ate little, talked less, and seemed incognito, always with his hand to his chin. He didn't drink, didn't smoke, and only drank water when thirsty.

"Willy is one of Loreto's liveliest characters," said Silvestre as he ate his chile relleno. "I mean lively as in unique. Don't let the look fool you. Want to tell him why you're barefoot, Willy?"

"I gave shoes up as a sacrifice to the *Virgén* of Guadalupe thirty-one years ago, when I almost died on the island. I promised her that if she allowed me to live, I would never wear shoes again, and I'm here now," said Willy, with a faint smile and a German accent.

"What happened on Isla del Carmen, Mr. Becker?" asked Julian.

"Call me Willy," he said. "The Japanese owned that island. They had bought the land from Mexican President Lopez Portillo who had a great relationship with the empire. He even signed lifetime extraction permits allowing them to mine it. The island itself was a good buy, but the salt that was there," he kissed his fingertips. "The purest salt in the world came from Isla del Carmen 99.5 percent sodium chloride That's why they bought the island. The Japanese couldn't get enough of it; they needed 10 million tons a year." Willy nodded. "Salt, freaking salt. That much high-grade salt was not going to be used for human consumption."

"Why don't you tell him who you are. " Silvestre interrupted.

"My full name is Wilhelm Von Becker. I was the best mining engineer in Germany, graduated with honors from the Technical Institute of München. Moved to California, the birthplace of American prospecting, and worked at mines in Nevada and Arizona. Eventually I got recruited by a Japanese-Canadian company called Argos Mining to come and manage the salt mine at Isla del Carmen. It was a particularly exciting project for me at the time because the mine wasn't built yet, so I was coming in to build the thing from scratch. The extraction process, everything, right from the get-go," Willy stopped, looked at Silvestre, almost as if he were censoring himself.

"It's okay, Willy. Tell him the story you told me—the *real* story," said Silvestre.

Willy nodded. "The thing that made this particular mine so interesting is that we built it around an evaporation model. To put it simply, we created a surface for the water to come up and evaporate. H2O with an extremely high amount of salt, when it evaporates, it leaves behind millions of tons of salt. By this point, it's important that you understand that salt is used for everything on earth, from bombs, to feed, processed food, to everything you and I are wearing one way or another. But most salt doesn't need to be that high of a grade. Demand for this high-grade salt is very specialized."

Willy took a sip of water, like he wasn't used to talking for so long.

"Business was good for the first three years. We built a town together, all of us, for the workers and their families. We even built a church that's still there, with a portrait of the holy Virgen de Guadalupe that I personally go get and bring to Loreto for the procession every year on December 12th, and return it to the church on the island," he said proudly, a moment, nostalgia settling in. "My methods of production had been almost perfected. Extracting 10 million tons a year wasn't easy; however, we required large amounts of freshwater to mix it up during the cooling process. We found only three wells on the north bay, but we needed more.

We kept moving southeast on the island, looking for wells, until one day, the drill broke through the surface. Naturally, us being miners, we were intrigued. We heard an echo. We threw a rock. The splash, I still remember, it was so far away. The darkness was so captivating. Even after all these years, I still get goosebumps," he looked into his glass of water. "The next day, we made a hanging ladder and sent in two men. They began talking of a giant fluorescent cave below. We made bigger hanging ladders.

We kept this up for weeks, obsessed, like boys playing an intense game. We drilled bigger holes, used a crane to lower a rope ladder, and we finally made our way down with some generators. I still remember the first time I set foot inside that cave. I felt a rush, like a true explorer of the likes of Pizarro and Vancouver. Then I looked up and saw it, *Bocamía*. I named it at that precise moment. The name just came to me because everything around me sparkled — the walls sparkled and radiated a light of their own. Crystals, stones, petrified coral, shells, and salt. It was a majestic cathedral.

"Something came over us," Willy continued. "It was our secret. We, the miners, had discovered something of our own. We decided not to tell the owners of the company. We decided not to tell anybody. We figured it was better that they didn't know. Within *Bocamía*, there was water, but there was also a beach. I called a geologist friend of mine and when he saw the cave, he told me the coral could be sold for millions on the black market.

I had never been a corrupt man, and I didn't do it because of the money. I was a mining engineer; this was a potential mine in the middle of nowhere. Coral of the same value as quartz and amethyst carbon-dated by him as millions of years old, materials that still needed to be tested, its uses unknown."

Julian looked at Willy with awe.

"Yes, Mr. Mayorca, greed began to consume me. And not just me, all of us. We decided to carve a big piece of the coral stone. I contacted Matsu Goya, the captain of one of the Japanese salt ships whom I had befriended over work and booze. We asked him to take some of the coral back to Japan to have it tested, and, also, to see if it could really be sold as a novelty.

To make a long story short, it turned out the coral tested positive for promethium, a rare element that has luminescent properties. At the time, the handheld videogame industry was booming in Japan, and there was a sudden need for all of the promethium they could get their hands on," Willy explained.

"So, soon enough, I brought in a diving team from the Netherlands and we began to plan a whole excavation. We followed the water to its thinnest point, which was at the southeast bay. There, we created an entryway that connected the heart of the bay with *Bocamía*. We used explosives and had to time it with heavy work on the salt mines so the workers wouldn't suspect anything. After millions of years, our cave was exposed for the first time. We began exploiting it for all of the promethium we could carve up. For me, the cave became the joy of my life, but I still had the extra pressure of the salt mine."

Willy took a drink of water.

"As I began to pay more and more attention to our promethium scheme, naturally, since you can't serve two masters, the salt mine began to decay. The first year that we underproduced, Ottawa asked me what the problem was. I told them that we weren't finding freshwater sources and convinced them to double our water prospecting budget, which I used to build a giant dock within *Bocamía*."

"We made millions of dollars extracting promethium. I don't want to say that we made 100 million, but we probably made more than that. We made it in about three to four years. We never discussed the location of our cave with anyone. Only one Japanese company with small crews who were sworn to secrecy knew about the mine's location. And the same *petit comite* who had discovered the mine were the ones who worked and operated the business, day in and day out.

All of us became millionaire pirates. Matsu Goya, our merchant, had to pay us in cash, U.S. dollars. Over time, with everyone holding large amounts of cash, we began to distrust one another," Willy said with deep sadness. "In a way, it was funny. On the island, there really wasn't any use for money, and we all had so much of it."

"As our promethium shipping grew, our salt production waned. The first year, we were down to seven million tons of salt. The next, five million. Then we bottomed at three million tons — 30 percent of our capacity. You could say it was because I had lost interest. Ottawa sent a team of engineers to scope their once-moneymaking island. They looked all over her and didn't find a trace of our *Bocamía*. That's how clean we kept our cave and how good we had built our access and logistics. We designed it so that you could be standing on a ship right in front of it and you wouldn't see the entrance." He touched his chin, a slight smile on his lips, a light glow of pride in his eyes.

"Money is *not* the root of all evil, the *love* of money *is the root of all evil*," he continued. "I know this now. I kept my money in holes in the ground. We all kept our money in holes, away from each other. Can you believe that? During the day, we worked together, and at night, we would dig holes to bury our money, separately from one another. It was a tough dynamic, because we would almost never leave the island.

I didn't leave Isla del Carmen for over two years at one point. The others were in the same position, and since we had kept Bocamía a secret, we all had to mine it ourselves. Eventually, we began tapping the salt mine's talent pool, but we did most of the work ourselves. So even though we were all multimillionaires, we lived worse than the laborers who mined salt. We worked twice as hard as those bastards," said Willy with some disdain.

"There's a poetic air to madness. I look back now, and it's so obvious. I couldn't see it then, but I see it so clearly now. At this point, the conditions for the workers at the salt mine was very bad, and since management was absent, they unionized. Eventually, Paco, one of the few laborers we'd recruited to mine promethium, got drunk with some of the salt miners and told them what we were doing. He told them we were making so much money and we were all burying it in holes throughout the southeast bay. *So much cash is buried in holes*, he told them.

And on March 17 of 1985, the term 'Bloody Sunday' took a whole new meaning for me. I can still see them coming over the hill. Matsu had just left with a full cargo, we were all freshly paid but too tired to dig. We were all at camp, sitting, guarding our money, half-trusting each other, strangely greedy and lonely. The people, the laborers, came chasing after us with machetes, makeshift weapons, pokes, and iron bars.

They caught us, guilty as charged, with our hands in the jar, nowhere to run. Ten million dollars cash, right in front of them, and this was just what was in our hands. They knew there was more. The workers organized — each of them took one of us and they began unleashing the worst of human nature upon us."

"*Where did you bury the money? Where did you bury it?* they would yell. We would dig, sometimes we found some, sometimes we didn't. When push came to shove, a lot of us had forgotten where we had buried it. At this point, the people began getting greedy themselves and they started stealing from each other.

They went wild. They had collected a total of $66 million dollars, and they didn't know what to do with it. They began cutting each other's heads off, and they killed most of the miners. I survived because I told Cayetano, my torturer, that I had buried $20 million in a single hole, which I believe was true, but that we had to continue looking for it closer to the southeast bay. We had disguised the original entrance to *Bocamía* with twelve boulders around it. I told Cayetano to look over one of the boulders—that's where I had buried my treasure. He looked over it like an eager little boy, and when he did, I pushed him into the deep cave below," said Willy.

"From there, I hid for days, until all the workers who were still alive had fled — most of them with millions of dollars, some with hundreds of thousands, all with the intention of disappearing. That was a strange time for me. Everybody I had worked with was dead or gone. I was tired, hungry, thirsty. I walked back to the salt mine and it was empty; nothing sadder than a mine without a single soul. I went into the mess hall and ate whatever I could find. There were no ships, no dinghy, no tender, not even a kayak.

I stayed on the island, roaming aimlessly from place to place with no purpose. One day I saw a ship approaching. It was company men from Ottawa. I hid in the bushes, too embarrassed to talk to them. At that point, it was better to have them think I was dead. And they did; they thought the whole town went crazy and that everyone had disappeared off the face of the earth. They took three months, scrapped what they could, and when they explored the island and found a couple of their old laborers' and miners' decaying bodies, they decided to shut down their operation completely and end their investments at Isla del Carmen. The company declared everybody missing and returned to Ottawa.

The whole time they were there, I was hiding among them, like a ghost. They never saw me. After they left, I continued to roam the island. I began to feel guilty over everything that had gone down. The level of corruption that I had unlocked within myself, the way I had failed this wonderful island. In town, the company people had left the small church untouched. I got nostalgic because I had built it with the laborers during my first years. I remember sitting there in front of the picture of *La Virgen* on that day and weeping." He choked up.

"I felt her warmth for the first time. I continued walking around the island for months, not really wanting to get off, but I also didn't have a way off. I was stuck there but fine with it, in a state of delightful suffering as we say in Germany. But one day, I was walking toward the southeast and from the crest of the hill, I saw Matsu and his fleet, a bigger fleet, coming into *Bocamía*," said Willy.

"I don't know what I thought, but I was so happy to see Matsu; he was my friend. I had brought him into this racket. I went into the cave through our boulder and ladder entrance. When Matsu's ship entered the cave, I was still nervous. I hadn't talked to anyone in months, but the way those ships entered Bocamía, they felt threatening, especially for someone in my mental state," Willy said.

"Matsu gave a welcoming speech to all of his men, over 100 of them. He explained that everybody that used to run this island was dead and that all mining operations had been ordered to cease, meaning this their last chance to raid it clean. *Promethium is very valuable in Asia*, he said as they all went to work. For a week I watched them, wanting to get close to Matsu, but scared, still living in my own head.

Those days I spent in the cave, mixing undetected with the working men, like a faceless stranger, another miner-pirate with nothing to lose, looting my own home, working beside them, sharing meals with them, sometimes quietly, sometimes speaking their language. I floated through space, saw them from what I now understand was a hallucinatory-survival trance. Twenty ships came into *Bocamía*.

They extracted all of the minerals they could, a complete blitzkrieg and disregard for nature. They took it all, leaving the cave empty. Hundreds of millions of dollars on twenty pirate ships. When I saw that all of the men were getting back into their respective vessels, I realized

I didn't want to leave. Little by little, they left the island and I went deeper into my cave, hiding, and the last of Matsu's ships left *Bocamía*. Moments later, I felt this bang! " Willy struck the table..

"I had been too caught up in my experience to realize that Matsu or someone had put explosives all over the mine, its dock, its entrances. The smell of sulfur hung in the air. I was wedged in pain between thick boulders and heavy debris, instantly awoken to a new reality—a physical reality of pain, agony, and survival. I freed myself from the bigger pieces of rock that were on me and began an upward climb.

The first night, I tried to climb out, but I was trapped. I was shaken, stuck in a corner, destined to face the death of a miner. I remembered the image of the *Virgén de Guadalupe* that I had seen at the church. I prayed to her and that night she appeared to me, the *Virgén*. She wiped the blood off my face in between the crystal rocks that still had an eerie glow to them.

"She whispered, *Take off your shoes, my son, for the ground on which you are standing is holy ground.*"

"I did, I took them off, I begged her to let me live." A tear ran down his cheek. "At that moment, I realized what I had been missing. That existential void was filled. Regardless of my suffering, after the *Virgén* herself came down to wipe my tears, I felt inspired, alive, I told her, *Mother, if I survive, I will never wear shoes again. The whole earth will be holy ground to me, because you have blessed me with your presence*, and she actually nodded, to me, a mortal. She, the Mother, nodded to me.

"*Walk to the image of me that hangs on the salt church and you will be saved*, were that last thing I heard her say before she faded back into luminescent rock dust. It took me three days to crawl and push out of *Bocamía*. But I did it, and with her strength, I made it to the surface of the island.

"My struggle wasn't over yet," Willy continued. "It took me three weeks to walk from the southeast to the north of the island in my condition, plus it was winter. I didn't realize it at the time, but the luminescence from Bocamía had created a layer of dust that kept me warm and protected. It gave me energy when I needed it. Outside on the surface, walking barefoot hurt, every step… but I didn't cover my feet, I kept my part of the bargain with my Lady. When I made it to the salt church my feet had bled so much that I lost consciousness on the bench in front of her portrait.

I was so happy that I had made it… I remember telling her, *I made it*, as I took a seat at her majesty's presence. Next thing I remember, I was in a hospital in Loreto, where they were administering serum via I.V… you see, on the exact day that I had made it to the salt church, December 12th, her namesake, was the same day that Father Ramón came and got her majesty's frame to take her to the procession in town. He saw me there, and since I was so fragile, he was able to carry me over his shoulder and take me aboard the panga that had brought him."

CHAPTER 85

Pirate Nonsense

THE NEXT MORNING, JULIAN TOLD Denise to go online and research everything she could find about Isla del Carmen. He told her she'd need to brief the crew about her findings that afternoon. Later, he went back to Catacumbas and bought maps and books about the island. He called Silvestre to recap the previous night.

"Take everything you heard with a grain of salt," he told Julian. "Sometimes, people in Loreto, we exaggerate things.."

"Yeah, I know. I still think there's something worth looking into," said Julian

"I just wanted you to know that if you need any help from me or the club, we're here for you."

"Thanks, Silvestre. I have a question, do you know who owns the island now?"

"Technically, the city of Loreto does. But, the Mexican National Parks Commission runs it. They're the ones in charge of issuing hunting permits."

Julian thanked him for the information and went back aboard the yacht.

He laid out a large map of Isla del Carmen on the salon table and called a meeting.

"Okay, guys, this is Isla del Carmen. Denise, can you tell us what you've learned?"

"At 37,000 acres and only eighteen kilometers away from Loreto,

Isla Del Carmen had a very productive salt mine at one point," she said. "There are bird species endemic to the island and a bighorn sheep colony whose numbers are growing because there are no known predators on the island."

"That's your history lesson," said Julian. "Now, I have some information that could help us. The old mine's facilities are located on the north end of the island. That's where we'll find the church and some historic landmarks," Julian said as he showed them pictures of the town from his books.

"The yacht we're looking for was spotted closer to the southeast bay. There's a legend in town that there's a cave somewhere between the boulders," he said.

"Is the cave large enough for a ship like *The Durango*?" asked Denise.

"If what my source told me is true, you could fit five or six *Durango's*… It's a huge cave supposedly."

"What? How?" asked Denise.

"Well, while some were mining salt, others were illegally mining rare earth and coral. They even had a dock within the island's belly. The cave became known as *Bocamía*," he said.

"So what's the plan, Skip?" asked Denise.

"Let's swing by the island. We'll stay on the south side first. We'll anchor like tourists, then tomorrow, we can take the tender closer to the southeast bay to see if we spot the mouth of the cave."

An hour later, they were on their way to Isla del Carmen. The ride over was smooth. Denise took the helm while Julian read books in the salon. That night, they anchored in the south bay.

Julian was up to see the sunrise the next morning. And by 08:30, the hot sun was beating down on the yacht. Everybody was eating.

"I made an explorer's breakfast," said Rubio. "Chilaquiles, omelettes, flour tortillas, bacon, and salsa."

Only Ernie was able to eat it all. Afterwards, he grabbed his camera and lowered the tender.

Denise handed Julian a C.B. radio. "Call me if anything goes down."

Julian grabbed the radio. "I'll take care of your husband, don't worry."

"I don't want you guys caught up on some pirate nonsense."

"Too late," said Julian, as he boarded the tender to look for *Bocamía* cave.

They went around the southern tip of the island in search of the southeastern bay. When they came around, the bay opened up like an oyster. The beach was larger than Julian expected.

"Let's go ahead and beach it," he said.

Ernie steered the tender straight.

Julian felt the sand between his hands. He looked at it as if expecting it to glow. He smelled it, but he hadn't developed the knack for distinguishing minerals.

They walked around the beach and hiked up one of the mountains. Ernie took pictures and shot video. It was nice desert vegetation and hard rocks. They walked around for a bit, didn't see anything, didn't really know what they were looking for.

"There's supposed to be bighorn sheep on this island," said Julian.

"There's also supposed to be a huge yacht in its belly," said Ernie.

Once back aboard the tender, they went around the bay.

"Get up close to the rocks. I want to see if there's some sort of entrance," said Julian.

They went through the southeast bay, getting as close to the rocks as they could. Julian studied them from all sides; nothing seemed to stick out. There was an arch about fifty meters from the beach. They went through it five times since something about it struck Julian — it couldn't be seen from the front since the entrance was at an angle.

This reminded him of something Willy had said: *You could be standing right in front of it and not see it.*

Then he saw it. The arch led to a stone wall — no entrance, but under its crevice, there was an opening.

"There, there! You see that?" Julian pointed.

"Where?" Ernie asked.

"Right there. There's a little wake. You see how it beats against the rocks?" he pointed closely.

Ernie saw it. The rocks ended where the water began.

"That's it! *Bocamía*, my mouth. You see how that looks like lips?" said Julian as he pointed at the slit between the rocks. "Pull up closer."

It was almost as if there was a tiny space, a wind tunnel, or a slight current between them and *Bocamía*. Ernie pulled the tender as close as he could to the rocks. Julian took off his shoes and jumped onto one of the boulders that led to the water. He walked to the end of it and dove into the sea. He went under the rock wall that resembled a three-foot tunnel. The ocean helped push him as he held his breath.

This was a bad idea, he thought as he felt the wall above him for a second too long.

But the ocean pushed him and he made it into the darkness. He could breathe; there was stillness and silence. He was surrounded by immensity and a unique smell of sulfur and humidity. He reached for the walls, but struggled to make it against the current. When he did find a way to hold on, the rocks were slippery and slimy, covered in seaweed. He looked deeper into the cave as his eyes adjusted to the darkness. There was depth to *Bocamía*, but he knew he shouldn't go any farther.

I'll return tomorrow with dive gear.

He made it to the edge, jumped back into the water, and as soon as he did, he felt something pulling his leg. He swam with the current, but was unable to move. Something was pulling him, like strong ropes wrapped around his leg. His skin bubbling, suction cups attached to it. He felt his leg lose circulation. The wake was gaining on him, water going over his head. He was trained not to panic, but he was losing control.

Oh Christ!

He grabbed his inner leg and felt it. A tentacle sucking his skin. It was a damn squid.

He swam against the predator. He pulled and tried to focus on the light beyond the wake. He held his breath, wave and wave out. The fear of the open ocean surrounded him, the physical pressure of the squid, a bit of water in his mouth, coughing, out of breath. The wake getting higher, the fear stronger. This was it, the moment of death. Julian felt it, and fear overwhelmed him. But he was still conscious. In that moment of panic, he remembered the Victor Frankl he had read. He decided that he was not going to be a victim, wasn't going to be scared. But quickly that thought opened up new possibilities. Julian realized that if he set his focus just a step beyond death, it wasn't that bad. Death didn't feel as heavy as life.

Maybe I should just let go.

But no. He swam and kicked, but nothing dislodged the squid. He reached the surface, gasped for air. He swam for the rocks on the tunnel that connected both sides, dove underwater, went out three feet, and finally made it over to the other side. The squid was off his leg, but his muscles were swollen. He floated in the sunlight, belly up.

Ernie, relieved, came up in the tender.

"Jesus, Julian. What the hell is wrong with you? Don't ever do that again."

Julian still belly up, was not answering.

"Julian!" Ernie, terrified, turned off the engine, grabbed the rope that was attached to the tender, and dove over to his friend.

He was breathing, but very slowly.

"Are you okay?"

Julian barely opened his mouth. "Yes, but very tired," he whispered, out of breath.

Ernie towed him back to the tender. He gave him a cold electrolyte drink and Julian sipped on it. Ernie went full throttle towards *The Cecilia*, yelling at Julian.

"Don't ever do something like that again! Fuck! You hear me? You just jump into the water, into what? Into the abyss. What were you expecting?"

"That was it. I saw it, felt it, *Bocamía*" said Julian with a faraway smile and a raspy whisper.

CHAPTER 86

Fried Calamari

JULIAN WAS FEELING A BIT loopy when he got to the yacht. Images flashed through his head. The darkness from the cave had affected his vision. The bitter sulfur was still stuck in his nostrils. His leg was swollen, reminding him of the damn squid that had let him go only when he reached sunlight. He had felt the pull of death, its allure, he even considered giving into it. Julian still felt a rush when he remembered the feeling of letting go. Poets were right —death was but a door.

After a nap, he took a warm shower and was wrapped in his towel, lying on the bed in the master stateroom when there was a knock on the door.

"Dinner's ready," said Rubio.

"What are we having?" asked Julian through the door.

"Fried calamari," said Rubio

"Ha!"

Julian put on fresh clothes and headed out.

After dinner, he asked Rubio to bring out the best bottle of mezcal in the liquor cabinet.

"Did you tell them about today?" Julian asked Ernie.

"I did. You're a real son of a bitch, you know that?"

"But I saw it! Well, I saw darkness, and I'm not talking about death. I'm talking about *Bocamía*, the cave," he said with excitement.

"What do you mean?" Denise asked.

"I swam under a wall and popped out on the other side. There was darkness, silence, stillness. I made it to the rocks. There was a depth to that cave that I could begin to sense. We need to go back tomorrow, with full diving gear," said Julian.

"What?" Ernie snapped. "You almost died out there! When I got you out of the water, you looked like a bloated fish, and now you're saying you want to go back?"

"I'm saying that *we're* going back," Julian replied. "I'm not diving there alone."

"I'll dive with you," said Denise.

"What?" said Ernie.

Denise looked at her husband with the stare of death.

Ernie sighed.

"If he needs somebody to dive with, I rather do it than you. I'm a much better diver." Denise held her stare.

"This is what we're gonna do. We are going to move the yacht to the southeast bay. Rubio will stay on board. Ernie, you take the dinghy. Denise and I will dive. Is everybody good with that?" asked Julian.

"No, not me," said Ernie. "I don't want you diving there tomorrow." He looked at Denise.

"What? We are not doing this. You are not doing this. You don't get to tell me what risks I can and can't take," she said.

"No, sweetheart, it's not that. It's just that it's really dangerous, and then some *thing* bit his leg. Did you see?" Ernie pointed at Julian's leg, which bore the red marks of the Kraken's tentacles.

"A goddamn squid. But I'm taking my speargun tomorrow. If I see that thing, we're having squid all week," Julian said as he high-fived Rubio.

"What do you expect to find in that cave? Do you expect to see a megayacht just abandoned there? Wake up, Julian! If they're hiding a yacht that large, there could be anything. You said so yourself. What about the darkness?" said Ernie.

"We're bringing lights," said Julian.

"Listen, if somebody built a layer, there could be security. I can't let you two scuba over there.

Julian took a moment, allowed his own euphoria to wind down, and looked at his friend.

"Listen, man. Thanks for saving me out there today, but this is the mission! And today, with that squid—yeah, I almost died. I saw the tunnel, and, yes, I almost took a step too close to it. But I was unprepared. Tomorrow we go prepared."

A long pause.

"Why do we even need to find this yacht?" Ernie asked. "What's so important that we're risking our lives over finding it?"

"I'm doing it for Alberto. He asked me personally to look into it. He's been there for me and has been a phenomenal business partner to all of us. And we're here now. I know that we're close to something. I don't know what exactly, but I can feel that it's something that's gonna change the game."

Ernie just shook his head in silence.

"Tomorrow, I just want to take a look near the place we went today. That's it. After I get a little more of a visual picture of what we're looking at, then I can call Alberto and figure out what we can do next."

Julian expected some sort of reaction from Ernie but got nothing, just complete stoicism.

"And, Denise, you don't have to go. Ernie, if you don't want to skipper the dinghy, that's fine. Rubio, you're on dinghy. You two stay behind on the yacht," Julian said, looking at Denise.

"I'm going with you," Denise said. She stood up, gave her husband a killer eye, and exited.

CHAPTER 87

Dragón

J ULIAN WAS UP AT THE crack of dawn and went for a swim in the still waters. When he returned, Rubio served him a cup of coffee. He pulled anchor, went up to the bridge, and moved the yacht to the southeast bay.

"Rubio, lay out all of my dive gear, check the tanks and hoses, and you know what? Bring out the BladeFish," he said.

Ernie and Denise came up to the bridge.

"Skip, we want to talk to you," said Denise.

"Julian, I want you to know that I back you 100 percent. It's just that I was so worried for you when you went under," said Ernie.

"I know, and I appreciate that," said Julian.

"And even though Denise is my wife, she makes all of her own decisions when it comes to the things she gets involved in. That's how she was when I met her, and that's how she is now," said Ernie.

"Okay, bring it in," said Julian, extending his arms. The three of them hugged. "You two..." Julian thought of a million things to say, but just left it at that.

"Alright, help me anchor this baby." He slowed down near the bay.

Julian doubled-checked the scuba gear and Denise strapped a Go-Pro camera on her visor. "I'm recording this dive."

The ritual of their morning dive resembled young warriors preparing for battle. The field was the ocean; their objective was diplomatic.

"We're just going in to see. 'Observe and report,' as they say," said

Julian, strapping a knife on each leg.

He loaded up his small speargun and strapped it to his side.

Ernie stared at him. "'Observe and report,' right?"

"Well, just in case," said Julian with a smile. "Rubio, you and Reyna stay aboard the vessel."

"You got it, Skip."

"Make something good for lunch," said Julian.

"Well, I'm gonna wait for that Kraken."

Julian laughed.

They boarded the tender. The sea felt glassy, smooth. No chop, just a reflection of the morning — a clear, sunny, South Baja day.

"There's more visibility than yesterday," said Julian as they pulled up to the arch.

Ernie wedged the small anchor into the rocks. Julian and Denise dove into the water. Denise had a line that ran from her to the BladeFish.

"Let's stick close to the rocks. You see where there's a crevice? That's where the access is," Julian said as he pointed at the lips of *Bocamía*. "From there, we enter the cave. Let's throw on our lights, stick to the rocks, get a sense of space, and reconvene inside." He took his last breath of fresh air, put on his mouthpiece, and dove.

Denise followed. Both were like natural ocean organisms, swimming in their element, close to the rocks, under the lip of the entry to the cave, through the clear blue water, into a shift toward darkness. Julian shone his light on the depths and couldn't see the bottom. They kept swimming close to the rocks as the cave began to unfold.

Somehow, in the movement of his light, Julian saw a sparkle below him. He turned the light off. Meters below, there was a glow. An allure, a pressure, ringing in his ears. Julian turned his light back on and looked at Denise. He gave her a thumbs down, indicating a desire to continue descending, and she responded with the okay sign. The cave went deep and the deeper they went, the brighter it got, a luminescent glow coming from the void.

Ten meters. They stopped and decompressed, popped their ears and moved their jaws. The water was becoming warmer and the rocks prettier; they felt open. All the boulders were lined with glowing crystals. Fifteen meters. Decomp. Okay, hand gestures. Called by the void to dive deeper.

Twenty meters got very green, much lighter and denser. The water felt thick. Okay, hand gesture. Twenty-five meters. Saltier ground. To Julian it felt rocky, like it could have been a cave within the cave. He was sure that if he went farther out, they could go deeper, find the source of light.

He began to walk on the cave floor. His bubbles began getting bigger, his gauge read only ten minutes of air left. He was convinced that he could reach more; the strong currents began calling to his pressured ear. He was ready to go farther. Then a touch on his shoulder. It was Denise. She gestured, *follow me*.

He did. Back toward the rocks, up a couple of meters. Denise felt around, moved half a rock, and exposed an anchor. They smiled through their masks, grabbed the chain, and used it to climb back to the surface, one yard at time, pulling up like prehistoric creatures attached to ocean crevices. When they reached the surface, they filled their vests with air and floated. In front of them, in the semi-darkness of a clean, soulful light coming in from the cave's ceiling was the biggest yacht they had ever seen.

Beautiful, long lines, tall tower. Julian and Denise looked at each other, amazed but not wanting to say a single word, scared that they might awaken some sort of beast. They went around the back of the yacht. They couldn't quite read the name. It began with a D. Julian flashed his light. It read *Dragón*.

For some reason, revealing the name of the yacht made Denise gasp. It was almost as if with that gasp there was a loud, continuous sound. The water around them began to move and a light shone stronger on the *Dragón*. Julian looked beyond the bow. There was an inlet that continued through the cave. At the very end, the walls were moving, a gate was opening. Two small boats came toward them, fast.

Julian felt it; these men were bloodhounds. "Bladefish."

Denise handed it to him and he turned it on. They bit on their mouthpieces, went two meters below the surface, and made their way back with the help of the underwater motor.

Exiting the cave was difficult. The currents weren't budging, and even though the Kraken didn't come out to play, Julian felt him near.

There are more than vibes to this place, Julian thought. Underwater, his gauge marked zero minutes. He held his air. They made it through the darkness of *Bocamía*. As soon as they reached sunny waters, Julian broke the surface and spat out his mouthpiece.

Denise, much cooler, had preserved a little more oxygen for herself. Ernie reached them within seconds, thanking God for his wife's safe return.

CHAPTER 88

Flowers

"**L**ET'S GO. WE NEED TO get this yacht moving," said Julian as he took off the wetsuit. "I'll raise the anchor. Ernie, you take the helm."

"Yes sir," said Ernie, as he climbed the ladder.

When they were underway, Julian stood on the bow, letting the wind ruffle his hair. He wore swim trunks, a t-shirt, and top-siders. Rubio came to him, holding fresh mimosas. He gave one to Julian while he sipped on the other.

Denise approached, recently showered, wearing a light dress over neon swimwear, looking hotter than ever. Julian never really saw Denise in that light, but something about that afternoon, after having explored underwater caves together, and the way her hips swayed as she walked towards the bow, made the flame within him stir gently. Rubio offered her a mimosa, knowing she would say no, but hoping that she would accept it.

"I'll have an orange juice," she said.

Rubio served it in a champagne glass.

"That was crazy out there," Denise said. "Did you see those guys coming in? How did they do that?" she asked as she held her wet hair. "They just opened the mountain."

"Well, either the guys that came in are Ali Baba and his forty thieves, or they built a gate. My money is that they built a gate," said Julian.

"I'm still in shock," she said

"Is it too much for you? Do you want a simpler life?"

Denise smiled. "Who, me? I'm a pirate at heart, Julian. I love this. Ernie might complain, but he's branded. Certified pirate."

"I'll drink to that."

They clinked their glasses.

"Tell your husband to take us back to Loreto."

Julian took a shower, then went up to the galley and snacked on fish tacos. Rubio made small talk, but Julian had things on his mind.

What to do next? Notify Admiral Gomez first, or reach out to Alberto?

Denise came into the salon, sat on the computer, and began uploading files from her GoPro. Julian made his way next to her.

"We can't be sure that was *The Durango*," he said.

"Well, I know it read *Dragón*. But how hard is it to change the name of a yacht and call it something else?" Denise asked.

Julian raised his eyebrows. He looked around his own yacht, at one point called the *Almost Heaven*.

"I'll tell you what. Take a look at those videos from our dive, but let's be meticulous, like scientists, and not make any assumptions. I need you to find everything you can about *The Durango*. Its history, where it was made, how much it cost, what technology was used, who built it — everything. And not just what's on the internet either. I want you on the phone with these people, get to know them."

Denise was interested. She took out her notebook and began jotting things down.

"I want to know what happened to the yacht when Bracho was captured. I want to know everything. I think Axel Cuevas was her first captain. I want to know everything about those years in Cuevas' life. I never saw him during that time. I need to know what we're looking at. I need the details from you in order to get the big picture."

The perfect project for Denise. She could dive deep into research, get to the truth. She made notes.

"And why do you think Don Aldo Ruiz is interested in finding this yacht?" she asked.

"Well, it's a $200 million yacht to say the least. You should get the design blueprints. But be discreet, don't be blatant. We're poking around in secret. Once we know for sure that the yacht we saw is *The Durango*, we'll contact the necessary people. But, for now, we keep everything shut."

Denise nodded. "What about the people that came in?"

"Let's not focus on them now. When the time is right, we'll zero in on them. The yacht will lead us to them."

Early South Baja afternoon, Loreto in front, Isla del Carmen behind. Julian stepped onto the deck with his satellite phone. He called Alberto Fontana's office.

"Hello." Almost a whispered voice on the other end.

"Margot?" said Julian.

"Yes," she continued in a low voice.

"It's Captain Mayorca. Can you be a dear and put Alberto on the phone?"

"Oh, my. Haven't you heard, Mr. Mayorca? Alberto is dead." She let out a wail.

"What!?"

"They shot him as he got down from his car. Seventy-three bullets, Mr. Mayorca. They almost split him in half!" She screamed, sobbing uncontrollably.

Julian felt a rush of doubt, disbelief, as if it were a sick joke. It had to be one of those stupid holidays where people lie for fun.

"What day is it?" he said, angry.

"I'm sorry?" she said.

"What day is today?" he repeated.

"It's Friday," she said, still weeping.

Margot wouldn't lie to him, wouldn't joke like that. She was a serious lady.

"What about the bodyguards? The guys protecting him?" he asked.

"They killed two of them as well," she said in tears.

Julian took a second. A giant scream stuck in his throat. "When's the funeral?"

"Closed casket is tonight, at our Lady of the Boulders. Burial is tomorrow morning." She sighed and let out a whimper.

"Hang in there, Margot. This is very hard, but hang in there. He was a good man," said Julian, with a whimper of his own.

"A very good man, Mr. Mayorca. You have no idea," she wept.

He could hear her wipe her tears from 1,000 kilometers away.

Julian entered the salon. Eyes red, sobbing, stressed.

"What's wrong?" asked Denise, standing up from her desk.

"They killed him, they fucking killed Alberto," Julian cried. He laid down on the sofa, face up, his inner arm to his face.

"What, who?"

"I don't know." The yacht slowed down. They were approaching Loreto.

"Denise, go up and help your husband. I don't want him crashing my yacht, not today," Julian said with a sob.

Rubio sat next to Julian as the Jordans docked *The Cecilia*.

"It's just not right. Damn it! Why?" he wailed.

Rubio held him, "I don't know, Skip," he said as he began to cry profusely.

The Jordans came in as soon as the yacht was docked. Rubio was holding Julian. He let go.

"Denise, buy a plane ticket for me tonight, out of Loreto."

"I can't," she said.

"What do you mean? Just buy a ticket!"

"No. I mean, you can't go on an airplane after scuba diving," she said.

"What do you mean, no? This is an emergency. I'm sure nothing will come of it. I need to go to Alberto's funeral," Julian said.

"Like hell, you will. You'll decomp, get the bends, or worse, pop a blood vessel. An aneurysm, stroke. Absolutely cannot risk it. I know it's Alberto's funeral, but we dove deep today — twenty to twenty-five meters," said Denise.

"What should I do?" Julian asked.

"Send some flowers, Skip. Let's send the biggest floral arrangement we can order. Those bastards," Rubio mumbled through tears.

Julian laid down on the master stateroom bed. He was caught up in emotions. Sadness to the level of physical pain near his chest, anxiety, Inexplicable doubt, fear, stress, confusion, sadness. His life was a constant storm. Even when the sun was shining, there was a sand storm hitting him in the face.

"Fuck this," he mumbled as he got up and washed his face.

He put on jeans, a dress shirt, Dr. Martens, and a black cashmere blazer. He packed a weekender bag and shut off the lights.

"Hey guys, I want to make it to the burial tomorrow morning, so I'm going to take the bus out of town," he said.

"Our love is with you. We know how close you two were," said Denise. She stood up and hugged him.

Ernie did the same.

"Do you want me to go with you?" asked Rubio.

"Yeah, we could all go. Let's just rent a car," said Denise.

"No. There's a lot going on right now, so you three better take the yacht back to La Paz. We'll touch base in a few," he said as Reyna came up to be petted.

Julian walked on the Loreto boardwalk and when he got to the station, bought a ticket for the first bus to Ensenada. He got a window seat near the middle of the bus, sat down and slept. It was a thirteen-hour ride from Loreto to Ensenada. When he woke up, it was pitch dark. He stayed awake until the sun began to rise. They made it to Ensenada at 6:15 a.m.

Heading into town, Julian felt like he was being carried by the force of two spirits. One was the spirit of death, lurking like an enemy in the periphery. The other was the spirit of greed. He felt it near, like a stranger making eye contact at a bar or coffee shop, but foreign like a new neighborhood in a well-known city.

He got a taxicab to the Coral Hotel & Marina, where the only way they would let him check in at 8:00 a.m. without paying for the previous night was if he got a suite, so he did. It was a nice room that overlooked the marina. The funeral began at 11:00. It was a powerful Catholic ceremony; the casket was walked from the hearse to the plot by six men. Two were his sons, Alberto Jr. and Ruben, ages twenty-two and twenty. The others were his brother-in-law, Xavier Cho, his compadre Guillermo Alarcón, and two of his nephews. There was live *banda* playing at the burial. They played a Sinaloan rendition of Sinatra's "My Way," titled "*A Mi Manera.*"

At the gravesite, the weepers, like a centuries-old fresco: the wife, torn; the lover, Tatiana, devastated; both women hugging each other, comforting themselves in the knowledge that the man who put them through so much was now gone, forever.

Julian watched the surreal scene. He found it overwhelming how everything came together. Then into his field of vision came a truck from the funeral home. It was delivering all of the floral arrangements from the closed casket service the day before. There were dozens of them, mostly modest, but then came the big ones. Baja Air & Sea's was beautiful. Denise had listened to Rubio and sent a flower arrangement. Sergio Cho, the richest man in Mexico, had sent a nice one. Don Aldo Ruiz had also sent an arrangement. There was one, however, that was bigger than them all. It read: *Rest in Peace Old Friend - Axel Cuevas.*

Julian felt the sting of hate.

CHAPTER 89

The Piss

"*RESPECTFULLY MASTER THE ART OF deceit, one is a warrior, the other a prince*," was written on the stall of the toilet where Julian was urinating.

Nothing else around him, only penis in hand. The funeral party had been too sad for him. He had spent his time mostly with Margot, who was still inconsolable. Alberto's wife served her husband's favorite red wine, Gran Ricardo by Monte Xanic. Alberto's compadre, Gilberto Alarcón, the Mexican ambassador to Canada, was among the guests of honor. Julian went up to greet him when he was off of his phone.

"Of course, I remember meeting you. Alberto spoke about you often," he said.

"I'm still in shock over what happened. Do you know who ordered him killed?" asked Julian.

Gilberto looked deeply into his eyes, as if doing an inspection for trustworthiness. "We are not sure yet, but it's looking like the order came from Samuel Bracho."

"What about Axel Cuevas?" asked Julian.

"Julian, we know he's your cousin. How do you expect me to trust you with information regarding him?" Gilberto replied.

"Axel and Bracho pulled a fast one on *me*. They've fucked me over before. The only reason they didn't kill me was because it was inconvenient. I know the two bastards work together. And trust me. Alberto was more family than goddamn Axel ever was. All I need to know is, did Axel assist Bracho?"

Gilberto nodded.

Julian didn't want to believe it.

He knew it, with every inch of his body, but wanted to embrace disbelief, if only to be able to hold off weeping and bending over in inconsolable pain. "But what about Don Aldo? I mean, he also knew about the project," he said.

"Listen, Don Aldo was here last night at the closed casket service. He was hurt. He really liked Alberto. He told me that he owed his father a personal favor from when he was governor, and that he was devastated that Alberto died before he could make amends on that debt. I talked to him; he was angry. I think he really wanted to be a part of the Punta Colonet Port project," Gilberto said.

"Evening gentlemen," said Xavier Cho. Julian had met Xavier only once, years ago. When he began talking port business with Gilberto, he didn't mind that Julian was right there, listening.

"My uncle is pulling out of this port deal," he said. "He just told me that without Alberto leading it, there's no port, there's nothing. Besides, this deal just got way too hot."

Xavier Cho turned and walked away.

Gilberto's eyes followed him, calmly. "There you have it. Just look at who benefits if the port deal is off."

"Why would Bracho want to kill the port deal, though? Do you think it was out of retaliation because Alberto didn't sign with them?" Julian asked.

Gilberto Alarcón took a moment. "I'm working with Canadian intelligence, and we believe that Bracho was freed from prison by a man named Pascual Pizante."

"Balboa port captain—from Panama" said Julian with a quick whisper, as if everything made sense.

"You know him?" said Gilberto.

"I knew about him. He taught a class at the Mexican Naval Academy a few years before I entered," said Julian.

"Really, what class did he teach?"

"Counterterrorism. I remember, because of his reputation. Do you know what they called him?"

Gilberto shook his head.

"Mr. Terror," said Julian.

"Well, now Mr. Terror is president of the International Council on Ports and Harbors. Basically he represents the mafia that runs all of the ports in the world — the shipping magnates, interests at sea. At this point, if they couldn't join Alberto and the Baja port from the ground floor, they would rather kill the deal than compete with their existing ports. Pizante is more interested in destabilizing Mexico," Gilberto said.

"Why do you think that is?" Julian asked.

"Well, we haven't proven anything. But we believe that he wants to separate Baja from Mexico."

"What?"

"Yeah, he wants Baja California to be its own country. He wants to destabilize the region as much as he can, to feed insurgency, create guerillas, force outcasts, mass migration," he said.

This information hit Julian hard, like the news of divorce hits a child.

"And why is Canadian intelligence invested in all of this?"

"NAFTA, trade agreements, Canadian mining is stronger than American mining. They've got to protect their own interests."

After the party, Julian went out drinking alone. Bar after bar, saddened, astonished by the way life throws a curveball after a changeup, and how often sweat is followed by blood. He imagined Mexico without Baja. It couldn't be. Mexico had its problems, but to separate Baja California, create another country, that sounded absurd. The whole idea sounded entitled, perverse, ridiculous. Just when he thought that Bracho was the end of the line, Mr. Terror himself entered the scene. Julian began to feel paranoid.

Why did Gilberto Alarcón give me all of this information? Aren't intelligence agents supposed to be silent and covert? Julian's mind blurred into possibilities, but in reality, he was taking a piss, alone at a shithole bar with poetic inscriptions on the wall.

CHAPTER 90

El Rey Sol

THE NEXT DAY, JULIAN'S PHONE rang at 8:47 a.m. It was Fabio, the CPA.

"*Pinches cabrones*. I just heard what happened to Fontana," he said. "I was out on a fishing trip, completely off *el pinche* grid. I come back and the news hits me like a hurricane," he said. "*Pinche* Ape. I loved that guy," his loud voice breaking.

"Yeah, they buried him very quickly. There weren't many remains," said Julian.

They went back and forth for a while, mourning their friend.

"Listen, Julian, we need to do something. We need to get all of the files from your dealings with Fontana. I know he held onto all the paperwork, especially everything that has to do with the yacht," Fabio said.

"What?" asked Julian.

"Yeah, you know, Agencia Mayorca, the thing with the yacht," said Fabio.

Brief panic. Julian not knowing what to say. *Had Alberto told Fabio their secret about their "acquisition" of The Cecilia?*

"I don't know what you're talking about," he said.

"Look, Fontana told me everything. That's how him and I were. But that's not the point. The point is, take my advice, break into his office if you have to. Take your paperwork for Agencia Mayorca and Baja Air & Sea and bring it back with you to La Paz," said Fabio.

"Okay, fine, I will."

"And while you're at it, I need you to do me a favor. There's a hard drive sitting next to his computer. Bring it back with you and give it to me when you come into town," he said.

"What?"

"Listen, I'll explain everything, just text me when you get to La Paz. I'll pick you up at the airport, " said Fabio.

When they hung up, Julian called Margot. She wasn't at the office, so he tried her cell. She was still in bed, crying. Julian told her to get ready because he was going to take her out for breakfast. An hour later, they met up at El Rey Sol, which claimed to be the first French restaurant in Baja.

The place had an air of sophistication. Margot ordered eggs benedict, and Julian had the machaca. Afterward, they had coffee and eclairs.

"Margot, I need to go into Alberto's files. I need to get the paperwork we shared."

"I can't. The police, an investigator came by yesterday. He told me not to touch anything."

"What investigator?" asked Julian.

"Sanchez. He was from the state judicial police."

"Well, I need to go in there, so if you don't want trouble, maybe just give me the key and I'll go get it."

"I don't know, Captain Mayorca. I don't want to give the wrong impression."

"Listen, Alberto would rather have *me* have the files than some bull-shit cop," Julian said.

Margot just looked at him.

"You are good at what you do. I'll tell you what. After what happened, I know you're in shock. It's a horrible thing to go through. Why don't you take a nice, long vacation, and when you're ready to work again, you can come down to La Paz and work for me. You'll love it there," said Julian.

"I don't know, I've been here in Ensenada my whole life. I couldn't figure going to another town," said Margot.

"Maybe just come down and visit. You can stay in my guest bedroom. La Paz is similar to Ensenada, but it's much nicer," said Julian.

"Careful, this is my town," said Margot.

It took another twenty minutes for Julian to convince her to give him the keys.

Julian went into Alberto's office. There was a neatly organized file cabinet. He took the files that read *Agencia Mayorca* and *Baja Air & Sea LLC*. When he was looking, he came across two thick files that read *Punta Colonet* and *Punta Colonet Port*. He grabbed them both. The hard drive was exactly where Fabio said it would be. He disconnected it from the computer and took it with him.

When he returned the keys to Margot, he handed her $500 in cash.

"What's this?" she asked.

"Oh, it's just a little gift from me to you."

"Julian, I don't need this," she said.

"Oh, I know you don't need it. It's a gift. You were always so nice to Alberto. I wanted to get something nice for you, but I didn't have time. So, you get something nice for yourself," said Julian.

Margot got teary eyed and hugged him.

"If you ever need anything, I'm only a phone call away," said Julian.

Julian walked around the Ensenada strip and bought a few souvenirs. After clearing his mind a little bit, he picked out a card from his pocket and dialed Gilberto Alarcón's number.

"I'm in Valle de Guadalupe, at Decantos winery," Gilberto said.

"Well, I've got something I want to give you," said Julian.

"Come over and have a glass of wine."

Julian got a black car to take him to the winery. The car waited for him as he went in. Gilberto was sitting with a small group of people. He introduced Julian as his friend. The sommelier poured him a house red, which was delicious.

"I've got to give you something, but it's gotta be in private," said Julian.

Gilberto looked around, like a spy on a hunch. "Gentlemen, please excuse me."

The two men stepped outside. Julian pulled out a little leather bag he had bought at the strip.

"It's everything Alberto had on the Punta Colonet Port project," said Julian.

"Why are you bringing me this?"

"I need you to find Samuel Bracho. If this information helps even a little bit, if you can use your connection with the Intelligence community and tell me Samuel Bracho's whereabouts... I want you to call me, and give me this information, because I will avenge our brother's killers," he said.

Gilberto Alarcón smiled and took the bag from Julian's hands. Julian didn't go back inside. He asked the driver to take him to the Tijuana airport.

CHAPTER 91

Bayardo

Denise had gotten a return ticket for Julian. When he got to the airport, there was chaos. His flight was canceled and the AeroBaja counter was closed. There were no flights to La Paz. Red and black communist-looking flags were raised everywhere. *Strike!*

"What?" said Julian when he caught up to a girl wearing a red and brown AeroBaja uniform.

"Yeah, this company has done it to us one last time. They just fired fifty people. We can't take that. We're all shutting down, going on strike," she said.

"But I have to get to La Paz," said Julian.

"Well, tell the airline to pay us more," she responded.

"That makes no sense!"

She shrugged and walked away.

Julian went to the restroom and splashed water on his face. Afterward, he looked at the departing flight monitor and saw there was only one flight to La Paz and it was leaving soon. It was a company he had never heard of before called VuelaMX! He made his way to their ticket counter. There was a line of about sixty people in front of him.

The girl with the VuelaMX! uniform spoke over the P.A. system. "There are no more flights to La Paz, Loreto, or Cabo."

The next available flight was 24 hours away. Julian thought about staying in Tijuana, but he missed the sea. His face must have shown his frustration, because a smiling gentleman approached him.

"Hey, do you want to get on that flight to La Paz?" asked the man.

"Yeah, why?"

"I'll sell you my ticket."

"What?"

The stranger handed him the ticket.

"It says non-transferable, *Bayardo*."

"No, no, you see, I got my wallet stolen yesterday, and when I reported it to the police, they gave me this document."

The old man pulled out an official piece of paper that read: *State of Baja California Judicial Police; Mr. Sixto Bayardo, reported his wallet stolen along with his identification. This will serve as temporary I.D. while the new one is being replaced.*

Julian grabbed it. "You think it'll work?"

"It has to. It says right there that this piece of paper is my new I.D. Just take it!"

"Well, how much do you want for it?" asked Julian.

"A thousand," said Bayardo.

"What? Hell no — that's a lot."

"Well, I'm sure somebody here will buy it."

"I'll give you $500," said Julian.

They eventually settled for $750.

"But what if it doesn't work?" asked Julian.

"I'll give you my number. Call me and I'll take you out to dinner," said Bayardo with a smile.

Julian took down his number, dialed to make sure it was correct, and the two men made the exchange.

The security agent called his supervisor, who authorized Mr. Sixto Bayardo to pass through the gate with his temporary I.D. He rushed over to Gate 17 where VuelaMX! was stationed, a small counter in the basement of the terminal. He could see the Embraer 120 jet on the tarmac. They didn't use jet bridges. People boarded the plane via stairs. Everybody was aboard and Julian didn't see an empty seat.

"Mr. Bayardo," said a voice.

Julian looked for his seat.

"Mr. Bayardo," said the female voice again.

No reaction.

She touched Julian's shoulder. "Excuse me, are you Mr. Bayardo?" said a very pretty stewardess whose name tag read Clarissa.

"Oh, what? Um, yeah, Bayardo," said Julian with a slight smirk at the pronunciation of his new name.

She looked suspiciously at Julian, turned around and went into the cockpit.

Julian thought his scheme was up.

When she returned, she asked a female passenger sitting in the front seat to stand up. That passenger did.

"Here, Mr. Bayardo, please take a seat," she said.

"You don't have to throw her out of the plane," he said.

Clarissa laughed. "Oh, no, she works for us. She can sit in the jump seat."

She closed the door and pulled down the flight attendant seat. The other passenger smiled and sat down. Julian strapped on his seatbelt. Engines on, the door closed, and Clarissa gave the security spiel about air pressure and floating devices.

The Embraer took off. Turboprops spinning. It rose smoothly against a crosswind. During the flight, Julian took out his company papers and began reading them. Financial statements, letters of intent. Julian was shocked, completely unaware of how much work had been done to hold his two companies together. Eighty minutes later, the Embraer landed in Loreto for a layover. A handful of passengers got off, others came on. Clarissa did her safety spiel again, but this time she looked directly into Julian's eyes.

Light flirtations emerged between the two of them. Clarissa would graze his shoulder with her hip as she walked down the aisle. She put a smile on Julian's face. He forgot some of his worries while they traveled through Baja California skies. When they landed in La Paz, Julian gave her a piece of paper.

Underneath his number, "Bayardo" was written next to a drawing of a smiley face.

Clarissa smiled and put it in her pocket.

CHAPTER 92

Ribeyes

FABIO PULLED UP TO THE airport curb. He was driving a big red Dodge pickup truck that still had unmarked dealer plates. He got down, they hugged, expressing condolences.

When they jumped inside, Julian felt the fancy dashboard. "Damn! Is that stingray?" he said with a smile.

"Yeah, I just picked it up right now. It's completely custom," he said. They went to Buffalo's for dinner.

"So I got my company papers," said Julian as he picked at his salad.

"Did you bring the hard drive?" Fabio asked.

Julian set it down on the table. Fabio grabbed it, put it in his briefcase, and continued eating.

"Why did you ask me to bring it?" asked Julian.

"The thing is, Fontana had some offshore accounts. Nothing too big, under five million. But I helped him set up those accounts and all of the passwords are stored here," Fabio said, pointing to the briefcase.

Julian looked at Fabio.

Waiters came and replaced salad plates with ribeye steaks.

"Don't get the wrong impression, Julian. I want to move these moneys fast so his wife can access the funds. I'm not trying to steal from a widow and her family," Fabio said.

Julian believed him. He knew that he was a standup guy like Alberto. That night, they continued talking, drinking, and eating in their friend's memory. The two who'd been introduced by Alberto Fontana now bonding over the departed.

"Tell me the truth. Why were you so interested in me getting my company papers? Was it just so you could get the hard drive?" asked Julian.

"Well, yeah, but, like I told you, Fontana told me about your yacht. I know that you guys came upon it from some dead gringo."

Julian looked away.

"Hey, Mayorca! Don't worry about it. You're *my* client now. I'm going to protect you like I protected Fontana, that's what I do," said Fabio.

"I just thought that that was our secret," Julian said. "I didn't know that you or anybody else was in on it."

"Fontana and I did a lot of business. He told me things that could have sunk entire industries. And you know what I've done with that information?" said Fabio.

Julian waited.

"Nothing. I'm a confessor's confessor. I'm a vault with those that I trust, and a stranger to those that I don't. I mind my business, except when forced, or moved. I mean, I can be a pretty ruthless enemy," he winked.

Here it comes, thought Julian, the natural exception to the rule, the *I'm not corrupt, but…*

"You're not the only client that I shared with Fontana. I've got one client in particular. You know the Ardiente Casinos that have been popping up all over La Paz and Cabo during the past five years? I do all of their payroll and accounting here in South Baja. Anyway, I've never met Don Aldo Ruiz. I deal mostly with business managers and other accountants. But I'm gonna be honest with you — I hate that business. I see how much they rake in. Ardiente Casinos are robbing this state blind, and the people are just giving their money away. Those machines are so rigged. Nobody inspects them, and when they do, it's just for show. It costs Ardiente $10,000 to buy those 'inspectors' off. Fontana knew this; he knew I hated their business, but he didn't care. He would laugh. After all, he was the one who introduced me to them, when they first opened shop in La Paz.

"*Why don't you fire them as clients*, he would often ask me. But the truth is, I make good money from them. Not nearly enough as what they're taking out of this state, but they put substantial profits on my books for me to look the other way. So I'm morally conflicted, but last week when I went up to Ensenada, Fontana invited me to have dinner at his house. We spent a great evening." Fabio looked away.

"Looking back, it was our goodbye." Melancholy and nostalgia in his voice. "We're talking, and the subject of Ardiente Casino comes up. He tells me that he had gone to Don Aldo for protection on his port deal. I remained quiet, and he keeps talking. Eventually, one subject leads to the next, then he tells me that Don Aldo asked for help finding a missing yacht, and that you were the man at sea on that operation. I thought that that was the strangest thing, so I asked him, 'Why does Don Aldo want to find a yacht that's been off the radar for so long?' And Fontana tells me, 'Because there's over $120 million in cash hidden aboard that boat.'"

Julian's jaw dropped. "How do they know that the new owners didn't take it out?"

"Fontana told me that Don Aldo had confided in him that only he and Bracho knew about the safe aboard, that even Axel Cuevas, who skippered that vessel for years, had no idea about it. He even told me that they used to laugh at him behind his back."

Even after everything, Julian couldn't help but feel bad for his cousin getting laughed at.

"I bet he knows about it now," said Julian.

Fabio nodded.

"And what about Bracho? How do we know the yacht isn't already in his possession and he's the one hiding it?"

"I've got a source inside the port captain's office. He told me Axel talks about finding that yacht often. They don't have it," said Fabio.

Julian thought about the cave and the darkness where *Drágon* was docked. He couldn't make it seem like he knew where this yacht was.

"Well, there you go. They're hungry for that yacht. We're up against Axel and the whole port apparatus. How do we expect to beat them and take their money?" said Julian.

"Of course, Axel is looking for it. But, come on, you and I both know that Axel is a shit seaman, a shit sailor, a bad captain. Good at politics, but has the sense of ocean of a plastic bag. As for who owns it, who knows? My guess is that the Knights sold it for pennies. Michoacanos are not sea people."

The waiter came and offered dessert. They declined, but asked for more wine.

"Why didn't Alberto tell me this information himself?" Julian asked.

"He wanted to, but he was waiting to tell it to you in person," said Fabio in a tone that left Julian speechless.

"Listen, I don't know if you've found that yacht yet, but if you ever do come across some money floating around, feel free to tell me, and I can help you—as they say—*launder it*," said Fabio.

"I trusted Alberto like no one else. Are you of the same character?" asked Julian.

"I'm not made of the same character as that great man, but on my brother Fontana's memory, I would never tell Don Aldo, nor breach your trust," said Fabio.

The two shook hands. Fabio paid for dinner.

When Julian got home that night, Reyna wasn't there. He fell asleep on the couch.

CHAPTER 93

A New Age

THE CECILIA WAS DOCKED AT its marina slip. When Julian went aboard the next morning, she felt a little disheveled, like how yachts get when they've been out at sea for a while and they haven't been thoroughly cleaned. Rubio arrived five minutes later with cleaning products. Twenty minutes after that, Denise arrived carrying her briefcase.

"Reyna is with your neighbors," said Rubio.

"Why?" asked Julian.

"Well, they were going out to the beach, and her kids wanted Reyna to go with them."

"You know, when I return from trips, I really like to see my dog," he said.

"Okay, Skip. Won't happen again. How was the burial?" Rubio asked, hoping to shift some attention away from him.

"Tragic. I'm devastated." Julian briefed them on the details, including floral arrangements. He finished by saying, "Just so you know, I'm working on a plan. Not going to let those bastards get away with it." He turned and looked through the window out to the sea.

Silence hung in the room.

"Julian, I've been waist-deep into research of *The Durango*," said Denise. "A German company called Anchorwerks built it, but they are impenetrable and don't publish any information. However, they do issue short press releases when they deliver a yacht to one of their customers. About *The Durango*, they said it was designed by a company called Guffen Haus."

Denise took out printed articles and handed them to Julian.

"Guffen Haus is the complete opposite. They love the spotlight; their projects appear in yachting magazines and they're constantly being interviewed. I read through tons of press and I finally found this article that came out in *Yatísta* magazine six years ago. The reporter asks, *What's the craziest thing you've ever integrated onto a yacht*?" Look at the answer." She pointed to a section of the article.

I mean, I've put a basketball court on one and a bowling alley on another, but one that was particularly challenging, I was asked to design a vault about the size of a closet, and mind you, the yacht was pretty much built. So, I didn't know where to put it. Finally, it came to me, and I put it under the helipad, but the challenges didn't stop there. I couldn't just insert a vault that size because the metals required made it way too heavy. The yacht's beam wasn't going to support another ton of metal plus a helicopter, so we did what is called a concealment safe, something very well hidden and lightweight."

Julian smirked as he finished reading.

"Not only that, with the GoPro video I took, I was able to do a 3D mockup."

"What?" said Julian.

Denise and Ernie showed a rendering of both yachts matching up.

"3D mapping! I looked at all of the specs, and the data adds up. *Dragón* is *The Durango* or *The Durango* is *Dragón*. And if there's anything of value, it's probably in that safe," said Denise.

The area beneath the helipad on the rendering was circled red.

Julian nodded in silence, almost as if he were dozing off.

"What are we going to do, Skip?" Ernie asked.

"We wait. That's what we're gonna do!" said Julian.

"Wait? Why?"

"We need to figure out what we need to do and how we're going to do it. There are too many moving parts to this and I'm still too emotional about Alberto. We need some time to think. We need to formulate a plan."

"Okay," said Denise, "what's our first step?"

"First step? I've got to make a call," Julian said, rubbing his chin.

"Who are you calling?" Ernie asked.

"My *padrino*."

CHAPTER 94

"Bloody Insurgency"

ADMIRAL GOMEZ MET UP WITH Julian that afternoon. "It's a goddamn shame what they did to Fontana. Mexico City knows, but someone up high is protecting them. They won't touch Axel as long as Bracho is alive," Admiral Gomez said in his usual fast speech.

"Does anybody know where Bracho is?" asked Julian.

"I don't!" said Gomez, disappointed.

Julian looked at him for a moment. "Admiral, I found it," he said with a whisper.

Gomez tilted his head as if not following.

"*The Durango*, I found it!" said Julian.

"What! Who else knows?" the Admiral asked.

"No one. Well, I mean, just my crew," said Julian.

"Where is it?" said Gomez.

"It's in a cave."

"What! A cave?"

"Yes, we saw it, but it's now christened as *Dragón*."

Almost out of instinct, Admiral Gomez picked up his phone.

"Wait, before you call anyone…"

Gomez put the phone down.

"The people who are hiding the yacht, they came in fast. They've built a gate to the cave. A mountain that opens and closes. I don't know who they are, but they aren't your usual *malándros*. They're sophisticated, swift, and I wouldn't doubt they're up to their necks in weapons," Julian said.

"And what do you suggest we do?" asked Gomez.

"Find out who really calls the shots on Isla del Carmen. I was able to look into its history, but I couldn't get a straight answer about who currently calls the shots there," said Julian. "The place is in bureaucracy hell, owned by the city of Loreto, run by the National Park Commission, but leased to an organization that breeds bighorn sheep for an unknown reason.

Not only that, the island's mining history with the Japanese, Canadians, and Germans—add that to the yacht's past ownership, plus the alleged deal with the Knights of Michoacan, and you've got yourself a cluster. I wouldn't just stroll in there without knowing what we're dealing with, because obviously somebody big is bankrolling all of this."

"Do you think that it's Bracho and Axel who are behind Isla del Carmen?" the Admiral asked.

"None of my sources think so. They told me the Knights sold the yacht for cheap."

"What else do your sources say?" said Gomez with a smile.

Julian took a moment, gathered his thoughts. "I do have a contact. He works with deep intelligence. Told me that Bracho and Axel work for Pascual Pizante. You remember him?"

"Mr. Terror!"

"Yeah, apparently he's the one that broke Bracho out of prison," said Julian.

"Mother… " said Gomez.

"What do you know about Pizante?" asked Julian.

"Pascual Pizante is a living legend. Arms dealer, diplomat, military man, guerilla insurgent, mercenary with a head for business and an incredible record. He taught that class at the academy, but when Noriega's government fell in Panama, he lost his protection and diplomatic status. He went underground for years, and eventually returned even more powerful."

"Yeah, he's port captain in Panama. Also presides over Council on International Ports and Harbors," said Julian.

"Jesus. I don't know what these guys are up to, but if Pizante is involved, something is going to explode," said Admiral Gomez.

"You better believe it," said Julian.

"But why did he free Bracho? What do those two have together?" asked Gomez.

"Listen, Admiral, I want to tell you something that I heard, but…"

"Well, what is it? Just let it out!"

"The thing is, I don't want to start a war," said Julian.

The Admiral looked intently at him. "My boy, if Pizante's involved, the war has already begun."

"My sources believe that Pizante wants to destabilize Mexico in order to eventually separate Baja California and create a new country," said Julian.

"Bloody insurgency!" said Gomez.

"Yes, as you can see, we have a complex situation," said Julian.

"The only way to debilitate Pizante is to crush Bracho and Axel!" said Gomez.

"Let's not focus on Axel right now. My source is getting me Bracho's location. Once I have his whereabouts, I will come to you. We'll get that *cabrón* first," said Julian.

The Admiral smiled, proud to see his protégée making grown-up decisions. "Good. I'll find out what's going on with Isla del Carmen. Once I have all of the info, we'll regroup and figure out what we're going to do," said Gomez.

"Yes, sir, but don't ruffle any feathers just yet. We need to strike at the right time."

"Don't worry; we won't make a move on *The Durango* without your involvement," said the Admiral.

"*Dragón*"

"What?"

"The yacht's name is *Dragón* now."

The Admiral stared at his godson. "This is a new age for Baja. We're fighting a ruthless enemy. We've got to sting fast and swift, before the chain of command finds out what we're up to. Because once it does, it's too late."

CHAPTER 95

A Poem Titled *Islet*

THESE WERE INTENSE TIMES FOR Julian. He wanted to make wise decisions. The millions of dollars in cash supposedly hidden on *The Durango* came to mind often, but he knew he needed to be patient and wait for some balance to be restored. After Alberto Fontana's murder, he felt Bracho and Axel had become too powerful; he had to hold off, at least until Admiral Gomez had some information for him. Days turned into weeks. Time has a way of leaving its mark on people, and Julian was no different. His face showed his grief over his friend's death. He needed to get even.

He'd reached out to Gilberto Alarcón in Canada, hoping to get some intel, but there had been no answer. He thought about flying to Vancouver, where he'd met Gilberto, but then he realized the embassy was probably in Ottawa.

I'm not gonna just show up in Ottawa uninvited, not just yet, he thought.

He was stressed. Denise had gone back to business. She had booked a yacht charter for the weekend. It was a bachelorette party—twenty girls, hungry for freedom.

Aboard *The Cecilia*, there were penis decorations everywhere; male gigolos and Lucha Libre stripers were on the schedule.

"Damn, these La Paz girls know how to party," said a happy Rubio when they had their staff meeting.

"This is awful," said Julian.

"I've got to go deliver some materials for Greg. I'm taking a small boat up coast," said Ernie.

What Julian really wanted was to go on a hunt. He felt like that was the only thing that could help him unwind. He missed his rifle. He remembered the .308 Winchester he had sold to the Crimeans, and craved holding it in his hands, squeezing its trigger and firing a shot.

"Why don't you and I go up and see Greg instead of staying around here for that bachelorette thing?" said Julian after their meeting.

"What about Rubio? We can't just leave him behind with all these women," said Ernie.

"Ha! Please! He loves it!" Julian said.

Ernie arranged a thirty-five-foot Cabo fishing boat from his usual Mexican Navy contact. Julian loaded up all of his hunting gear, his handgun, and the triple-barrel shotgun. This time, they took Reyna.

"Why all the weapons?" asked Ernie.

"Don't know what kind of animal we're going after, don't know what's in season," said Julian.

They sailed up to Mercenary Point on a Friday morning. They fished along the way, and Julian journaled, something that he hadn't done since he was port captain. He cleared his thoughts on paper, and the night before they got to Mercenary Point, he penned the following poem:

Capricious of the sea; serpent, celluloid, a tree.
The stars mock dynasties
And me
I love

He stopped it there. They anchored at an islet that looked like a trident. Ernie made spicy grilled fish burritos for dinner. The following morning, Julian swam near the islet. When he returned aboard, he opened his journal and wrote the word *Islet* over the poem he'd written the previous night, giving it a proper title.

CHAPTER 96

The Watering Hole

ERNIE WAS A PRO AT getting in and out of Mercenary Point Ranch. They anchored the Cabo boat at the neighboring bay and took the tender to the special access that was through a small cove. A lot of work had been done on the property.

"Yeah, they built this access about six months ago with some materials that I brought them. These guys are really hard working," said Ernie.

"I can see."

The little house they'd purchased from Jazz was upgraded and surrounded by palm trees.

"Who goes there?" said a thick Russian accent.

"It's the KGB! We finally caught up to you!" said Julian.

Yakov came out from behind a boulder. "Damn it, Julian! Don't joke like that! I could have killed you," he said.

"Oh, right, I forget — you probably have this place boobytrapped."

"Not precisely, but yeah, I am the boobytrap. Come here, let me give you a hug," said Yakov.

"I like what you've done with the place."

"Wait until you see the cabin," he said, leading them through the palm trees.

"Holy shit, the gods have descended from Mt. Olympus," said Oleg when he saw Julian.

Oleg was wearing an apron and fully immersed in the kitchen. Julian noticed there was a new wood-fired oven in the corner. The room smelled good, of foreign recipes and local herbs.

"It's lamb," Oleg said. "We've got a small herd. You might see them roaming around. Me and Yakov skin them and go through the whole process. We collect the herbs, and even chop the wood."

"Well, it smells delicious," said Julian.

The men got acquainted with the property.

"I was thinking about staying here, as long as you don't mind being our host for a couple of days," said Julian.

"My friend, you can move in with us if you want, but if you're gonna stay here, we work the land. We all eat well, but we work hard. Just ask Ernie" said Oleg.

"Yeah, he told me that he helps you out whenever he comes up here. I wouldn't have it any other way."

Julian and Ernie went back to the boat to get Reyna and their equipment. That evening, they all ate dinner outside. The lamb *au* wild herbs was delicious. When it got dark, Julian washed the dishes and Yakov made a bonfire.

"I feel like going on a hunt. Do you still have that rifle I sold you?"

"Do I have it? I love that rifle, wouldn't trade it for the world," said Oleg.

"Good, I'm gonna have to borrow it. I want to go look for a stag," said Julian.

"Julian, around here, bullets are a prized commodity," said Oleg.

Julian opened a cartridge bag he'd brought with him. It had 100 rounds inside. "Thank goodness I just renewed the membership to my gun club."

The men laughed.

"Bring it out, I want to see it."

Oleg brought out the Winchester. Julian held it in his hands. It felt like an extension of him.

"You know, I miss this rifle," said Julian.

"Don't even think that you're getting it back."

"Well, that's too bad." Julian removed his triple barrel shotgun from its carrying case. "I had even brought this bad boy, just in case you guys wanted to trade."

"Let me see that," said Oleg.

"Well, we'll keep it—for insurance until you return our rifle, how's that?" said Oleg as he felt the shotgun in his hands.

"Sounds fair," said Julian.

As Oleg was falling asleep in the hammock by the fire, he told Julian, "Follow the trail, and about five kilometers east, there's a watering hole. If you get there before sunrise, you might catch something."

The next morning, Julian got up at 4:04 a.m. He put on his camouflage and with only Reyna to keep him company, went on his hunt. He carried twelve rounds, one in the chamber, six in the strap attached to the butt of the rifle, and the rest in his vest pockets. He followed his compass east, relying mostly on his sense of direction.

Life all around him was asleep or pretending to be asleep. He walked at a quick pace, Reyna behind, her nose to the ground. Julian was alert. Every dozen steps or so, he would take out a big flashlight and shine it across the bush, looking for those shiny deer eyes to pop out. He picked a spot by a big tree and remained calm. He took a drink of water from his canteen and gave some to Reyna. As the sun lifted behind the purple moonglow, he saw at a distance what appeared to be the watering hole. He headed toward it.

When he was about 150 yards away, he set up next to a big boulder within perfect view of the hole. He was hot and perspiring, so he took off his sweater. As soon as he finished, something moved towards the watering hole. He picked up his rifle, and with his breath still out of synch, he put his right eye to the scope. He could see an animal moving, but only slightly, as light was still fighting the battle against darkness. As he looked, trying to distinguish the animal. The sun rose ever so gently and the animal's reflection was cast on the water. Julian saw it—a California mountain lion.

"Oh shit," he whispered to Reyna.

Reyna, a dog. The mountain lion, a cat. Loud barks.

The huge feline looked up and ran full speed towards them. Julian's heart raced. Through the scope, he could see the beast bolting towards them, hungry for meat, coming in at full tilt. Julian thoughts tried to quiet his mind, realizing he had in his hands a single-shot rifle. He held his breath. The mountain lion took a leap and Julian shot it in the neck. Dead center through the throat. Julian was close enough to get sprayed with blood.

When the beast hit the ground, it was choking on its own pulp. Julian went up to it, pulled out his knife, and finished the job. Reyna was petrified, cowering behind the boulder, aware that her bark had almost cost her master his life. Julian tried to pick up the corpse, but this was a big cat, over seventy kilos.

"Goddamn, this thing would've chomped on us no problem," said Julian looking at Reyna.

Eventually, he grabbed the mountain lion's back legs and dragged it back to the ranch. It took him three hours in the rising morning sun.

"What the hell, Julian. I thought you were gonna kill a deer?" said Ernie.

"Well yeah, that was the plan, but he came at me. I was about to be his breakfast." He dropped the mountain lion on the ground and rested.

"Jesus!" said Oleg as he rushed out and looked at the beast.

"Good job, Julian," said Yakov.

"Yeah, too bad we can't eat him," said Ernie.

"What? Of course, we'll eat him," said Oleg.

"We can't eat a predator. What parts would you even eat?" Ernie asked.

"You know nothing," said Oleg. "Cats make the best burgers. Yakov, grab the legs."

The Crimeans took the mountain lion to their work area and began skinning him. Julian went around the back to rinse and freshen up. From there, he could hear Oleg tell Ernie, "Yeah, in Siberia, I once made burgers out of a white tiger. This little cat is nothing compared to that. But it's okay. It will probably taste good; it has good meat."

CHAPTER 97

Refuge

FOR THREE DAYS, ERNIE HELPED Yakov build a deck and Julian helped Oleg cure the mountain lion's meat. They treated it with spices, salts, herbs, and softened it with liquors and milk. They used every part of the feline, only disposing of certain veins and tissue. They made sausages, put the skin out to dry and separated all of the teeth.

Julian had never worked like this in a kitchen, he thought about Rubio, he wished that his friend could be here, working and learning besides him. Just being around Oleg was a lesson in it of itself. On the fourth day, Oleg and Yakov made burger patties with the soft mountain lion meat.

The bread, they had made from scratch, and served it with tomatoes and lettuce from their garden. The mayonnaise, they had made with eggs from their own chickens. Accompanied by sweet potato chips, crispy and lightly dressed with fresh-made ketchup. Julian ate two epic burgers. Afterward, he went on an evening walk. When he returned, Ernie was by the deck ,waiting to talk to him by the beach.

"Skip, I talked to Denise. I think we should go back to La Paz,"

"Why, what's going on over there?"

"Sir, we have a business to run," said Ernie.

"Yea, I know. But since I've got this whole thing in my head, I'm out here like—how do you say it? Centering myself. Like a zen warrior, I feel stronger with each passing day. I need this refuge," Julian took a moment to gather his thoughts. "We lost a lot of power when Bracho and Axel killed Fontana... and the only way to recuperate is by centering within."

It was one of those moments where Julian could sense what Ernie was trying to tell him, but perhaps couldn't grant himself permission to speak freely.

"I get you, sir, but I have a wife," said Ernie.

Julian knew something about Ernie, something not even his wife knew. But today was not the day to talk about it.

"Yeah, you're right. Go back. I'll stay here with Reyna. I need to clear my head," said Julian.

"Sir, Denise asked me to ask you — what are we going to do about *Dragón*?"

"Tell her to never talk about that. *I* will let her know what we're going to do when we're ready. Until then, silence."

"Copy that, sir."

"This is like a stew. You don't put in the squash at the same time as the potatoes. Something big is cooking, and I need to wait to make my move."

"That's why you're the captain."

The next morning, Ernie left on the Cabo boat. Julian stayed behind with his weapons, his dog, and his phone. Mercenary Point Ranch became not only his refuge, but also the place where the real hunt began.

Once someone falls into Baja time, it's easy to lose track of the days. But that's what Julian wanted, that's what he needed. He worked the land, cleaned the house, raked the garden and peeled fruit. He left his satellite phone on, but nobody called. He grew out his beard and didn't shower. Days went by and his mind began to change. He stopped thinking loudly, which was the most important thing for him. He began to focus only on the day's affairs. Whenever a thought about Bracho, Axel, Alberto Fontana, *Dragón*, or Regina Dahlgreen entered his mind, he'd begin deconstructing it. He'd focus on the desire within himself to manifest that thought. He often thought about power and his own personal desire for it. To the Crimeans, Julian seemed absent, trapped in his head. Oleg would throw more and more work Julian's way, just to see if he broke. He didn't, but he grew quieter. Around day sixteen at Mercenary Point Ranch, the weather began to change, cooler evenings and shorter days. With this weather, the doves became easier to hunt. He and Reyna would go on evening dove hunts. They would then pluck them and grill them with rosemary for dinner.

One evening they were biting into doves when Oleg spat out a pellet. "It's the pigeon chest that's really delicious."

Julian nodded.

"So, what's going on with you, J? Are you taking a vow of silence?"

"No," his voice cracked. "Not really."

"Do you want to talk about something, or do you want me to leave you alone?"

Julian took a second, "Well, I'm just making peace with myself. I'm not sure if I want to go back. I like the country life," he said.

"Yeah, I like it, too," said Oleg. "But it's different for me, because I already did everything that I had to do. You know how old I am?"

"What?"

"Do you know how old I am?"

"No."

"I'm sixty-nine. I ruled a country for fifteen years. And before that, I did everything you can imagine!"

"Dang. Sixty-nine. I thought you were like fifty-eight."

He scoffed. "Yeah, I could kick any fifty-eight-year-old's ass. I don't know what's going through your head, and unless you want to tell me, I don't like to guess. But I'll tell you this. How old are you, Julian?"

"I'm forty-seven."

"You are a young man, and society needs you because you are good. Out here, Yakov and I are refugees, but we don't care, because we came from nothing. We came from pig shit, and I made it to my golden palace. In the end, did I let it go to my head? Yeah, maybe a little, but I was good for a while; I was good to my people."

Julian could only imagine everything that went through Oleg's head. No wonder he spent long days cooking and working.

"You know out here, it's different. Plants to grow, pots and pans to clean, and lots of thinking. No politics out here, only the still voice of conscience. And you know that I think of my days at the top. I don't want to, because I'm not a dweller, but out here, there's dwelling to do. The only thing I wish is that somebody I respected would've asked me when I was young and on my way to the top, 'What's your goal in life?' Julian, what do you really want to achieve? And be honest with me. Don't give me no hogwash bullshit."

Julian cleared his throat. "That's the first time anyone has ever asked me that. Everybody always assumes that I already know."

"Well, don't you?"

"I think I did when I was really young. When my parents died, I wanted to be a sea captain, you know, a rescuer wishing I could've been there to save them. That's it, and I achieved that. Well, I didn't achieve it, but I became a sea captain, the best sea captain I could become, and that made me port captain. Then Axel stripped it away from me in such a heartless manner. That hurt me, and I hadn't been hurt like that since the day my parents drowned.

"To answer your question, I think, at this point I just want this *life force* to fly out of me. I often feel like I'm chosen. Actually, I know I'm chosen. It sounds insane, but I really believe in destiny. And I'm not talking about not taking responsibility for my actions, because believe me, I feel responsible for everything I do. I'm talking about being a warrior. There's more to the battle than can be explained, but it's like I currently reside in the heart of combat, and all that's left for me to do is to war on, and I can't ask too many hard questions right now. I just have to do what's right in front of me, take the next step, and have faith that the following step is going to be revealed, then the next one, and the next one. I don't know where the victory is, but I'm willing to make the hard choices and take it by force if necessary."

Julian to a swig of vodka.

"To be totally transparent, I'm at peace with being a warrior. Seeing those around you die, or worse, betray you, losing parts of themselves with every move, selling themselves out, selling their lives short…"

"Julian, you are more than a warrior; you are a conqueror. You are both fierce and honorable. I give you my blessing." Oleg touched Julian's forehead and gently carved the sign of the cross with his thumb. He stood up. "You're lucky I'm here. I'm good at keeping secrets."

"Thanks, Oleg."

Soon after, Oleg went to his chamber. Julian watched the stars for hours that night.

CHAPTER 98

The Long Road Ahead

Twenty-seven days since Ernie had left, and Julian was fully immersed in life at the ranch. Oleg and Yakov would speak Russian, and Julian practically understood. He had talked to Denise five days prior, and she assured him that business was doing good.

"Yeah, we've been doing sunset cruises with the yacht, so a little bit of money has been coming in every day," she said. "Do you want us to come get you?"

"No, thanks. Not yet."

One morning, Julian was playing fetch with Reyna on the beach. Reyna would go into the water chasing a stick, come back, and do it again; she was a happy dog. He went into the house and got some water from the jug. He heard his satellite phone ring and went over to where he kept it plugged in.

It was an unknown number, but he picked up anyway.

"Julian, this is Gilberto Alarcón."

"Gilberto, what a pleasant surprise!"

"Yes, I have something for you; *he lives in a pink mansion in Santa Rosalia.*"

"What?"

"You want to settle the score? Bracho lives in a pink mansion in Santa Rosalia. Did you copy that?"

"Yes, I copy," said Julian.

The call was over.

Julian made himself some coffee and enjoyed the afternoon.

That night at dinner, Oleg brought out a clear bottle of liquor. "It's homemade vodka. I made it out of potatoes, but I think it's good."

Yakov went to bed early; Julian and Oleg stayed up.

"Oleg, did you ever have to kill anyone?"

"Why do you want me to answer that question?"

"I'm faced with a decision that could change my life," said Julian.

"Is he family? Is the person you are going to kill family?"

"No"

"Will killing this person solve all of your problems?"

Julian shook his head.

"Have you ever killed anyone?"

Slight shake.

"Do you still feel like you must kill this person?"

"He killed my brother," said Julian with a long stare.

"The first time I killed a man, I was fourteen. The man I killed, he had taken my mother's land after my father died. From the time I held that knife on, I became a fugitive. I joined the Army, didn't return until five years later. It turned out there had never been anyone looking for me. They had blamed it on a gambling debt. The man had plenty of enemies and people who wanted to see him dead. I ran and hid for years, even fought in a war, and nobody was even chasing me. But, you see, that's what killing does to you. It makes you a fugitive, even if you get away with it," said Oleg.

"Do you regret killing the man?"

"No, never. But that's not the point. Guys like us, we're marked. *Chosen*, as you say, and the battle is real. Your only decision is if you're going to participate or be on the sidelines!"

"Well, I'm already participating."

"But I sense something else troubling you. What is it? Are you concerned for your soul?" Oleg asked with a smirk.

Julian took a moment. "Not really. Well, I'm a Christian."

They looked eye to eye, then a burst of laughter.

"Then, that answers it. I've got a Bible inside and it clearly says in the book of Exodus *Thou shalt not kill!* It's right there in the Ten Commandments."

Julian thought for a moment. "Some time back, I met a pastor. He told me that I could never lose my salvation if I just believed in Jesus."

"Well, do you?"

"What?"

"Believe in Jesus?"

"Yes, I mean, sure," said Julian.

"Well, I don't know much about religion, but I know one thing, it doesn't give you a free pass. Nothing does," said Oleg.

"I'm not talking about a free pass. I'm willing to pay for my actions," said Julian.

"But are you willing to pay the ultimate price?"

"No, but I'm willing to negotiate." Julian smiled.

Oleg laughed. "I'm not sure that's how it works. But I'll tell you something. Also, right there in the book of Exodus, it says no tattoos. Tattoos are as bad and as punishable as murder."

"Well, I don't have any tattoos," said Julian.

"You don't have any tattoos? A sailor with no tattoos? A captain?" Serious disbelief from Oleg.

"No. I always thought I'd have tattoos, but I just never got around to it," said Julian.

Oleg took off his shirt, revealing a world of complex tattoo art. The skin on his chest, shoulders, upper arms, back, and torso was completely covered in ink. A star on each shoulder, a full blown picture of Lenin on his stomach, skulls, dragons on each side, Madonna and child, a ship with a huge sail, a bold tiger, Russian eagle crests, eyes on the upper chest, knives on the clavicles, a giant cross with text and flames above the left kidney, and a universe of other markings connected by intricate colors, designs, and patterns. He had a swig of vodka, grabbed his shirt, took a few steps and looked back. "Let me know when you're ready, Yakov and I give you first tattoo. We'll ink you right."

"Will do," Julian laughed.

Oleg went inside.

The next day, Julian thanked Oleg for his words. "I've made my decision, and I need to get out of here."

"You will be missed. Is there anything we can do for you?" Oleg asked.

"Well, trade me my triple barrel shotgun for the rifle."

"I don't want to, but I'll do it only because it's pigeon hunting season and we need a shotgun. If not, I wouldn't trade it."

"Oh, I'm also going to need to borrow your truck."

"What? My truck?"

"Yes, I'll bring it back in less than a week," said Julian.

"Do what you have to do," said Oleg.

As Julian was walking out the door, he looked back. "Reyna, she needs a place to stay. I'm afraid she'll bark on my hunt."

They both looked at the canine who put her tail between her legs.

"This is her ranch anyway," said Oleg.

Julian drove the old truck out of Mercenary Point Ranch that afternoon. He wanted to make sure that he'd make it through the winding dirt road and onto the highway before sunset. Oleg had packed him lamb sandwiches and a flask of hot coffee for the long road ahead.

The truck was a smooth carriage pulling its weight north. Highway One was desolate. Julian tuned in to an AM station and thought about his mission ahead. It was just after 10 p.m. when he made it to Santa Rosalia. He didn't want to attract any attention, so he found beachside parking outside of town and slept until sunrise.

In the morning, he went into town for coffee and a warm roll of bread. Dirty jeans, long beard, old button-up shirt, stench of ranch, and an old truck. Julian blended right in with the locals. Nobody looked at him for a second too long, nobody thought about him — just another working *cachanilla*. He drove around town looking for a pink mansion. He was unsuccessful until about noon, when he took a cobblestone path up a street called Luciano Road.

CHAPTER 99

The Mule
that Paced Past Midnight

THE MANSION STOOD LIKE AN old presidential palace covered in dust. The pink coloring was washed into a soft intestine-like hue. Large palm trees swayed in the wind. There were black vehicles outside, Suburbans, pickup trucks, and ATVs. Julian parked his truck up the street where he had a good view of the front door. He made note of the cars, of their licence plates, and observed that an entourage of white Suburbans didn't leave for the night.

The next day, Julian left his car and walked farther up the hill, around the mansion up to the nearby hill top. From there he had a view of the mansion's backyard. He was standing there, watching the empty pool, when Samuel Bracho stepped outside to smoke a cigar. He was shirtless, wearing shorts and slippers. It was strange, but Julian actually felt respect for the man, some sort of fixation. Maybe it was the thought of a worthy adversary.

One of his guards came outside with him and looked Julian's way. He ducked beneath a bush. He wasn't able to hear them, but he had a clear sight of the two men smoking, talking, plotting. When Bracho was finishing his cigar, Julian heard a noise up on the hill top. Scared, he turned around and saw a mule chewing a plant.

"*Órale.*" It was an old ranchero asking a mule to move.

The ranchero herded six mules. He guided them to a thin trail and

Julian followed them. Three kilometers out, they reached a stable. Julian headed back toward the mansion, meditating along the way.

When he returned to his truck, the white Suburbans outside of the mansion were gone. He drove around town and found them parked outside of the port captainship office. He parked across the street and put his seat down. He staked out, waiting for hours when he saw Axel Cuevas come out of the office.

"Oh, there you are, hello cuz," Julian said to himself in a funny voice.

Axel got into a Suburban accompanied by his goons and they drove south out of town.

Julian knew what he needed to do. That night, he bought some steaks and went off-road and around the hilltop. He made his way to the mule ranch. The mule herder was named Adalberto. Julian introduced himself as Sixto Bayardo. He even gave himself a compelling backstory — a ranchero from La Ventana who was scoping out a small piece of land up in the Sierra that he had inherited.

"It was my uncle's ranch. He didn't have any kids, so it goes to me. But I think that it's way up on one of those hills," he told him. Julian asked if he could camp out on his property until the following day.

Adalberto agreed and made a fire. Julian grilled steaks. After dinner, he brought out a tent for Julian. The next morning, Julian told his host that he needed a mule to head up to his uncle's property, but didn't know when he would return.

"How about I trade you a mule for my truck?" Julian offered.

"Your truck looks like it's in really good shape. Why would you want to trade it for a mule?"

"I want to go up to the property, but then I want to keep going, you know, up the Sierra."

"Well, I think that's not a fair deal. I'm giving too little for too much," he said.

"Okay, why don't you throw in the tent and camping gear?" said Julian.

They shook hands a minute later.

Julian picked a mule named Freddie. It was a good trade for the old pickup truck; he knew the Crimeans would be mad if they ever found out how he'd gotten rid of the truck, but at this moment, he didn't care. Julian was beginning to unfold his handiwork like a mason laying a stone before a stone.

He loaded the mule with his rifle, water, and camping gear. The next morning, he headed out to the bush by the hilltop where he had a good view of the mansion. He took out the Winchester, loaded it, and set up with a rock comfortably beneath him, observing the world through the target, waiting for the perfect moment.

After two hours in the sun, Bracho stepped outside by himself to smoke a cigar. Julian didn't think twice. He shot him through the center of the eyebrows.

Bracho dropped.

Julian reloaded and looked again. Waited. Twenty seconds later, his guard, the same one from before, came out to check on him. As soon as he stepped outside, Julian shot him through the throat.

He stopped, reloaded, picked up the two hot casings, packed his rifle in its case, strapped it to the mule, hopped on. He hit its sides with the sole of his shoes where spurs should have been, and with natural tempo, Freddie began pacing, then jogging through the Sierra, up the hills and down the valleys.

Life was happening all around Julian, and he couldn't help but think of the road ahead. His plan was to traverse Baja, from the Sea of Cortez in the northeast, through the desert all the way to the Pacific Ocean in the southwest. He figured that when he made it to the other side, enough distance and time would have passed between him and the murders. But soon, he saw in this walk revindication, a cleansing of sorts.

It wasn't just him who saw it in the light; it was the spirits of the desert, the ones who graze from generation to generation in search of a new bearer, the ones who mark the rites of passage that men must take when they become great or perish. The sun came up behind him, hung over, and rested before him, but he and his mule kept pace. Julian was silent, a still transformation was taking place within. At night he would set up the tent and start a fire to keep warm. Every day he would feed something to the fire. The first day, he burned the rifle.

"That's all the evidence," he whispered to the winds.

The next morning, he tossed the steel that hadn't melted along with the empty caskets in separate ditches and buried it all. Three days after the killing, his thoughts began coming back. He felt the persecution, he knew that people were after him, people he didn't even know.

The rush of killing became a slow cry for help, one that he was keen on burying in that same desert. Solitude became his refuge, Freddie the mule was his only partner. He felt certain satisfaction in walking Baja. The long days helped him meditate on his actions. He knew what he had done; he didn't need atonement, he needed safety, and somehow he felt the desert give him that.

His commitments began coming back to him. He had broken his pact with Admiral Gomez about getting Bracho. But it was better that way, completely silent. He had turned off his satellite phone since talking to Gilberto Alarcón, and had no intention of turning it back on until he made it to the other side. His mind began making its own justifications, its own pilgrimage in defense of past actions. Somehow in Julian's mind, pacing through the Vizcaino desert would distill some hidden knowledge or secret about the act of killing. But, no, it just made him grow old of sunburn and fatigued of spirit.

Freddie was a good companion. He had a nose for water. Julian would boil it before drinking it. For food, they ate cactus, prickly pear when they could find it, and, if not, pitaya fruit. He would pick the spines off with his knife. Sometimes he'd boil the cactus, other times, he would eat it raw. The desolation added to the hole Julian felt in his chest. It wasn't guilt, but a giant emptiness he was experiencing.

His mother had once told him that hell was the absence of God. In this case, he didn't feel evil, simply the absence of good. He wanted to be back home..

Santa Rosalía is 160 kilometers northwest of Bocana, where the desert ends with Sierra hills bearing the Pacific beyond. When they made it over the last hill, they camped on the summit, and Julian made a fire. At dusk, he burned his camping gear and his extra clothes. He kept only a few possessions, including his handgun, his satellite phone, and his wallet. Somehow, these things had power over him, they anchored him, persuaded him to choose a life outside the desert.

As they were making it down the mountain early the next morning, Freddie tripped and broke his front leg. He couldn't stand up. He cried, he moaned. Julian knew that there was only one thing he could do. He shot the mule with his handgun and pushed him into a ditch. It felt somewhat like a proper burial. It was strange, almost sacrificial, but Freddie never made it out of the desert.

Julian walked to the Pacific Ocean solo. He soaked himself, washed his hair and body in the salt water of salvation. He smiled for the first time in his new life; he was baptized a man in the drink that connects the whole planet. Afterwards, he laid out on the beach, content. He walked south, seven kilometers, to the village of Boteque.

Once there, he remembered that he had a wallet with money. He used it to buy an electrolyte drink, razor blades, clothes, fruit and all of the newspapers he could find. There was a small hotel in town. He got a room, showered, shaved, and went out for tacos. When he returned, he slept on a bed. That night, he dreamt of a mule trotting alone in the desert forever, never making it to the promised land.

CHAPTER 100

Finger on Pulse

FIVE MEN ENTERED THE OFFICE of the Secretary General in Mexico City. These men were not known in the department; they had never been there. But on Wednesday, they entered the office of Licenciado Gamboa like they owned the place. The five men were all in their sixties; three of them wore cowboy hats and two of them suits. They weren't wearing any badges, as is strict policy at this office.

Our source near the event said the men closed the door behind them, and a look of fear came over Gamboa. It's clear each of these men represented one of the five cartels of Mexico, who combined, run a payroll bigger than the federal government. It's also clear that the purpose of their visit was to express concern over the death of Samuel Bracho, who was considered protected by a previous agreement.

Just the day before, after plenty of confusion regarding Bracho's death, the Mexican federal police claimed responsibility. According to mexileaks, an anonymous site run by Mexicans abroad, Bracho was considered untouchable, since each of the five cartels had some sort of business with him—not to mention the respect they felt for him since his escape from prison and reappearance in the underworld.

For this publication, the death of Samuel Bracho came as a relief; because, as you know, he was responsible for burning down our headquarters in Tijuana, killing Margarita Salazar, Raquel Inzunza, and Alfonso Reyes, good people who had families, dreams, and promising careers. But something about the way Bracho was killed surprises me.

The federales had been protecting him for so long. Why would they suddenly kill him? Was he no longer valuable to the organization? I don't think so. I think his death came as a surprise to all of them. Maybe old accounts caught up to him, maybe it was a rogue mercenary or an equalizer. It is these other possibilities that I am taking the liberty of raising because I believe the criminals who run Mexico are scared. They are scared that all of the bodyguards, the bulletproof trucks, the political connections, the police coverage, and the guns can't protect them. They must know they are as vulnerable as everyone else when they enter the arena of violence. Death has its own karma, and in this case, it caught up to Samuel Bracho in the form of a single bullet to the forehead.

The federales took responsibility for Bracho's death because they'd rather be viewed as heroes who finally caught the criminal who escaped, than as another inept institution made of people who don't know what's happening under their very noses. The hero perception works great for the media, but not so great for the cartels who pay for the public servants' mansions.

It's hard to imagine these five men fearing death, but if the cartels are coming together to ask for explanations, it means that bottom lines were hurt. It is difficult to estimate the fortune that Bracho left behind, but Globe magazine put it at $3.7 billion in liquid assets alone at the time of his capture nearly a decade ago. Since then, various sources have said his wealth was raided by some of his closest associates, including then-governor of North Baja, Don Aldo Ruiz.

After his escape from Almoloya, however, Samuel Bracho began an aggressive campaign to re-establish his connections, recover his enterprises, and grow his wealth—some say, scavenging everything, he could get back. Supposedly nobody knew where he was, but after his death, it became clear that he ran his entire operation out of an old mansion in Santa Rosalia.

It's unknown how business in the underworld is going to continue smoothly after this event. Bracho was a man who, during his last years, brokered shipments of all kinds and sold weapons to everyone in Mexico, including police forces, military, and narcos. He also held stakes in mines all over the country and a casino infrastructure made of slot machines in barrios. No wonder Mexico has often been called a bloody circus.

It's easy to laugh about our own corruption and the veil of impunity that exists in the world's twelfth largest economy, but I want to know what our country is going to be called during the wave of violence that's going to take place while the markets adjust, because I can assure you one thing, it won't be funny.

This piece first appeared under the title "Bloody Circus" in the space assigned to *Finger on Pulse*, a signed editorial by Pablo Heraldo, published weekly in the pages of *Gazeta*.

Julian read Heraldo's words and knew it was time to go home.

Chapter 101

Viral

"You know that expression, *Rome wasn't built in a day*?" said Ángel, the driver of the blue truck.

"I'm sorry?" said Julian, who was sitting in the passenger seat.

"*Rome wasn't built in a day.*" You've heard that before?"

"Yeah, yeah, I have."

"Well, I like to add: it wasn't brought down in a day, either. The systematic destruction of a nation is like cancer. It takes years to grow, and then it spreads quickly," said Ángel as he held the wheel.

Julian was trying to not make conversation, but Ángel was excited, talking enthusiastically about what everyone else was talking about, Samuel Bracho's death. Distrust in the government's story was widespread, and somehow, there was nostalgia about Bracho. People defended his life, like that of a worthy bandit, and folklore around his death began to emerge. Whether in favor or against the official narrative, Bracho was the viral topic of the day, on the tip of everyone's tongue.

"So, do you usually pay for people's gas in exchange for rides?" Ángel asked.

"No, I was whale watching at Puntabreojos, met up with my family who came down from Maneadero. I didn't want to ride the bus down to La Paz. Figured this way, at least I get to meet nice people," said Julian.

"Well, how do you know you'll get a ride from a good person?"

Julian took a moment. "I only ask for rides early in the morning. At that hour, the road is mostly decent people who make an honest living."

"Interesting. what a keen observation." Ángel looked at him, intrigued. "And what do you do for a living, Bayardo?"

"I'm a fisherman," said Julian, as he looked out the window at the winding Baja.

Hours later, they spotted La Paz from miles out, looking stunning, sexy, elegant, inviting. Julian understood why some called it the pearl of the gulf, because from the last hill, the city looked like a giant oyster. When he got closer, there was a little bit of traffic to enter the city. As they drove in, Julian realized that there was a Mexican Army checkpoint.

The Army was looking for guns, which concerned Julian because he had his .45 pistol strapped to the inside of his left ankle.

Thank God I'm wearing jeans, he thought.

The soldiers looked through the truck and made them step down. They never touched Julian, however. He exhaled with relief when they let them through.

Twenty minutes later, he thanked Ángel and asked to be dropped off on the next corner, which was four blocks from his house. He walked the final stretch and unlocked the door with a key he kept in his wallet.

Home, the feeling of sanctuary. Julian had left a mess. That evening, he cleaned his house and cooked dinner. He felt like being alone, gathering his thoughts before entering the world of reality the following day. Before he went to bed, he turned on the news. There were so many theories about what had happened to Samuel Bracho. People were making up myths about the man; one TV analyst was saying that he was killed by Navy Seals with orders directly from Washington. Another said that a Twitter poll concluded that most Mexicans believed Don Aldo Ruiz had been behind the hit. But as in all things, the reality of the situation was better than fiction, and, in this case, it had been a lone shooter, who was now safely back home. Julian felt protected behind this curtain of misinformation. He knew that with so much speculation and interests floating around, no investigation would ever link back to him.

CHAPTER 102

Values

*P*ERSONAL HISTORY IS ETCHED ON *the skin*, was the thought in Julian's mind as he looked at himself in the mirror while he shaved and noticed the marks the desert had left on his face.

He got a haircut and called Admiral Gomez. An hour later, they were talking in his office.

"They beat us to it, Julian, what can I say? Bracho had a lot of enemies," said Gomez.

Julian thought about the past weeks since Alberto Fontana's funeral. Part of him wanted to come out and tell his *padrino* that he shot Bracho, but pacts made in the desert didn't allow him. "Yeah, but at least they got to him, and that makes our lives easier."

"What do you mean?"

"We need to get Axel. Especially now that his boss is gone. He'll be like a chicken with his head cut off," said Julian in a rather aggressive voice, one that the Admiral didn't recognize.

"Have your thoughts changed regarding Axel's life?" asked Gomez.

"No, I don't want him dead. I want him in jail. He's got to go."

Admiral Gomez took a second. "Do you have anything in mind?"

Julian raised an eyebrow. "What did you find out about the island where a *Dragón* sleeps?"

"Well, turns out the city of Loreto doesn't own Isla del Carmen like we thought. They have a claim to it, but in reality, it's owned by a Japanese firm called Sendai Corporation. These guys are doing some crazy research involving Cimarrón bighorn sheep. Part of their spleen is being used to cure cancer, or to prolong the effects of a medicine that cures cancer, something like that. It's our understanding that once the Cimarrón are big enough, they ship them alive to Japan, where they get treated to intensive lab work," Gomez said.

"So, why are they hiding the yacht?" Julian asked.

"We think somebody at the Sendai Corporation bought it on the black market, took it to the island to remodel it, and they're waiting on an opportunity to take it back to Japan under false paperwork."

"Who owns Sendai Corporation?" asked Julian.

"The Goya family, but they're in Tokyo."

"Matsu Goya," whispered Julian with a light smile.

"What? You know him?"

"I've heard about him. He used to be a salt merchant in the days of the mine. He made a killing out of selling illegal promethium," said Julian.

"Well, he's making a killing now," said Gomez, as he showed him reports on Goya's wealth and high standing in Japanese society. "Whatever the case, he lives like royalty."

"What about his Mexican operation? Does he keep an office?"

"Yes, they do, but it's nothing. A shell corporation. It's basically an information booth about the bighorn sheep and the treatment they use it for. We believe the office is only a front that deals with bribing politicians and filing paperwork."

At this precise moment, Julian had all the information he needed, and everything felt aligned. Power had returned, and with Bracho's death, a balance had been restored. He felt ready to strike.

"I know what we're going to do, but I have to let you in on the big secret," said Julian as he leaned in and lowered his voice. "In the bow of the yacht is a compartment where we believe there is over $100 million in cash."

Gomez's eyes lit up, but remained speechless.

"We need to go in there, retrieve that money, expose that yacht, blow the lid on the island ,and on Sendai Corp for corruption. But get this — we're gonna pin everything on Axel."

"Wow, Julian, I mean, it's going to take some planning." He was hesitant, his shock was sincere, but Julian could tell that Admiral Gomez was thinking, strategizing. "Before we move on to operations, which, trust me, there's a lot of ground to cover, I want to know, how are we going to pin everything on Axel?"

Julian exhaled and took a moment to gather composure.

"Axel used to be Samuel Bracho's captain when the yacht was called *The Durango*. We tell that story to the media, saying that Axel's personal enrichment is based on the illicit sale of the yacht, and you know he's not going to allow anybody to poke around his finances because there's dirt everywhere. So we'll accuse him of peculation, abuse of power, and influence trafficking, then make it seem like he used his job as port captain to protect Sendai Corporation interests regarding the yacht that he'd sold them. We'll expose him, get him fired, and we'll work nonstop to have him arrested."

Admiral Gomez looked steadily at Julian. "What about Pizante?"

"If everything they say about Pizante is true, then the death of Bracho is weakening him, so when Axel falls, it will be a huge blow. We'll have Pizante right where we need him, because, so far, he's remained in the shadows. Let's see if this will push him into the sunlight," said Julian.

"Somehow, I can't help but get the feeling that you've been planning this," he said.

"Admiral, this is the time to strike. I don't want to be worried that Axel will continue to grow. I want to weaken him to the point that he breaks."

"Just be careful, Julian. Hate can change a man."

"Hate? No, I don't hate Axel, but I need to destroy him. His party is about to come to an end."

"You know, Julian, you had me at $100 million. We get that money, I support you against Axel with my complete force."

"That's what I'm talking about," said Julian, extending his hand. Gomez shook it. They gave each other homework and agreed to meet again in three days.

CHAPTER 103

Homework

JULIAN HAD PLENTY TO TELL his crew, but didn't know where to begin. He didn't want them involved in the retrieval of the money.

They can't be on full disclosure; it's too much money we're speculating with. If we actually retrieve the money, of course, I'll share it with them.

He convinced himself it was for their own protection, and although that was true, the other part was that he felt a bit of greed. His crew suspected there was something aboard *The Dragón*, but they didn't know specifically about the cash. Julian almost felt guilty for not telling them, but like a cheating husband, he overcompensated and took them out to Palermo's for dinner.

"Tonight, let's not talk about business or about whatever's on the news and social media about Bracho and our enemies. Tonight, I want to celebrate, drink with you, who are my real family. I know that I was gone for some time, but let's create new memories here, now," said Julian.

They all raised their glasses and had a toast. Julian ordered angel hair pasta with tomato sauce and another bottle of red. Even though Rubio was the only one keeping pace, Denise and Ernie were in on the fun, too.

"Why don't we go out on the plane tomorrow?" Denise offered. "It's been so long since we've flown together. We took her out last week. Some clients wanted to go to San Juan de La Costa for lunch, this great little spot we'd never even heard of. You guys have to let us take you."

"Well, you know I'm game," said Julian as he paid the bill.

The following day, the crew of four flew around La Paz, carefree, leisurely, enchanted by their own freedom and the beauty of it all. The restaurant at San Juan de La Costa was called Antonia's and it was spectacular—seafood laid out on the table, homemade flour tortillas, rice, beans, beers, and tequila flowing for Julian and Rubio, live banda played local favorites. Julian laughed at the ridiculous lyrics. One in particular went, "*Let me be a dog and bury my bone in your backyard.*" The joy of laughing that hard brought a tear in Julian's eye. They flew back to La Paz in the afternoon. Julian was sauced. He asked to be dropped off on the yacht and fell asleep at 7:00. The next day, they went out to sea.

Julian skippered the yacht to his favorite local spot, Isla Partida. Afterward, Rubio made fish tacos for lunch. It was incredible how much Julian had missed Rubio's *sazón* for food.

"I've been in contact with Admiral Gomez, and we've drafted a plan regarding *Dragón*. But first, you all need to be up to date," he told his crew during lunch. "The yacht is owned by a Japanese company called Sendai Corp. It was sold to them by Axel Cuevas, who used to be her captain when she was called *The Durango*. These guys are corrupt. Sendai Corp ties back to Matsu Goya, who's been a pirate, raiding Baja California since the 1960s. And Axel is using his power as port captain to protect him."

Denise looked angry. Ernie wanted to know more.

"So, this is what we need to do. I'm going to advise Admiral Gomez on the tactical part of the operation. So, starting tomorrow, I'm going to be working more closely with him. Denise, given your track record with social media accounts, and the way you've been taking great pictures and promoting them through internet forums..."

"It's Ernie that takes all of the pictures and videos," Denise interrupted.

"Yeah, the both of you. I need you to focus on one thing — we need to expose Axel Cuevas for the criminal that he is. Your job will be to handle the web strategy. We need to give him a trial by social media, make him look guilty to the maximum degree, because after the lid is blown off, we're going to find a way to put him behind bars," said Julian.

"How do we do that?" asked Ernie.

"Press releases!" said Denise.

"So the bighorns are being used for medical research?"

"Yeah, they take them back alive to Japan, where they remove their spleen once they're ready. They fatten them here in Baja because, for some reason, when they've tried to fatten them in Japan, they never reach their full size. Something about their natural terrain," said Julian.

"You know what we need to do," Denise interrupted, "contact Greenpeace, the environmentalists, animal rights activists. They'll jump all over this."

"Now you're thinking," Julian said.

"Now, the biggest thing is to coordinate the tactical operation with Gomez and the media operation with you, with me as a middleman. So, get the ball rolling because I'll meet with Gomez tomorrow and I need you to have a plan we can present to him," said Julian.

"Ay, ay, Skip," said Denise.

That evening, after they'd docked *The Cecilia*, Denise began her research. If she was going to attack, she was going to do it right. Julian loved that about her. He was certain that media operations was something Denise could do masterfully.

CHAPTER 104

Tactical Media

JULIAN AND ADMIRAL GOMEZ MET early on Thursday morning. The excitement about retrieving the money was tangible.

"I've put together a team of four Hawks, our most elite unit. Counting us, that's six people who are in on this," said Admiral Gomez.

"Plus, my crew," said Julian.

"What are *they* doing?"

"Well, they found the yacht with me, and they're handling the media side of things."

"Okay, so, you've got people, and I've got people. How are we going to do this?" Gomez asked.

"Well, I think we should split it evenly between you and me, and we each take care of our own as we see fit."

"Right down the middle?"

"Whatever we find, half to you, half to me," said Julian.

Gomez took a second to think things through. "Well, that's easy for you, because your crew isn't going to be there to see exactly how much money we'll be getting."

Julian smiled, "I thought the Hawks were your guys. I thought they were loyal?"

"Yeah, they're more than loyal. But pirate law is pirate law. If we're raiding it for ourselves, the raiders split it evenly. Plus, once people see the money in cash, shit changes. We raided a home in Veracruz once. Everybody went crazy, you know $100 million. That's half a room, about

200 briefcases. It's not like it's going to be easy, just walking out of some cave with that much volume," Gomez said.

"Then, what do you suggest we do?"

"Well, I was thinking about retrieving the yacht, and once it's here, we go to work on getting the money out," he said.

"But, as soon as Mexico City finds out that you have the yacht, Don Aldo Ruiz has contacts, and he knows about the money in the bow. Why else do you think that he told Alberto Fontana to poke around? He'll move quickly, send his people to retrieve it, and once the establishment knows about the cash, you can count on us not getting a single dollar," said Julian.

"You're right. If we're going to retrieve the money, it needs to be *in situ*. It's just that $100 million divided by two is $50 million each. If we split it within six people, it's only $16 million. There's a big difference between the two numbers," Gomez said.

"It's easy—you and I split it, you take care of your people and I take care of mine how we each see fit. But let's not fry fish we haven't caught," said Julian.

"Yeah, but militarily, I don't strike until I know exactly how it's going to go down. One wrong play and we'll get killed for that money, whether it's the Hawks because they felt robbed, or Don Aldo a year later. We have to get the money, just us. We've got to come out looking clean, innocent, and the Mexican Navy in South Baja has to look heroic; that's our job," said Gomez.

"And pin it on Axel! Simple, we want it all," said Julian with a grin.

"We could always just pin everything on Axel without touching the money," said Gomez.

They took a second, looked at each other, and let out a loud laugh simultaneously.

"Yeah, and let Don Aldo and his friends just walk in and take it all? Never," said Julian.

"In that case, let's go tactical media," said Gomez.

"What's tactical media?"

"It's when you use your media team to engage in the attack."

"Like actually have them there while we capture?"

"Exactly!"

"Wouldn't that give away our strategy?"

"No, that's the trick. The media team creates a curtain of smoke and mirrors. We have to get them to focus on specific things and away from us. That gives us the time to go in and take the money ourselves, even if it takes us an hour," said Gomez.

"How do we begin?"

"We need three boats, the media team, led by your men…"

"Woman," said Julian.

"What?'

"My media team is led by a woman."

Admiral Gomez paused for a moment. "We need another boat for recovery—that's you and me. We're the money team. The third boat is for the hawks."

"Okay, so what's our operation going to look like?"

"First, one of the Hawks opens the gate to the cave with a transmitter that de-scrambles all signals. They go in and make arrests, light the place up with firepower if necessary, secure the location. Second, we go in, straight to the *Dragón*. I was able to figure out what vault it is from the links you sent me. It's basically a hidden exterior safe, so I know what we need to do. Those are tricky to get into, but the good thing is, they're not real vaults, they're more for concealment. The door has a way to pop out if enough pressure is applied, but I don't want you to worry about that. Leave that area to me."

Julian nodded.

"Once we clear our opening and we have access to the goods, we call in tactical media. We exit with the money. Tactical stays behind covering the story, focusing on the Hawks, the arrest, the island, and the exterior of the yacht. Then, I call in large backup and blow the lid off this thing up the chain of command. And once that happens, tactical media needs to get out of there, quick. They have to hurry to make the story go live within minutes of the backup arriving. The island, Sendai Corp., Axel, the corruption, the whole bit needs to be national news by that same afternoon."

Julian looked at his mentor. "Wow, good to see that great military mind of yours in action."

No reaction from the Admiral.

"When do we strike?" asked Julian.

The Admiral took a second. "Take your yacht out to Bahia San Dolores, halfway between La Paz and Loreto. I know a private cove there. It's a great spot to leave it anchored. I'll pick you and your team up by sea at 0400 on Sunday morning."

"Perfect, send me the coordinates," said Julian.

CHAPTER 105

Game Theory

ERNIE SHOWED JULIAN A TWO minute video of bighorn sheep roaming Isla del Carmen.

"I rigged the bottom of the plane so it could hold a couple of Go-Pros."

"Good quality stuff," said Julian.

"Yeah, we flew out to Isla del Carmen and took a bunch of pictures. It's quite the sight. Really sets the contrast," Denise said, showing Julian photos of the bighorns suffering in Japanese labs. "Turns out there's a Japanese animal rights organization called *Dobutsu Life* that's on to Sendai Corp. They'll be getting our press releases as well."

"Good, that's what we need, everything ready, because we're going to strike on Sunday." Julian looked away and then turned back to Denise, who was sitting next to Ernie. "By the way, you guys have a way more hands-on role than I'd originally had thought."

"What do you mean?" Ernie asked in almost instant disagreement.

"Admiral Gomez calls it 'tactical media,' which means that you guys are coming in with us to capture the island."

"What? So we're actually going into the line of fire?"

"Well, we're not sure if there's going to be any fire, But we need you guys there with your cameras. We need to create a curtain of press, and we'll need it to be like clockwork," said Julian.

"Fuck, Julian. You know how I feel about exposing my wife," said Ernie.

"And you know how I feel about you getting in the way of my life," Denise said. "We've been working on this for so long, Ernie." She calmed down and grabbed his hand. "It's okay."

"I just…"

"I know," said Denise, and the two held hands. After their moment, Denise looked back at Julian.

"Truth is, we believe there's something of great value in the vault underneath the helipad and Admiral Gomez and I are going to retrieve it," Julian said. "We don't know what's in there or how much it could be worth, so I don't want you guys to think about that. But I really need you to operate at a higher level. If there's plunder there, we're splitting it down the middle with Admiral Gomez. You know I'll play fair and bring it into BAS and take us to a whole different level. But I need you guys to focus on the tasks directly in front of you right now. This is a complex operation, and tactical media is no joke."

"We trust you entirely. We're with you 100 percent," said Denise.

"You've never let me down Skip. Let's do this!" Ernie hugged Julian.

"What's the plan, Skip?" Denise asked.

"The reason we're doing tactical media is not only to keep attention off of us as we survey the yacht for loot, but to make the Hawks look good. They're an elite force of the Mexican Navy. Admiral Gomez asked us to make sure that credit for the capture goes to them.

"This is the plan," Julian continued. "We need to write the press release and have the media strategy ready to launch. Then, after the capture on Sunday, you're going to come back to shore, add the new pictures, videos, and finish adding any details. Then, you send all of the information to this one email, arman@newzagency.mx. He's Admiral Gomez's contact for massive PR attacks."

Julian handed Denise a card with the email address and a password written on it.

"What's this?"

"This is the email you're going to use to leak the story. Log in from anywhere. It's an encrypted email. We can't have anything tracing back to us."

That afternoon, Ernie and Denise went to Cabo and stocked up on adventure gear, new generation GoPros, and other camera supplies. The next day, they had another meeting with Julian.

"So, here's the plan. We're leaving early tomorrow. We're going to anchor *The Cecilia* in a private cove up coast. From there, the Mexican Navy will pick us up and take us to our destination. It's important that you guys, the media team, do a complete capture—the yacht, pictures, video, and references. After everything is done, you'll go to Loreto. There, a man named Silvestre Greene will pick you up at a specific location. He'll take you to the offices of the Pistol & Rifle, a club that I'm a member of. From there, you'll send the complete press package to that email. From there, you should drive north. Stay in Ensenada for as long as you have to."

"What?"

"This is going to be a huge hit on many levels. You need to be out of the picture until everything settles."

"How long do you think that will be?"

"I have no idea, but if there's retaliation from Axel, they're going to come looking for us. Be prepared to spend time away until I tell you it's clear," said Julian.

That day, Denise and Ernie packed their bags, gear, cameras, and computer into their Tacoma pickup and handed the keys to Julian, who handed them to Rubio.

"You'll drive this truck to Loreto tonight, give it to Silvestre Greene, and you'll get on the first bus back. We need to leave tomorrow early by boat."

He was gone a half-hour later. As Rubio drove the Jordans' truck up Highway 1, Denise and Ernie finished the press release and packed their tactical gear.

Julian gave them a call. "It's important that you wear your balaclavas the whole time you're with the Hawks. It's better they never know your identity," he said in a hushed tone.

"What?" said Denise.

"Your masks!"

Everybody was aboard *The Cecilia* at 0800 the next morning. Rubio looked tired, so Julian let him rest the first couple of hours into their journey north. Clear skies, fair wind, no wake. Julian was happy to be at the helm of his yacht. The sun glimmered on the water. Julian asked Ernie to put on some tunes. He selected a new band Julian had never heard before called Woods. Good melodies, awesome vocals. Soon enough, Julian wanted a drink. Rubio came up to the bow just in time with fish tacos and margaritas. Denise took the helm and they anchored at Bahia San Dolores at 16:45.

By 22:00, everybody was asleep except Julian, who was up in the tower taking swigs of mezcal, looking at the clear ocean night, anxious for the morning, when fortunes would change hands and destiny would unravel in his favor.

CHAPTER 106

Sunday Morning

"**B**EING ON TIME IS BEING five minutes early," said Admiral Gomez as he threw a rope over to *The Cecilia* from a black tender at 03:54.

Julian caught the rope in the still darkness. He pulled the tender closer and tied it to the yacht. The Jordans jumped into the tender in full gear: half wetsuits, amphibious shoes, cameras in waterproof cases, black vests with PRESS on the back, hats, and sunglasses. They greeted Admiral Gomez and put their masks on, like bandidos about to rob a bank.

"Good, don't take those masks off until you're clear in Loreto. We don't want anybody to know who's anybody. It's for your own protection. A big mission like this can trigger retaliation," Gomez said.

Julian went back inside the yacht and said goodbye to Rubio, waking him up. "We've got to go on a mission. Stay here, take care of our lady. I should be back before two days. If I'm not, wait a week, then take *The Cecilia* back to La Paz and contact Admiral Gomez at the base. If neither of us is back, your last stop is Fabio. Understood?"

"Yes, skip." Rubio stood up and gave Julian a hug. "Take care of the crew, boss."

"Haven't I always?"

Rubio nodded. "We believe in you, we trust you."

"*Gracias.*"

Once aboard the tender, Julian put on his mask and the rush set in.

At 04:21, the tender arrived at a seventy-foot Challenger with a robust, well-built hull. With four tenders above deck, hanging from cranes like resting bats, the ship appeared aggressive, delivering on its promise.

There was a strange tension aboard. This was a serious mission, but since information had been given in bits and pieces, the lack of unity on board was expected. Julian, Ernie, and Denise sat in silence with the six-member company of Mexican Navy elite forces, known as the Hawks. On this operation, the Admiral was their commander. The Challenger went full throttle, pushing fifty knots for over 100 nautical miles. When they finally spotted Isla del Carmen, the Admiral called a general meeting. The main room aboard the boat was filled with people wearing black clothing, masks, and heavy-duty gear.

"Okay, this is a special operation — for all of us. First step, Hawks open the gate, then go in there and make arrests. Flash-bang and scare the shit out of them. If you can do it without casualties, better. Make sure everyone is bound and held. We're expecting anywhere from twelve to twenty people to be stationed on the island. When they're subdued, you give us a call and the media team will go in."

Julian scoffed. "You're sending six Hawks? How many people are you expecting? There's…"

"Relax," said Gomez. "Didn't you six-stop a mob of 250 armed peasants?"

"It was 350," said one of the Hawks.

"See. What's twenty people for you?" asked Gomez.

"That's 3.34 each," said one of the Hawks as he cocked his gun.

The other strapped a big knife to his leg.

The Admiral looked at the Hawks, then at Julian, and back at the Hawks. "Afterwards, media will be getting coverage. Gentlemen, they are here to make us look good, so treat them right! In third position, team *Dragón* will enter the cave in the Challenger and survey the yacht," he looked at Julian. "Hawks and media need to capture a complete visual inventory of the cave, and like you saw in the brief we sent, it's a big one, so go deep; we're here to figure out the story, to get to the heart of the matter. Are we all in agreement?"

"Yes, sir!" said the two teams as an actual unit.

The plan seemed viable enough to execute. All of the different teams had been briefed separately regarding their exit strategy. Team media was going to ride the tender to Loreto and the Hawks were going to wait for additional Navy forces. Admiral Gomez and Julian had been careful, calculating, and smart in assembling the teams.

The Challenger decelerated in front of the entrance to the cave where stones that looked like old soldiers stood petrified. One of the large Zodiacs was brought down from the deck and placed carefully upon the water. The Hawks boarded and rode like a kettle of predators staring into a newfound food source. They shot over towards the wall of land that had a custom built entrance disclosed as part of the mountainside. Julian was nervous, the Admiral was not. The leader of the hawks was carrying the most sophisticated descrambler for this type of gate. Admiral Gomez had an engineering unit build it. He had full faith in science and in his men. The wall opened and the Hawks went into Bocamía.

From the safe distance of the Challenger, Julian and Gomez looked for glimpses of the battle. Ernie decided to lower his own tender, and he and Denise waited for the call.

"Go, go," said Julian as he reached over the rail towards the tender where his crew sat.

The second tender entered the cave. Julian and Gomez, alone in the Challenger, waited. Through the small opening at a distance, they couldn't see anything happening inside the cave, but with their sixth sense of strategy, they could visualize the battle being executed. When they got the go-ahead from the Hawks, the *Challenger* went forward into *Bocamía*.

Chapter 107

If Dragons Could Roar

THE CAVE WAS NOT LIKE Julian remembered it. Perhaps the feeling was based on the difference in the entry method. The Challenger fit well within the cave, which was Japanese engineering at its finest. Entering *Bocamía* through the big gate was empowering. Admiral Gomez could maneuver his ship easily through it, like a canal in an affluent city. The Hawks had captured nine people, seven Japanese and two Mexicans.

The Hawks got them to turn on the lights. And even though there were still plenty of dark areas to the cave, you could tell how incredible of a lair it was.

Dragón could be spotted in the belly of the cave. Shining beautifully, but uncomfortable over the amount of light it was receiving, like a creature who's been in the shadows of a cavern for so long that it becomes uncomfortable near illumination.

With its fresh coat of paint and stylish design, the yacht looked like a kidnapped heiress trapped in a dungeon of vile men waiting on a ransom. At a distance, the Hawks could be seen holding the Japanese men as the media team took pictures of each one.

Admiral Gomez threw the rope over and tied the Challenger close enough to the *Dragón*. He jumped between the two ships easily and stepped aboard the *Dragón* like a man sneaking towards prey. He hunched over, a small bag of tools in his hand, and a miner's light on his head. The two men walked towards the bow of the yacht in silence.

The helicopter pad was empty. The Airbus H155 that nested there in the days of *The Durango* was gone, sold, and probably in service of a jungle cartel somewhere in South America. There was a platform with a hatch that was secured with a simple lock. Admiral Gomez picked it with extreme precision. Once the hatch was open, there was a little ladder that led directly below to the master stateroom.

"Strange," said Gomez. "There's supposed to be a vault here."

"Damn," said Julian, as he heard a noise coming from deep in the yacht.

Julian shared a fear with all the men throughout history that have been in caves and risked startling dragons. Somewhere in its slumber, the yacht was beginning to awaken.

"What the hell was that noise?" Julian asked.

"It's the yacht. She's begging us to get her out of here. She wants to stretch her sea legs."

Julian scoffed.

"Yachts have a life of their own. You know that."

"Yeah, figuratively," said Julian.

"Shh… be quiet. Listen to her; she's trying to tell us something." The Admiral spoke with authority. "Let us find what we came for and we will liberate you from this cave."

"Damn, if our plan consists of you talking to a yacht, we *are* desperate," said Julian.

At that moment, the megayacht rocked slightly and Julian, the experienced seaman, lost his balance. His foot slipped off the ladder. He feared that he would fall, so he kicked out and put his leg up against the opposite wall. But the wall didn't hold; his foot went right through a false wall of thin plywood and drywall.

"Dang it. My leg is stuck. I think I cut myself," said Julian.

"Ha! Can't you see? It worked! She's guiding us," Admiral Gomez said as he helped Julian liberate his leg.

"Just a small cut, nothing too big," said Julian as he tied the red handkerchief Admiral Gomez had given him around his cut.

Julian regained composure and the Admiral beat through the wall with a hammer and cut it away with a small battery-powered saw. Julian stood behind him, throwing the broken plywood and drywall on the floor of the master stateroom below them. Admiral Gomez was following a pattern, making a tunnel into the wall, opening up small areas that were surrounded by heavy, impenetrable walls. Like a miner in search of El Dorado, Gomez turned on his light and continued digging patiently into the belly of the *Dragón*. He would listen to the walls, feel them for their hollowness, and strike at precise spots.

The men kept breaking through wood and mining the bow of the yacht for forty-seven minutes, until they reached a steel door. It had no lock, no handle, nothing. Admiral Gomez looked through his bag and pulled out a thin tool that Julian didn't recognize. He slipped it underneath the door. He added a wrench to the back of the tool and worked it like a jack. The door began to lift, creating tension in the steel. The steel compressed until Admiral Gomez couldn't turn the wrench anymore. Julian grabbed a hammer and began beating the wrench, making everything even tighter, tensing the steel enough for it to show a crack. Julian lifted the hammer and beat the wrench with all his might. The door became harder, firmer, and Julian struck the wrench again. A snap came from the side and the door popped out. Admiral Gomez grabbed it and opened it, pulling the steel door towards them.

Gym bags, duffel bags, satchels, briefcases, black plastic bags, backpacks — there were nothing but bags in the safe. In the darkness, Julian's sense of smell became more acute. The density and the heat created a damp scent that he and the Admiral recognized immediately as money. Paper money carried a unique smell when humid: slightly moldy, not quite repugnant, almost smelling like iron in the blood or chlorophyll in plants; strange, but the money trapped in that room smelled like a living thing.

Julian smiled. "Let's finish what we came here for!" he said.

The pair went to work carrying two or three heavy bags up to the deck at a time. They would jump ship with the bags and load them in the main hall of the Challenger. Gomez would take bags to the ladder and Julian would take them from there. They did this 105 times over almost three hours. Excitement gave them adrenaline.

The safe was finally empty. Julian and Gomez were drenched in sweat, breathing the somewhat fresher air on the deck of the *Dragón*.

"What about the evidence?" asked Julian.

"What evidence?"

"Chief, we just broke through wood and panels on a luxury yacht. I even cut myself earlier. I think somebody's going to notice the mess we made," said Julian.

"Nah, don't worry about that, I've got forensics in my back pocket. Anyway, I have a plan. Take the Challenger and skipper it down to Bahia San Dolores, to where *The Cecilia* is. Once you're there, transfer the goods aboard your yacht, and skipper her down to La Paz. Leave the Challenger anchored there at Bahia San Dolores. I'll send someone to pick her up."

"What do I do with the money once I get to La Paz?"

"Stay at the marina. Don't unload anything from the yacht. Wait for me; we'll do it when we're safe at the base and I'm there. I'm trusting you with my life's work — don't screw this up."

"I won't, Chief. Take care of my crew."

"I'm dismissing them as soon as I head up there, before I even call backup," the Admiral said.

They lowered the remaining tenders from the Challenger and the Admiral went deeper into the cave looking for his Hawks.

Julian held the helm.

"Bless my journey Jesus, guide my hand and let be wise with this money," he prayed softly. Even though he didn't want to create any wake inside the cave, Julian skippered the *Challenger* out of Bocamía as fast as he could.

PART V

Underworld

CHAPTER 108

Dreams of Bolivar

WHEN PASCUAL PIZANTE FIRST HEARD about the death of Samuel Bracho, he immediately thought it was Don Aldo Ruiz who'd sent a hitman. He remembered Axel Cuevas warning them against killing Alberto Fontana, but Bracho and Pizante had decided to go ahead. Pizante felt a slight aftertaste of failure, but he swore to continue on with his fight. Baja California was now his main focus.

Stopping the Punta Colonet Port had been a great move toward his plan to destabilize Baja. Further building international distrust in business related to Mexico, causing investors to lose money, forcing the World Bank to file a bad report, causing billionaires to back out by killing overall enthusiasm. Killing the Punta Colonet Port had been great business for Pascual Pizante, who felt like he'd single-handedly decided the fate of the whole peninsula.

He couldn't see Baja succeed; he needed the region to come to its knees, so he could force people toward an insurgency. Yes, it was strategic, but for Pizante, this operation was personal—it was his legacy. He knew that the Mexican hold on the Baja California peninsula was weak, and if the right picture was painted, Baja Californians would support a separation from the Mexican Republic.

After they had killed Fontana, Pizante focused on destroying a different industry, local airlines, a strong link between Baja California and the rest of Mexico. AeroBaja, the airline whose hub was La Paz, had a growing dissatisfaction among its workers. The airline, which had been losing money, status, and flight routes since its heyday in the mid-1980s, was still a large source of employment for the city of La Paz. Thousands of men and women worked in the air and on the ground to connect South Baja with parts of their own country that often seemed so far away.

The day after Bracho's death, Pizante continued with his plan. He bribed Alfonso Otto, the union leader of AeroBaja's *sindicato*, with $75,000 to call for a general strike. Not all of the money went into Otto's pocket. He hired agitators and propagandists, paid off the police and the airport authority. It was a professional strike, executed to the highest International Workers' Association standards. The anarcho-syndicalists did their thing. Within hours, and with nothing to tie him to the strike, Pizante destroyed another source of income for thousands of families in the region, unleashing hardship onto a productive segment of the population, forcing them to lose jobs, migrate, drink more, gamble, pawn, and take other predictable paths of destruction that could benefit the man formerly known as Mr. Terror.

Pizante had always been a good strategist when it came to offensive roles. After the AeroBaja strike, he continued his active work in media, sponsoring stories about the decay of Mexico's economy, crime, strikes, etc. He was a master of selling destruction to a wide array of outlets. Ten days after the AeroBaja strike, Pizante formed a small council in Panama. He named it "The Bolivar Council," which was a cover to talk about his operations in Baja with elite members of international agencies that he trusted. Their plan wasn't just to separate Baja from Mexico, it was to make an entirely new country, one so close to—yet so far from—the United States, one that could be its Switzerland, its offshore paradise. He'd have a blank canvas to implement better ideas on capitalism and democracy, an advanced society.

"Imagine a country birthed in the new millennium, empowered by progressive ideas and technologies, and best of all, that country could be in North America. We could define the new first world," Pizante said during one of his talks.

On the advice of some members, Pizante began to distance himself from anything that smelled like Samuel Bracho.

"What about Axel Cuevas? What are you going to do about him?" asked one of the council members after Bracho had been shot.

"I have a long-term plan for Axel. I can make him governor," answered Pizante.

The Bolivar Council was a success.

The following day he called Axel Cuevas and asked him to abandon all business interests that were tied to the deceased gangster.

"Basically, everything except the training programs," said Axel.

"Exactly," answered the commandant.

Pizante had a new plan; Samuel Bracho's murder had been a blow, but now the grand architect was revealing his framework.

CHAPTER 109

The Shrewd Servant

Ever since Bracho had caught a case of lead to the head, Axel Cuevas's hustle had intensified. He didn't want to abandon all the projects that had been so difficult for him to regain. He didn't understand Pizante's logic, but orders were orders. Axel began to give Bracho's business entirely to his distributors; these were millions of dollars, hundreds of thousands of slot machines spread throughout Mexico, mines that were being dug, piracy and pornography distribution centers, unimaginable things that added up to over a billion dollars in value. Pizante told Axel not to make any money from liquidating Bracho's assets, but Axel was shrewd.

He'd give every business back to a distributor on one condition.

"Samuel Bracho is dead. I don't want a kickback, but let's just say that you owe me a favor. There's going to be a time when I call and need something from you. When that time comes, be ready."

Naturally, they all agreed. When they questioned his motives, he would say that Bracho's replacements were more international types who had enough of a fortune and had other business interests. The net of distributors who had worked under the lead thumb of Samuel Bracho was given a free pass from his servant. The lords of the underworld approved of Axel; they vowed their friendship with him.

Things were different in his other operation. Axel tightened his grip on the police training and weapons program. He and Pizante began bringing in trainers from all over the world to teach courses throughout

Mexico. The program became a huge success because they gave local government lines of credit for weapons and equipment purchases that included discarding the old weapons and training with the new ones.

Axel made all the right friends, but he also made many enemies in government because of his high standing. People noticed that he wasn't an average politician, not even an average *rich* politician. It was clear that Axel represented interests far above his head. He continued on this route using his power and influence to forward Pizante's cause, like a soldier marching into war, unaware that he's carrying destiny on his own shoulders.

CHAPTER 110

Sundays in the Sun

Regina Dahlgreen loved spending Sundays with Axel. He usually showed up at her house in Cabo around 10 a.m. with breakfast. This morning, it was Puebla style *chilaquiles* and orange juice. She opened the door to her estate and gave her man a kiss.

He grabbed her and ran his hand up her thigh. "Wow, you've got some legs, girl."

"Yeah, I've been doing yoga again. Can you tell?"

"Wow, I can feel," said Axel.

"Wait, let's eat first," said Regina. "I'm starving."

She grabbed the food from his hands. The table was set, coffee was made, and they sat down and feasted on crunchy tortillas with mild tomato salsa.

"I love chilaquiles," she said.

"Yeah, I'm still waiting on the day that you invite me to try the ones *you* make," said Axel.

Regina hit him in the arm. It was her way of defending herself against such mockery. Axel damn well knew she was a woman of many talents, but cooking wasn't one of them. She joked about it often, saying that whenever her chef or maid didn't work, she would just stare into the fridge, imagining what the things inside of it were, then settle for ordering in or eating out. She wasn't proud of her lack of skills in the kitchen; deep down, she knew that if push came to shove, she could make herself a sandwich.

"But I didn't come to this world to eat mediocre sandwiches."

"Such a snob," said Axel.

"What? You don't cook either!" said Regina.

"Bullshit! I have a signature dish: Axel's…"

"Baked lamb."

Regina joined him in the hand gestures he always did when saying the name of the one dish he made.

"Ha, you're so proud of that dish."

"Yeah, it was my grandpa's. He brought it over from the old world," he said

"*The old world?* Listen to yourself. It's called Europe. Are you living in the sixteenth century?"

They laughed while eating breakfast and drinking orange juice.

Afterward, they went in the pool and began to mess around. Axel caressed her breasts.

"Stop, they might see us," said Regina, wrestling to keep her top on.

"None of your employees are here, it's their day off."

"Yeah, but they might come back for something," she said.

He kissed her gently and continued to fondle her. Regina began to kiss him violently. He held her down and she almost resisted when he pulled off her swimsuit bottom and began to touch her. Regina's moan, when Axel made love to her, was warm and candid, like a spring note in a down tempo album.

"Laughter is the best aphrodisiac for me," Regina used to tell Axel when they first started dating.

"Being naked is the best aphrodisiac for me," was his usual answer.

These were Axel and Regina's Sundays—relax by the pool, go out on the yacht, make love, go eat at a nice restaurant, maybe play a little lawn tennis. Since they were both so busy, they had made a pact a year prior that they would spend every Sunday together. Regina had come to love Axel with all of her heart.

Early in their relationship, she had her doubts about him, but her feelings toward him changed drastically after they made their Sundays together a thing. Even if it was the emotional attachment of spending the first day of the week with a loved one, Regina grew closer to the man she was engaged to. Axel began treating her with the familiarity of love, something that Regina craved, and since she didn't have anyone, Sundays with Axel filled a huge void in her life. Regina had even spent a couple of Sundays with Axel's parents, Gene and Luisa. They loved her, and she loved them.

"So, when are we going to talk about the wedding?" asked Axel.

"I told you that I don't really want a big wedding. Why don't we just do something small? Something intimate, just for us," she said.

"Honey, do you have any idea how many people I know? And if any one of them found out that they weren't invited to my wedding, they would flip. I have commitments. You're not marrying just anyone, you know."

Regina's face grew sad. But even in sadness, her beauty radiated.

"What's wrong, mermaid?"

"It's just that I don't have anyone to invite."

Axel held her tight and kissed her forehead.

"I have my employees, associates, but no family, no friends from childhood. I only have you," she said.

"Aw, sweetheart, even with all of the people in my life, the only person that really matters is you. It's not going to be *you* and *me* anymore — it's going to be *us*," he said as he continued to hold her.

They remained silent for a moment, Axel feeling her vulnerability. He imagined himself a lion embracing a lioness.

"Can we at least set a date?" he asked with a chuckle, breaking the silence with a lighthearted question.

"Yes, April," said Regina.

"Okay."

The two kissed gently on the lips. Like most Sundays, they spent the rest of the day out in the sun. Axel took a nice nap on a lawn chair by the pool. When he awoke, Regina was doing yoga in her bathing suit, the magnificent sea behind her, while the sun played its game of light. Axel enjoyed looking at his fiancée stretch like a cobra—her toned legs, her amazing curves and abs. Axel knew this was the woman he was going to spend the rest of his life with. It was strange for him, the womanizer, to have fallen so hard in love, but she was someone tender in his heart, a flower in the barren desert of harshness that had become his life.

His phone rang as he smiled in appreciation of his mermaid. It was a call through an app he had installed on his phone called Covertia, a clandestine service that re-routes calls a million times, making communication untraceable. He knew it was Pascual Pizante.

Axel stood up and answered the call, like the habit of waking up early and being on time that Pizante had drilled into him during what seemed like a lifetime ago.

"What did you do?' said Pizante in his strong voice.

"I'm sorry?"

"You're all over the news. You hit every international station half an hour ago. There's an immense PR attack going on against you right now," said Pizante.

"What? What does it say?"

"It's about Isla del Carmen. What happened on that island?' Pizante asked.

"Nothing," said Axel.

"Well, they're blaming a huge international conspiracy on you involving obscure animal research. And, get this, there was a cave within the island and inside that cave, *The Durango*, Bracho's old yacht that you used to skipper," said Pizante.

Axel was speechless.

"So, I'm going to ask you again: what did you do?"

"I know nothing about this. This is fake news!"

"*Fake news?* You are a fool, letting them play you like this. Fake news? I invented that term, you know that?" Pizante was heated. "They're trying to get to me, but they won't beat me at my own game. It's impossible!"

"Sir, I won't let them get to you. I owe you my life, Captain," said

Axel, whose voice shook as he felt his phone vibrate with messages, emails, texts, alerts, tweets, everyone trying to contact him, everyone wanting to know something that he knew nothing about. "What do I do?"

"Call a meeting at your bunker. I'll talk to Zev. I won't be there, but I'll connect via Covertia."

"Yes, sir."

"I expect you to handle this like a pro. We are fighting an all-fronts war, so we'll make a plan and win this," said Pizante.

"Who is behind this?" Axel asked.

"The Mexican Navy. The discovery was led by Admiral Gomez." Pizante kept talking, but Axel's mind went places.

He thought of the Admiral who despised him. Gomez had told Axel he hated him to his face when he'd tried to sell him a weapons program. He also thought about Julian Mayorca, his cousin and the Admiral's godson. He could picture Julian like a coyote, lurking behind this attack.

"Get to Los Barriles, call the War Room together and I'll connect," said Pizante, interrupting Axel's thoughts.

"Yes, sir," he answered.

"You're one of mine, Axel; I leave no man behind."

"Thank you sir."

When they hung up, Axel began looking through his phone. Friends and acquaintances had all sent him articles and links to what the press was calling the biggest corruption case in Baja history. Clearly an exaggeration and a direct attack upon his person. He put his phone down and got dressed. He put on the blue cap that read *Captain*, which Regina had given him.

"Where are you going?" said Regina as Axel began to change.

"*We're going.* I'm going to need you to take me on your bird to my bunker at Los Barriles. I think the shit just hit the fan for me."

"What? What happened?"

Axel showed her his phone and an article titled "Axel Cuevas, the criminal with a badge who runs the operation Samuel Bracho left behind."

"Oh no," said Regina. "Is it true?"

"Of course it's not true, but before you go questioning me about something I know nothing about, please help me! Can I count on you?"

She nodded.

"My boss called an emergency meeting at my bunker where we're going to figure out a counterattack. Please fly me there," said Axel.

Regina ran inside and got ready. Twenty minutes later, they were up in the air.

CHAPTER 111

War Room

"**Y**OU CAN BE A REAL prick, you know that?" said Regina while still in the pilot's seat of her chopper.

Axel had asked her to fly back to her estate. "Come on, honey. You understand. I just can't let you know *all* of my business. It's better that way, legally, and ethically, and…" He began to move towards her, smiling for the first time since the news attack.

Regina let him give her a small kiss on the lips. After a momentary feeling of joy, she sighed and became sad. "I can't go through all of this again. Don't lose this war, Axe."

He kissed her. "I don't lose. We don't lose. I love you." He exited the aircraft.

Moments later, he entered his bunker and she flew away. The meeting began a little after 8:30 p.m. He spent all night preparing to defend himself.

Pizante, who was connected through Covertia, began the conversation.

"It's clear that this is an attack against all of us, so we must fight it with all of the intelligence available. They want us to abandon Axel, to leave him out to dry, to sacrifice him and think we're saving ourselves, but they don't understand that we're never gonna do that. We have plans of our own, long-term plans that can make everybody in this room a billionaire. So before we get into our strategy, let's see what's ahead."

They all shared links and went around discussing the PR attack that had just taken place. Then Pizante excused himself, telling them that although he would remain connected, he would mute his microphone since he would be busy working on a mainframe strategy from Panama.

Everybody in the war room assumed a role. Axel's platoon leader was Zev, his trusted bodyguard and military strategist. Then there was Franco, his first mate at the port captainship, the man he'd been training in nautical affairs for two years. Pamela, his publicist, was sitting next to 537-pound Liviano Pompa, a CPA and president of the Baja Academy of Public Accountants. At the opposite end of the table sat Elmer Rivas, the fiercest attorney in Baja California.

"Charges have been brought against you for the crimes of peculation, corruption, and money laundering," said Elmer.

"*Speculation*?" asked Axel.

"No, *peculation*, which means stealing public funds or property," he said.

"They can't prove anything. What are they saying I stole?"

"There's a whole list of things, but most of it is fluff. This is nothing."

"Basically, your accounts have been frozen due to a loophole in the law. Once someone is charged with *peculation* and money laundering, a judge can order an immediate freeze on your accounts," Liviano interrupted. "But this is really strange. It's not even Monday morning and the bank has already taken action. We've never seen them move so fast. People are working on the inside track against us."

"Are they looking to detain me?"

"No, you've been charged, but no arrest warrant has been issued. I did receive a subpoena from the fifteenth circuit court, based out of Mexicali, North Baja California."

"What the fuck does that mean? Are they going to come and get me?"

"Not yet. They want you to testify, and, after that, probably make you turn yourself in."

Axel scoffed. "Turn myself in? Who's the judge?"

"Olivares, Prospero Olivares," said Elmer.

"Can we get to him?" asked Zev.

"Impossible, the guy lives underground," said Elmer.

"I'm sure there are ways," Axel interrupted.

"No, Prospero Olivares *literally* lives in a bunker underground. He gets more death threats and attempts on his life than anybody else," said Elmer.

"What about giving him money?" said Liviano.

"We believe that if given the opportunity, he would use the same payoff money to do the exact opposite and actually corrupt other authorities into incarcerating Axel."

"What about other authorities? The governor, our friends?" Pamela asked.

"I just got off the phone with the governor of South Baja California," Pizante interrupted over the speaker. "He says he won't touch you. As long as you don't leave the state, he won't send you to face Olivares in North Baja."

"What about the port captainship?" Axel asked.

"Keep your job. At least we'll know where they're going to attack," said Pizante.

"What do you mean?" asked Liviano.

"Remember, being charged with something doesn't mean guilty," Elmer said.

"Exactly," Pizante agreed. "If he keeps the port captain job, the focus will follow us there. If we have Axel resign, he'll lose clout and the media is going to pick at him from every angle. At least this way, they'll come looking for Axel at his office, and we can control the narrative to a certain degree."

"Do we issue a statement?" Pamela asked.

"Yes, draft one up and send it my way so I can revise it. I'll get my own media apparatus to begin releasing articles in favour of Axel," said Pizante.

"Can't we just make all of this ridiculousness go away? I mean, it's hearsay!" said Axel.

"Nobody wants to touch this case right now, even if some of our other friends in government handled it for insane amounts of money. It would have to begin in a week or two, after everything has calmed down, but the problem is that we need to move fast," Elmer said.

"And legally? What can we do?" asked Axel.

"The way they implemented the freeze on your money has got to be a first. They're claiming that they're gonna *study* your accounts."

"Study?" interrupted the fat accountant.

"Yes, exactly, so I will be filing an appeal. My firm's already working on it. It will be ready in the morning," Elmer said.

Things were complicated for Axel, and even though Pizante wasn't saying much, he was hearing every word and simultaneously making plans with a team of his own.

CHAPTER 112

Primos

THE CHALLENGER RODE SOUTH LIKE wildfowl chasing the setting sun. Julian Mayorca was focusing on his skippering; getting back to *The Cecilia* was helping him keep a sharp mind and a calm demeanor. He didn't want to think about the bags of money in the main room below deck since the curiosity created anxiety. He'd told himself he wouldn't take a single peek inside the bags until they were safely aboard *The Cecilia* and far away from this boat.

Julian got to Bahia San Dolores a couple of hours before sunset. He smiled when he saw what was anchored in the heart of the bay, *The Cecilia, a* true princess in the court of nature. He pulled the Challenger smoothly up alongside it.

"Ahoy!" he yelled with enthusiasm.

Rubio came up to the deck. "Jesus, Julian! Did you join the Navy?"

"No, just a little Navy transportation to ease transit."

Rubio jumped ship, grabbed the rope, and jumped back, securing one yacht to the other, pirate style.

"Listen, I've got some bags in the main room below. We need to load them all up in the master stateroom."

"Ay, ay, Skip." Rubio was glad that his boss was back.

"What the hell is in these things?" asked Rubio as he was helping Julian move the bags from one vessel to another.

"Papers, documents, Mexican intelligence…"

Rubio took a couple of bags in silence, and when he returned, he murmured: "Yeah, right. If you don't want to tell me what's in here, fine, but don't expect me to buy that shit."

"Just relax, Rubio. I only have an idea about what's inside the bags. I haven't taken a look yet. I want to load them up in my room and then I'll run through them," said Julian.

Rubio did some more inaudible mumbling.

"Look, you're probably the person I trust the most in this world. I promise you I will share information with you when it's ready to share, but right now, we need to focus on getting out of here with all of these bags."

"Copy that," answered Rubio.

The bags barely fit inside the master stateroom. They could have organized them better, but they'd rushed because Julian wanted to leave Bahia San Dolores behind.

"Let's go. Let's bail out of here," he told Rubio.

Rubio pulled *The Cecilia*'s anchor and they left the Challenger behind.

Julian was pushing it, feeding the yacht thirty-five knots per hour.

"Are we going all the way back to La Paz tonight?" Rubio asked.

"Why? You got a problem with that?"

"It's not a good night, Skip. She's choppy. I know we're in a hurry, but if it was any other night..."

He was right, the sun hadn't set, but it was going to be a nasty night out on the water.

"And you know that I don't hold helm at night, Skip."

He called Admiral Gomez.

"The Challenger is anchored and we're making our way down, but it's choppy as balls out here," said Julian.

"*Cabrón*, if anybody can handle weather, it's you. Plus, I trust you with my millions for a reason. I know you make right decisions. But I got to go; they summoned me to Mexico City already. It's gonna get real tough for us. Be smart, Julian. Tread lightly," said Gomez.

"Why is it going to get real tough? We did a good thing, we caught the bad guy!" said Julian.

"Don't be naive! The chiefs know there was money aboard the vessel. They also know it's gone. They're gonna try to bleed me to get to the money, but I'm not budging. All I can tell you is hide for a bit with it all. Lay low," said Gomez

"Roger that, you tough old son of a bitch," said Julian with admiration for his friend's bravery.

They made it to La Burra that night. In the darkness, Julian anchored at a small bay he only knew as Cape OK. They found good shelter from the turbulent waters. That night after dinner, Rubio watched a documentary called *Elephant in the Room*. It was about solitary elephants in European zoos. Julian, however, went into the master stateroom and opened the bags.

The first bag he opened was big and square with a handle. It looked like a fusion between a kid's bag and an oversized briefcase. Inside were clear plastic bags filled with cash. Thousands of hundred dollar bills sticking together, sweaty, dense, the smell of plastic, sea, and greed mixed into one. Julian felt a rush with each bag he opened. A millionaire many times over, the boundless possibilities.

He'd always been a rich man, recently a wealthy man, but now, wow, he was overwhelmed, and a strange presence began to fill the room. He started looking over his shoulder every few seconds. He felt a sense of responsibility for the money. So he began counting it, dollar by dollar, bag by bag.

He separated the bills by denomination. Although they were mostly $100s there were plenty of $50s $20s and $10s to be accounted for. He laid all of the bills out on the bed. It took him hours just to organize them by denomination. Then he began counting the $100s. He lost track of time. He spent hours counting the money. By 9 a.m. the following morning, Julian was exhausted. He'd counted up to $11,287,940—eleven million, two hundred and eighty-seven thousand, nine hundred and forty dollars. But there was still so much money left to count; it was at least ten times what he'd counted. He'd really underestimated how long it would take. He organized the money he'd counted in one-, two-, and three-million dollar bags. All the money he hadn't counted, he arranged into the other bags as best as he could so he wouldn't lose track of where he was.

By 10:00 that morning, the cash was perfectly organized back in the bags in a way that was countable. Julian was red-eyed, tired, but disgustingly and unequivocally rich. Like a beaver ready for winter, he took a bath and went out into the salon where Rubio had made lunch. They pulled anchor and Julian asked Rubio to take the helm back to La Paz while he took a nap on the tower. With fresh air hitting him in the face, he dreamed of nothing, like the stones that rest forever in the bottom of rivers.

"Skip, Skip, wake up," Rubio began shaking Julian.

Julian awoke like somebody in the middle of a trance. A zombie, only ninety minutes into what could have easily been a four-hour nap.

"Skip, it's Axel."

"What? Axel? Where?"

Rubio pointed to the horizon. It was *La Capitana*, his old ship, coming towards them.

"*Puta madre*," he said as he stared at the yacht coming in.

"Rubio, put on some coffee and bring me a cup as soon as it's ready," Julian said as he took the helm and slowed down. *La Capitana*, in front of them, did the same. Julian watched Axel get on the tender and ride toward them. He pulled up to *The Cecilia*. Julian went down and caught his rope.

He helped Axel aboard his yacht. "How are you, cousin?"

"Well, not as good as you, I presume," Axel said. "I'm involved in some sort of shitstorm that I don't even know about and I'm trying to retrace my steps, and they lead me back to Admiral Gomez, your *padrino*. Now, why would your godfather want to crucify me like this? What the hell is going on, cousin?"

"Wow, Axel, good to see you too," said Julian with a smile.

Axel grabbed him and put Julian into a headlock, forcing him to the ground. "Don't condescend me! What the fuck is going on?"

"Why the hell are you at it again with me? Get the fuck off me, you piece of shit," said Julian, trying to push back but stuck in an unexpected wrestling position.

"Your *padrino*! Why is he out to get me?"

"Nobody's out to get you."

"Tell me the truth!" yelled Axel as he pushed Julian's head into the floorboard.

A crack and a loud voice. "Get off of my captain." Rubio was pointing a small revolver at Axel.

"Ha, will you look at that? My people will absolutely kill you. They would chop you into little pieces if you damage a hair on my head, *Coolio*, or whatever the hell your name is. Tell your man to stand down, Julian."

"I didn't ask him to come out here," Julian said. "I didn't even know he had a gun."

"I'm ready to die. I'm ready to go, right here, right now; I don't give a damn. And if you go with me, my death will be worth double. I came to this world to die, and to die in a gunfight is an honorable way to go. Shit, my grandfather died in a gunfight, and I'm named after him, José Rubio."

Axel let go of his cousin and sighed as he sat down on the deck. Julian sat up, pulling his shirt down.

Rubio put his gun down. "You two talk it out, like the *primos* that you are. I'll be back with some coffee," he said, as he turned around and entered the yacht.

"Damn it, Axel. I don't know what you're talking about. Rubio and I have been out at sea for a week," said Julian.

"Oh, yeah, where exactly?"

"None of your business. Why do you care so much about what I do?"

"First of all, I'm port captain. I have a right to ask."

"Yeah, you hold that job only because you took it from me."

"And I'm about to take a lot more if you don't show me some respect," Axel said.

"Look at you, with the big balls. I get it, Axe, you've got to prove yourself. You felt overshadowed by my successes, fine. But where's the love? Gene and Luisa didn't raise you to..."

"Oh, shut up! You don't care about them. You don't care about anyone but yourself. You taught me to be like this! Why should I care a single bit about you?" Axel interrupted, disturbed upon hearing his parents' names.

"Yeah, man. I had my own issues," Julian said.

"You could have helped us, but you never shared your wealth. You grew up with us, my parents guarded you, they guarded your money—they didn't let you spend a dime until you were smart enough to know better, and then when you got it, you abandoned us. When mom needed it the most, you wouldn't even give her anything. So ungrateful," said Axel.

"What? How was I supposed to know she needed money? She never asked me," said Julian.

"Of course they weren't going to ask you. It embarrassed the shit out of them."

"Well, that's on them," said Julian.

"You see, that's exactly what I mean! You're so full of yourself, so self-assured. I try to be nice to you, but I somehow feel that you're behind this, Julian."

"Behind what?"

This attack! And if that's the case, if you're behind Isla del Carmen, and all of this bullshit, I will forget you're family and I'll fuck you up. Last time, when I took your job, I saved your life from Bracho—they wanted to kill you—just like I tried to save your friend Alberto Fontana's life."

Julian sensed Axel's anger, but to him, it seemed misdirected. He looked at his cousin the way a child looks at an ape in the zoo—a species so close yet so incredibly far.

"You don't stand a chance against me, Axel."

Axel looked at him in disbelief.

Rubio came out holding two paper cups with lids. "Here, have some coffee like civilized people." He went back inside.

Julian took a sip, looked at *La Capitana*. "*Primo*, I was an asshole, always caught up with myself because I suffered great loss at a young age. I sheltered myself. It wasn't personal. But tell me, what can I do to help *now*?"

"You can tell your *padrino* to back off."

"I had nothing to do with that, Axel. The Navy hates you, they know you were a soldier for Samuel Bracho, they know you skippered his yacht. They're coming after you, for your own choices. You have to understand that this has nothing to do with me," said Julian.

Axel took another sip of his coffee.

"Fuck!" He threw the paper cup overboard. "Fuck, fuck, fuck, fuck…"

"Will you calm down? This is why you're in trouble. You're acting like a maniac," said Julian.

"Fuck! But you're right. You *can* help me."

"Sure, anything you need," said Julian.

"Let me borrow some money," said Axel in a low voice.

"What? How much?"

"Two million dollars."

"Two million dollars? Why the hell do you need two million?"

"My fucking accounts are frozen. Can't use my own funds, so I'm facing a lot of shit. Can you do me a solid, for old times sake, and spot me two mill?" said Axel.

"Well, it's not going to…"

"Can you spot me two mill, yes or no?" Axel interrupted.

Julian took a second. He fantasized about walking into his stateroom and getting one of the small bags and throwing it at Axel while saying, "*Get out of my life you useless piece of shit*," but he couldn't do that. No one could know that he carried that amount of cash aboard. He took another second.

"Okay, I'll give you the money, that's what we're here for, *primos*."

Axel smiled. Almost a tear in his eye. Nothing is more sentimental for a materialistic person than the thought of someone giving him money on his own terms.

Axel didn't move from the deck.

"What?" asked Julian.

Axel made a hand gesture.

"Now? I don't have the money now!" said Julian.

"Oh, I thought you had it in cash," said Axel.

"No, why would you assume that?"

"I don't know. I once heard my folks say that your parents had left you five million dollars. I always imagined you having that money in cash," said Axel.

"Well, that's bullshit. They didn't even leave me half of that. But, whatever. Me giving you this money is a big sacrifice. Don't you think for a second that this is easy for me. I'm only doing it to prove to you, that no matter what, I will be there for you," said Julian.

Axel gave Julian a hug, but he continued to linger.

"What?" asked Julian. Axel did a hand gesture. "What?" he asked.

"If you're going to write a check, make it out to CPA Liviano Pompa," said Axel.

"Jesus, Axe. I don't have my checkbook. Would you relax? I'll have my accountant figure it out with you tomorrow."

"Sure thing. Just have him call me, early though. I don't want to have to come looking for you again. And turn on your goddamn phone," Axel said, but continued to stand there, this time touching his stomach.

"What the hell was in that coffee? I'm going to have to use your head," Axel said, making his way toward the door of the yacht.

Axel entered the salon. "Nice yacht, man. We should plan a day when we all go out together," he said as he walked quickly toward the master stateroom. He grabbed the silver door handle.

"No," Julian said. "My toilet is broken, use the one straight ahead."

Axel let go of the handle and used the other head. Julian locked the door to his stateroom and headed up to the galley. Five minutes later, Axel exited with his shirt well-tucked. Julian was waiting in the salon with a cold bottle of water. He handed it to Axel, who thanked him.

"You should give me a tour of your yacht," Axel said.

"Maybe some other time. We just came back. She's pretty dirty right now," said Julian.

"Are you hiding something from me?"

"Yeah, my dignity," said Julian.

Axel laughed.

They walked back outside. Before Axel got on the tender, he said, "Don't forget about sending me the money tomorrow. I'm counting on you."

"I won't."

"Oh, and Julian—cash, if possible," said Axel with a smirk.

"Sure thing," said Julian.

The tender-headed back towards *La Capitana*.

The Cecilia made it to its marina slip.

CHAPTER 113

Two Sticks to Make a Fire

J ULIAN SLEPT NEXT TO THE money. The following day, he knew he had
to get the two million he'd promised his cousin. It was strange how,
on the one hand he was holding him over a barrel; on the other, he was
helping him out with the money.

But what can I do?

He wanted Axel off his back. He tried calling Gomez, but the Admiral
wasn't answering his phone—he was being questioned by the Mexican
president about the Isla del Carmen operation, which the government
only cared about because of public opinion. What they were secretly
grilling him about was the money they knew was aboard. Money that
Don Aldo Ruiz had promised government officials.

Julian set up a meeting with his CPA.

"Rubio, Fabio is coming aboard. I want you to do me a favor and
strap your gun to your belt," Julian said.

"Belt? I'm not wearing any belt. These are basketball shorts."

Julian laughed at Rubio's clothes: sandals, basketball shorts, and a
scrawny tank top.

"Nah, it doesn't matter. Just put the gun in your shorts, or change
your shorts, but act natural. Just have it on your waist. I want this guy to
see that we're both strapped."

"Who? Pappa?"

"Yea!"

Rubio laughed and went for his gun.

Fabio entered the salon, grinning. "What the hell happened, Mayorca? Oh man, when I saw the news, I knew it, I knew it, I knew it. You were right there."

"Shh… you don't know anything," Julian interrupted.

"Oh, right—top secret," said Fabio as he glanced at the gun, took a second, looked around, but didn't lose the smile.

"So, why'd you call me?" Fabio asked.

"I want to know if I can trust you."

"Trust me? I'm the one who told you about the money."

"Okay, and? What do you want in return?"

"I want to manage it, launder it, yield some earnings, and help you with the financial decisions. And, obviously, make my points. The honest way."

"And you won't screw me? Because you need to know that the Admiral is my partner on this, so be sure that this is life or death money," said Julian.

Fabio raised his right hand and took his left to his heart. "Listen, I swear an oath to you, and in honor of my friend Alberto Fontana, may he rest in peace, and with Rubio as my witness, I will stand by your side and fight your battles as if they were my own."

Julian nodded. "Come with me," he said as he walked to the master stateroom.

This time, Rubio couldn't help his curiosity, so he came along, silent, but gun in waist.

Julian opened one of the bags he had counted and Fabio yelled with joy. Rubio's face went white.

"Right now, I've counted up to $11,287,940, but it's only these five bags."

"Wow," Fabio exhaled as he took a seat next to the bag of money, grabbed a handful of it and smelled it. "This is incredible, just amazing. It's also highly dangerous."

"Yeah, don't you think I know that?"

"First of all we have to get a full count, down to the last bill. We have to do it somewhere safe. You shouldn't keep this cash on the yacht for much longer."

"Yeah, I'm waiting for Admiral Gomez, but he's in Mexico City facing the powers."

"Well, I'm gonna work on a plan, something I can present to you and the Admiral, to get this money somewhere safe," said Fabio.

"You do that. In the meantime, I need you to take two million and give it to Axel Cuevas. He needs it in cash."

"Julian, what's going on with you and him? I thought that he was the sonuvabitch who..."

"He is," interrupted Julian.

"Do you know why he hasn't been arrested?"

"No! Admiral Gomez was supposed to orchestrate federal prosecution, but it's all booked up. We did a big trial-by-media thing, but that alone won't lock him up," said Julian

"So, from putting him behind bars to giving him money? That's a pretty big change of heart," said Fabio.

"The thing is, he came to me yesterday and begged for two million, saying that I've never given him anything in my life, he resents me for it. I don't want to give it to him, but I already told him yes, just to get him off of me."

"Damn extortionist."

"Yeah, I thought I'd talk to you, maybe you could help."

"Help with what? You already agreed to give him the money," said Fabio.

"Fine, then just take it to him," said Julian.

"Sure, I can do that for you."

"I don't know, make him sign some sort of personal loan. Don't make it look like the bills came from where they came from."

"Do you think he knows about the money on the yacht?"

"He came aboard yesterday. I think Bracho might have told him about the vault," Julian said..

Fabio took a moment. "Don't give him the money."

"What?"

"Don't give him shit. If you give him cash, he'll know that you have the money from the yacht. It's a trap."

"And if I don't give him any money, he'll continue coming at me. I know how he is!"

"Julian, I'm gonna come clean with you. I'm the one who got Prospero Olivares, the judge from Mexicali, to enforce the anti-peculation law and freeze Axel's accounts," said Fabio.

"That was you? I thought that had been Admiral Gomez."

"No, Prospero Olivares is a personal friend of mine. He used to be close to Fontana, too, and he's hungry to get Axel. He did a private investigation and believes Axel was behind Fontana's murder. But, he doesn't believe there's a murder case just yet, so when the media jumped on Axel, we linked and based on the available financial information, he personally pressed charges for stealing public funds AKA *peculation*. Once that was done, because of my connections in the financial world, I got the Secretary of Hacienda himself to validate Prospero's order quick and officiate the freeze on Axel's account."

"Why did you make those moves? And without informing me?"

"When I saw the PR disaster that Axel was involved in, I didn't know for sure that it had been you. I was hoping it had been, but at that point, the money was irrelevant to me; getting Axel became about payback for Fontana's murder."

"But it was Bracho who murdered Fontana, not Axel," said Julian.

"Those two didn't act alone. Probably more people behind them, too. But, listen, the laws of power say we must obliterate the enemy. If we leave them a little to hold onto, it will grow into strength and they will use that force against us. We must crush them when they're down."

Julian nodded. "So what do I do about Axel?"

"I spoke to Prospero earlier today. He told me that he would've locked him up already, but that he ran into a brick wall. Here's what I would do; you give *me* the two million that you were going to give *him*, and I'll process his ass. Prospero isn't just a judge, he's a badass judge, a magistrate, up in Mexicali, one who's feared and revered. The brick wall he ran into when trying to process Axel was made of money. If I take those two sticks up north, with all of the scandal going on, we could finally get Axel Cuevas," said Fabio.

"And what am I supposed to do? Just sit here and wait in Axel's jurisdiction?"

"You need to move your boat to somewhere private and we need to get the money out of here before he comes back around looking for it," said the CPA. "But we need to act fast. Let's make a decision. Let's take the two million up north and put it in the judge's hands. It's not for him; he's an honest man. It's for the whole machinery to function in our favor."

"Tell me a little more about him; why should I trust him?" said Julian.

"He's a real clean-cut guy, but his hands are tied. He told me he has all the pieces to crucify Axel beginning with these corruption charges, but ultimately for the murder of our brother. But the powers over him are stopping it. Nothing a few million couldn't solve. Plus, the flame on Axel's stake is already lit; all we have to do is add a couple of sticks."

CHAPTER 114

Notes from the Underworld

*I*SLA DEL CARMEN IS THE *biggest scandal in the nation. One can't walk a block in Mexico City or go to a supermarket in Torreón without hearing chatter about this incredible act of corruption. An island off Baja California's coast was the epicenter of rare dealings for a Japanese company known as Sendai Corp.*

Isla del Carmen, which has an intricate interior canal system with a disguised retractable gate, a dock for large vessels, and many other obscure contraptions, was used to store and transfer strange goods to the empire of the rising sun and back. Our current estimation is that the Japanese company spent over $250 million in developing and maintaining the island and its cave. Admiral Gomez, head of the Mexican Navy in South Baja California, was responsible for the discovery. His office released pictures of the island, along with reports on their investigation, which went by the name of "Bocamía," a beautiful name for a place that's the modern equivalent of a sacrificial den.

One of the areas of the cave is now being referred to as a tortoise "cemetery" because thousands of endangered giant tortoise shells were found piled up. The deaths did not stop at our shelled friends. The Navy also found over one hundred bighorn sheep heads dissecting in a special sanatorium. Photographs of this brutality can be seen in the following pages; however, our editors warn you of their graphic nature. Sendai Corp. made the following statement last night in Japan, where the government is facing pressure from Mexico to discipline Sendai Corp.'s actions.

"We regret the misunderstanding between our company and public perception. We assure you that this scandal regarding the Mexican island is based on exaggeration and lies. We, as a corporation, do operate a station on the island, where we use endemic species to further our research into curing many ailments, among them the plague of our generation, the Goliath known as cancer. This disease does not fight a conventional war, and neither do we. That is why part of our research requires specific plants and animals to give their lives for science. We are aware of the moral and ethical dilemmas that accompany our line of work, and we do not expect the world to understand what we do. But we do expect everyone to be able to benefit from the fruits of our labor. If you look at our line of products, our prices on life saving medication are always the lowest and that is because we are a private company, whose intention is to help cure diseases through groundbreaking research."

Navy forces became aware of Bocamía because of the ongoing search for The Durango, *the infamous 220-foot yacht that once belonged to Samuel Bracho. Admiral Gomez said in a statement that there had been reports of a large vessel that matched the description of the yacht around the island, and that upon further investigation, "a can of worms opened up." He concluded by saying he and his team worked around the clock to handle the operation with care. The yacht had been missing since early into Samuel's Bracho prison sentence, and it turned out to be stored in the heart of a cave. As of today, there has only been one person charged, Axel Cuevas, the controversial La Paz port captain.*

Peculation, money laundering, and a half-dozen corruption charges have been brought against Cuevas by the 15th District Court out of Mexicali. As the investigation continues, everything still points to Cuevas as being the largest beneficiary of the Isla del Carmen scandal. According to various sources, up until last month, Cuevas was receiving monthly installments of $30,000 from Sendai Corp., also known as some serious hush-money. He claims that he is innocent and that his assets have been frozen illegally. No financial statements have been released as of today.

The investigation also concluded that Cuevas was the original yacht captain aboard The Durango, *and therefore had a vested interest in seeing the yacht restored. During Samuel Bracho's imprisonment, it is believed that he was the one who brokered the deal with the Japanese. When asked, Sendai Corp. denied having a relationship with Axel Cuevas or knowing anything about the yacht, stating that someone in their middle management had cut a deal directly with the people involved and that their headquarters was conducting an internal investigation of its own.*

The company didn't provide any names but stated that they have been operating legally in Mexico since the 1950s, and plenty of people in government benefit from the work taking place in Baja California. This statement doesn't look good for Cuevas, who hasn't been arrested, despite being charged with serious felonies. He's also retained his current job as port captain. His own PR attempts have been weak and have only turned the public further against him. Across social media, thousands have tweeted the hashtags #Axelmustpay and #axeAxel. Mexican news outlets have published extensive pieces on him, some detailing his rise to power as a soldier of the recently deceased kingpin Samuel Bracho.

Cuevas was Bracho's friend, yacht captain, and played a key role in his escape from prison. One article noted that recently, Axel used his power as port captain to do business on Bracho's behalf, collecting money and expanding influence through government contracts. With all of the overwhelming evidence against Cuevas, it's strange that no arrest warrant has been issued or that he isn't being publicly asked to resign by anybody in leadership. Maybe officials aren't sure whose orders to follow, or maybe they're still trying to see through the smoke and mirrors and are wondering why the Mexican Navy (read: Admiral Gomez) launched this tremendous offensive to destroy Cuevas.

Even if that's the case, the federal prosecutor has not formally addressed Cuevas' crimes. The federal prosecutor seems more eager to discuss the active role Prospero Olivares, the magistrate out of Mexicali, unconstitutionally played in the charges brought against him than on the crimes themselves. We at Gazeta *believe that no arrest warrant has been issued because somebody big is still protecting Cuevas, somebody deep inside the justice system. We dare suggest that Axel Cuevas tread lightly because history has proven that once the masses want a lynching, they get one — it doesn't matter who it is.*

Ten days after the discovery of Bocamía, Axel Cuevas still holds the title of Port Captain of La Paz and is still president of the Baja California Port Captains Association.

Notes from the Underworld was a series of editorials published by the *Gazeta* newspaper. They were signed by Pablo Heraldo, whose goal was to demystify the criminal underworld and expose its operations. Heraldo won a *Plume d' Or* from the French Free Press for his columns on the *Bocamía* Scandal. He couldn't attend the ceremony personally, so he sent Samantha Reyes, the daughter of Alfonso Reyes, one of the victims of the Gazeta building arson, on his behalf to make a speech about the press in hostile *laissez-faire* regions. The French Free Press gave the Pablo Heraldo Foundation a €200,000 grant to continue its investigative reporting.

CHAPTER 115

Cut / Uncut

L UCK IS THE MOST IMPORTANT thing in a person's life, but it's also a thing to be learned. Axel had mastered the art of being lucky in his late teens. He'd learned to lean on his good looks, his smile, his ability to rise to the top like foam. He knew when to keep quiet and he knew that letting his rage out at a specific person, at a specific time, could be very useful. But right now, Axel's grasp on luck was being shattered by the events around him.

He'd been lucky he wasn't prosecuted when Bracho was sent to prison; he'd been lucky to escape when *The Durango* was sieged by bloodthirsty Michoacanos; he'd been lucky when he was stranded on the tender for months and survived only because he was found by Pizante's forces. But now, alone in his office in La Paz, he didn't feel so lucky.

Charged with felony corruption, his accounts frozen, his cousin Julian, who had promised him $2 million, was nowhere to be found, and what hurt the most was the fact that his fiancée hadn't returned his phone calls in over two days. He sat in his office chair, angry that it was all coming down.

"Fuck, you fucking fuck!" he yelled as he took the Glock handgun from his drawer, put it inside his waistband and walked out the door.

Regina loved Axel, but she couldn't be by his side as his world fell apart. She had witnessed the fall of her father, the fall of her mother, and her own fall from New York socialite grace. Her survival instinct had kicked in and she was on autopilot, shielding herself from her boyfriend, who was on a cascade down. Her yacht was anchored near Bahia Salamandra, off the coast of Magiasuelo. She was, in a way, that same girl who had left New York behind, a small player in a big world. But this time it was different; her experience in Baja had turned her into a savvy woman.

Her desire and ability to fight for herself had elevated her perspective. Her relationship with Axel had pushed her to become more aware of her surroundings. She learned how to protect her own interests. Seeing Axel discredited, dishonored, and weak gave Regina mixed feelings. She cared for him, but she didn't want to be anywhere near him; he was toxic. She questioned her love for him, but was unable to pick up the phone when he called.

She didn't want to talk to him; she didn't want to be near him. She wanted to disengage, disassociate, and let the storm pass. She felt guilty over her attitude, but prefered to go out on her yacht, where she could experience a little freedom. Although she didn't want to relive her past, she couldn't help but think of her father. She grabbed a red notebook and a pen, headed up to the tower where the breeze was comforting, and decided to write a letter.

Soren Dahlgreen
Butner Federal Correctional Institution
North Carolina

Dear Father,
Time has passed since we left our old life. I sometimes think about it. I think about you and mom, especially our days at sea, those magical summers that I hold dearly in my heart. I've never written to you, and even as I'm writing to you now, I know that I'll never send this out. I know in my heart of hearts that I will never contact you, not once call you, or go visit you. But I write to you today to tell you that I love you. No matter what, I love you.

I don't know if you're wearing an orange jumpsuit, or if it has stripes. All I know is that I never want to see you in one of those things. I take pride that I never knew about your businesses. Whenever my friends, well, the people who I thought were my friends, asked me "How could you not know? Weren't you just fooling yourself? Turning a blind eye?" I could answer honestly that I didn't know. And in those moments, I was so incredibly proud of you for guarding me. If you're surprised that I wasn't angry, don't worry, it came later. But, now, my anger is not directed toward you.

I'm not here to talk about rage and grudges. I have learned that it's best to put away those things; and, besides, I was given a better shot at making it than most people. If I add it all up, I guess I'm still a millionaire—although I fear I must begin selling some of my assets since I am running out of cash. My business is not generating nearly enough to make ends meet, and my fiancé (yeah, I'm engaged) is facing a mess that has me stranded, alone with my thoughts.

Instead of thinking about him, I'm thinking about you. He reminds me of you so much. Axel, my Axel—so complicated, so ambitious. He, unlike you, is messy. He thinks he's smooth, but he doesn't clean up his messes. I feel bad, because I'm running away from him now. He asked me to borrow money—$2 million. Can you believe it? I mean, I don't have it; I told him I didn't have it. I didn't sail off because he asked me for money. It was a feeling that made me do it—a feeling that I didn't know how to respond to. To be honest, I think the fact that he got to that position of vulnerability disgusted me. The disgust made me feel evil, and that scared me. It was the fear of my own ability to shut off that made me turn my head.

I don't know if I'm hiding, running away, or simply taking a break. Anyway, I figured some days at sea would help, so, I'm anchored off Salamandra, in the same bay where you and mom celebrated your fifteenth anniversary. The Dream On is doing great. Congratulations on having such great taste and getting this wonderful yacht. I still remember when we christened her and brought her down to Baja. You'd be proud to know that even though it's been a challenge, I've *managed to maintain her at her prime. Like the best of the best, she responds nicely, but in the stillness of this bay, I can tell she misses you, Capt. Soren.*

I don't feel lonely or confused anymore. I feel your love, father, and for that, I thank you!

Your daughter,
Regina Dahlgreen

Julian Mayorca had been circumcised as an infant. It was only by co-incidence that it had happened on the eighth day. Later on, when his mother Cecilia read scripture that mentioned Jesus being circumcised, she remembered that her own son had been taken to be cut when he was exactly eight days old. She told Julian that it hadn't been a coincidence, that it had been God calling him, preparing him for a life of blessings. Julian believed her from that moment on. And even though he wasn't religious, he hardly questioned the hand of God in his life, and when he did, he always thought it was better to enjoy it and receive it then to question it.

These thoughts began to saturate Julian's mind. Thoughts about his circumcision, his mother, and his early years.

"How much is *that*, Skip?" said Rubio.

Rubio's tone of excitement awoke Julian from his thoughts about his foreskin. They'd been counting money fifteen hours a day for nine days straight.

Julian scribbled some numbers on a notepad. His hands were swollen from counting, his mind pulsating from the intoxicating smell of moist paper money. He looked up.

"$187,638,955," he said.

"What?" Rubio's voice cracked.

"It's one hundred and eighty-seven million, six hundred and thirty-eight thousand, nine hundred and fifty-five dollars," said Julian.

Rubio gasped. "You wanna do a recount?" Dead serious.

"No, no, no, I don't want to count a single dollar for a long, long time," said Julian.

"But there weren't any singles. The smallest denomination was fives and there was under $2 million in fives."

"Shh, shh, stop. Let's just organize it by bundles and put the money back in the bags," said Julian.

"Where's Gomez?" asked Rubio.

"*Admiral* Gomez! You count a little money and you think you can forget rank?"

"Sorry Skip, where's *Admiral* Gomez?"

"I don't know. He hasn't contacted me."

"Hopefully, the heads of state aren't impaling him for this money," said Rubio, half joking.

"He wouldn't crack," said Julian with a raspy voice.

CHAPTER 116

Madison House

A WEEK HAD PASSED SINCE they'd finished counting the money and still not a word from Admiral Gomez. Ernie and Denise had been asked to take a vacation and not return to La Paz until captain's orders. They peacefully drove north to Ensenada. Fabio was their only contact with the outside world, but Julian and Rubio were still waiting for him to return from Mexicali. It was a strange time for Julian. Samuel Bracho's murder haunted his conscience in waves of angst.

His idle mind was torturing him with the guilt that he'd tried to bury. In these moments of cold sobriety, when there was only bad television to watch and canned food to eat, he felt fear far superior to what he'd felt in the desert. It was the money, the large sums of cash, that made the existential hole bigger. All the money in the world, but only crap to eat and nothing to drink. This wasn't his style.

He'd agreed to bring his yacht to Madison House, a mesmerizing mansion built by Beth and Paige Madison, the wealthiest lesbian couple in North America. They'd built the house for comfort and partying, but for seclusion as well. It was a slim building carved into the corner of a cove, built low into the high cliff. Its main entrance was by water since the house had its own grotto below, where *The Cecilia* was docked. The most impressive feature was the waterfall they had built as a curtain to the mouth of the grotto. The space had been the site of many parties in the 1990s, but since then, the Madisons had been vacationing elsewhere, and their house had fallen off the radar.

Recently, Miguel Ceballos, a client of Fabio's, had purchased the house and had begun restoring it. Fabio approached him and convinced him to rent his house as-is for a personal emergency. Fabio paid Ceballos $100,000 to rent the property for a month in complete secrecy.

The interior of the house was comfortable, with big leather couches and a big TV. Julian appreciated the security of knowing he was right above his yacht, where the fortune of a small nation was sitting, like a useless lump in a forest of nothing. Everything was fine, but Madison House had a strange air to it. Perhaps cave-life was what Julian disliked; it wasn't his calling to be in hiding, attached to something that couldn't be out of his sight. The money had been taken from one cave to another, as if it were destined to be in darkness. He didn't know what to do but wait.

He and Rubio had been at Madison House for over two weeks and Fabio hadn't returned. They were running out of supplies and were down to two small meals a day. Their cell phones didn't get reception and Julian's satellite phone was broken. They *did* have Mexican cable TV and a collection of 1990s CDs that included a lot of Mariah Carey. The hunger and the sensation of emptiness was driving Julian mad, causing him to forget about the blessings.

Rubio was a different story. He was a natural caveman, spending most of the time down at the grotto, lying on a beach chair on the damp sand near the water and close to the yacht and its cargo of cash.

Julian thought he'd developed some sort of cave syndrome, like the one Cassandra developed with her captives.

Rubio was lying on the dark sand, smoking a thin cigarette, cut with a tad of hashish. Keeping an eye on his lady with his revolver next to him. Julian went aboard *The Cecilia* and lowered the tender. He exited through the waterfall like a hungry bat being chased by daylight.

It was a little after 3 p.m. and the sun was still strong. Julian went fast on the tender, gliding over South Baja waters like a manta ray. He had seized the day and left the money behind. No matter how much cash it was, it wasn't going to hold him down. He defied the laws of greed. He remembered there was a small store at the lighthouse nearby. He sped up. The breeze blew and a smile formed on his face.

CHAPTER 117

Seawolf Lighthouse

JULIAN MADE IT TO THE lighthouse about the time that Tadeo, the owner, was arriving to replace his son Cleo for the evening shift. Tadeo and Cleo were both fat. They had the friendly way and innocent faces of simpletons. The little store at the bottom of the tower was the typical little market with old metal shelves that held chips, snacks, and chocolate. Julian grabbed a banana and an orange that were near the counter, ate them, and went for the beer. He downed a Pacifico and opened another one. He grabbed chips, supplies, beer, and groceries. He loaded the bags on the tender and turned on his cell phone. There was reception for a second, but when he tried to dial, it disconnected and read NO SERVICE. He went back inside the shop.

"Is there anywhere I can get reception?" he asked the shopkeeper.

"No, it's really bad here, but there's a telephone in the bar upstairs," he answered.

The bar at the top of the lighthouse was a gem. A real hole-in-the-tower with a couple of arcades, a jukebox, and Christmas lights around a stained mirror. The tower's windows were open and the breeze came in uninterrupted. Every now and then, the wind would gently rattle the bottles, producing an echoing sound, visions of liquor touching ice cubes in a short glass came to Julian's mind.

I'm thirsty.

Lizzette, a pretty, big-bodied girl, popped her head from below the bar. She was cleaning.

"Hi, I need to use the phone."

"It's a dollar, or free if you buy a drink," she said, standing up and drying her hands on her pants.

"What do you recommend to drink?"

"Honestly, I make a great vodka cranberry," she said.

"Great, make me one of those."

He went over to the phone and called Admiral Gomez. It rang, but went to voicemail.

Julian sat down and had a sip of vodka cranberry.

"That's a damn good drink," he said.

"Yeah, I beat it in the martini shaker so it comes out cold. I like the vodka a bit burnt."

"Wow," said Julian as he thought of heaven in a glass.

The phone rang. Lizette reached for it.

Julian stood up and rushed over. "Sorry, darling. Please, let me get this. Might be for me."

Lizzette hesitated but turned away.

"Hello," Julian said.

"Hello," said a faraway voice.

"Is that you, *padrino?*"

"Damn it, Mayorca, where the hell are you?"

"Right now, I'm at the Seawolf Lighthouse, having a drink with Lizette."

"The little lighthouse by Bahia los Estrados?"

"Yeah."

"Stay put, I'm going to come get you," said Gomez.

"Isn't it better if we meet at the…"

"Shut up, don't say it. All the lines are hot right now. I've been looking for you for days — and I'm not the only one."

"Yeah, no cell service."

"Just stay put. I'm taking the chopper."

"You got it, chief."

He hung up the phone and finished his drink. He went over to the jukebox and put on "She's the One" by The Beta Band. He asked Lizette for another drink. The second cocktail was even better than the first.

"So, how long have you been here?"

"Me? My whole life. My whole family lives here."

"And how do you like it?"

"I wish I could get out of here," she said.

"Well, maybe one day you could come on my yacht," said Julian.

Liz peeked out the window and looked at the tender. "That's not a very big yacht."

Julian laughed. "No, that's just my tender."

Liz continued cleaning.

"Do you have anything to eat?" asked Julian.

"Yeah, we've got our famous empanadas."

"Famous, huh?"

Liz laughed. "Yeah, they're really good."

"Fine, bring me a couple of those and some salad if you have any," said Julian.

"Don't have any fancy salads, but I can slice up some tomatoes and avocados, add a little sea salt if you'd like."

"That sounds perfect," he said.

The empanadas were soft and tender with thick grey meat that was something between steak and seafood.

"Delicious," said Julian.

"It's seawolf," Liz told him after he'd finished.

"Well, it's the best damn seawolf I've ever had," said Julian.

"Have you had much seawolf?" asked Liz.

"Just a little, *un poquito*," said Julian.

CHAPTER 118

Ringwormed

Axel Cuevas was driving around in Regina's Land Cruiser. The last thing she had done for him was let him borrow her car, a small price to pay to cut him off. He figured that since he hadn't heard from her for over two weeks, the car was basically his. The Land Cruiser represented something that he could hold onto. His life was slipping away; he could see it clearly.

Pascual Pizante, his boss, the man who had protected him and had put him through the fire, was lifting his blessing, even if just a little bit. He could sense himself falling from Pizante's grace. The thought scared him. At this point in his career, Axel had developed a knack for reading the board, and the chips didn't look good.

"*Pendejo!*" he yelled.

His money frozen, his life on the line, scrutinized by every asshole possible. The media was on him every day; he had to shake them off. One newspaper had even found his Los Barriles bunker and had done an exposé on it. Things were getting out of hand. He had to settle this. But how? With whom? Goddamn Pizante wasn't passing information downstream; he was damming it up, the way the Colorado River never gets to its Gulf of California delta.

All the favors he called in from the underworld came back negative; Axel had the stench. No warrant for his arrest yet, but it was coming. It was close. He felt like he had the stigma of a branded criminal. What surprised him the most was the fact that the people who *did* want to shield and shelter him were involved in massive turf wars with one another, fighting over street corners where they could put slot machines and sell dreams for a peso and a yank of the lever.

"Yeah, you remember Turco, that vato is no longer family," said Gabriel Eduarte, one of the men who offered protection if Axel worked for him.

"What happened?" Axel asked.

"He started cutting into my business, my area, and I couldn't allow that to happen."

At that moment, Axel saw through Pizante's game. Giving Bracho's street businesses to the distributors created turf wars and challenges for law enforcement. It was a disruptive practice aimed to further his agenda, destabilize the Mexican government, and feed insurgency while all along growing his influence by selling more weapons and training programs. Pizante had told him that he would never leave him behind, but right now, Axel wasn't feeling any love from the man from Panama.

Axel had been staying at his parent's house in La Paz. It was one of the only places where he felt safe. His parents, however, were scared not just for *his* life, but for their own. They wouldn't throw him out of the house because of their values, but it was like Axel was a teenager all over again, only worse. He was a grown man facing complicated problems. His parents couldn't help him. He needed a different place to go. He drove toward Regina's house, desperate. It was his only shelter and he'd wait for her there forever if needed. A gun was strapped to his side. He wore jeans and Ferragamo shoes that made him look like the gangster that he was. He didn't trust anyone, and if a crazy reporter, or somebody crossed a line, he was ready to use firepower. Fueled by rage, he was capable of anything. His phone rang.

It was Zev. "Boss, I just got a call from Pascual. I know where Mayorca is."

"What? Where?"

"He's close. Come pick me up and I'll take you," said Zev in a thick accent that could be mistaken as a mumble.

"Where are you?"

"I'm in Los Barriles."

"I'll be there in twenty minutes," said Axel.

Axel picked up his sergeant, who was excited like a Boy Scout on his way to a campout.

"I know those coordinates. There's a fucking lighthouse there," said Axel as he drove at 90 mph down a two-way highway with trailer-trucks coming up the other way.

"How did you get these?"

"Pizante sent them to me, and wanted me to take care of him. But I figured I might as well let you in on it." Zev took a moment to admire Axel's eagerness. "Let's finish what we should have finished the day we got here."

"You've got that right!" Even though he was excited, Axel was concerned over why Pizante hadn't called him directly.

The reality was that Pascual Pizante, being the forward-thinking mastermind that he was, had been investing heavily in technology over the past years. He paid well for services that were reserved for intelligence operators. He had communications agents, backdoor channels, phishing pools, and every tool money could buy to retrieve any digital information he considered relevant.

Over the past ten days, Julian Mayorca had become the Bolivar Council's enemy number one. His cellphone had been ringwormed. Tagged with a tracking algorithm that moves around and becomes undetectable. All it took was that brief moment when Julian reached for a signal near the lighthouse to immediately pin his location and notify Pizante of his whereabouts. Less than thirty minutes later, Axel and Zev were armed and on their way to get Julian Mayorca.

CHAPTER 119

The Scapegoat Walks Itself to the Slaughterhouse

"J*UST KEEP ON KEEPIN' ON, just keep on doin' it, baby*," Julian sang as "Keep on Lovin' Me" by the Whispers played from the jukebox.

He sat at the bar with a smile on his face and the lightness of being of someone who's faded on the perfect amount of solvent and juice.

"Come on girl, dance to this song with me," he told Liz.

"What? I don't know how to dance to this."

"Oh, come on, neither do I. Just go with it." He grabbed her.

Julian pulled her close. She let loose a little, turned around, and grinded on his crotch like somebody who was waiting to go wild. She was a good dancer, had the beat. Julian had the grin of good booze. He was feeling warm and friendly.

"What are you doing?" said a loud male voice.

Julian looked up. It was Tadeo, the shopkeeper from downstairs.

"Daddy, we were just dancing," said Liz.

"Dancing? You call that dancing? I told you that if I caught you tricking again, I would…"

Tadeo took off his shoe and threw it at her. She ducked and the shoe hit Julian in the face, right on the cheekbone. It stung like the punch of an adolescent boxer.

"*Ay wey*, my eye!" he moaned.

"How much did she charge you?" Tadeo yelled.

"What?"

"Are you tricking? You better not be pimping yourself again! You ungrateful piece of scum!" Tadeo pulled her hair.

She screamed. "Get him off of me, get him off of me."

Julian was holding his cheekbone.

"Jesus," he said as he stumbled about, barely seeing the stars he was supposed to see.

His eye and nose felt swollen, almost blinding him. He went behind the bar and grabbed a can of beer. He placed it on his cheekbone; it helped. He opened the beer and drank it; that helped more. The father-daughter brawl continued. Julian escaped the scene and headed downstairs to the little store. He opened the refrigerator and put a steak to his face.

"Ahh," he sighed in relief.

The little bell that was attached to the main door rang. Two men entered. Julian turned around and caught a glimpse of their silhouettes. He ducked. It wasn't his cousin accompanied by an Israeli bodyguard; it was his cousin accompanied by the angel of death himself.

Payback has a way of showing up unexpectedly. Julian dropped flat on the floor. He could see his cousin's shoes, and behind him, the man's boots looked like hooves.

"Do you think the son of a bitch is still here?" said Axel.

A loud noise came from upstairs. Broken glass and cracked wood, maybe a shattered bone or two. Axel and Zev hustled through the store and up the lighthouse towards the bar. As soon as it felt safe, Julian ran out the door. It was comforting to be outside.

The evening was still warm, but the colors of the sky had changed; they had shaded, but remained soft against the blondeness of the sun. He took a breath, ran down the dirt road, jumped to the wooden planks that led towards the tender. As he looked up to the sea, at a distance, he saw El Grande, the big Bell 360 INVICTUS helicopter flying in. Behind it, a second helicopter, then a third.

"Backup," he whispered.

"Hey, Mayorca!" a yell from the top of the lighthouse. It was Zev holding a rifle, taking aim at Julian. Axel was next to him.

"Got you, cousin," Axel yelled.

Julian kept running toward the safety of the sea. Zev fired a shot. Julian felt warm inside. No pain, not a single noise. Seconds later, the warmth began transforming into coldness, into fear.

Chapter 120

Underworld

THE WORLD IS A HARBORING place. It gives birth to all alike. The good, the bad, and every kind of in-between. But the laws and the people who make them forget to mention the existence of another world, one that shadows their own. The Underworld, where ancient pacts and modern weapons have as much influence as traffic routes or bags of money. It all matters and it doesn't at the same time.

The place has saints of its own: Malverde, Franklin, Napoleon, and Lazarus are among them. Certain names are forbidden and others are encouraged. The point of the Underworld is to bring more people into its claws, into informal economies and Rasputin schemes. A lack of understanding abounds; confusion sets forth and the times all melt into one. There is no ocean or sky, but a river called Hades runs through its core. Other people's friends, but none of your own, are there. Some are bored, others tortured. There is a clear rupture, some claim to see a light.

Once more a void; four white walls and no clocks.
It spirals down into a heaven
And in a room see games.
God playing complex brilliancies
For even what we dream of, the truth is still a mystery
Reality, blood, engagement
This is a whisper.

CHAPTER 121

A Letter to the Innocent Bystander

A T LEAST TWO NAVY HELICOPTERS *trailed a Toyota Land Cruiser through the desert coast. The passenger aboard shot at the choppers, using a high-powered rifle. The Navy claims it didn't fire back.*

"We knew Axel Cuevas was in that vehicle. It was our strategy to pursue him, corner him, and hold him until we could get to him from land. I would say that we succeeded in that," Admiral Gomez said about the operation.

There are so many things that amaze me about this operation. One of them is how a gunfight between two enemies at such a high level is still the way things are solved in this part of the world. Even though Cuevas had been charged with many crimes three weeks ago, no arrest warrant had been issued until minutes before the helicopter chase.

What happened at the Seawolf Lighthouse that we're unaware of? Why was the Navy there? Why was Cuevas there? The official version says there was an anonymous tip that Cuevas, desperate for funds, was selling weapons for cash, and upon receiving this tip, the Mexican Navy acted with the warrant.

Witness accounts suggest there was one civilian casualty, an unknown "Juan Doe," an innocent bystander caught in some sort of crossfire. Supposedly the Navy took the body by helicopter, but they're denying any casualties.

The Navy is playing a hard line on this, releasing the least amount of information in the most calculating way. Who will be charged with this murder? Will we ever know or will there be the expected Mexican impunity? I'm appalled by the joke our institutions have become. The paradox of our country is the quality of our people but the poverty of our institutions. So, it is to the honor of that innocent bystander that we dedicate this editorial.

How many deaths are too many? Why must it always end badly for the innocent, for the nameless, and for the poor? What troubles us is that there is no real investigation into the shooting. Why is there nobody looking into the death of this innocent bystander? Are we so blind that we let the affairs of a few chieftains hold power like an ape's grip on our democracy? Are we that callous and cynical about our nation?

At least for now Axel Cuevas, one of these little chieftains, is finally behind bars. The Navy held him for three days, then Admiral Gomez released him to the federal government who sent a plane for him and took him to Mexicali to stand trial for his role in the murder of Attorney Alberto Fontana. That's just the cherry on top of a long list of corruption charges Cuevas is facing.

Cuevas was a man who covered his tracks. Even after the military establishment went after him and the media lynched him, they couldn't process him. It took a judge out of Mexicali, one judge with enough co-jones to actually get a murder charge against Cuevas for the gruesome murder of Alberto Fontana, the distinguished attorney and businessman from Ensenada. The obvious truth is that Cuevas is a man who has been deeply protected from the inside for years. Even in the last month, when his name and his face became international synonyms for unhinged Mexican corruption, he still held his job and titles.

It's a case with a lot of holes. For instance, what about Admiral Gomez who clearly went on an offensive against Cuevas? Will he pay for the death of the innocent bystander? The problem in Baja California is that we hold ourselves to a very low standard. We have carved out a system in which mediocrity is rewarded, so we continue on a downward spiral. Corruption brings our quality of life down, and the Mexican system is built on it.

The PRI, the party that built the current system, built it with holes *in it to allow corruption. Now, with the new parties that come in, they don't close the holes, they stretch them out for themselves. These holes are now big enough for more corruption. I write this with a heavy heart, but Mexico has championed the democratization of corruption! Axel Cuevas is the example of a young, new class of politician who rose with the same corrupt tactics that have been the norm for the past 100 years. Let's just be grateful that this land is noble and continues to give us its riches despite being pillaged by every government since 1492.*

Mediocrity is very expensive in the long term, and we are paying for our own ignorance, for our own selfishness. It might seem like this scandal is something far away because it's not in our neighborhoods. But, I assure you, these actions affect the lot of us in deeper ways than we'd like to admit.

Axel Cuevas wasn't granted bail. His trial begins tomorrow in Mexicali. It's already clear that if a guilty verdict is reached, the underworld of crime will push back, retaliate for one of their own. Reports have come out that various cartels throughout Mexico support Cuevas and have issued threats to anyone who gets in the way of his freedom. It is hard to imagine Southeast Mexican cartels having a say about a Baja California port captain, but Axel had a business selling weapons programs to anyone who could pay, so governments and cartels were his biggest clients. He is believed to have plenty of friends within the structure of organized crime and narcopolitics.

Mr. Bystander, forgive me, I know I promised I would assume your innocence, but it has come to the point of this editorial when I must intrude. Why were you at the shootout? What if you're the cause of all the chaos witnessed on a tranquil desert coast? What if your identity is secret because you are the missing link, the last piece of a puzzle that doesn't fit anywhere. How come the Navy hasn't released pictures of you, Mr. Bystander? Why are they holding your card so close to their chest? I guess we must assume your innocence, because death is the great purifier, the great deed that paints the path for all.

So, Mr. Bystander, Admiral Gomez, and Axel Cuevas meet at a light-

house in the middle of Baja California. The lighthouse has been known for prostitution since the time of the Revolución. Then two helicopters chase a Land Cruiser over twenty miles of dirt road. So many questions. Did they arrange a meeting? Did they have drinks at the lighthouse? Were words exchanged? Was there a deal made? Was a pact broken? I wish I knew your identity, Mr. Innocent Bystander. I bet that if I did, I could tie this whole thing together. But why hasn't anybody claimed you? Perhaps you were a lonely person, unloved, or a migrant from a faraway land.

Since we are an institution of commitment, we will put our money where our pen is. We will pay $100,000 to whomever proves the identity of the innocent bystander. We need to find out the truth, because the era of the chieftain needs to end. We don't need bossism in government. We need to get these bosses out of the Navy, out of the captainships, out of the police forces, out of Congress, out of the Senate, and into prison. Axel Cuevas is a start, but what about all of the other ones? We need to cut away all these larvae, all these parasites that cling to a system that is only covered in blood and feces that degrade us all.

Come forth. Let's put a name to this innocent bystander. Let's solve this piece of the puzzle that might free us from another living, working threat—Admiral Gomez, the Navy chieftain who, from growing criticism about his involvement in the capture of Isla del Carmen and the subsequent persecution and arrest of Axel Cuevas, has responded with an all-out PR campaign, marketing himself as a whistleblower of truth.

The world is changing; our enemy is adapting and they're using weapons more powerful than guns. The modern enemy is working hard, deceiving, manipulating. They're using tools of mass persuasion that blind the common folk into supporting unnecessary wars. Help me, dear reader. Let's change the course of this country, of this world, of humanity!

In order to collect the $100,000 reward, informants must send an email to reward@bajagazeta.com with as much information about the suspected bystander. Information must be presented in a single PDF document that includes pictures, contact info, and an explanation of why this person is the innocent bystander we're looking for. The informant with the *correct facts will be paid in a single installment. If the person desires to remain anonymous, we can arrange for a third party to claim the reward. If the reward goes unclaimed, the money will be donated to a foundation of our choice.*

This editorial was signed by Pablo Heraldo and published by *Gazeta* three days after Axel Cuevas's arrest.

CHAPTER 122

Breaking the Seal

J ULIAN MAYORCA FOLDED THE NEWSPAPER he'd finished reading. He sat up in the hospital bed, still bandaged up and attached to the IV pole. He felt the need to go on a walk. The doctor had told him walking would help him pee.

He had lost a kidney to the gunshot and was a little worried that he hadn't urinated since the operation. He needed to "break the seal" in order for the operation to be considered a success. He remembered nothing after being shot; he lost blood and fainted. After he regained consciousness, the doctors briefed him about his condition.

The Navy hospital in South Baja was treating him with the utmost care. He was the Admiral's godson and was brought in by his helicopter. Every update was reported directly to the Admiral.

"Mr. Mayorca, you have a visitor," said the nurse practitioner.

Julian walked slowly toward the waiting room and saw the most beautiful woman in the world, Regina Dahlgreen.

"Hi, gorgeous," he said with a smile.

Regina came up to him and hugged him tightly.

"Ouch, careful. My other kidney might come off," Julian said.

Regina pulled away, frightened.

Julian laughed.

"Jerk! You scared me!" She laughed.

"I never thought you'd come visit me, not in a million years, but it makes me so happy," he said.

"Julian, after I heard what Axel did to you, I remembered some of the things you'd said to me. And to think that he shot you," said Regina.

"Well, he didn't shoot me. He gave the order. His bodyguard shot me."

"Zev?"

"Yeah, whatever his name is. You see, that's the difference between him and I. I would've taken the shot myself," said Julian with disdain.

"You're a real hands-on guy, huh?" she said.

"Well, if our roles were reversed, he wouldn't be here talking to you now," said Julian.

"What is it with you guys? What happened between you for there to be so much hate?"

"Well, it's my fault. I wasn't nice to him when we were kids. I never bullied him or anything. I just never minded him. It wouldn't have been a problem, but I grew up in his parents' home and they absolutely loved me. Even today, if I go over there, their faces light up. It's just, Axel was always such a strange child. Sure, he developed social skills, but..."

At that moment, Julian realized Axel was gone, in jail, and *he* was the one sitting next to this wonderful woman who fueled him from the inside out. He smiled and exhaled in relief. The thought of Rubio, and the millions of dollars in the grotto, probably not too far from him, quickly entered his mind.

"But you know what? I'm not going to waste a single thought on Axel anymore."

He placed his hands on top of hers. There was a light tan line on her finger where her diamond engagement ring had been. She sighed, but left her hands under his.

"Julian, I'm leaving Baja California," she said with an odd head movement.

"What? What do you mean?"

"I'm taking my yacht and sailing out of here," she said.

"When are you coming back?"

"I don't know. I'll probably come back to visit, but I'm tired of living here. I don't think I belong in this lifestyle."

"This *lifestyle*? What are you talking about?"

"You guys, the Mexican way, and Baja. It's just all so intense and messed up in a lot of ways. You know life is different in other places. People live their whole lives without getting into the amount of shit I've had to put up with in the past four years," she said.

Julian took a moment. The beat of his heart increased with the knowledge that this girl was going to leave without giving him the chance of becoming *his* girl.

"You know, before I saw you last time, when you picked me up at the airport, I had just had one of those sessions about leaving Baja. I actually sat against the border fence in Playas de Tijuana once, thought about going stateside forever, and living life like a civilized man. I'm a dual citizen. How many people would want that? I could go, hold a job, weekends, family. I could do it, you know? And maybe if I would've done it, it could've saved Alberto Fontana's life, or maybe Axel wouldn't be in jail now if I would've just gone away. But I couldn't do it. I'm too involved, I know too much. I have a sense of responsibility."

"Yeah, well you're your own breed, Julian."

"No, I'm not. I just know that it's people like you and I who can actually make this place better."

"Maybe this place doesn't need to be better. Maybe we're wrong and it's people like us who actually make it worse."

"No, I'm always right," Julian said.

They laughed.

They sat in silence. Julian looked at her. "Where are you going?"

"New Zealand."

"I've always wanted to go there."

"Yeah, I remember you said something once," she said.

At that moment, the sun began to set and a strong orange light crept in through the cracks.

"Can you do me a favor and raise the blinds?" Julian asked with a convalescent swagger.

Regina stood up; her skirt pressed against her toned legs. She pulled it out and it hung a little looser, beautifully. Beyond the hospital was the Sea of Cortez in all its glory—mellow waters, turquoise colors, two islets painted by the setting sun behind them.

"This is what does it for me every day," said Julian.

Regina crossed her legs.

"You know, between the loss of blood, transfusions, and anesthesia, I had some heavy nightmares. Hallucinations, really. At one point, I saw the sea destroyed. It was as if a hand came in and snatched it dry. I saw the bottom of it, all muddy and filled with pestilence. I was alone and I heard a voice say, *They're coming for it, they're coming for your sea!* So, it's up to us to protect it, we who have the money and the connections to do good because everybody else that has the power and the money uses it for evil," he said with a saddened tone.

"I admire you, Julian, but right now, I have none of that. I spent years with a man whose friends are now calling him 'the pest.' I'm *persona non grata*. And money? I don't have much of that anymore."

"What are you talking about? You're the wealthiest person I know."

"It's gone, Julian. I've got less than a million in cash, and with the way my yacht burns fuel and the expenses of my house, I'll be dry in six months, at most. I've got friends in New Zealand. They said that it's super chill over there and there's money to be made," she said.

"You know, the grass isn't always greener on the other side. You can't keep doing this. You ran from New York, now you're running from Baja. This is your life. We're destined to repeat patterns if we don't change."

"First of all, I guarantee you the grass is greener in New Zealand. That's literally what they're known for—*greener grass*. And, two, I've changed. I'm not the same girl that had to break into my own house when I first got to Baja because my attorney was taking it from me," she said. "Plus, what do you want me to do? I tried making money here. It's not working out for me."

"Sell some of your stuff."

"You know how much trouble I'd get into for selling my house, yacht, or helicopter? All my shit is tied up in legal limbo. Nobody can really buy them from me. You know how things are."

"Well, there's gotta be something you can sell. What about all those expensive paintings you have at your house? I'm sure your modern art collection is worth millions. It's impressive."

"Julian, they're all fake. Counterfeits. It was my dad's hobby. He loved to impress his friends by telling them they were real. Everybody thought he had a billion-dollar art collection. But, no. It's shit. Fugazies, like everything else in his life," she said, almost whispering.

"Your father was a great man, even if he lost his war. He fought. Don't judge somebody who was good to you, regardless of what he did to others."

"That makes no sense," said Regina.

They both smirked.

"I know it doesn't. It's called love."

Regina turned around and he looked into the universe within her eyes. Julian grabbed her head and gently kissed her forehead. She hugged him as he held his lips against her third eye. They felt each other's vulnerability.

"Julian, I can't." She pulled away.

"If it's about money, I've got plenty. I can help you. I already thought about a hundred and eighty-seven million ways I can invest in your company," he said.

"You don't understand. I need to leave," she sighed.

"If you're scared, I can protect you," he said.

"Look at how good you protected yourself!"

Julian's wound dressing itched; it felt tight.

Silence set in. Regina stood up, her silhouette against the sun.

"Regina, you're like me, branded. You're attached to this land. You won't be able to ignore that, but you know what? Go to middle earth. Hopefully you'll find what you're looking for there. But, if not, just remember I'll always be here, and you'll always be *here*," Julian poked his heart with his index finger.

"You know, after I got shot and was bleeding to death, I learned something. Love reaches through the darkness in the form of light. I hope my love reaches through the Pacific Ocean, and that every time I think of you, you feel it. Because *we're* not done with each other. But I won't stop you." He rubbed her cheek with his thumb. "I'll pray for you," he said.

A tear rolled down Regina's cheek. She grabbed his right hand and kissed the back of it. She then stood up, and walked away.

The sound of her steps going down the hallway stuck in Julian's mind. Afterward, when the sun had finally set and the only thing heard in the hospital waiting room was the air conditioning unit flapping up and down, Julian walked to the restroom and emptied his bladder.

About the Author

Rick Zazueta resides in Baja California alongside his wife, Geraldine, and their two kids; Maximo and Larissa. When away from his duties, he plays professional croquet as a member of the Mexico national team. Baja Air & Sea is his first novel.